YOUNG GODS

J. DANIEL BATT

YOUNG GODS

A DOOR INTO DARKNESS

STORYJITSU

ALSO BY J. DANIEL BATT

The Tales of Dreamside

Visions of the Future

Printed in the United States of America
Second Printing, 2016

ISBN 978-0-9906385-5-1

StoryJitsu
Sacramento, CA 95742

www.StoryJitsu.com

Ordering Information: Quantity sales. Special discounts are available on quantity purchases by corporations, associations, and others. For details, contact the publisher below.

Orders by U.S. trade bookstores and wholesalers.

Please contact us:
(916) 674-2288
sales@storyjitsu.com

For the inhabitants of the Red House—
You've shoved joy into every minute of my life.
Thank you.

To Tristan—
You were the door to my new world. Find the door to yours.

"I tell you that all these things—yes, from that star that has just shone out in the sky to the solid ground beneath our feet—I say that all these are but dreams and shadows; the shadows that hide the real world from our eyes. There is a real world, but it is beyond this glamour and this vision, beyond them all as beyond a veil."

—From *The Great God Pan* by Arthur Machen

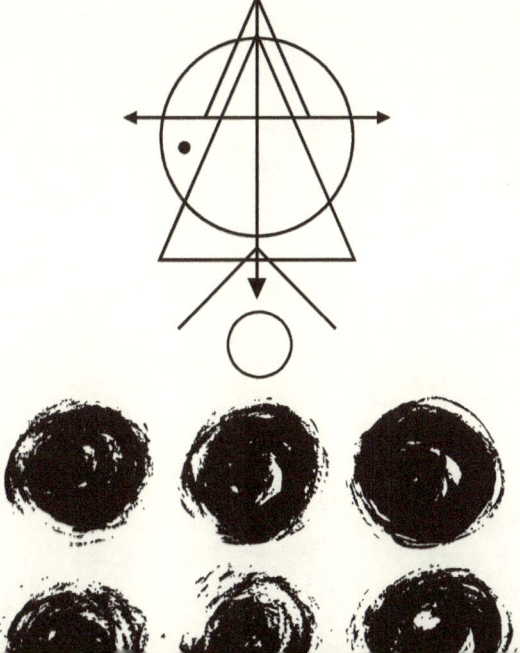

PART I

THE DOOR

CHAPTER ONE

THE SPLINTER KEY

T HE BOARDS DID NOT CREAK. The hinges on the ancient ash door, carved with large, twisting, serpentine symbols, did not squeak. They opened wide but noiseless. The rays of light from the thin windows, hundreds of feet up the walls, were unbroken. The hulking bodies guarding the room fell to the ground without scream or thud. The soft shadows of the intruders melted into the darkness. No alarm was raised.

On the far side of the room, having dispensed with the guards, a tall man, thin as a shadow, stared at a single drawer embedded in the massive, faded ash wall. Behind him, on the floor, laid several bloody creatures, their charcoal wings overlapped and blanketing the ground.

Next to him stood a shorter, much wider man surveying the damage, a look of astonishment on his scrunched-up face. "Unbelievable. I didn't think we could do it. There, I said it. Splendid!" He spread his arms out wide. "Find me a more guarded room. There is none. No other individuals, save the Princes themselves, have stood here." His stubby hand waved around the room and he brought his foot down hard on a lifeless wing. The wing snapped with a sharp crack. "And here they lie." He ended his sentence with a sniff. His name was Mr. Mu and his companion, the thin one, was named Mr. Hu.

Mr. Hu spoke, "*Yes.*"

His voice was almost absent of sound. It was felt more than heard. The sub-sound slithered through the room like a snake.

"*I am sure,*" said Mr. Hu, obscured by shadows, staring at the lock on the drawer. His finger twice rose to touch it and retreated, "*You only get one chance at these things.*"

Mr. Mu touched one of the bodies. "Blast, this was an expensive endeavor." He had a face closer to a basset-hound than a man. His eyes, cheeks, chin, and mouth drooped in a series of arcs into large jowls. His fox-red eyes were plodding in movement, yet precise in gaze. From his ebony tweed jacket, covered in patches and sewn with strange scribbling symbols, dark and crimson, he pulled a purple velvet box and opened the pale gold clasp. He drew out an obnoxiously large, darkened cigar and returned the box to his pocket. As he brought it to his mouth, with his other hand, he drew a line in the air and the tip of the cigar fell off. He placed it between his lips, and, as he drew in his first breath, made another motion with his free hand and the cigar flared brightly. In the dark, the amber glow revealed their desecration of the room. A line of bodies were strewn from wall to wall, their wings, arms, and legs broken and contorted.

Mr. Mu turned back around and the glimmer of the cigar lit the gold of the drawer's handle. With a glint, it shone back. The handle's two far sides pulled apart and melted against the wood. Three small circles the size of large coins rippled across the face of the drawer. Slowly, the circles began flow up the wall.

In awe, Mr. Mu pulled the cigar from his mouth. "Well done." As he moved the cigar downward, the pools of metal formed back into a clasp and hardened.

The two stared.

"And now?"

No answer came. After a moment of silence, Mr. Hu, the taller one, swiftly grabbed the cigar from his associate's hand and held it up against the gold. As soon as he had done so, the metal, again highlighted in the cigar's glow, dripped up the wall.

"*Stand here and smoke.*"

Mr. Mu plopped the cigar back into his mouth, careful to keep it aimed at the gold, and mumbled, "My cigar was the sixth key?"

"*Fire.*"

"They made the final key fire? We're in a room made of wood. Dry boards. Kindling everywhere. How clever."

"*Fire. It will all end in fire. It is not the final key.*"

The metal had flowed upwards and formed into three separate handles each now hanging against the wood. Mr. Hu snatched the cigar from Mr. Mu and held it close to each handle. He waved it quickly in front of each, then repeated the motions slowly. Nothing happened. He leaned into the handles, now at eye level for him. He returned the cigar to his friend and took a step back.

They waited. The only sound was the occasional sniffing of the shorter gentleman.

After three minutes, Mr. Mu stomped his foot, "Now I'm pissed! What else is there left to do?"

"*Wait.*" Mr. Hu glanced at one of the many pocket watches dangling from his jacket pocket, "*Six and a half minutes. Just about.*"

Three small, thin-lined squares appeared an inch around the handles. Shallow at first, they deepened until they ended with a small snap.

"*Patience was the key. He does nothing quickly.*" He pulled the first drawer out, it was short—less than six inches deep. He turned towards the table behind him, walking nimbly between the bodies. He did nothing to avoid their now-fading wings.

"Let's have a little clear space here." He sharply took out an ebony cane that had been sheathed to his side and used it to prod and push the body off of the table, huffing as he did so. The winged man fell to the ground with a thud. The taller one placed the drawer on the table and returned to the wall, removed the other two, one after another, and laid them next to the first.

They peered into the drawers. A rolled, blood-stained heavy cloth sat in each. They pulled the first out and, with care, opened it on the table. Inside was an inch-long shard of dark and aged wood, rugged and rough.

The taller one stood up, the small skulls that served as buttons on his jacket rattled. He tapped them out of habit, "*Of course.*"

They unwrapped the second cloth revealing another similar wooden shard. It was rough, nearly the same length as the first, but uniquely jagged. They placed the two together on the first cloth and pulled out the third roll. They unwrapped it, again on the table, and stared aghast.

It was empty inside.

After several heavy moments, Mr. Mu said, "They won't be pleased about this."

"*No, they will not.*"

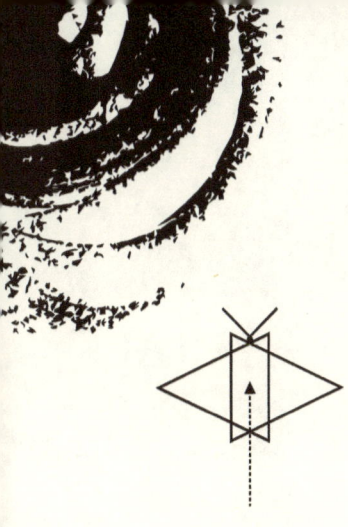

"Listen to them, the children of the night. What music they make."

—Bram Stoker

Chapter Two

MIRACLES IN THE DARK

Tuesday, January 31, 2012

T RYAL SIGHED, growing impatient as he waited for his brother Roland to wrap up a conversation with what was becoming a very talkative daddy longlegs. "What is the spider saying?"

Roland knelt in the hallway as the four others circled around. Lit by the electric cyan of the Incamna Aquarium's nighttime security lights, Roland's nose hovered above the spider waving its front legs in strange patterns. His straggly dark hair fell forward and stretched like a canopy over the arachnid as they chittered back and forth.

Tryal leaned over his brother's shoulder. Roland nudged him away and pressed his face closer to the cold concrete. "Leave me alone. This isn't easy. This one's a bit gabby."

Kaly twisted a thin strand of her brown hair around a finger, leaned into Tryal and whispered in his ear, sending a shiver down his back. "Sometimes I think he makes this crap up."

Tryal kicked at her and a bit of snow that had clung to his shoe flew up. She stumbled away from the white blur. Tryal laughed, "If he's making it up, we're all making it up."

Janae's soft voice spoke from the corner of the room, "At least we're not just barging in."

"We're learning," Kaly said. "Step one: Talk to the bugs."

Roland looked sideways at her. "Spiders aren't bugs."

Kaly replied, "Then how come you can talk to them?"

Roland muttered something undecipherable, a quick series of chirps, clicks and purrs, and bowed to the spider. "We have roughly twenty minutes before the guard finishes his nightly dump. The spider . . ." Roland leaned his ear back down. "Um, excuse me. *Mister Lycos the Araneae Lord* says that the security guard walks out of the office and swings through the rooms south to north. That should give us another few minutes if we hear him. Let's go." Roland stood, his silhouette stark against the blue security lights.

"The spider knows when the nighttime rent-a-cop takes a poop?" Cody flung his backpack onto his shoulders. He loomed over the others. Cody was powerfully built—an inch or two above six feet, and as wide as a Cadillac hood.

"The spider is keeping us out of jail while we attend this stupid stunt of yours." Roland walked down the hall, glared back at them, his dark eyes disappearing in the shadows. "Stay quiet and keep up."

Tryal glanced back over his shoulder.

When was the bad thing going to happen?

Only the empty hallway with its sea-green speckled carpet lay in their wake. His hands dripped with sweat as he gripped the strap of the Doctor Strange messenger bag slung across his shoulder.

Kaly squeezed his arm. "Let's go." Tryal followed. Her steps were delicate and precise. She had sharp features, a slight tinge of freckles across her nose, flowing dark hair, and a smile that pulled a bit higher on the right.

Cody started after, stopped and held out a hand to his sister, Janae, who sat cross-legged in a corner. "C'mon, sis, I want you with me. I want you to see this."

Janae let him lift her up. She was dwarfed by Cody, almost half his height, thin, and had the habit of hanging her head, staring at the ground—a habit that made her look smaller still. She squeaked, "Do you really have to do this?" She tucked her hands into her dark jeans embroidered with hot-pink skulls.

"Trust me. You guys will want to watch this." Cody put an arm around her and they walked together down the long hall from the aquarium's entrance room to the displays. "Besides, this is the fun way to do it."

The five of them moved as shadows, their faces flickering in the scattered patches of blue light. They rounded the corner and Tryal paused. Kaly squeezed his hand and grinned. "It'll be okay. Not everything turns out as bad as you imagine it will."

Tryal crossed his arms. "But it usually does."

She ignored him. She loved the sneaking around. Last week, it had been a low-security military base (and the trunk of a Corolla, although that had been an accident). Before that, they had driven up to Mount Rushmore and climbed up to Washington's chin. Bad things happened but they always managed to survive. Tonight, it was the Incamna Aquarium. Incamna shouldn't have an aquarium. It was a small city in the Panhandle of Nebraska, surrounded by prairie, sand dunes and the sparse forest of the Wildcat Hills.

They meandered through small glass displays of tropical fish, a shadowed room with a kaleidoscope of reflecting light.

Kaly broke the silence. "I think we need a name."

Roland disappeared around a column. "Yours is Kaly. It's sewn on your underwear."

Kaly turned around and punched Tryal in the arm.

Tryal jerked back. "What was that for?"

"He's *your* brother."

Tryal grinned. They weren't really brothers. They had been adopted together and had been foster brothers before that. One night, years ago, in the overly crowded Hartsell Home for Foster Children, Roland had walked into the bunk room to find Tryal getting beaten up. Roland had dived in, smacked the other kids around, and they had been together ever since. Later, Roland discovered Tryal had deserved the beating for stealing an iPod from one of the other kids.

Kaly spun around, stretching out her arms. "Seriously, look at all the cool things we can do."

In the tank next to her, an eel, long and velvet, swam out of the murky waters up to the glass. Kaly screamed.

"What is it?" asked Roland.

Tryal put an arm around Kaly as she jumped back. "It's okay. Something in the tank, some fish, scared up. She's fine." He pulled her close. "You're fine, right?" Maybe this moment of surprise was the bad thing he had been anticipating.

No. That was too easy. It would get worse. It always did.

Roland grunted, "Shut up. The guard may be dropping one but he isn't deaf." Roland walked away, glanced over his shoulder and smiled. "Besides, if you wanted Tryal to hold you, I'm sure you just had to ask."

Cody said, "I think it's just one more room over. The tanks are getting bigger."

Janae put her hand on one with several large clown fish swimming in lazy formation. "These are huge."

The dark door in front of them opened to reveal a large pool with a metal rail surrounding it. Flashes of green and blue danced on the room's walls and surfaces. Light like electrical branches crawled across them.

Tryal grabbed onto the rail and leaned over. It was larger than the city pool, orange light from the exit sign reflecting off its smooth surface, like a gigantic mirror. Under that, dark shapes moved.

"Cool," said Tryal. Murmured agreement emanated from the others. All except Kaly. He turned back to see her still in the doorway. "We were just teasing about your family. They're great."

"It's not that," she said as she pulled her arms behind her back.

Tryal remembered. "It's the water? You do hate it, don't you?"

Kaly nodded.

Roland hung over the edge, dangling a finger in the pool. "You almost drown as a kid?"

"No. I don't know. I just don't like it," Kaly said.

"Well, it loves me!" Cody had climbed over the guard rail, and stood leaning above it.

Kaly rubbed her forehead.

Tryal said, "Another headache?"

Kaly nodded. "Yes."

"You seem to be getting a lot more . . ."

Janae interrupted, "Cody, are those real sharks in there?"

"Yep!" Cody leaned forward and pulled himself back against the rail, over and over like a six-year-old on a playground.

"Dog sharks. Hammerhead. Nothing like a great white," Roland said.

Cody smacked the edge of the water. "They still bite."

Kaly had walked closer to the edge with Tryal's arm around her waist. She said, "Before he does this, can we come up with a name?"

"Serious?" Roland groaned. "Then we are now officially Captain Roland and His Amazing Talking Animals!"

Janae said, "Roleo!"

Cody frowned. "Let's call ourselves the Locals."

"Stupid," said Tryal. The few lights from inside the pool flickered and Tryal shivered. Beads of sweat formed across his forehead.

Roland knew this look. "You okay?"

Tryal's eyes darted around the room. "I don't know. I think so. Whatever it was, it's gone."

Roland turned around and took inventory of each of the doors into the room, just in case. "Umm, ya. Sure."

Kaly had inched forward and stood near the guard rail. "We should call ourselves The Voice!"

Roland went down on his stomach, leaning far over, splashing his head in the water. "Team Electric Bunnies."

Tryal let go of Kaly and stared into the pool as the large dark shapes swam underneath. "Kaly, 'The Voice' sounds like a woman's magazine."

Kaly twisted a finger through her long brown hair. "It's just that we all hear voices."

Janae stood between Cody and Tryal. "That makes us sound crazy."

Cody hung a foot over the edge. "Can I get on with this?"

Roland said, "Ya, by my clock, we have less than ten minutes before that guard walks through again. If you're jumping in, you might want to take off your pants."

Tryal said, "So, you're going to do what now?"

Janae grabbed Cody's arm. "You're not thinking about jumping in? That's a shark in there."

Cody smiled his big signature smile. "Just watch." He hung over the rippling surface of the pool, whispered a few words, and let go of the rail. Cody's huge body fell forward into the massive tank.

Janae screeched, "Cody!"

Where there should have been a splash, there wasn't. The waters spread below him and Cody landed hard on the dry floor of the tank, the waters standing in a column around him. He waved, completely dry and grinning broadly.

"Wow! Cody, how did you figure that out?" asked Janae.

Roland waved his hand in the column of air and ran his fingers through the wall of water. "That's just. Wow!"

Cody looked up, still grinning. "I know."

"We are gods," Janae said.

"We're too young to be gods," said Roland.

Kaly stood back from the rail. "Then we could be 'The Young Gods.'"

Roland snorted. "Fine. Hey, Cody, time to get back up here. About five minutes left before mall cop starts his rounds."

Tryal said, "This is serious Moses-level crap you've done here. How did you . . . How did you?"

Cody started moving across the bottom of the pool toward the ladder near them. The water separated where he walked. "How do anyone of us do what we do? I don't know. I just talk. It understands and I understand it. I just work to get the words right and the guts to ask."

He held up a hand to the water's surface as a small dog shark swam by. The shark saw his wiggling fingers and bolted for them. It broke the water's edge and missed his fingers by less than an inch, slammed into the ground and flopped around, shocked that its belly wasn't full and it was suffocating. Cody had grunted and leaped back. Tryal spun to see what had happened and bumped into Janae, already hanging over the edge.

Janae shouted, "Watch it!"

Tryal grabbed hold of her arm. "I'm sorry. I just didn't."

From the tank, Cody called up, "Janae, what's a matter?"

Roland whispered back, "Stop with all the shouting. She's fine, mister over-protective."

The lights flickered again and everything turned dark. Janae squealed again. Tryal pulled on her arm. She was sweating and his hands were wet from the rail. His hold slipped. Janae lost her balance and tipped forward with a splash.

Roland shouted, "What was that?"

Tryal leaned over and scanned through the rippling water. "Janae? "

"You let go of her?" Roland shouted.

Cody's voice, echoing against and amplified by the water, sounded, "Is Janae alright?"

A shadow moved outside the doorway and a deep, gruff voice spoke, "What's going on in there?"

Roland muttered, "Blast."

Tryal yelled down to Cody, "Janae fell over!"

Cody shouted back, "What?"

The room grew darker as the shadow blocked the entrance cutting off all the light from the hall. "Who's in here?" His last words were lost under a rumble issuing from the tank.

The tank trembled and water splashed over the edges, flooding the room. In an explosion, the water erupted from the tank. Tryal and Roland were slammed against the ground, choking through the water filling their lungs. The world went black and the sounds were hollow in the pounding of the water. Tryal flailed, his fingers scrambling against anything they touched, searching for a grip. The flow pushed him and he smacked hard upon the back wall.

The coursing water battered the standing aquarium tanks and glass sprayed across the room. Janae screamed in pain but Tryal couldn't see where she was. He tried to look around. His eyes stung and his vision was a blurry red. As if in a half-speed strobe, he saw glimpses of the room, the aquarium lights reflected from the flowing water, a shimmering dance of bright shards. In one of the glimpses, he saw a dark shape rise from the center of the large tank. Cody. His tall body and broad shoulders were unmistakable, even in half-glanced silhouette.

Cody bellowed, "Where's Janae?"

A voice answered back, angry and sputtering in confusion, "What the heck did you do, boy?"

"Tryal, where's Janae?" Cody demanded.

Tryal scrambled. Why was Cody blaming him? What had he done? Tryal replied, "What? She's . . ."

"Where is she?" Cody raised his hands and Tryal felt the water spinning around him.

Roland ran to Cody. "Stop! Let him go."

The water spun Tryal up and around, his body helpless against it, a marionette on its strings.

Roland punched Cody, sending the tall boy to the floor. Roland yelled, "Janae's right over there."

Cody pushed himself back up, rubbing the side of his face where Roland had made contact. "I was just scared."

Roland leaned over him, extending an arm back to Tryal, "What were you going to do?"

Cody stammered again, finally standing, "I, uh . . ."

"Get control, brutus. It was an accident. You were about to hit Tryal—the boy that would never hurt anyone. Or punch back. Now get your sister."

Janae stirred and mumbled a weak, "Help." She was hurt and struggling to stand, silhouetted against the scattered light.

Behind her a voice grunted, "Gotcha!" She was pulled back into darkness.

Cody roared, "Janae!"

Roland tried to be louder, "Hey, we're sorry!"

The security guard's voice came from the right, "Then follow me. Her and the rest of you are sitting in my office until the cops arrive."

Cody shouted, "Let her go! She's hurt."

"Or what?" asked the security guard.

"Seriously, haven't you been watching?" Roland asked, gesturing at Cody, "That freak did all this. All this!"

"What's wrong with you kids? Try anything and . . ." the security guard stammered.

Cody stepped towards the security guard as a wall of water rose up around him.

Roland glanced between the shadows. Cody and the security guard holding Janae. Roland dropped his shoulder and rammed Cody back to the ground. "Stop it! You're out of control!"

Before Cody could move, Roland spun around and swung, punching the surprised guard squarely in the jaw. The guard stumbled backwards, dropping his hold on Janae. Janae stumbled into the light, falling and slamming into the ground. Blood spread into the water around her. Her arms and legs had been sliced by the glass.

Roland shouted, "Tryal, Janae's hurt. Get her out of here."

Tryal still stood where he had been when Cody advanced towards him.

Roland shouted again, "Move it, little brother. Go!"

As he stepped towards Janae, Tryal was struck with a feeling that he was missing something. He took a quick inventory—Roland, Janae, Cody, Kaly . . . Wait, where was Kaly?

"Kaly?" he said her name anticipating her to answer softly next to him. But no answer came. Again, louder, "Kaly?"

"Get Janae. Let's go." said Roland, helping Cody to his feet.

"Kaly!" Tryal shouted. No answer came. Kaly wasn't in the room. "Where did Kaly go?"

"Are you serious?" asked Roland.

Tryal stopped listening. He had splashed towards the exit, stepping between the security guard and Janae. "Kaly!" he yelled down the hall. The sound made a gonging echo against the glass of the various tanks.

"Get back in here! I can't help both!" Roland left Cody's side and moved towards Janae. "Stupid. Tryal." Tryal never heard that.

Instead, they heard Tryal's distant shout from far down the hall, "Kaly?"

The entire room began to buzz, the remaining lights all flickered. The water turned to steam, billowing into the few lighted places in the aquarium.

"What's happening?" Roland said. "Cody?"

"Uhh, not me."

"Where's the rent-a-cop?" asked Roland.

A moan issued near his feet in answer. Roland kicked at the lump and it groaned again. "Now, stay down and stay away. We're leaving. Don't follow us. Or next time, I'll let my friend here really go nuts."

Roland bent and pulled a small piece of glass from Janae's arm. "Pick your sister up and get going. She's hurt." He ran a hand across the bleeding girl's cheek, her wounds open and deep. "Real bad."

CHAPTER THREE

GODS BETWEEN WORLDS

K ALY HAD RUN OUTSIDE WHEN CODY LOST IT. Her head hurt and grew worse with every moment. The headaches had been getting sharper over the last few weeks, but she didn't want to admit it. Running helped, so she ran. She ran through the narrow halls and pushed on a door under a red, glowing EXIT sign, bursting out into the still, cold air. The amber lights on the building and in the alley flickered briefly and something buzzed behind her.

A dirty hand grasped her elbow. She spun and found herself inches from the face of an old, hunched-over man with a long, dusty beard. His drab, brown cap reached down to his bushy eyebrows. The man grimaced and gasped as if in pain, pulled her close even as she stepped away, and rasped, "The oceans have turned against us! They send dark things against us. Dark things from the depths!"

A sharp pang stabbed in Kaly's head. Catching her balance, she pulled free of him and moved towards to the back door of the Aquarium. She glanced around, and stumbled as the man moved right behind her.

"Dark things, things unheard of." He grabbed her again and held on tighter. The old man's face was crinkled like paper. His eyes were sunk into his head, their sockets noticeable through the thin wrap of skin over them. His voice rasped and the words spat out with a steady spray of phlegm. "It's you, isn't it? I've heard of you. You've been gone for so long, they all believe you dead. But it is you."

Kaly's head throbbed—a spike being driven through her temple. She grabbed her head. A migraine—sharp, nasty, and electric.

"Get out of here!" a voice shouted from the door behind her. She turned around and was relieved to see Tryal there. His hair fell into his eyes as he rushed up next to her. "Leave her alone."

"Even the Red One is frightened, they say."

"Get off," she shouted. Tryal pushed his way between the two, forcing the old man to let go and back up.

As the old man staggered backwards, his face went still and he stared at Tryal. His body remained almost lifeless for a few moments. Slowly he spoke, "And you . . . you will be a god."

The old man's eyes drilled into Tryal. Tryal found it hard to move. His limbs went rigid and he stared back.

"But you're still tied to this side, aren't you? That's good. That's very good. They won't be expecting that." The old man reached down and grabbed Tryal's hand and pushed something into it. "Take this. Please. I don't want to go back. You have to take it. I promised. They'll know." The old man glanced at Tryal's closed hand and muttered something indecipherable. "It's yours. It will always be yours."

Tryal pulled his hand back, pushing the old man off of him, "What are you talking about? Get away." Kaly grabbed onto his arm. Her eyes shut tight against her headache.

"Don't tell them you saw me. I can't be found," the man staggered away, "They'll find you soon enough. Don't tell them you saw me. Don't tell them where you got it from. I'm sorry. I am. But they'll know."

Tryal watched the old man slowly back away. "Hey, wait. It's cold out. You shouldn't be walking around out here."

The man started around the corner. "Dark things from the oceans. They betrayed us all." He took another step and was past their view.

Tryal followed after. As he walked around the corner, he paused. Kaly came up behind him and asked, "Where did he go?"

All that could be seen was the now gently falling flakes of snow between the shadows, houses in the distance, and a blue dumpster against a wooden fence.

Tryal looked at Kaly and then down to his hand. As he unfolded his fingers, he revealed a silver locket and chain. Kaly picked it up and examined the strange designs running along the casing. She slowly pried it open.

"It's a mirror." Scratched, stained hazy white along the edges, but it was a mirror. "There's something written here." She held up the opposite face of the locket.

Tryal took it and read,

FACE TO FACE
SHOW ME TO MY BROTHER.
BETWEEN TWO WORLDS,
I'LL OPEN ANOTHER.

"That's . . . different." Kaly asked.

"Yeah, I guess." He closed the locket and handed it to her, "Here. For you."

She put it in her pocket and wound her hair around her finger. Just having it made her anxious. She could feel a buzzing sensation growing in the back of her mind. "I think my headache's getting worse."

He shivered, "The others will be out soon. We'll go back home and I'll get you some aspirin."

Kaly softly leaned into him as they walked to the Jeep Cherokee door.

"Roland has the keys, so, um . . . I guess we're waiting."

Tryal put his arms around her as they leaned against the door. They stood for a minute in silence as the snow fell around them.

She glanced up and ran a finger across his cheek. "I've always wondered why you didn't dress more Goth."

"Are you serious? With the black fingernails?"

"The pentagrams draping from your neck. Ya." She grinned.

"Because of Door?"

Kaly winced, "Don't do that. Cody talks to water. Not Mr. Splashy." Cody talked to water. Roland talked to spiders and bugs. Janae talked to storms. Kaly talked to the future. More often, the voices talked and she listened. Her gift wasn't like the others. She couldn't change anything. She heard what she had called "the whispers from tomorrow," voices that were barely discernible, muttering about things that might happen. They were sometimes right.

Tryal groaned. "Because of my friend."

"Yeah, and you know it creeps me out when you call her . . . it . . . that."

"I talk to her as much as I do you."

"But you've never even seen her."

"Kinda. That one time I did," Tryal brushed the back of her hair.

"Why do you call it . . . I mean why do you call her Door?"

Tryal thought for a moment. "When she first said who she was, one of the names she gave herself was 'the Doorkeeper.' I liked thinking of her like that. She was a door."

Kaly smiled at him. "That's a bit nicer."

Tryal coughed, "What'd you expect? For me to be morbid and all depressed?"

"Sure. You hang out with Death. Actually hang out with Death. The dream of every Goth in this school."

"Could be my ticket to popularity."

"The King of the Goths?" Kaly smiled and looked up at him, caught by his green eyes. Those bright green eyes.

Were they brighter now than before?

She leaned forward and kissed him. His eyes went wide and he wasn't sure whether to return the kiss or . . . And then it was over. Kaly put her head back down.

Tryal stayed immobile. Dazed. "That was, uh, new."

Kaly muttered, "Ya." Then, slowly, she looked back up and said, "Where are the others at?"

"Right here!" The Aquarium door swung open with a bang and Roland marched out. "No thanks to you and your boyfriend."

Cody followed, carrying Janae in his arms. Blood dripped from her arms. Blood stained her sleeves. Blood everywhere.

Kaly shrieked and ran over, "What happened? Is she okay?"

Cody muttered, "The glass hit her when I . . . "

"No. She's not okay," Roland pushed past, "We need to get her to the hospital. Now." Around them, the winds roared and blew the snow sideways.

Tryal turned, "I'm sorry . . . I . . ."

"You're useless. You just stood there. Like always." Roland pushed his hand into Tryal's chest, slamming him back into the snow. "You're the biggest coward I know."

Kaly went and grabbed Janae and helped her into the Jeep Cherokee. "Get her some towels. We can wrap her up." They pulled a tattered green blanket from the back and covered Janae, setting her in the backseat with her head on Kaly's lap.

Roland walked around them, "Now get in before the cops show up."

Tryal brushed the snow off his pants and his book bag, and shuffled to the driver's side of the car, glancing back at the rear door of the aquarium. "I can drive."

Roland grunted, "No."

Tryal started, "But . . ."

Roland shouted, "No time for stupid arguments. Janae is hurt." Roland pushed Tryal hard, "I'm driving." He climbed in, shoving Tryal and causing

Tryal's knee to smack the full ashtray sending their mother's cigarette butts across the floorboard.

"Idiot," Tryal said.

Roland slapped Tryal's head, "Selfish little brat."

"What we cannot speak about, we must pass over in silence."

— Ludwig Wittgenstein

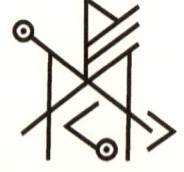

Chapter Four

THE GREAT DESERT

O N THE EDGE OF THE SAND sat Mr. Mu and Mr. Hu. They enjoyed coffee in a street-side cafe' of a small village. Strung around them lay the drying bodies of the restaurant's patrons. The wind rose and batted one of the patrons' separated heads against the tan bricks of the cafe' with a clunk. A vulture squealed above as it drifted a little lower on each turn.

Mr. Hu, his tall frame arching over the table, stared out at the desert, his elbows on his knees and his body folded uncomfortably into the too-small seat. The wind whipped the sand behind him. The desert rippled away from them like the spreading of a sheet.

"In Arabic, it is known as *As Sahra' al Kubra*, the Great Desert. Sahara," said Mr. Mu, his belly pressing against the buttons of his hand-tailored suit. His hand gripped a fork and his other held a cigar as he took turns nibbling on the end of each. His black, thin, glossy hair was matted against his head. His features were darker still, dark eyes set inside dark rounded sockets against a pale face. Mr. Mu's lips were thin and jutted, following the crest of his long nose. "Could you pass the sugar?"

Mr. Hu did not move. He stared across the sand. The sugar appeared next to Mr. Mu's cup without any intervention.

Mr. Mu sighed, "You spend too easily. Our riches won't last." He tapped his spoon against the edge of his glass, "You're mulling."

"*It is what I do,*" replied Mr. Hu, his voice thin in time.

"Stop it, please. You're depressing me." Mr. Mu tugged at the carcass laid out on a plate in front of him. "You know I can't eat when I'm upset."

Mr. Hu turned his long neck and scanned across Mr. Mu's ample frame and returned to gazing across the desert.

"Well, it's true," Mr. Mu continued. "I simply cannot eat when I am depressed, and I am always depressed when you are mulling. You only mull when something is about to go wrong." Mr. Mu jammed what resembled a clawed foot into his mouth. It might have belonged to a raccoon at one time. "You are never wrong."

Silence hung in the air. Between bites, Mr. Mu said, "So?"

"*So what?*"

"So, what is going to go wrong?"

"*Oh, that.*"

"Yes, that!"

"*You will not like it.*"

"Do you hear that?" Mr. Mu said, pointing his fat fingers at a corpse seated near him. "Do you hear that? He wastes time by telling me that I won't like it. Does he think there is a type of wrong that I would enjoy? A calamity awaiting us that would be to my liking? Perchance something that I have been waiting for?" He twirled his finger at this, and with a literal squawk said, "Tell me at once."

"*I think one of us shall die soon.*"

"Oh, that. That's all? Never mind, then. Can you pass the ketchup?" Mr. Hu stared at the sand and the ketchup did not move. Mr. Mu grunted, "And what leads you to that?"

"*The third key.*"

"I know. Without it, we can't move on. Yes, it does not upset me." He had picked up the bottle of ketchup and had begun shaking it over his plate.

"*We must do our jobs.*"

Mr. Mu shook the bottle harder, "No, we don't have to."

"*If we don't, then what would we be?*"

Mr. Mu smacked the back of the bottle, sending a splat of ketchup across his plate as he said, "Free men."

"*We are not free.*"

"Oh, I am quite certain I am. I am free to do what I want. To eat this bite." He nudged the head of a corpse with his heel, "To kick this fool's head. To ignore your inane driveling. To walk away from this job."

"*We must honor our pledge.*"

"That is your mistake right there. You use words like 'pledge' and 'honor.' Stop that type of thinking. Stare at the facts. The proper word to describe our condition is 'employed.' As in, we are 'employed.' Nothing more. We can choose to leave this current employment."

"*He is not his father.*"

Mr. Hu shuddered at the mention of their current employer. A beastly, hulking man known for bashing the heads of his friends open like ripe fruit. A tyrant of many names—Danor, Taranis, the God-Slayer, the Bastard Usurper.

"Hades!" Mr. Mu spat on the sand, "No, he isn't. His eyes see nothing beyond his own walls. We will leave and he cannot follow."

"*He's crueler than his father was.*"

"He is a fool and we are fools for staying in his pay."

Instantly, Mr. Hu reached out his long hands, grabbed the fork from Mr. Mu's hands and jammed it into Mr. Mu's eye. The eye popped with a sploosh. Mr. Hu reached his long fingers all the way around Mr. Mu's fat head and jerked, snapping his neck efficiently. Mr. Mu's eye dripped across his jacket as his body slumped to the ground.

In a single step, Mr. Hu leaned over and pulled out the cigar case from his dead partner's jacket. He opened it and retrieved a single stick—a splinter. The piece of wood was dry and gray. Mr. Hu held the splinter up to the noon sun with his thin fingers. He blinked as he heard the screaming of a throng far off in the distance (or in the past).

He reached into his own pocket, removed a blood-red cloth and unrolled it on the table. He placed the splinter next to two others. The cloth was bright against the stained metal tables.

The wind roared and, in between shutters, he heard a sound of flapping wings. A shadow fell across him and from behind, his friend's familiar voice spoke, "You coward! I should've known. You were planning to kill me from the start. I hate when you do that."

"You lied ."

"You trusted me. First promise of our relationship is to never trust the other. You made a grievous tactical error." Mr. Mu walked over to his dead body and bent over. He searched the top breast pocket and pulled out two small cases and placed them in his own pocket.

"I did not. I have the key along with the other two and we are now within range."

"And possibly the end of all."

"Yes. But we'll have done our job ."

"You're a fool. He's daft."

"But he pays."

"Is the job always more important than existence to you?"

"The job is our existence ."

"That is drivel and . . ."

"Enough. We must be off." Mr. Hu stood. His long legs pulled him up, resembling a crane.

Mr. Mu had finished searching through his former body's pockets, transferring each personal item into a new pocket, "Would you prefer to do our long quest on camels? Or perhaps a flying carpet?"

"*A carpet should work.*" Mr. Hu was already walking into the blowing sand.

"You don't know where to go, do you? No. Of course not."

CHAPTER FIVE

CALLING ON THE WIND

THEY RODE IN QUIET THE FIRST FEW BLOCKS. Roland focused on the road, Tryal kept turning around to check on Cody and the girls, and Kaly held Janae tightly. Cody sat huddled over, glancing at Janae and the returning to stare at the floormat. Tryal thought he heard Cody muttering. Maybe praying.

"Which hospital are we taking her to?" asked Tryal.

"I think Incamna United is closest. It's a piece of crap, but it's the closest," Roland said. Incamna was a small city but it had somehow developed two hospitals: a public-owned one, Incamna United, and the Catholic Grace Hospital on the other side of town.

Roland rubbed the inside of the windshield. "Dang! I can't keep these windows clear." Twice in the five minutes they had been driving, he had pulled the car over and scraped the front windshield with an empty CD case. The storm was growing stronger and Janae grew more still.

The streets of Incamna were walled by short-lawn houses and the rising profiles of the bluffs they sat against. They were empty tonight, draped in amber streetlight. Fresh snow had covered every footprint and trail. Most of the streets went downhill toward the east. The journey was slow in the driving blizzard. Behind Tryal and the others, as they weaved through the streets, rose the hills of the Pine Ridge forest, the beginning of the Black Hills. Tonight, those old trees and valleys were entirely hidden by the clouds. The car windows and the wheel-wells were collecting the ice and debris kicked up by the tires.

Roland flipped on his blinker to turn left. He pulled at the steering wheel and nothing happened. He slammed on the brakes, pulled at the emergency brake between the seats and went outside. A moment later, he opened the car door back up, "Get out here and help kick this snow off the tires."

The front passenger tire was stuck in packed exhaust-stained snow. He started to kick the snow out from underneath the wheel well—a slow and tiring job. He resorted to scraping some of it out with his hands when kicking failed. This trip was taking forever. What if they didn't make it? Their friend's life hung in his and his brother's incompetent hands. He freed one tire and quickly moved to the back passenger-side tire.

Roland turned up the heater and the warm air streamed out of the defrost vents. Tryal warmed his hands on the dash. Roland eased onto the highway and headed south; much slower than before. The road disappeared after only a hundred feet and Roland gripped the steering wheel as the wind buffeted them from the right. He downshifted to second and they slowed to 20 miles per hour.

Tryal said, "This is not good."

As she cradled Janae in her lap, Kaly grabbed a strand of hair and twirled it around her finger over and over. Cody pulled the two girls close, Janae's head still resting on Kaly's knees. Kaly's arms were slippery from a blend of blood and sweat, her hair damp. Kaly's head throbbed. A voice spoke in her head, *Soon.* She rubbed her temple.

A minute later and they had slowed below 15. The winds rocked the Cherokee back and forth. The snow blew across the highway and large drifts had formed. They plowed through several with only the smallest notice. Each successive drift hit the Jeep harder.

They stopped with a jolt. Kaly slid forward, dropping Janae's head off her lap and against the back of the seat. Her sweat streaked on the beige vinyl. Kaly quickly pulled her back up, "I'm sorry. I'm so, so sorry!" Tryal's face smacked the dash. He pushed himself off, his lip bleeding. Roland turned on the emergency flashers and went out, once more.

Tryal and Cody followed, "What's happened?"

"We're stuck. We've plowed into a large drift." Roland climbed back in and shifted to reverse, the wheels spun and the Jeep didn't move. He shifted into first and the truck didn't even rock forward. He stepped out again and walked around to the back. "We're not moving. The snow has already started to form behind us."

Cody muttered, "Maybe I can help."

Roland lifted an eyebrow. "Think your Moses' schtick can work on this?"

Cody said, "It's water, isn't it?" With that, he cupped a chunk of snow, held it to his mouth and began to whisper.

Around them, the snow stirred. In a flash, the drifts ahead of them turned to steam and the road cleared.

Tryal beamed, "Holy! Nice job!"

Roland was back to the Cherokee, opening his door, "Well done, Goliath. Let's . . ." The wind slammed the door back shut. Around them, the wind roared and the snow still piled along the sides of the road blew back across the pavement. Within a minute, the road was blocked again.

"Get in!" Roland yelled. Cody started to lift up more snow. Roland grunted, "You can control the snow but not the wind."

"We need to wake Janae up. This can't be chance. She's hurt and the weather goes berserk?" Tryal asked.

"Cody. My idiot brother has it right. Get in," Roland said.

The three got back in and looked at Kaly and Janae. "Wake her up. She has to call this off," Tryal said.

"You think she's doing this?" Kaly asked.

"I'd put money on it," replied Roland. Janae could talk to the weather. The storms would talk back; she would ask them favors, they would listen, and often respond. Often, her relationship with the weather went beyond words. Even when she was silent it listened to her.

"Yes," said Tryal.

Kaly said, "How am I supposed to wake her up?"

"Like this," Roland said and moved his fingers by her ears and snapped them. Janae didn't stir.

"Like what?" Kaly said.

"Wait." Tryal reached out, brought back a handful of snow and dropped it onto Janae's face. She gasped and shook her head. "Now, start talking to her!" Tryal said.

Cody leaned in. "Hey, little sister, you need to wake up. We need you."

"Louder!" said Roland.

"Janae, we need you. You have to tell the wind that you're okay," Cody continued.

Tryal added, "Come on Janae! Help us. I think it believes we're trying to hurt you. Tell it to calm down."

Janae's thin lips moved. The Cherokee continued to sway as the winds pushed against its right side. The snow had started to drift across the hood. They were being buried.

"That's right. Come on girl. Please. Tell it to calm down. We're stuck, it's blocked our path. Please just tell it to stop," said Cody.

Janae's eyes opened as a slit. Kaly brushed away the strands of her brown hair from her eyes.

"Come on, I know you're with me! Tell the wind to stop," Cody said.

"You have to. Tell it you're okay!" Kaly placed her hands on both sides of Janae's head.

"Mmm, plleah nnoh," the words drifted from Janae.

"That's right. Stay with me. Louder! Tell it!" Kaly's eyes watered.

Janae's eyes started to close.

"NO! STAY AWAKE! You have to do this! We need you to do this! Please" She was sobbing as she shouted.

Tryal dropped another handful of snow onto Janae's neck. Her eyes snapped open, she stiffened and arched her back, jutting out a cry, "Aaaaaww."

"Crap!" Roland pulled back. Janae's body loosened and Kaly pulled her in close.

"Please! Tell the wind to stop! Tell it you're okay!" Cody said.

"Mmmm aah'm ohkaey uhhh plleah sssstohp," Janae said, her lips trembled.

The Cherokee stopped shaking. The wind stilled. Tryal opened his door again. The snow was falling straight down now and the amber lights of Incamna around them glowed.

"Yes!" he shouted.

Kaly hugged Janae, "You did it! You did it! You did so good!"

"Let's dig ourselves out now." Roland climbing out to the front of the vehicle. Tryal and Cody followed.

"Wait, I have an idea," said Tryal, "Get back in. You'll want to be in here if this works." He sat back in the truck and Roland cocked an eyebrow in disbelief.

"What's your idea, Einstein?"

"Kaly, is she still awake?"

"Yeah, barely." Kaly brushed the snow off of her neck and wiping her face with her own shirt.

"Let's see if she can get the wind to clear our way."

"Can she do that?" asked Roland and Kaly in unison.

"Stupid. Look. Did you just see what she did? I think it actually cares about her. She's never given it directions. It's always just responded to her emotions without her saying anything. She's always been protected by it. Just now, I think it thought we were the ones hurting her. It was trying to stop us. If it cares that much about her, I bet she can give it a few small directions," said Tryal.

Roland shrugged. "Wouldn't hurt to try."

Cody brushed the few loose strands from Janae's face. "I need you to do one more thing, Janae. Can you hear me? Are you still awake?"

"Mmmm eahh."

"Sounded like a yes to me," said Roland.

"Janae, the wind's stopped, but we're still stuck. Can you tell the wind to clear the road so we can get you to the hospital? Can you do that for me?" Cody asked.

"Mmmhh ah."

"Janae, we need you to help us. Can you ask the wind to clear the road?" Kaly pleaded.

Tryal leaned in, "Janae, please do this. This is the last thing we'll ask of you. Just tell it to clear the road."

Janae's eyes opened. She whispered something.

Roland started to open his door and Tryal shouted, "Close it!" With a jolt, the back of the Cherokee lifted up and moved forward. A sharp wind came from behind them and leveled the snow ahead. The air was filled with white. Now, they couldn't even see the road. The car continued to shake. Tryal grabbed hold of the oh-crap bar and the center console, Kaly pulled Janae close to her, and Roland clicked on his seat belt and grasped the steering wheel. The back end continued to lift up and drop down with a thud time after time.

"I'm not sure this was that smart of an idea," said Roland.

"Yeah, neither am I," responded Tryal.

The air swirled around, a deafening roar louder than a jumbo jet.

The car started to move forward. The braked tires were sliding across the ice on the road. Roland popped the emergency brake off and shifted the gears into neutral.

"Why did you do that?" said Tryal through gritted teeth.

"At some point, we're going to stop sliding and hit solid pavement. I don't want to flip the Cherokee when we do."

Tryal grimaced. "No! No! No!" as the Cherokee sped up. He dug his hand into a thin tear on side of the seat and pushed his feet against the floorboard.

"We just hit seventy! We're going to die," said Roland, "and it was your idea." The car jolted again. "Oh, no, oh, no," muttered Roland.

The white sheet of snow that had surrounded the Cherokee dissipated and the road in front of them opened up. The wind had blown the highway clean in front of them. The large drifts on either side of the lanes left a tunnel, an invitation, straight down the center. The road was clear except for the thin layer of ice resting on top.

"It worked!"

"And now we're going to die!" Roland struggled to pull his arm free enough to put ahead of him. Half a mile ahead, was a semi, jackknifed across the center divider with the trailer overturned, dumping frozen cattle across all four lanes. Roland tugged on the steering wheel and simultaneously, against all of the lessons of Mr. Martin (his tenth-grade driving instructor), jammed the brake pedal far into its holding. The accelerating car gracefully slipped into a spin, moving like a top down the highway.

Kaly's tears gushed and she sobbed, sucking air between rhythmic piercing cries. Her panic filled the car, Tryal's arms went to gooseflesh, and Roland's jaw clenched.

If they had looked back to Kaly, shaking and bawling on top of the bleeding Janae, they would have pissed themselves. Her deep heaving set a tempo and she herself, her skin, eyes, her very self, were glowing. The strobing, dampened light was blue and growing more intense with every breath she took. Her eyes were sealed and she showed no sign that she knew what she was doing. The light grew and pulsed, faster and faster. Its aura line touched Cody on the neck and he twitched. It was cold. It pulsed once more, less than a second later, hitting the boys again, seeping the heat from them. Their eyes rolled back and their grips released. Once more, further out, past the Cherokee's body, the light flashed and cooled the boys into unconsciousness. The spinning vehicle was feet from the heap of frozen cattle.

The blue light flickered and strobed, Kaly's eyes sprung open, her throat struck a high sustained octave, and the glow, the bubble surrounding them exploded, lighting the highway for a mile in a sudden burst of white.

They were gone.

The cattle truck, the stiff bovine carcasses resembling spilled coffee grounds, sat in the highway between the hardened walls of snow, alone.

"Turning and turning in the widening gyre

The falcon cannot hear the falconer;

Things fall apart; the centre cannot hold;

Mere anarchy is loosed upon the world,"

—From The Second Coming by William Butler Yeats

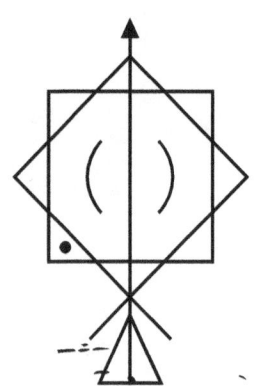

Chapter Six

DIRECTIONS

THE VOICE WAS SOFT but Tryal jerked awake in surprise.

i need you

The thought of Door, of Death, hung over Tryal as he awoke in a hospital bed, and he called back to her, but no answer came.

He opened his eyes. "You need me? That's a first."

He waited. There was no response. "What do you need? You know I hate it when you do this!"

The room was empty. Only the muted voices of nurses talking in the hallway drifted through. He ran his left hand down his right arm. An I.V. had been started below his elbow, and based on the pinprick marks, they had trouble finding a good entry point. His left leg, above the ankle, was in a cast. There were gashes along his body, but none too deep nor wide, until he touched his face. His left cheek had four stitches on a cut running between the bridge of his nose and earlobe.

He was in pain. He was in the hospital.

Okay. Now how did I get here and how do I get out? thought Tryal.

There was a moment of confusion and then the memories surfaced. They were driving through the storm . . . he shivered. Something was missing. Big chunks of time.

Taped to the television was a note, scribbled in Kaly's handwriting: "Sleepyhead, we're in B9. Glad you're OK."

He pulled himself out of bed. His mother had brought a new set of clothes and laid them on the chair in the corner. He dressed quickly, knowing he didn't want Kaly to see him in a white hospital gown. His cast had acquired a few signatures (along with a crude drawing from Roland), one was Kaly's and the other one looked like Janae's.

So Janae had been up and around. That's good news. Maybe.

A pair crutches leaned against the corner, obviously for his use. He picked them up and hobbled past the unused bed closer to the door. He turned the corner and started down the hall.

He'd never been in this hospital before. This was the one hospital that other people in Incamna avoided. The facilities were nice, the people weren't.

A few minutes later and he was lost. He had moved into a section of the hospital that was creepy by any description. The smell of decay was floating in the air. People shuffled in and out of their rooms. Several overhead lights were burned out. He was in the hospice section. He continued walking, determined to get to the large doors marked "EXIT" at the other end of the hall.

A gurney was rolled out by a frumpy nurse looking like a bulldog. She parked it in the hall and Tryal stared. A body lay on it, covered by a single white sheet. He walked towards it. Reaching the foot of the gurney, he quickened his pace to get past it.

An arm shot out from under the sheet and yanked him towards it. He dropped the crutch with a clang and a breeze blew past him, the sheet fell revealing the pale skin of a dead face. An old woman, closed eyes sunk into their sockets, skin pulled tight to the bone, lay there, motionless. The grip was tight.

The eyes opened and stared at Tryal. They were black, without any white. From her slit, dry lips came a drawling, gurgling voice, "There is more than one door to the Zwischen, into the Blend. Find her, the girl who is awake past midnight and her sulking guest. Inside her house, behind the red cloth, is one more door back. Go there. She can only be safe there."

Tryal whispered to the blank face, "Who?"

The woman's dry lips continued to mutter but her voice grew deeper, "The wolf will run free. Much do I know, and more can see of the fate of the gods, brothers shall fight and fell each other. You stand in axe-age, and then a sword-age, a wind-age, a wolf-age, ere the world falls. And you will be drained to reknit it all and hung to begin all anew. Stand watch of . . ."

A gruff voice shouted behind him, "What are you doing?"

Tryal panicked and turned to find the nurse staring at him. She pushed him away from the body. As he glanced back to the old woman, the sheet was over her face, her arm tucked nicely underneath.

"I'm sorry. I didn't mean to. I dropped my crutch and stumbled," said Tryal.

"Where are you going?"

"To room B9. My friends are there."

"Then get there, now!"

"I would, but I'm lost." Tryal didn't mean to be that honest. His first re-action was to get out of there as quickly as possible, but the words just spoke themselves.

"Straight out the doors behind you, to the left. It's in the urgent care section. Now get going." Nurse Bulldog grabbed the ends of the gurney and started pushing it, leaving Tryal blankly staring at her back. "I said get going."

He turned and left through the doors.

Tryal shook his head. Directions from dead people. Strange. But not the strangest thing he'd encountered. Tryal's life had always been difficult. It had also been odd.

At first, there were the things he could see, things that no other five-year-old saw, which others attributed to an over-active imagination. Then strange forms visited, moving in and out of his room at night.

Finally, there were the voices. Late into the evening, ambulance sirens would wail out on the highway a few blocks from his house, and the walls in his room would begin to ripple. The voices never came unless there was misery and pain nearby in the world. The voices were many at first. They were unintelligible voices further down a hall, close by but just beyond reach. They grew louder night after night. In the beginning, Tryal strained to hear them, to make out the words. If he could just grab hold of a single syllable, the rest would unravel.

The volume stayed low at first. It became deafening as the months rolled on. He would pull the pillows over his head, stuff cotton in his ears, crank his music up, anything to mute the voices. Sleep at night was chased away and his grades plummeted as he routinely slumbered in class.

Then the interventions from his foster parents and teachers began. He kept lying: "I just don't get the classes. It all moves too fast." None of the work surpassed him, he was bright and he knew it. At the depth of the spiraling descent, he broke into his foster-father's liquor cabinet and drank himself to a stupor. He woke the next morning in his own vomit on the back porch as his foster-father beat him across his back with a belt.

The voices stopped after that night. Months passed.

Sleep returned. His grades improved. His foster-father's belief in harsh beatings as discipline was reinforced and repeated. After another runaway attempt, they were removed from that foster-family and moved to Vera's house by the woman who would ultimately adopt them and they would call "Mom."

One night, amidst the falling snow, as he crossed the intersection, a voice came. It spoke one word.

i

In the following nights, he heard more words.

sorry fear sorry

Strange, scattered, and disturbing, but they were words, not just background noise.

"Sorry? For what?" Again, no response. Weeks passed and Tryal waited for the voice to return.

Again, near the end of March of his eleventh year, Tryal was making the trek from the SavMart to his house in the middle of the drifting snow. This night it had ceased snowing. The wind blew the settling snow into sculptures with soft lines. He had stood underneath the amber street light watching the drifts grow.

do you fear me

Slow to respond, Tryal said, "No, not anymore. Who are you?"

The voice, in words and thoughts, poured through his mind.

i am your end all of your ends the last the door threshold silence beyond silence death

The words came without pause or change in tone or cadence. They were akin to words read from a dictionary. No pauses. No inflection. Words.

Tryal asked questions and the voice answered. The voice asked questions and Tryal answered. The two talked far into the night until Roland found him the next morning, shivering and huddled against the streetlight. The conversations since were both frequent and long. A tenuous companionship formed between the young boy Tryal and his new friend, Death.

CHAPTER SEVEN

THE PIT

WEDNESDAY, FEBRUARY 1, 2012

THE OLD MAN NAMED MAORI was wrapped in burlap and his beard fell out underneath his hood. He tugged at the camel's reins and did not smile as he said, "The Sahara is the best place to find meteorites. It's not that more land here than anywhere else. The desert would be cruel if she simply hurled stones down at travelers! Nothing moves but the sand. And the rocks that fall here, they stay untouched, if they are even looked upon."

Mr. Hu walked ahead, his long legs stepping with ease over the drifting sand. Mr. Mu did not fare as well. He paced several feet behind the third camel and breathed heavily with each step. He coughed, taking in a gulp of sand as it stirred in the air around him. His coughing fit brought him to his knees. Mr Hu looked over his shoulder and stopped.

Despite the heat of the sun, Maori shivered. Something was wrong about these two. His lips started to form the word "djinn," but he caught himself knowing that to breathe the word in the presence of an actual one was to invite ruin.

Mr. Hu held a long finger to his mouth.

Mr. Mu picked himself up from the ground. "He wants you to stop thinking so loudly. You are bothering him and you are bothering me. Isn't that right, Mr. Hu?"

Maori shivered again. Mr. Hu was vaulting forward again, leaving light footprints in the sand with his long legs.

Mr. Mu coughed. "I think I will set up lodging here. You simply need to find your door and come back to me and I'll be waiting. Walking is for worms." He grimaced and hurled a handful of sand at Maori, "I said to stop thinking! I am tired, I am hungry and you think so loudly it is like the buzzing of flies. I should eat you and solve two of my problems at the same time."

Maori stood with his arms limp, unwilling to move. The air blew sand into his mouth and he breathed, the grit raking against his throat. He coughed.

Mr. Mu stood up, took a step towards him, raised his hand and moved his finger in a curling motion. Maori's throat tightened and his vision blurred.

"*We are here.*"

Mr. Mu said, "Thankfully."

"*Drop him. He will be needed soon.*"

Mr. Mu grinned, a smile full of teeth resembling those of hacksaw blades, hundreds of sharp small teeth lined along a white edge against two thin lips. Mr. Mu dropped his hand and Maori fell to the sand, coughing and holding his throat.

The old man clawed and rushed towards Mr. Hu, "This isn't," he coughed, "this isn't where we were," another cough, "where we were going."

Mr. Mu had walked up behind Maori still struggling to gain his footing. He said, "If Mr. Hu says this is it, your response should be 'Where is the shovel?'"

Maori held out his hands. "But we did not bring a shovel."

Mr. Mu kicked him squarely in his spine, "Then dig with your hands!"

Maori fell forward, sand cramming into his mouth.

Spitting, he said, "Dig? For what?"

Mr. Mu drew his foot back and said, "You're not digging. Dig!"

Maori clawed at the ground, his stomach clenched against the bile creeping back up.

"Digging is right?" Mr. Mu asked.

Mr. Hu studied the ground, "*Yes.*"

Mr. Mu's saw-blade teeth flashed in the sun. He pulled a cigar from his pocket and waved it in a circle. It lit itself and he drew a long pull on it. The smoke lifted away.

The sky had grown dark and twinkled with stars. Something was wrong. The sky was too large, the horizon too close. It was growing closer. It was near them and they were upon a rock of sand in the expanse of sky and stars. The sand poured around them falling into the nothingness of space.

"You should dig faster, little man," Mr. Mu said, bending over and holding his cigar out, waving across the abyss as if Maori hadn't seen it.

"What have you done? Where are we?" Maori asked.

"*We have slipped beyond your world.*"

"What I think the bloke's saying is that you've stumbled across a booby trap, you boob," Mr. Mu said.

"You told me to," Maori said.

"Yes. It means you are close to finding what we need and you should KEEP DIGGING!" Mr. Mu shouted. Maori dug faster, scrambling and spraying the sand as it wheeled away into the infinite sky.

Mr. Mu pulled opened his pocket watch and looked at the receding circle of sand. He said, "At most we have 30 seconds."

"I'm digging, I'm digging." Maori was crying now, "What am I digging for?" The tears were in lines down in his face forming mud along his cheeks. Quietly, he cursed, "*Bara nail!*"

"Tsk! What horrible language, but a great question!" Mr. Mu hunched down, looking over Maori, "Mr. Hu?"

"*I do not know.*"

"What? Allah, we're going to die!" Maori said. The word "die" echoed.

Mr. Mu leaned over the hole. In two voices he said, "That's odd."

One of the voices came above Maori and the other below him, from the hole. Maori leaned over into the hole and screamed. He was looking at a reflection of the three of them. No, that didn't seem right. He leaned forward and touched the reflection and it touched back.

Mr. Hu leaned over, his long nose an inch from Maori, "*You've found the spot.*"

Mr. Hu leaned forward and unraveled a crimson cloth and pulled out the three splinters. One by one he dropped them into the hole and they floated in the center. The third one fell as Maori grabbed Mr. Hu's legs, the sand inches from the hole.

The falling sand stopped.

There they stood, floating in the abyss on a disc of sand, peering into a hole that showed them copies of themselves. Mr. Hu inched forward. The weight of his foot increased ever so slightly. He looked down the long stretch of his legs. The sand underneath him and Maori was darker—mud. Maori, still bawling and huddled, had wet himself.

Mr. Mu spoke, "You know that I'll stand with you after this. We are one. But brother, cousin, I would press you to consider caution in this next act. You cannot turn back. Nothing, no one can undo what you are about to do."

"*You and caution.*"

"Do not jest. I am serious."

"*Yes. We both are,*" Mr. Hu said, reaching and pulling Maori up by his arm. Mr. Hu extended a long finger and sliced through Maori's wrist. His hand fell away.

Maori screamed in agony, "Oh! *Wald il hawyaa!*"

Mr. Mu took a step back, his heels on the edge of the spinning disc of sand, "Is that the final key?"

"*No. Your splinter was. This is bait.*"

Mr. Hu held Maori's bleeding wrist over the hole and it drained into the mirror reality, filling the hole where the splinters rotated. Mr. Mu grimaced at the word "bait," and drew long on his cigar, holding the smoke in without breath.

"My hand? Oh, my hand!" Maori screamed, "WHAT DID YOU DO? WHAT ARE YOU DOING? MY HAND!"

"I am not killing you. Be quiet."

"OH, MY HAND! MY LIFE! KILL ME NOW!" Maori wailed.

"You did just cut off his hand. Screaming is to be expected," Mr. Mu said, his tongue tip coursing his top lip, "It's my favorite part."

Mr. Hu squeezed Maori's wrist. The blood spurted and stopped. Maori screamed and fell to the ground as Mr. Hu released him. He burrowed his face into the wet sand, clutching his wrist. He twisted towards the stars spinning in a rush around them and his scream turned into pure horror as at first he saw a cross of cubes, each block falling into and out of each other. A grotesque, massive head resembling a distorted, phantasmic wolf rose as a shadow in front of the stars and fell down upon them.

Then it was gone.

The stars stopped spinning. The Sahara Desert slept as if nothing of the infinite terror had ever happened. They were still standing, except for Maori, where they were when the world disappeared. A third man stood above where Maori had dug. A dark man—not a dark-skinned man, but truly dark as if deepest night had a color.

Maori stammered, "A midnight man . . ."

The man slavered over Maori. His eyes froze Maori's screaming lips and Maori's bowels released. He spoke, a voice that started beyond the stars above them and ended at his lips, "Yes."

The Midnight Man turned to Mr. Mu and Mr. Hu. "I hunger." The last thing Maori heard was the Midnight Man snarl, "Is that my first?"

Mr. Hu nodded, and there was no longer the Midnight Man but the rushing mouth of a great smoldering monster. Then darkness.

"Ocean is more ancient than the mountains,

and freighted with the memories and the dreams of time."

—H. P. Lovecraft

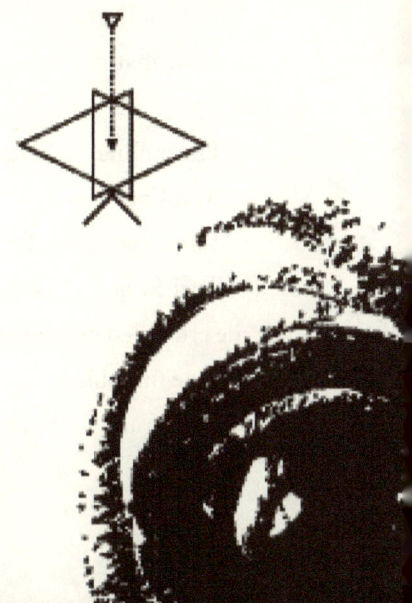

CHAPTER EIGHT

WATER, WATER EVERYWHERE

THE ROOM WAS FILLED WITH CHATTER when Tryal walked in.

"Sleepyhead, you're awake," Kaly hugged him, nearly knocking him off of his feet and causing him to clasp his crutches.

"Welcome back to the land of the living," Roland said, his back against the sink and mirror, arms folded.

Cody only grunted at him, still angry from the aquarium.

"Now that you're back, could you try and put a smile on his face?" asked Kaly.

"I'm smiling," said Cody.

"And I'm Wonder Woman," said Kaly.

"I'll call you that if you promise to wear the costume," Roland smirked.

Tryal turned to Janae in her bed. She looked up at him and back down at the crumpled bed sheets. "You okay?" Tryal tapped her bed with his crutch.

Janae mumbled, "Ya."

Tryal grunted, "Sorry. I should've—"

Kaly spun, "What? We did awesome! We got her out, through the storm and—"

Roland coughed, harshly. "Here we are, back to the whole 'super team' thing again. Who are we kidding? 'And in other news, earlier today a young girl gets cut up looking at the fishes and our mighty heroes The Young Gods were there to save the day.' We're pathetic. We're like the Wonder Twins. She bleeds and all you can do is try to get an answer from the future. Heck, you got a busy signal. And me? What do I do? I talk to bugs. We talk to things—that's it. We should be called 'The Answering Service.'"

Kaly wrapped her arms around herself and leaned against the wall. "I'm sorry. You're right. The voices just aren't . . . I don't know . . . Consistent. Maybe if I practiced like Cody. Worked harder." She lowered her head and rubbed the back of her neck. "I just thought, we've done pretty good for ourselves. Shouldn't we be proud? We actually did something."

No one responded. Kaly sighed and walked over to the sink and turned on the faucet. She splashed a little water on her face and stared at her reflection in the mirror. She leaned down once more and splashed some more water on her face. The locket slipped out of her shirt and dangled in front of the mirror. Kaly looked at the reflection of the locket in front of her, letting it spin and reflecting the light from overhead. It was a beacon, sparkling over and over again. Its silver face was bright under the lights. It slowed its spin and she realized he had been a bit mesmerized by it.

Escaping her trance, she spoke, "There's something written on the back of this. It's weird."

Tryal walked over, reached out and took it. He remembered it had some strange designs but had overlooked them. On the other side, its edge was formed into a molded rim along and shaped in a braided knot. Inside this, in relief, was a symbol:

"I don't even know what that is," Tryal said.

Roland said, "What are you talking about?"

Tryal said, "A locket some homeless guy gave us."

"Throw that away. You're going to get hepatitis. And then you're going to give it to Kaly," Roland said.

Cody said, "When?"

Kaly said, "Outside the aquarium. I ran out and this guy grabbed me. Tryal came and pushed him off."

"Tryal to the rescue!" Roland said, "Guess you weren't entirely useless back there."

Tryal said, "He was looney. But he gave us this locket with all these strange symbols. It's just . . . I don't know . . . Kinda cool. Kinda weird."

"The story of your life. Although with more weird and far less cool," Roland said.

"It reminds me of those crop circles," Kaly said, running her finger along its edge.

"Ya, it does." He turned it over. The other side simply had a large circle on it, almost closed, the one end narrow and sharp, the other done in the shape of a hook:

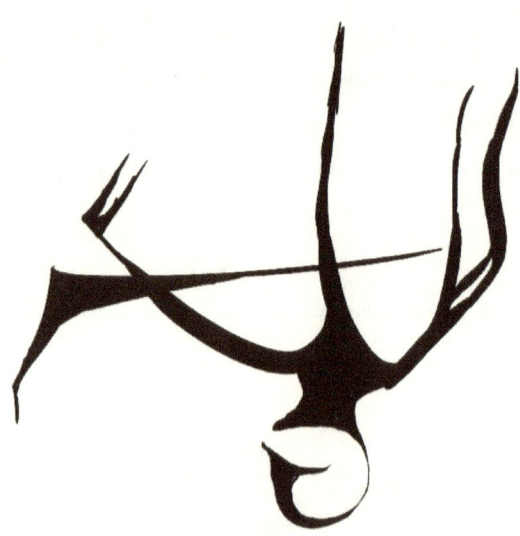

Tryal read aloud from the inscription inside, "Face to face, show me to my brother. Between two worlds, I'll open another."

Kaly winced, putting her hand to her forehead. She was getting another headache. She tried to ignore it and said, "Cute rhyme, but it makes no sense."

Tryal said, "It's a riddle."

"Of course it is. All strange things given to you by strangers are a riddle, Frodo. So do we have to speak the answer in Elvish?" Roland asked.

Tryal smirked, "No. And it's Elven. Not Elvish."

Roland laughed, "Loser."

Tryal smiled, ignoring Roland, "A mirror. Look at the locket. It is a riddle. The answer is a mirror. 'Face to face, show me to my brother.' The locket is a mirror inside. Another mirror is its brother."

He turned the locket over and over in his hands, moving his thumb across the odd symbols along its outside. He opened it up again and scanned through the words and stared at himself in the mirror of the locket. The image shook, and for a second, he saw a double image—himself staring into the mirror and overlaid, in a phantom outline, his own face much older, bruised and beaten, a strange tattoo like the one on the locket across his cheek. The double image was gone and his own face stared back at him. What was that?

"Well, are you going to do it?" asked Roland.

"Do what?" Tryal asked, lost in the reflection.

"Uh, hold it up to another mirror," Roland said.

"Oh, ya," said Tryal. He slowly brought the locket up and turned it so both mirrors faced each other.

Nothing happened. He continued to look at the strange tunnel created in the mirrors reflections.

"Nothing is happening," Tryal said.

"What did you expect? A magic Narnia door to open up?" Roland asked.

Kaly said, "Well, ya, kinda. You are Mr. Freaky. Weird crap seems to follow you around."

Tryal shook his head.

Was that something moving down the tunnel? What was that?

He squinted to see but the reflection in the mirror had grown hazy—blurry. He tried to focus. He shut and opened his eyes but nothing improved.

The door to the hospital room opened. A nurse stepped in, young, with flowing red hair, a freckled complexion and bright green eyes.

"How you doing?" Roland asked her as she entered.

"Settle down. She's not here for you," Tryal said.

The nurse ignored Roland's words but Kaly still caught the look of surprise on her face as she scanned the room. The nurse had taken a slight step back.

Had she heard what they had been talking about?

The nurse looked at Cody and smiled. He returned the grin.

Roland raised an eyebrow. "You two know each other?"

Cody narrowed his eyes.

Kaly continued to rub her neck. Another headache was forming. She heard the voice again in the far back of her head.

Watch her!

Kaly shook her head.

Where was this coming from?

This voice felt different. This voice didn't come from outside. It came from deep inside her. It wasn't her own thought, and yet it spoke in a familiar tone. Was she going crazy? Maybe she truly was the strange one in the group of freaks.

"So, how's our patient?" The nurse walked over to Janae and checked her I.V. bag. Cody sat up and moved to the other side of the room.

"I'm okay," Janae said, wiping her nose on her bedsheet.

"That's good. I'm Michelle and I'll be taking care of you for the rest of the day. I need to switch out this I.V. bag," she said as she handed the new bag to Cody. "Could you hold this?"

After checking Janae's vitals, the nurse asked, "Have you been sleeping well?"

Janae hesitated and then said, "Not really. Just can't stop thinking."

Low in volume, just above a whisper, but deep like a voice heard under water, came the call, "*It's time. Come over.*"

Roland raised an eyebrow at Tryal.

"Ya, I heard it too," said Tryal.

Cody, looking between Tryal and Roland, asked, "What was that?"

The lights in the room flickered and the television turned on to a screen of crackling static.

The nurse had backed away from Janae and scanned around the room.

Kaly saw her own reflection and screamed. The mirror had turned to a view of water and leaked. The sink overflowed and poured onto the ground. Janae's I.V. bag popped and the liquid splashed across her and the nurse. The nurse screamed.

All around them, water poured into the room. The windows outdoors had turn to a view of water. They began to sweat and drip onto the floor. Then they cracked and burst, as did the mirror, the water quickly rising in the room.

"It's the locket! Close it!" Kaly said, rushing to grab it out of his hands. She stopped and grabbed the sides of her head. The dull buzzing of the headache had changed into sharp needles. A migraine. She grunted and leaned back against her closet.

"Close it!" Roland screamed at Tryal and plodded over to him.

His fingers were already on the opened locket. "It won't close. I can't close it." Roland grabbed it and pushed against both sides as hard as he could. The locket didn't budge.

Cody moved to the room's door and pulled. "What's happening? The door is stuck!"

"Come over." The voice came strong, loud and deep.

Cody stood up and shouted, "STOP!" The water paused mid-flow and hung in the air. The small waves that were already chest-deep froze and the water stopped as if turned to ice.

Michelle, the nurse, stared in rapt horror.

"Thanks," said Roland, who relaxed, and shook his wet sleeve in a mock attempt to dry out.

It was in vain. As fast as the water stopped, it began again. The cascading water rushed into the room. Janae stood up as the surface of their small lake had completely covered her bed. Michelle ran to the wall and madly pressed the red "call nurse" button. She still searched the room, her eyes wide with fear.

"Stop!" shouted Cody again. Nothing happened and the water continued to pour in. "STOP! STOP! STOP!" He was red in the face as he shouted these words, his fist balled and his knuckles white.

Kaly shouted back, "It's so cold! It's like ice!"

Janae slipped under the water and back up, "It's salt water. Sea water." As if to prove her right, a small brightly colored fish leaped out of the water and swam past.

"Who cares? We're still going to drown," shouted Roland. The sound of the water pouring into the room was deafening.

Tryal struggled to shut the locket and Roland waded back to him, "What are you doing? We've got to get out of here."

"I've got to close it," Tryal said.

Tryal said, "Help me."

"Here. I've got an idea." Roland swam across the room to the door and pulled the fire extinguisher from the room. He turned back to Tryal, "Set the locket on the counter and back off."

Tryal had barely set the locket down when Roland heaved back with the red extinguisher, the hose flapping from the side, and swung down like homemade sledgehammer. The locket shot out from underneath and splashed into the water.

Cody swam over to Janae. He slipped and his head went under the water. As he went under, he heard a voice, "I'm here. I'm waiting." He thought, that's not the same voice. It spoke again, "Come for me, Cody. Come find me." He jerked up and brought his head above the water. Why had the voice said his name? Had he recognized the voice?

"Find it!" Roland and Tryal both sunk under the water, madly combing the floor. Janae and Kaly had paused and stared at the large, dark shapes, half-swimming, underneath the roiling surface. The surface of the water reflected the shape of the mirror behind her. In the churning water, it resembled a black, smoking door.

Tryal broke the water and lifted the locket up, its chain dangling, "I've got it."

"Did we shut it?" Kaly asked just at the same moment Janae asked, "What are those things?"

In answer to both, the splashing waves froze. For a brief second, every ounce of water turned to snow, sending shivers through them as they stood drenched. All traces of the water and the dark shadows underneath its surface disappeared. The mirrors were mirrors again, the windows were windows, their clothes were dry. The only reminder was the slight smell of salt water in the air and the taste on their lips.

Michelle, the nurse, ran terrified into the hallway. Tryal watched her leave.

Did a few of the shadows follow her?

Kaly turned to the bathroom and threw up as she reached the toilet.

Tryal can carry it. I don't want it, she thought. The other voice in her head bellowed as she hurled up her hospital breakfast.

We could use it.

She argued agains the voices. *No. It's horrible!*

Roland grunted, "The whole room smells like fish now."

Tryal sniffed. "You're right. It does smell like fish. That's strange."

Cody ran a finger across the mirror, "Stranger than the mirror becoming a waterfall?"

"No. But still strange," Tryal said, "It was salty."

"So?" asked Cody.

"It's sea water."

Roland replied, "Again, I ask 'so?'"

"We live in Nebraska! The closest sea water is a thousand miles away. Why not fresh water? And why does it smell like fish? This water didn't come from your pipes. It didn't come from here."

"Between two worlds, I'll open another," Cody quoted.

"And why water? It was supposed to . . . I don't know, make a door. Narnia, blast it!" he laughed to himself. "It doesn't make sense." He pulled out the locket and held it up.

He stared at it and said, "Look at it. There's nothing on this thing that even hints of water. No symbols, nothing. Even in the language of weird, this doesn't make sense. This type of stuff usually comes with some cryptic warning label—I'd expect huge splashing waves on the outside. Or some guy drowning. There's nothing but these weird symbols."

"Keep that closed," Roland said.

Tryal flipped the locket over. "It's closed."

Roland stood up, fighting off the shakes from the sudden temperature drop. "Too much weird for me. I need a walk," he said as he left the room.

Tryal dropped the locket on the counter. "Ya, me too." And he left after, turning the opposite direction down the hall.

None of them saw Cody lean down, pick up the locket, and place it in his pocket.

CHAPTER Nine

MEETING OF THE MINDS

MR. MU POURED FROM A SMALL GLASS VIAL etched with strange carvings. It was nearly empty except a small amount of a red liquid at the bottom—a strange shimmering substance the color of blood but squirming as if alive. He rubbed a dab of the blood-colored fluid between his fingers, careful to put the top on the vial, and held it up to the streetlight. He muttered, "This is wasteful."

Mr. Hu stood next to him. Both of them were wounded, black ooze dripping from several cuts. "*Go faster. They are coming.*"

Mr. Mu drew with his finger in the air, the red on his fingertip in sharp contrast to his pale skin. There was no unexpected noise nor lights, but their bodies began to mend, their shredded clothes reformed. In a few seconds, they were as before.

Mr. Hu coughed and held out his hand. A thin line of deep crimson was still cut into it.

Mr. Mu rubbed the bridge of his nose, "I don't know. Cover it, I guess."

Mr. Hu pulled his sleeve down over the cut, "*That was a first.*"

Mr. Mu said, "We don't have much left. This was a foolish use."

Sleet fell on the streets of Denver, Colorado. It melted and puddled at their feet, reflecting the overhead streetlights.

Mr. Hu spoke, "*You blame me.*"

"Blame you? Yes, I blame you. We released a beast and the beast turned on us. We still haven't been paid and we wasted much on escaping and healing. We have less than a vial remaining."

"*We completed our task.*"

"A task we should have fled from! We were fools."

"*Quiet. They are here.*"

The limo slinked through the downtown streets, the lights of the building reflected on its dark windows. It slowed in front of Mr. Mu and Mr. Hu and a door opened.

Climbing into the large passenger compartment, the two sat down across from three gaunt and elderly gentlemen. They were skin-on-skeleton thin. Their eyeballs rattled in their sockets, the darkness behind them made a crescent over the milky white balls. The joints of their fingers were carved to the bone. Gentlemen Skeletons.

"Makepeace and Sniffles," began the center Skeleton, looking between them.

Mr. Mu leaned forward, "Those, um," he sniffed, "aren't our proper names."

The Skeleton smiled, his thin skin pulling back across the bones, "Yes, but they do seem to be much more descriptive than Mu and Hu. Besides, your previous owner is gone—you should let those old names go."

Mr. Mu said, "It is Mr. Mu and Mr. Hu. We don't answer to anything else." He sat up and brushed a hand across his black jacket as if dusting some unseen piece of dirt away. "Now, we have a contract that requires your sign-off. Can we proceed with business?"

The Skeleton spoke, "No."

Mr. Mu coughed and spat, "No? What do you mean 'no'? The job is done.

The beast released. Sign off on the contract and pay us."

The Skeleton looked through the windows, past Mr. Mu. "You released the wrong one."

Mr. Mu snapped a sharp look at Mr. Hu, "We were meticulous. We found the path and the path led to the Pit. It was guarded and it was hidden. If it wasn't the right one, then your instructions were in error."

"Diversions. Those were all diversions."

"Diversions? The path was precarious enough that . . ."

The Skeleton leaned forward, spitting as he spoke, "Stop! You know he's the wrong one."

Mr. Mu and Mr. Hu shared a glance. Mr. Hu shrugged. Mr. Mu turned said, "Yes, we had disagreement as to the wisdom of releasing him." The leather seat squeaked as he shifted. "Next time, perhaps, it would help if we were given better insight into your goals."

"No."

"No? You want us to stumble in the dark?" Mr. Mu asked.

"Our goals are our own. You had a job. You failed," replied Mr. Center.

"We unlocked the locks and released the creature that was there. You have the writ. The contract states that you are to sign it, seal it and turn it over to us. All it needs is a final stroke. We are done with this contract."

The Center Skeleton howled, "You released a monster! We called for a weapon. You let loose a nightmare! Do you know what you have let loose?"

Mr. Mu coughed, "We, umm, imagine that we have," he rubbed his hands together, "Umm, released one of the Foundation Beasts."

"Yes! Yes! Think of what that means. From the darkness before the worlds. Here. Now. We are alone. Cut off—" screeched the Skeleton on the right.

The Skeleton in the middle slammed his hand into the other's chest, "Quiet. Our troubles are not their concern."

Mr. Mu smiled, "Our only concern is our payment. We have fulfilled our contract. Pay us."

"Here is your writ but your contract is still unfinished." The Skeleton held out a small piece of paper. Mr. Hu took it from him and read it. It was true. He winced as the top edge of the final symbol crackled and creaked as black ash. It was almost all finished but that small piece of the carving. He could draw no flow of Color from this. It could not be spent. The finished writ would give them access to their full payment—an unimaginable amount. Unfinished, it was worthless.

They had risked their very lives in this last task and they had nothing for it. Mr. Mu leaned forward and then back into his seat. He stared out the window into the lane of buildings. "Please, when you have audience with your Master, can you remind him that while we serve him out of contract and debt, we served his father out of the loyalty of our hearts."

Mr. Center opened a space between his thin lips and spoke, "But, our Lord and, ahem, Master is willing to give you the option of making it up. You can have the full amount if you locate someone and deliver him to us. In fact, we will double the payment. Twice the flow of Color will be yours. And you will be given freedom from report. Free birds, the two of you."

Mr. Mu bit his lip and pressed his thumbs hard together. "Promises upon promises with nothing delivered. Your Master will speak of flow and gold and glory as I dig and move this earth and he holds another in case mine breaks."

The skeleton on the right sat upright and pointed at Mr. Mu. "Hold your words! That is the King of the Blend you speak of, the one that sits on the Seeing Father's Throne. He holds scepter, sword, and hammer together. I will gut you through and pluck you clean if you speak another sly word against him." His finger slipped across the black blade now in his hand.

Mr. Mu said, "Your dog needs a muzzle." He smiled, leaned back and said, "You don't need to proselytize us. We aren't members of the," he glanced at Mr. Hu, "What are they calling themselves now? The Blue Fist? The White Fist? Blue Blade." He turned back to the Skeletons, "We aren't members of the Blue Blade."

The right skeleton spoke again, "There is no resistance!"

Mr. Mu smiled, "Of course there isn't. Everyone loves the great Taranis!

Hades, I'm president of his fan club. This is business. This has nothing to do with politics. We work. We want payment, not contortionist-style contractual debate. We did the job, your client has not delivered payment, and now he has a new assignment? No more! Besides, what source of Color could he have to produce double the payment. The carving is useless without a true and dependable source of magic. No source means no flow!"

"One of the keys has been used."

A look of surprise washed over Mr. Mu's face and then just as quickly he made it vanish. He sat upright, his back straight, his fat fingers squeezing the glass in his hand.

"And who came over?" Mr. Mu asked, wrestling himself to keep a sober face.

"No one," the middle Skeleton spoke.

Mr. Mu struggled to stifle his surprise. Mr. Hu ignored the shocking statements and stared dully at the Gentlemen, their blank expressions mirrored in his own.

"A key was used but nothing came into the Blend," Mr. Mu glanced at Mr. Hu, "How can that be? Perhaps your source was mistaken—overlooked a floating body maybe. A key brings a tag."

"Not this time. The door opened to nothing and no one."

Mr. Mu smiled, "Are you sure your information is accurate? There is a bit of a disconnect between here and there."

The three Gentlemen remained still.

Mr. Mu waited, making eye contact with all three. He grinned a bit more, coughed and said, "Time is shifting, isn't it?"

Mr. Middle spoke, "Time between worlds is always in movement."

Mr. Mu said, "But this is different."

Their forms grew more stiff, although they gave not a quiver of movement in response.

"So you have larger problems than finding a misused key? And the reason you contacted us." Mr. Mu lifted his right hand to motion at Mr. Hu.

"Our Lord, and others, believe it was used by, ahem, a live one. One of the Traveling Men must have found them."

Mr. Mu said, "A live one? You mean, I assume, a generator? A source of the Colors?"

Mr. Center said, "Yes."

"Are there any of those still?" Mr. Mu asked.

Mr. Center spoke in a lower voice and tilted his head forward, "He believes it to be a specific one. He says it might be the ember boy."

Mr. Mu asked, "Of the Meyjar myth?"

Mr. Hu huffed, causing the three Gentlemen and Mr. Mu to pause. The Skeletons twisted their heads around like frightened forest birds.

Mr. Mu spoke quickly, "Forgive my friend. He has had a tickle in his throat for the past few days."

"Quite alright," the Gentleman to the left said, his small eyes seeming to float in their cavernous sockets.

"*No. It is sad that the old man has not given up that ancient obsession,*" Mr. Hu said, his voice resonating through the car's interior.

The Gentleman on the right swooned, knocking his head against his comrade's as his body went limp, his fingers loosened, and he dropped his knife to the limo's floor.

"Stop talking!" the middle Gentleman shouted as he pushed his unconscious friend to the side. That one rolled off of the seat and sprawled across the floor. "Look at that!" Mr. Middle was at the edge of his seat. Before Mr. Mu could react to him, Mr. Middle had shoved his walking stick into the bridge of Mr. Mu's nose.

"If he speaks a single word, I will not hesitate to kill you." He pulled his thumb back along the shaft of the stick, the stick shivered, and a small whirring sound hummed.

Mr. Mu regretted this meeting. Failure here would follow him for a long time. Death wasn't a worry. Reputation was. "Mr. Hu, please."

Mr. Hu waved his hand and leaned back against the seat.

Mr. Mu rubbed his neck, "If I may ask, why doesn't the old man come over and deal with this one himself? I mean, if it is the one he's been looking for?"

The Gentleman on the left folded his hands together, "As you would know, the doors to the other worlds are few. We may send words across, but only words."

Mr. Mu tugged on his shirt, "But surely, he could muster enough power to satisfy this obsession if it's—"

Mr. Middle squeezed the walking stick and pushed Mr. Mu back against his seat, "It is the old man's obsession which will fill your pockets. It is his obsession which will keep you alive. Do you understand?"

Mr. Mu shook his head and regained his composure. "I'm beginning to."

"The boy. And, if there are others, bring them. Bring them all to Thrudvang. Understand?"

"Yes."

"Boy." The Gentleman tapped his stick against Mr. Mu's forehead for each word. "Boy and the others, you stupid old crows."

Mr. Mu swallowed and asked, "Are we excused?"

"Yes." The Gentleman thumped Mr. Mu hard on the forehead.

Mr. Mu waved in the air and he and Mr. Hu were gone.

"Fools!" The Gentleman Skeleton slammed the stick against the seat and smacked his sleeping friend, "Wake up, you easy little idiot." He kicked him hard in the spine, sending a spasm through the sleeping Skeleton.

———

Mr. Mu stood atop of parking garage as the limousine sauntered through the wet night streets. He pulled a cigar from his pocket and lit it, "The boy."

Mr. Hu leaned over the edge, "*If I remember, the Princes had a few dissentors rumored to have appointed watchers for him.*"

"The, um, 'ember boy?'"

"*Yes.*"

"There is no boy."

Mr. Hu spoke, "*Agreed.*"

"We'll need to find him first."

"*Agreed.*"

"They're desperate."

"*And anxious.*"

"Things must be going badly over there," Mr. Mu puffed on his cigar, "And we're stuck with another job."

Mr. Hu said, "*Still no payment.*"

Mr. Mu pulled a carved vial out filled halfway with the churning blood-tinged fluid. "Well, that's not entirely accurate."

"*Thieving again?*" Mr. Hu shifted and the watches, skulls, and various items clipped to his jacket clicked and clacked.

"I am a crow," He stuffed the vial back in his pocket after pouring another drop between his fingers, "Yet, if this is actually a real live one, one that doesn't just smell of Color but actually makes it, screw them. It's ours and ours alone. I won't be duped again."

Mr. Mu bent down and scanned through the streets as Mr. Hu said, "*First step is to find a Traveling Man.*"

"That's not an easy thing. I haven't seen one for years. But, if we must, then," Mr. Mu sniffed and snickered, "Follow my nose!"

"She's mad but she's magic.

There's no lie in her fire."

—CHARLES BUKOWSKI

Chapter Ten

A PROMISE

F ROM UNDER THE FRAYED HOSPITAL BLANKET, Tryal groaned and stirred.

tryal

"Hhhhhh," was all he could muster at . . . what? His eyes focused on the harsh red numbers of the clock.

3:15. AM. In the morning. Crap.

tryal

It was now unavoidable and she wasn't going to leave him alone.

"Door, I'm trying to sleep."

tryal please i need you to listen

"I'm listening," he said and then thought, *But I don't want to be.*

i am sorry you do not want to listen but you have to

Crap, he thought, *Words and thoughts are all the same for her.*

yes they are

Minutes passed and she spoke again.

please listen

Another pause, it was so unlike her.

i have to go away

"Sure." She'd left him several times. For days at a time. Months some-times. Once, for nearly half a year. He'd asked so many times about where she had gone and she'd only respond, "Far away." That response was frightening. Where is "far away" for Death?

for a long time

Oh. "How long is a long time?"

i don't know, another uncharacteristic pause and she spoke, *everything ahead of me is*

"Yes?"

empty

"What's going on? Is something wrong?" He wasn't sure he wanted to hear the answer.

tryal i have to go away

"You've said that. What's wrong?

i have to go away

He started, "What do you . . . "

now

"Door, I'm real confused. I want to help you," he was now standing up in his hospital room, "You have to tell me what's happening."

tryal

"Yes?"

i am scared

Three words he'd never heard her say nor imagined she could. Did she knew what fear was? "What can I do?"

make me a promise

YES! "Yes! Anything."

take care of her

"Who?" Ahhh, he hated when she started talking like this. Half-thoughts. Assuming that he knew what her pronouns referenced. So frustrating.

take care of her take her to the lake she isn't safe here

"Who? What lake? There are hundreds of lakes. What lake?" Okay, there weren't hundreds of lakes but there were a lot of them. Which one did she mean? He continued, "Safe where?"

promise me

"Take care of who?"

promise me please

She was stuck and he was scared he'd never get an answer before she went silent. "OKAY! Yes! I promise."

good-bye tryal i love you

"Who is she, Door?" He had meant to say, "I love you, too."

Nothing.

Absolutely nothing.

"Who?"

Again, still air and the darkness of the room were all that spoke. And they said nothing worthwhile.

"Who? DOOR? What lake? DOOR? DEATH?"

The air shuffled as the air conditioner kicked in, filling the void with a hum. Tryal was alone. His face was still as he thought of the vague promise he'd made.

CHAPTER ELEVEN

LABYRINTH

ROLLING OUT OF BED, Tryal stood on the cold linoleum in his hospital room, confused and shaken. His dreams were quickly retreating. The image of flames and steel stayed with him. Death's voice still haunted him, *take care of her.*

He had made a promise, something he didn't do often. But Death, she could always maneuver him into doing the things he didn't want to do.

Tryal had to get out of this small and lonely room. He slung his Doctor Strange bag over his shoulder. It was lighter than normal. No school books. Probably a notebook, a few pencils, and a pack of M&Ms. He fished for and found the M&Ms and popped one in his mouth.

Maybe Roland's awake.

He walked out and through the corridors, past the silent rooms of sleeping children, each step confirmed that he wasn't just going somewhere but that he was being led. He decided it was time to turn off caution and go by gut. It always worked. Death had left him a challenge and taken a promise. He had wrestled with it, he concluded, throughout his dreams, and now he was just letting God or the universe (he wasn't sure which) help him fulfill the promise.

Turn left. Turn right, to the elevator, down three floors, down another corridor, turn right, turn right to the edge of a staircase and—

Fear rushed back in. It was dark and he was alone. The staircases faded into the basement. He stepped onto the first stair, and then the next, and then the next. His cast clomped against the metal and made the descent difficult. At the bottom, he paused. Brick and shadows filled his vision. In the center of the room, along the walls and the ceiling was laid directionless steel and copper. This was the hospital's boiler room. The room danced with the faint lights of flame caged in iron bellies.

There was no door before him, just a bricked entrance caked with dirt, mold and cobwebs. If this was his great adventure, then this was the entrance to the cave where the dragon slept. He could even see the flames belching out as it snored.

He felt the compulsion to run.

Just turn around. Nothing's here. Leave.

He took another step.

There was no dragon. No great treasure lay under his scaly claw. Nothing to slay. And that was a good thing, as he was armed only with his hospital robe (which he was sure had opened wide enough that his small butt was showing through) and the remote control he'd picked up off his hospital bedside. Hardly the weapons of a warrior.

Tryal walked into the boiler room, twice ducking and once fanning unseen webs from his face. He'd been on enough of these stupid supernatural scavenger hunts to realize that this one was going to be a doozy. It would have been a relief to discover he was insane and none of this, not a single item, actually mattered. But experience had proven that line of thinking was surely going to come up short. Real short.

Four large boilers emerged from the haze of the heat in front of him, bolted down here decades ago. He started to look around. For what, though?

He couldn't answer that. It wasn't as if someone had drawn him a map. But that wasn't right. He did know what he was looking for. He was sure of it, but tried to push it from his mind.

protect her

Shut up! Why would "she" be down here? Who was "she?" And why was "she" so important to have one of the great forces of the cosmos lining up "her" protection service? Who was this "she" that Door wanted him to protect?

But he knew she was down here. This midnight quest would end with a girl.

He stepped around the third boiler. On the ground in front of the hulking pot, a mound of rags rested. But his mind shouted that was wrong. He stared once more at the heap.

And there she was.

It was a girl alright, huddled in front of the boiler, limp, and either unconscious or—no, if the alternative was true he had already failed in his mission. She was alive. He was sure of that for no other reason than he knew he hadn't been woken up in the middle of the night to protect a corpse.

"Don't touch." In his mind, the words hung above her limp sprawling body.

Why not? He hated arguing with himself.

First, she's on fire. And that was true. Without ever touching the thin gown she was in, flames were still on, above, and around her. He could feel their heat. She was absolutely consumed and still not hurt.

protect her

Death's words came back to him. Death wasn't there. She was still silent and "far away." He had made a promise and standing there gaping was not keeping it.

He glanced around for a blanket. He had to get the flames out. Cover her up, roll her over, throw water on her. Something. Where was Smokey the Bear when you needed him?

Was it the heat from the flames he felt? He stood ten feet from the open grated port to a hospital boiler, after all.

He put his hand in the fire and . . .

The flames didn't hurt. He didn't yank his hand back in pain. He didn't scream out in torture. He just stood there with his hands in the flames.

The girl. Remember the girl. Stop being impressed by the fireworks and protect her.

He knelt. She was, at the most, nine or ten. Maybe younger. Her features were sharp for her age—defined cheekbones, thin eyebrows, and thin lips under a small nose.

And fragile. Skin drained of color; her limbs were thin and nearly anorexic. Her eyes had begun to sink slightly into her skull. She was fragile, and likely quite sick.

He reached forward, intending on jostling her slightly, possibly turning her a bit more on to her side so he could pick her up. He moved his one arm under her legs and his left arm slid under her shoulders. She was light.

With little effort, he pushed himself up on his one good leg. She was nearly no weight against him at all. Standing entirely up, he turned towards the door and felt her stir.

Her eyes twitched, opened briefly and were gone.

Not just her eyes. She was gone. Had he imagined it? A slow puff of smoke, rose from the concrete.

He glanced back at where she had lay, but nothing was there.

Tryal stood alone in the large clanking and roaring boiler room of Incamna United.

"[I]t was a huge creature, luminous, ghastly, and spectral . . .

the hell-hound of the legend."

—Sir Arthur Conan Doyle

Chapter Twelve

SPELL-WORKING

Saturday, February 11, 2012

FOUR DAYS AFTER THE HOSPITAL released the last of them, they found themselves wasting a cold winter's afternoon in Tryal and Roland's house. Each of them sprawled out across the living room staring at the television. Their conversation never passed more than arguing over the channel and the occasional "Pass the Doritos."

Kaly pulled the curtains back a few inches, allowing a small shaft of light to fall across the floor and the wall behind the TV. The clock ticked closer to four and the light was fading outside. Through the small window, the lazy snow fell across the gray city of Incamna.

Kaly muttered, "It's still snowing." No one replied.

The popping of the electric baseboard heat could be heard. Cody stretched with his back to the couch and his feet where he could move them close to the baseboard and then back when his toes overheated. His right hand was shoved deep into his pull-over pocket, fumbling and twisting. He had developed the nervous habit since they left the hospital.

Tryal's foot was still in a cast and he propped it up on a green plastic, grated grocery box that served as a makeshift ottoman. He pulled his lower lip into his mouth.

Kaly glanced over at Tryal and he caught her look. They had been out of the hospital for days and they hadn't talked once about the locket. That dumb locket. He was scared of it.

It hates me. He smiled at Kaly. *At least she's holding onto the locket and not asking me to do it.*

If he had still been holding onto it, he wasn't sure that he wouldn't open it. He wasn't sure he had any choice in the matter now. The locket was powerful and made its own choices. The hospital experience had proven that. It opened on its own and refused to shut once it opened. It was a dumb locket with a small, fragile, soft metal hinge. Yet they had beaten it hard against the counter and it refused to shut.

Janae was curled up in the faded plaid easy chair, legs hugging her squashed chest, maple hair laying across her face, deep eyes peeking between the strands, pulling at her sweater with her teeth, and her right big toe exploring a steadily-growing hole in the fabric. A few crumbs of yellow foam had made their way on to the carpet in front of her.

From the 24" television, a band strummed as strange images of cats rolled behind them. Roland muttered, "They were high when they filmed this. They had to be." He sang aloud with the band, "I breathe to you. I dream to you. Light your fire."

"We need a fire." Tryal said it aloud before he even realized he had spoken. He hadn't even been thinking about a fire before he spoke. But then again, a bit far back in his mind, Tryal worked on a problem. Tryal wanted to fulfill his promise to Door. He was frustrated that so much time had passed and nothing had happened.

"It's 72 in here," Roland bit back quickly.

"We need a fire." Tryal stood now, glancing around the room.

"Hey, Repeat! You said that already!" Roland's hand gripped the remote control. An edge of tension arced through his body. Tryal was going to do something that was going to cause problems. He was acting weird again.

Tryal walked behind them to the old fireplace, knelt and pulled the grate from the front. Dust scattered. The fireplace was clean except for the dust. Not an ash lay on the bricks but there were the scorch marks along the sides and back.

Cody had sat up, his legs brought to cross each other, although he was as serene as ever. Janae had twisted in her chair and had brought her thumb to her mouth, close enough that Roland thought she might just suck on it—he had almost said as much.

Kaly stood near the far edge of the dining room table, her palms flat against its freshly-oiled surface, her fingers lighting against the crocheted center-cloth. She shut her eyes as the buzzing at the base of her neck started. Another headache.

Roland waved the remote control in the air as if trying to aim it at Tryal. "You're being stupid again. Knock this off and come sit back down. All of you sit back down. Except for Kaly. Since you're up, go get me a Dr. Pepper."

Kaly smacked the back of Roland's head, "Tryal, what's going on?"

"It's cold outside," came Tryal's muffled voice as he tucked his head into the chimney, "I thought it would be nice to have a fire."

Roland grunted, "The heat's already on. I'm toasty."

"Did she tell you to do this?" Janae spoke for the first time that day. They each knew whom she referred to.

"No," Tryal responded. He moved out into the living room. "Ya," Tryal spoke again, "Kinda."

Roland sat up at this and turned down the television.

"What's up?" Roland demanded.

"I'm not sure. I don't know if this will work, but I think what I've been missing these past few days was a fire."

"Missing? You lost a fire somewhere?"

"To find the girl."

"Kaly's right here. Say something nice about her hair and I promise she'll put out. You don't need to find another." Kaly's hand came quickly against Roland's head again. "Ouch, I didn't deserve that. You know he gets your engine going. You've just been cranky since you lost your cell phone in that little flood and your daddy won't buy you another one." Kaly glared at him but he didn't look at her.

"Not Kaly. A little girl," Tryal said.

"Oh, Tryal, that's sick." Roland said.

Kaly muttered to herself, "Dad's already bought me a new phone."

"Is this the little girl you mentioned that last night at the hospital?" Janae asked. Tryal stopped as he walked towards the kitchen entrance. Had he told anyone about the little girl? Had he told Janae? What was she talking about? He tilted his head to the side.

She answered, "You thought I was asleep. And I had been, but your whispering woke me up. I just figured you were talking to her. You were looking out the window. You mentioned a girl that had disappeared."

He had been trying to talk to Door. He had sat up with Janae one night and she had fallen asleep. Without thinking about his company, he had begun to ask Door a few questions about the disappearing girl. Disappearing? She had disappeared. Past-tense. Gone. He was afraid she wasn't coming back. He had stood there looking out at the soft south lawn of the hospital and had asked Death if he had failed her. He was certain he had. He must have gone too slowly. He must have missed something she had told him. How was he supposed to take care of her if she was not with him? At the same time, she hadn't been all there. From the first moment he tried to pick her up, she was lighter than she should have been. She was a little girl and should not weigh much. But she had not weighed anything at all. He had done something wrong. He had rushed it.

The spell required time. And him. And fire. Those were the three ingredients to bridge the gap. The first time he had missed the element of time. The last few days, he had had time and himself, but not fire. He hadn't been around fire since that night. How else was she going to come across? There was no other answer.

He meant to correct that oversight.

Tryal responded to Janae with "Yes" and moved into the kitchen.

"Where's he going now?" Roland called after.

Tryal went through the back door, needing to put his shoulder into it to push the piled-up snow back, and trudged through the drifts in his bare feet, oblivious to the stabs of cold running through his soles. He needed wood. He needed fire. He needed to keep his promise. There were some old 2x4s boards stacked on the side of the garage. Most of them would be soaked, but just maybe there might be a few underneath that were dry enough to catch a spark. He just needed a little. They had plenty of paper and there were lighters everywhere.

CHAPTER THIRTEEN

BORN IN FIRE

TRYAL BRUSHED THE SNOW OFF and started throwing the wet, and unusable, boards to the side, without any care to where they flew. Most landed in the snow. One slammed against the wood of the porch and nearly clipped Kaly's knee as she descended the stairs.

"Tryal! Watch it!"

"Yeah," Tryal said, and even that was barely more than a grunt. Just a few boards into the pile, the wood was dry. He had pulled four pieces, small cuts of wood, and tucked them under his arm. He stared at a longer piece, debating whether he could split it up in time or whether he should go with what he had in hand. The four smaller pieces would do. There was at least a half-hour, maybe more, of burn in the group. If he needed more, he could come back for this piece. He turned and went back in the house, leaving Kaly to stare after him.

"Tryal," she called. He didn't stop. He didn't even hear her. Now she was cold. Her headache had grown into throbbing pain. She heard a voice in her head, Stop him!

The promise. He had to fulfill the promise and for the first time in near-ly a week he saw an open door to the problem of the disappeared girl. He walked through the kitchen, forgetting to stomp off his snow-covered bare feet. The cabinet to the left of the sink had both matches and paper napkins. He'd make sure to grab a newspaper that laid in a cluttered stack next to the TV. As he shuffled through the cabinet, he could hear Roland prompting Janae.

"Spill it. I'm sick of asking. What else did he say? What else did you hear?"

"No. It's none of my business," Janae curled up further in her chair.

"You little brat. Start talk . . . " At this, Cody stood up. The look on his face was still calm, still stoic, but he communicated all he needed to.

Roland's voice sped up, "Okay, Chewbacca. It's okay. Nothing meant by it. Just trying to get some answers as to what's going on in my screwed-up little brother's head."

Cody stepped back, put his hands back into his sweatshirt pockets and fumbled with whatever he had in there.

"Door asked me to watch out for the little girl. I said I would. I have to do this," Tryal's voice came from the kitchen entrance as he walked into the living room and rounded the couch to grab the newspaper. Roland stepped in front of him.

"Okay. That's weird, but doable. So why a fire? Gotta send a smoke sig-nal? You trying to rescue Pocahontas?"

Tryal had grabbed the matches and had moved into the dining room where he dropped the four pieces of wood with a thud on the table.

"Ah, crap! Mom's gonna kill you!"

Tryal pulled the table back into the living room proper. He moved around to the other side, in front of the fireplace, and pushed the table further up against the couch, leaving a large area in front of the cement enclosure. Bending down, he started to roll up the paper. Kaly stood beside him and started to do the same.

"You are one sad little chica. We don't even know why he needs the fire. And you just start helping him out."

Kaly turned to stare at Roland, "It's a fire. What's the problem? So he's acting a little weird . . ." The voice in the back of her mind told her to Stop him! She had ignored it. Maybe she shouldn't be helping. The headache didn't make things any easier.

"A little weird? Kaly, he's completely lost his mind again, which is starting to be a weekly thing," Roland walked around the couch, carefully side-stepping Cody's impressive frame, "Peter Pan, would you just give me a simple reason why you need the fire?"

Janae said, "Has he ever been wrong when he gets like this?"

Roland grunted, "No."

Cody mumbled.

A moment passed, full of the sounds of the growling baseboard heater, the indiscernible mutterings of the TV, the wind slapping against the back door Kaly had left open and the steady ticks of the clock above the kitchen entrance.

Tryal said, "She was on fire when I saw her the first time. It was down in the hospital boiler room, right in front of the furnace opening."

"Who is this little girl? Freddy Krueger's daughter?" Roland said.

Kaly asked, "On fire?"

"Yes and no. There were flames everywhere, but she wasn't burning. I don't know. I can't explain it. I just need a fire. She showed up the last time there was a fire." He shoved the rolled-up papers into the enclosure on top of the iron grated platform. He grabbed the pieces of wood and created a Boy Scout tent and pulled out the matches.

"Whatever. You and Moses have fun with your 'burning-bush' girl and call me if anything happens. There has to be something more interesting on TV to look at than your butts." Roland plopped back down on the couch.

Janae and Cody had instead walked up and were peering intently into the fireplace as Tryal brought the first lit match against the newspaper. It quickly caught flame and moved across the folds and crinkles, jumping to the other pieces.

"Stand back." Tryal stepped back.

"How long does this take?" Cody asked.

"I don't know. She was already lying on the ground when I walked into the boiler room."

The fire clicked, crackled and grew.

Tryal continued, "But I went too fast last time. She wasn't all there." The fire had caught the boards and lengthened along their undersides, growing full in the fireplace with a few tips of the individual tongues lost up the chimney. "Longer than we think."

"Are you ready kids? I can't hear you!" The TV roared as Roland turned the volume up.

"Turn it down, please," Janae asked.

"Huh, what? Has your little match-girl shown up yet?"

"Oh, who lives in a pineapple under the sea . . ."

"Roland, turn it down!" It was Kaly's turn to demand.

"Oh, no? Our little fire-starter hasn't produced anything? Ah, too sad." On the note of sad, the remote control was pulled from his fingers. Roland glanced up, and Cody aimed the remote, turning the TV to a slight whisper.

Cody dropped the remote into Roland's lap as he turned his eyes down to him, "You're starting to tick me off, boy." Roland grabbed the remote and gave a shallow grunt as he did. Cody broke a thin smile and turned back as Roland pulled himself further down into the couch.

Kaly spoke from pure surprise, "Wow."

"Oh," Janae let a moan leak out.

Cody followed their eye lines and stared at the place in front of the fireplace where they were all looking. After a moment, he still couldn't begin to find what had shocked the girls.

Janae's hand moved up slowly and curled around his upper arm, "Move your eyes from left to right. You'll see her." Cody tottered on one foot and see-sawed to the other, pulling his eyes across the floor. One moment the floor was bare with nothing on it but the heaviness of the air and orange glow of the fire and then the next moment, it changed. Each of them, excluding Roland, could see it. It was like looking through heat vapor on a warm summer afternoon. The floor was waving and distorted, growing more so. There was something there. The boards on the floor, the fire in front of them, all looked warped, as if something pushed the air out of that space.

A bit of crimson appeared. Mostly faded, as if looking through sunglasses. There were a few more spots of color forming. As the painting in front of them grew more vibrant, they had all ignored the growing fire—a fire that was now sparking embers across the wood floor, each burning out before landing.

"Is this her?" Kaly questioned. Her headache throbbed but she was enthralled by what was happening.

"I think so. Same size." Tryal hunched over.

The image formed in the space in front of them. In a single moment, the girl's brown hair came into focus, followed by the details of her rag-dress.

Kaly muttered, "She's coming over." Her own words caught her by surprise. She didn't know why she had said that. Coming over from where? Had she given words to the other voice in her head?

Tryal shivered at Kaly's statement. He remembered the booming voice under the water in the hospital, "Come over." Yet Kaly's words might've solved a puzzle. Maybe this girl was coming over from . . . Well, wherever the voice in the water wanted them to go. So, where was that?

"Like the cat," Janae muttered.

"What cat?" Cody asked.

"Wonderland. The Cheshire Cat."

"Yes," said Tryal. It was just like that. Out of nothing the parts of a little girl were forming, slowly completing the puzzle. A few pieces were still to be found, so none of them moved.

But this wasn't Wonderland. This was Incamna, Nebraska.

Gooseflesh ran across Kaly's arms as she rubbed her hands inches from her face. Janae was cautiously moving closer to Cody, seeking out his huge frame to comfort her. It wasn't working.

"Big cat," Roland spoke just inches from Janae's back. He had moved from the couch and was now watching the magic forming in his dining room. "Once more, Tryal you win the gold medal for weird crap. This is way freaky. Fuhreeeeeakeey."

"Yeah, tell me about it," Tryal agreed with a smile.

"Is that blood?" Roland asked.

"Where?" Kaly couldn't see what he looked at. The little girl was dirty, looking as if she had slept in a back alley. Mud was splattered in patches on her dress—a faded burnt sienna color. But Kaly could see no blood.

"Under her. You're right." Tryal had seen what Roland had. "Janae, we're going to need some towels. They're in the kitchen pantry."

"I know where your towels are," Janae shot back as she walked into the kitchen.

"We're going to need to move her and get something on her head, if that's where she's bleeding." Roland moved in, pushing past Cody and Kaly, and bent to put his hand under her head.

Tryal grabbed his wrist, "No. Not yet. She's still not all here."

"Not all here? What part of her isn't bleeding all over the floor?"

"Look. She has no shadow." The fireplace's flicker danced shadows across the floor and the back of the couch behind them, but even though they were standing on the other side of the girl, with the fire beyond her, she cast no shadow. The firelight moved on the floor in front of them, again distorted, but not opaqued. Roland thought he could make out the slats of the wood through her thin frame. She was in front of him, inches from him, and yet, somehow, he could stare straight through her to the wood floor she lay on and the firelight reflecting off its varnished surface. Even while looking at the firelight, Roland hadn't noticed that the fire continued to climb inside the enclosure. Cinders were popping with far more frequency, several seeming to hang in the air.

"So we have to wait for what? When can we help her?" Roland asked.

"We are helping her. She's supposed to be with us. Just wait. It can't be much longer."

The small girl was covered in a dress that resembled kitchen rags, and it might have been just that. Her face was thinning, leaving behind her ba-by-fat. Her features were sharp and distinct from what he could see between the strands of ebony hair falling across her face.

Janae screamed from the kitchen, and the thudding smack of the wooden cabinets followed after.

Cody moved quickly to the entrance, running straight into Janae as she ran out. He put his arms around her and tried to steady her. She fought past gasps of air and pushed herself and Cody further into the living room, putting distance between them and the kitchen.

"A wolf," Janae stammered, "There's a wolf in there."

"You mean a dog?" Roland asked.

"Maybe a dog. I don't know!" Janae said.

Tryal said, "We don't have a dog."

"In the kitchen?" Roland asked, standing up and moving to her. None of them had heard anything and they all knew that the only dog to come to these houses belonged to that weird Korean lady three houses to the south.

"Yes. In the closet. I think it was a dog. It was something. Big. It growled at me.

While they stared into the empty kitchen, the embers flew. Two had popped clear of the fireplace and hung in the air to the right of the girl.

Roland grabbed a poker from the tray to the right of the fireplace grate and marched into the kitchen, turning sharply to the left out of their view. A moment later, he walked back into the living room shaking his head, "Janae, you sure you saw a dog? There's nothing there."

Tryal said, "Told you there's no dog."

"There was. I opened the pantry door and there were these two red eyes staring back at me. It growled." She pursed her lips. "I'm not making it up."

Roland's voice dropped to a slow, hushed whisper, "No, you're not." He stared at the dark of the kitchen entrance. "Grab the girl, Tryal. We need to get out of here."

Floating in the shadows of the doorway, two red eyes flickered. Without seeing a neck or teeth, a snarl rippled from the eyes.

Tryal looked between the eyes and the girl. "No, it's not done yet. Almost. A minute more. Maybe two."

Kaly coughed.

The red eyes were glowing brighter and the outline of something large and wolf-like began to pencil itself into the space held by the shadows.

The room itself had become hazy, filling with smoke.

"Tryal, you idiot!" Roland cursed.

"What?"

"You didn't open the flue. The smoke is filling up the house." To emphasize his point, the old Black and Decker fire alarm chirped from the living room, its high-pitched notes stinging their ears.

"Well, open it now," said Cody.

"I can't. The flue chain is on the inside of the fireplace. We have to put out the fire. Janae . . . go back and grab the towels, and grab a pitcher of water."

"No. What if there's another one waiting in there for me?" replied Kaly.

"The other way. To the bathroom! Get cups! A bucket," said Roland. "Cody. You do it. Tryal come here, we have to move her."

The red-eyed shadow had not yet moved but grew into the room. Roland glanced back over his shoulder as he was now crouching next to the girl's head. The beast's leg twitched and tugged against shadows. The creature tried to pull itself out of the darkness.

Roland shouted to Cody in the bathroom, "Forget the water. There's not going to be time." Turning back to his brother, looking for an okay, Roland nudged, "Tryal, it's now or never."

"She's not ready. A few more seconds. Please, Roland, I'm not sure I have a third chance to get her." And he wasn't sure. She wasn't bleeding the first time she had attempted to come through, and now she was. Wherever she was fading to and from, it was dangerous.

Tryal kept glancing between the girl and the red eyes. "I think that thing is here for her."

"Yeah, I figured that." Roland responded as a large "snap" cracked. A dark beast had pulled one of its legs free and had set it on the wood floor. Three faded claws poked through on its crawling paw. The fur lining the dark leg was just as transparent as the shadows it had pulled free from. That fur was as alive as the eyes, each strand twisting and flickering with the light that pressed against it.

Kaly continued to cough. Janae started to hack, a sound that was muted by the continued screaming beeps of the fire-detector

Roland said, "Hunch down. No, actually, get outside. We don't need you and the two of you will end up passing out if you stay here." The girls stood transfixed.

"Get out of here," Roland shouted and once more, a second snap echoed against the bricks of the fireplace. The two front legs of the dark dog were fully on the floor and the rest of its body was pulling itself from the sheath that was the shadows. It had tucked its snout down, trying to poke itself through a hole visible only to itself. In just seconds, it would be free.

The two girls hunched and raced towards the front door of the smoke-filled house.

"Here," Cody had returned with the towels. Without asking, Roland propped up her head, slid his arm under her shoulders and one more under her knees. She was light, but her weight was obvious against Roland's arms.

"Okay, she's all here," Tryal said. A bark sounding like the deep banging of a metal spoon against a cast-iron skillet rumbled from the shadow beast. The entire beast's body was nearly in the room, only its two back legs remaining. Its full body was larger than any dog Tryal had ever seen. It was as large, if not larger, than the lions at the Denver Zoo. Janae was right the first time—it seemed more like a wolf but he had never seen a wolf, nor a dog, that looked like this.

"RUN!" Roland shouted.

The beast snapped at Roland, its large, gaping mouth missing his elbow as he stood up with the girl. The beast pulled, barked and bit twice more as Roland, Tryal and Cody moved to the door. Its eyes were still as bright as the fire itself, shining through the smoke.

Out of habit, Tryal snagged his messenger bag resting by the scattered shoes. The boys cleared the front door held open by the girls.

A roar roiled through the smoke followed by a clear sound of cloth ripping as the large beast pulled itself free of the shadows and raced through the living room. Its final jerk free from the shadow-womb launched its hulking body hard against the dining room table, popping the table's leg clean free and bringing the entire table slamming down onto the ground, the porcelain vase, flowers, water, dishes, books, keys and cell phones crashing against the floor. Papers and a left-over bag from Arby's tumbled against the fire and ignited. The fire escaped the enclosure and spread through the room.

The beast's muscles rippled under its ebony skin and it launched forward to the door after the five of them, its eyes locked on the little girl held in Roland's arms, wrapped in flowered kitchen towels. As it left the dining room, one of the fallen cell phones begin to chime, its own ringing lost in the still blurting whine of the fire alarm.

The front door fell shut as the five of them raced down the front sidewalk and turned north, in the direction of Kaly's house. The large door exploded out, shards shot-gunned from its shattered shell and the beast growled through it, pulling the entire door off its hinges. It ran across the front stairs, clearing all four of them in one bound. Its front feet skidded on the icy sidewalk and then the entire beast spun around as its back haunches landed on the ice and carried the weight of its momentum full onto the slippery surface. It slid and tumbled into the snow.

"MOVE!" Roland bolted through the front yard, choosing the slow-moving resistance of the snow pack to the unpredictable ice on the sidewalk. The girls moved behind him, Kaly the furthest behind. Janae took a quicker step, pushed by Roland's loud voice, and tripped into the snow. Cody heard her grunt and swung his arm back to tug her up from the snow she had fallen into. Kaly had moved past her, and reached back to help her to her feet.

In the full light, the beast was larger than ever. Its hide was dark leather pulled across taut muscles that flexed hard with every movement. This was a creature of pure form and movement. Its shadow stretched out behind it. It reminded Tryal of the frozen moments of time caught in a movie film strip. Each frame blurred into the next, an inverted sparkler stream on a Fourth of July night. Where there should be the retina-burning gleam of the sparkler there were just deep shadows chained together and fading against the white of the new snow.

Even in the early twilight, its eyes flickered as lit flames.

The beast regained its footing, crouched and leapt again, landing in the snow four feet behind Janae. It hit its rhythm with its back feet and was once more in the air clearing the remaining four feet with ease, its wide jaws wretched open in a horrific way—nothing should be able to pull its lower jaw that low. As it fell onto Janae, it moved out of the shadows and the sunlight fell across its hide. It closed its jaws on the screaming, kicking girl.

And was blown away into a small dark wisp, more by the unveiled sunlight than the wind.

CHAPTER FOURTEEN

THE HOUSE ON THE LAKE

THE HOUSE HAD SAT NEAR THE LAKE for over a hundred years. The trees pulled close to the house; their limbs bent to protect it, as though its secret was far more important than their own. At night, the trees would whisper to each other, asking if either of them had violated the deep trust they had made with the house. Each responded that their loyalty was sure. The whispers were carried across the fields and the evening splashes of the lake. The children of that town heard the whispers deep in their souls and they knew to stay far away.

Until today.

Today, school had let out early with the rising snow. Caden Smith, his jeans dark with stains, jumped over the fallen corn in the field.

"Wait up!" Caden yelled between winded breaths. He stumbled as he reached his two friends, Sal and Eric, standing in front of the house.

"I'm telling you, Katie's cousin and his buddies went in it," Sal said.

Eric rubbed his hands together. "Naaa, they didn't. My brother says no one's been in there since it was built. If they did, they didn't come back out."

Sal kicked the snow at their feet. "That's just to scare you. Every town has a haunted house. They aren't real. People just like to make up stories to scare us."

"Maybe. I'm just not so sure," Eric jammed his hands in his pocket. This was a dumb day to forget his gloves. "I mean, what if they aren't stories."

Caden spoke, "I'm with Eric. I don't think we should—Ouch!"

Sal had punched him, "Have some guts. It's a house. It's not going to kill you."

Caden rubbed his arm, "But—"

Sal walked to the house, "You want to be cool? No one else in the sixth grade has done this. Go in this house, come back out, you'll be cool. No one will make fun of you then."

Caden ran to catch up with him. "Really?"

Sal punched him again, not as hard as the first time, "Who would make fun of the boy that braved the house?"

Caden smiled, "Not even you?"

Sal picked up a snowball and threw it at his face, knocking him on his butt, "I will always make fun of you. Let's go! I want to get home in time to watch the MMA championship tonight!"

The front door was unlocked and opened without resistance. That was the first surprise.

Eric said, "It didn't even creak."

Sal leaned his head in, "So?"

"This is an old house that no one has ever walked in. The door doesn't creak? My house door creaks and my dad is always working on it."

Sal grabbed his arm and pulled him inside, "Get in here and stop being such a baby! Keep that up and I'll tell everyone you're as scared as Caden."

Caden said, "You said no one would make fun of me anymore."

"I said I would. You get up here, too," Sal shut the door behind them.

Caden stammered, "Why did you do that?"

Eric said, "Ya, what if we need to get out of here?"

Sal said, "I keep telling you, there's nothing here. This house is empty. No one lives here. There's nothing to be scared of."

They stood by the front door as their eyes adjusted to the dark. Slowly, splotches of color formed into images. They were in an open entrance. To the left, an open door led to a kitchen. On the other side was a small living room with large high-backed couches. The house was old. The furniture felt older.

Eric rubbed his hand across the arm of the flowered chair closest to the front door. "It's clean. There's no dust. Anywhere."

Caden pointed down the hallway to an open door, "What's that?"

Sal followed his gaze to a large open room. A thick scarlet curtain that covered most of the far wall. Behind it, a violet glow shone. The light moved and rippled.

Sal spoke, "Someone's probably just covered up a TV that they accidentally left on."

Eric raised his voice, "In an abandoned house? In a house that no one was supposed to live in? Ever?"

Sal said, "Well, I don't know—Shut up!"

Caden had begun to stutter, "What, what are those?"

What they had originally thought was just a wallpaper design were actually little pieces of paper taped to the walls, hundreds of pieces of paper with small writing on them.

Caden read, "'Your courage will reap rewards for you.'" He read another, "'You will make a change for the better within the year.'" And then another, "'The coming month shall bring you much happiness.'"

Sal read, "'There are lessons to be learned by listening to others.'"

Eric read another one, "'Many people are seeking you for your sound advice.'" He whispered, "They're fortunes from fortune cookies."

Sal turned around staring at every wall, "There's hundreds of them."

Eric pulled one off the wall and said, "Thousands."

From deep in the house, a voice spoke, "Please don't do that."

Sal screamed, "Who's there?"

The voice spoke again, "Please put that back." The voice was closer this time. Caden was already fumbling at the doorknob. Eric spun around, looking for the source of the voice. As he looked in the direction of the kitchen, he froze and wet himself.

A gigantic, transparent head appeared floating in the air. It glowed white and moved towards them, "Just put it back. All will be forgiven. You can even stay for dinner."

Caden had opened the front door, ran screaming, and tripped on the stairs, sprawling face first in the snow. Sal and Eric wailed, ran out, tumbled over Caden and toppled on top of him. They scrambled to their feet and darted through the fence, a dripping trail of yellow following Sal across the snow.

From behind the frightened boys, the head spoke a final time, "It's alright. Dinner is almost here."

As they ran through the cornfield, they passed a little girl, bundled up in a large pink snow coat, her arms full of Chinese take-out bags. She laughed at the boys and shouted after them, "It's okay. He doesn't bite!"

The boys didn't look back and didn't stop running until they were inside their homes. When they saw each other the next day, they all agreed to not tell anyone.

The story about the house never changed. No one had ever gone in.

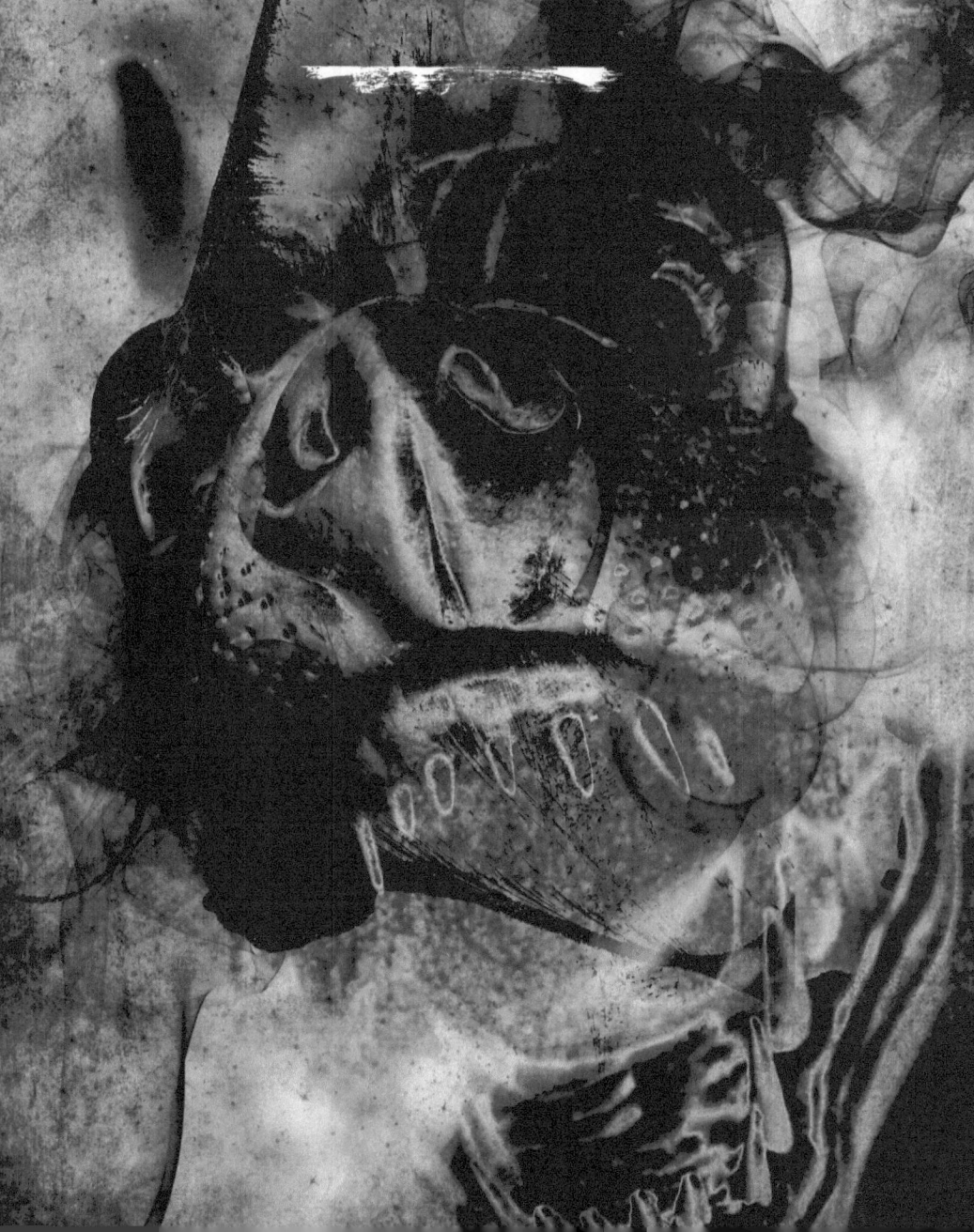

PART 2

THE CINDERS

CHAPTER FIFTEEN

THE NURSE'S TALE: EYES IN THE DARK

FRIDAY, JULY 20, 2004

MICHELLE AND PATRICK WOULD CROSS the thin dirt lane, jump over the small ditch the poor farmer made, and be in Wonderland, with its rows of corn, thick, tall and endless before them. They'd wake up before the dew had dried on the grass, race from one end of the field to the other, the leaves of the stalks slapping their face, raising welts on their cheeks.

There had been an unspoken rule that they never went into the field at night. Their parents never said they couldn't, that she could remember, but she was always sure that mom would yell and say something about coyotes roaming at night (they'd hear their yelps as they dozed off). Patrick and Michelle just knew that the edge of the ditch was the line. They could walk across the road if the basketball rolled out there, but if it rolled into the ditch, they'd just call it a game and pick it up in the morning.

"Hey." Patrick said as he slugged Michelle, and pointed.

Michelle followed his hand across the field, expecting to see a splash of lightning or a falling star. Instead, she saw the first set of eyes. They floated a foot or two above the ground, just on the other side of the ditch. They glowed orange and flickered slowly and without rhythm. Michelle was eleven and brimming with more curiosity than sense. Were they the foxes they'd seen earlier? She couldn't tell. Michelle stood up to get a better look and started to walk forward when her feet stopped. Just as she knew they weren't to cross the line, she knew she shouldn't get any closer. There was a mind behind those eyes and they weren't the eyes of some cute, fluffy, stupid fox pup.

"What is that?" Patrick asked. She felt as if she was looking down from a great height and a sharp edge. Patrick moved his hand to Michelle's elbow to steady her. Michelle didn't think he was even aware he had done it.

"Eyes."

"Eyes? I thought it was something burning." Then she saw it the way he did. The eyes were flames, dancing on a small, unseen branch, twisted by the breeze. There was no wind that night. As silently as the first set appeared, another set, a foot or two away, blinked into sight. The second set was stronger and stared directly at them. The eyes didn't move, but a moment later she felt a cry go up. Michelle couldn't make out the words and wasn't sure there was even a sound, but knew they had called to the others. Within moments, three more sets of Cinder eyes had blinked alive and each set looked at Patrick and Michelle. They named them Cinders because of the way they appeared, like a scorch mark on the air.

She had found herself pressed against the bushes that lined their house and led to their front door. The Cinders had each moved to the edge of the corn line and stayed there. She turned and walked slowly to the screen door at the top of the concrete stairs leading to their house. Michelle walked in. Patrick didn't move.

"Patrick! Come in!"

He staggered back in. His eyes were bloodshot and he moved as if he'd just awakened. They peered out the living room window at the eyes all pressed against the invisible wall at the far edge of the ditch.

In silence they went to their rooms and quickly dressed for bed. Michelle lay awake for a few hours until her body crashed into sleep.

The next morning broke and they were made bold by the new day.

"There's no prints," Patrick observed, feeling the dirt. He kneeled at edge of the corn as she crossed over the ditch.

"We didn't imagine it," Michelle said, pointing to a blackened cornstalk.

"I didn't say we did. They were here last night. I wonder if they could've been hanging from the stalks." He turned to examine the stalks.

"No scratch marks."

"They were lightning bugs. Or dragonflies."

"Ya." He stood looking at the ground and then at their brown-brick house and the wood split-rail fence around their lawn.

She took off racing down the rows as he chased behind. The day ran into the night as every day before. They played in the fields, came in at noon to eat their usual grilled cheese sandwich and tomato soup lunch, rode their bikes down to visit their friends, a few miles away, and ate dinner at their house.

That evening they played basketball as if the Cinders had never happened. But they had. Michelle didn't feel safe anymore. Wonderland was gone.

Michelle had gone for a simple lay-up and moved past Patrick with ease. The ball hit on the outside of the rim and she thought Patrick would rebound, but he didn't. It bounced across their large driveway out into the dirt lane, stopping short of the ditch.

Michelle raced after the ball and grabbed it before it rolled too far. As she reached it, she glanced up into the eyes of the Cinders. There were hundreds of them swarming at the edge of the corn field. In that moment, Michelle saw them. Rolling muscles under charred skin, taut in anticipation, serrated teeth licked by a brutal, black-stained tongue, claws larger than a game cat, and matted fur flowing from their bodies into a deep, damp smoke. Her thoughts swam in images of broken bones, pale in the moonlight, protruding from their leathery hide, grimaced expressions of hunger and tortured pain. Their eyes were large and not only flickered, but dripped fire that scalded the ground. She was pulled in, transfixed by their eyes, their orange, blazing eyes that danced with embers to join the stars above.

Michelle fell to the dirt road, startled, and quickly pulled herself up. She walked backwards to the house, each step slow and careful.

Then she screamed. One of the Cinders had moved out past the edge of the corn, past the edge of the ditch and was now standing firmly at the edge of the road, its shape sharp against the dirt.

"Patrick, what's happening?" Michelle's voice wailed. Then Patrick was at her side pulling her back.

"I don't know. Get in the house." They both turned and left the road at a sprint to the front door.

The light from the front door, from the porch light, from the street lamp, and the light from the dining room window all went out, leaving them in total darkness. Michelle grasped for Patrick's hand, found it, and squeezed with all of her strength. He backed up against her as they turned to the see the Cinders circling round about them. The world had become full of hungry, salivating candles.

"What do they want?" Michelle sobbed. She squeezed his hands and closed her eyes, expecting to hold off the impending torture, only to find that their eyes glowed as brightly in her mind as they did in the open air. With her eyes closed, her mind's vision of them was more defined. Their jaws, dirtied with the flesh of other creatures, slammed shut and opened in anticipation. Their muscles tightened as the Cinders on the front lines lowered as if to pounce.

Michelle opened her eyes to put out this image and rolled herself into Patrick's grasp. He reached both arms around her and held tight as the Cinders leapt and slammed against them, knocking them to the ground and into unconsciousness. Their teeth tearing into Patrick's legs, his arms, his sides. He screamed and they pulled him loose from her. She squeezed her eyes shut as his screams grew louder and yet further away.

Michelle awoke the next morning as if from a bad dream, in her own room. Her dad looked over her and her mom sat at the edge of her bed.

"Are you okay?" her dad asked. His eyes were puffy and red. He was still crying. He explained that they had heard her scream and raced outside to find her lying in the middle of the road, bloodied and bruised. They had discovered the shreds of Patrick's jeans on the driveway and drag marks in the dirt road leading to the cornfield. Her father had grabbed his shotgun and raced into the field. After several minutes, he called 911. The police arrived and they searched the field throughout the night as Dad stood outside the house, waiting for what he assumed was the large dog or coyote that had attacked them to announce itself.

Even after Michelle awoke, the search for Patrick, or Patrick's body, continued. For weeks, people pursued any lead or hint. They found nothing except for the scraps of denim in their driveway. No blood, no bones, nothing. Wonderland had been emptied of any trace.

"But now one age is ending, and God calls home the stars
And looses the wheel of the ages and sends it spinning back."

—From Spirits in Bondage by C. S. Lewis

Chapter Sixteen

FUJO

THEY STRUGGLED TO THEIR FEET and stood there alone, five dark strokes against a white canvas. Janae stifled a scream that instead came out as a wheezing sob and melted into Cody's arms. Her leg was untouched.

Kaly, Tryal and Roland scanned around, each anticipating the hellhound to pounce from somewhere yet unseen. Shrubs, fences, cars parked against the street—they were each suspicious hideaways for the demon dog.

Tryal's face dripped with sweat despite the freezing wind rushing past his cheeks. His T-shirt grew damp as it soaked up the perspiration dripping from his body. Ignoring the cold returning to his bare feet, Tryal asked the obvious question they were all thinking, "Is it gone?"

"I'm not sure. Please be gone!" Kaly quickly answered.

"It's gone," Roland responded, once more shrugging his shoulders to shift the weight of the little rag girl further against his chest and off of his forearms.

"I wish I had my spear," said Kaly, her heart racing.

Tryal tilted his head, "What did you say?"

Kaly stammered, "Nothing. I don't know." She didn't know why she had said that. Her head received a constant pounding from the headache and she struggled to make sense of what happened. In the back of her mind, she quietly heard the new voice again.

Get him out of here! Leave the girl!

She shook her head and shouted back to her thoughts.

No. No. No!

Cody marched Janae out of the piled snow, brushing her legs off when they stopped, "What was that?"

"Cujo's big ugly freaking brother. Freaking Cujo!" Roland leaned down and rubbed some of the snow where the beast had disappeared. "Fujo."

"Kaly, how did you not know that was going to happen?" Tryal's voice was laced with fear.

"I don't know," Kaly began to cry, "I only know what I ask about." The voices of the future were undependable. Maybe she had never heard the voices. Maybe she just made it all up to fit in. She was confused. She heard voices but not the ones that could help her. But she had heard from the future. She wasn't crazy.

Am I?

"Learn to start asking more," Cody's voice was shrill. His fears were painted across his eyes. He had imagined the dark dog chomping on Janae and ending her life. His mind had filled in the rest of his lonely life in that brief half-second.

Roland nudged Tryal, "This is ash."

Tryal said, "Huh?"

"Where the thing was, there's a bunch of ash," Roland looked back at the path they had taken from the house, "Just weird."

Tryal grunted, "Okay."

Roland shook his head and started walking, "Let's get moving."

"Stop!" Tryal yelled at his brother, "Where are you going?"

"First to get some help for little red riding hood here. And second, to get us as far from that house as possible."

"The house?"

Roland said, "Yes, the house—it's smoking. You didn't open the flue." Tryal then noticed the clouds of smoke that had started to push through the poorly sealed doors and windows.

"We have to get rid of the smoke. The fire might have spread. We can't let it go. Mom will kill us."

"Too late for that. Besides, you have a doggy treat on you? Fujo's still waiting."

"We have to do something."

"Get this girl to safety. You brought her here. She's your responsibility!"

Tryal's eyes caught Roland's and his shoulders dropped. He had briefly forgotten his promise to Door, to Death. He nodded at Roland in apology.

"Can't we slow down and think about this?" Kaly asked.

The two brothers shouted back in unison, "No!"

"We're safe. That thing is gone," Kaly continued to press her point. This was the exact opposite of what the voice in her head told her but she didn't trust it. If it said run, then maybe they should slow down.

Maybe this is what it feels like to go insane.

"It's 5—" Tryal looked at his watch, "5:26. It's going to get dark soon."

"So?" Kaly asked.

Roland said, "That thing disappeared in sunlight. What do you think will happen when it gets dark?" He glanced down to make sure that the girl was still alive, a move meant to reassure himself that she wasn't a hallucination.

Kaly grabbed a strand of hair, twisting it around her finger. She understood the problem clearly now. The places for the thing to leap out at them would multiply in the next few hours. Every dark corner was going to be a doggy door from the great beyond. In just a few hours, every place was going to be one big shadow. "We're not going to be safe anywhere."

"We need to get a car," was Roland's answer.

"Where are we taking her?"

"I don't know, but she's not getting any better out here."

"Let's just get her to Kaly's house and we can clean her up."

"Good for about another hour, but then Fujo pulls himself out of whatever Twilight Zone he was zapped back to and then we're back at square one. That thing was fast, frighteningly fast, but I don't think it can outrace a car."

"Can we call 911? The fire department? At least call Mom? We have to tell her what happened," Tryal asked.

"Got your cell phone on ya now, do ya?" Roland arched his back to shift the weight of the child in his arms, "Ugh! You're not fat, little girl, but you definitely aren't going to be the poster-child for Jenny Craig."

"Crap!" Tryal looked back at the smoking house, his ears now attuned to the far-off sirens of what could only be fire trucks, and realized his and Roland's cell phones were laying in the mass of crap that used to sit on the living room table before Fujo had knocked it over. Neither Janae nor Cody had a cell phone. Their dad had laughed at every suggestion of them. If they picked one up, he'd have made sure the phone would've been in pieces across the floor.

Tryal pressed his palms against his forehead, wiped the sweat from his eyes and glanced back once more at the house as he stood on the edge of the property. Smoke was now issuing from every window and pouring out of the shattered front door. They didn't need to call 911. Everyone for blocks would be able to see this. Just pray there isn't a fire. Just pray it's smoke damage. That and Fujo damage.

"Kaly, can we use your sister's car?" Janae had calmed down.

"Maybe. My mom won't be happy since I hadn't told her about it beforehand, but she won't mind much. The keys are on the hooks above the coat rack." Here they were: two orphan boys, an abused brother and sister, and then her. Nice, little Kaly with her real parents and her older sister away at college on a scholarship (and nice enough to have left her car for Kaly to use) and her one younger sister that still played with dolls.

I am the weird one, she thought.

The other voice replied, *Stop whining. Get him out of here.*

"Then can we have this talk on the way there? This girl is still bleeding and Tryal's little toesies are about to fall off in the snow," Roland walked down the street and the four followed. The sirens wailed. The fire trucks were just blocks away. "And hurry, we can't get slowed down by the boys in blue right now. I'm not sure any of us can explain any of this in a way that would make an ounce of sense."

They all raced down the block and across the street to Kaly's house. Kaly was just hoping her little sister was still at extended care and her parents were having a late night at work.

"Stacie? You home, yet?" The house was dark except for the hall light which was never turned off.

No response came.

She moved her hand inside and yanked the keys from the hook above the coat rack supporting several jackets and a mound of mittens, gloves, and boots laying against the wall. She snagged her own jacket and her sister's and shut the front door with care. Back outside, she flung her sister's pink coat at Janae (a perfect fit despite the difference of five years between Janae and Stacie).

"Got 'em." She announced and walked around the house to where the boys were waiting, huddled around the pale gray Volkswagen Jetta that peeked out of the last two months' of snow. The driveway and walks had been scooped clean every day by Kaly's dad, but he had let the Jetta amass its own monument of snow.

"Six people aren't fitting in this thing," Cody wiped snow from the front window with the sleeve of his shirt.

"Five. Janae and little Red Riding Hood only count as one person together. Maybe three-quarters."

"Red Riding Hood?" Tryal asked.

"She brought her own big bad wolf to the party. If you want, I'll let you dress up in Grandma's clothes." Roland's mouth twisted with a smile as Kaly unlocked the car and Tryal opened the passenger door for him.

"Give me the phone," Tryal said.

Kaly stopped. "What phone?"

"Your phone. You said you were going to grab it when you went inside."

"No. I didn't"

Janae, Cody and Roland all looked at him as if he had dropped his brains on the way here.

"She didn't? Okay, maybe I was thinking she should—It doesn't matter," Tryal said, "We need a phone. Can you go get it?"

"I'm not going in that house. It's darker now than it was ten minutes ago," Kaly said.

"The sirens are getting louder. Go get the phone," Roland sighed.

Janae said, "She needs clothes, too. She looks like she's Stacie's size." The little girl was about Stacie's size. Small, thin and about four feet, five inches. Tops.

"You're coming with me," Kaly said.

Tryal nodded and clomped back to the house, his cast made any attempt to hurry awkward. They walked in and down to Stacie's open room.

"Here, this'll fit her," Kaly grabbed the long-sleeved shirt that had been flung over the wooden desk chair and held it up to Tryal. It was white with tiny little lines of romantic poetry scribbled in a pattern across it. It was something only a 10-year-old girl would want to wear.

"Grab some jeans," Tryal said.

"And some underwear," Kaly added, opening the top dresser drawer. Tryal continued to look around. Thank God the closet was closed.

"Let's go," said Kaly

"Your phone?" Tryal stuffed the clothes into the messenger bag slung over his shoulder.

"Uh, I already had it. It was in my jacket I grabbed," she looked down at the floor. They didn't have to go in the house after all. They could've been blocks from here by now, maybe a good mile or two to somewhere safe, wherever that was. He still hadn't figured that part out.

They were back to the front door, nearly running through the dimly lit hall.

Kaly went out first and Tryal snagged Stacie's other jacket, a bright red woolen piece, from the hook by the entrance, and stuffed it into his bag. He started to close the door, looking back one more time into the dark house.

And there were the bright red eyes.

The flaming eyes against the skull-shadowed face of the giant dog were down the hall, twenty feet away at the most, floating out of Kaly's bedroom. Tryal grasped the beast's intentions. It had been waiting. This thing showed deadly skill in planning. It was definitely not mindless. It was not just a ghostly body. It was a ghostly intelligence.

The flames blazed as the beast caught Tryal's eyes, lighting the hallway in a haunting orange and yellow glow.

Kaly was already rounding the corner a second time when Tryal burst out, running at her, slamming the door hard against those piercing, burning eyes.

Tryal caught up to Kaly and heard Cody say, "Michelle."

"The nurse?" Roland asked.

"She said to call her sometime. I can't think of a better time," said Cody

Tryal grabbed Kaly, pushed her ahead of him and screamed at the three others, "GO! IT'S BACK!"

CHAPTER SEVENTEEN

VISITORS IN THE GARAGE

K ALY AND TRYAL AROUND THE CORNER of the house the second time just as an old blue Cutlass Ciera with Wyoming plates turned fast around the block and pulled into the driveway of Tryal and Roland's house. The automatic garage door on the smoking house went up and Vera, the boys' adopted mother, stepped out, her feet landing ankle-deep in the snow.

Tryal was supposed to shovel this! Then she scolded herself, "Please let him be okay."

Ten minutes before, she had received a call from the neighbor behind their house. The old woman had been blunt, "I hate to make a presumption, but I think those boys of yours have started your house on fire. There's smoke coming from the back door and about ten minutes ago, that youngest one, the one with the girl's haircut, dragged some wood from the side of your garage back inside. I've already called the firehouse."

Vera had then called Roland's cell phone and when there was no answer, she tried Tryal's. Her fingers fumbled twice over the numbers before she dialed properly and successfully rang the second call out. No answer again. Knowing she should've first called 911, she tried Roland once more before making the call bringing twenty-two of Incamna's finest to her front steps.

Still blocks away, she could see the blackened smoke clearing the tree-tops, her heart sped up and she forced the car to keep pace. Pulling into the driveway, her heart shuddered against her rib cage and she slammed her fist against the garage-door opener resting on the seat next to her.

One look at the front door sprayed in thin slivers across the old porch, the smoke billowing out of the torn door-frame, her prayers moved across her lips, "Oh, God, please let them be okay. Please let them be okay. Don't let them still be in there."

A few houses away, dog barked, loud and sharp, a gruesome sound, and her prayers were interrupted. She turned back to the garage as its still ris-ing door cleared her eye line. She instinctively ducked under the door as it jammed to a stop, peering between the smoke rushing out.

Two dark figures stood silhouetted against the overhead garage light, the fat one an easy two feet shorter than the thin, tall one.

The shorter one sniffed the air. A gravelly Scandinavian voice spoke from the smoke, "Three boys. Two girls." He sniffed again. "And something else. Maybe it's our boy. The Traveling Man was helpful."

The tall man next to him coughed and she grew dizzy.

The short one smiled, "Well, after some persuasion." He sniffed at Vera. "She'll do for now. Yes, quite nicely."

"Who are you?" Vera demanded.

"*Sleep.*"

The words poured as smoke through her ears and lungs and she slammed solid into the oil-stained cement, shattering her nose and splashing blood across the floor.

The shorter man waved the smoke away and the three of them disap-peared. The smoke drifting into the open air outside now rushed back into the vacuum left by the three absent bodies.

"Rered upp the [Devil] in the semblaunce of a black dogge . . ."

—ARREST RECORD OF JACK CADE, 1450

Chapter Eighteen

GO, GO, GO

TRYAL PUSHED KALY INTO THE DRIVER'S SEAT, slammed her door and ran to his spot. All five had piled into the car, Roland still clutching the little girl.

"Where's that thing at?" Roland said.

"In the house. It was in the house. It's coming. Kaly, start the car now. Please, just start the car," Tryal said.

Kaly fumbled through the four keys on the chain, grabbing the thin silver laser-cut bar which would start the Jetta.

The car jolted violently to the right with a large crashing sound. Tryal would have been sure they'd been hit by another car, that is if they still weren't in a driveway on the side of a house.

"Ah, heck no!" Roland had spoken as all of them had seen the same thing. Snarling from the shadows under the eaves of the house, the phantom beast was back and it was enraged. Its eyes were infernos against the black shadows, popping and spitting sparks into the cold air.

It reared back and then lunged again, both actions happening almost faster than the passengers could see. Its full weight was brought against the side of the car, denting Kaly's door and cracking her window into fine webbing. The mounds of snow on the car roof slid backwards and landed with a quiet thud on the ground and atop the phantom dog. The beast shook, paused, and then faded slightly, allowing the snow that had landed on its head to pass through it. It had turned into air.

Tryal had been the only one to see this. Adrenaline-laced realization coursed through him, "GET THIS CAR GOING!"

The dog was going to be coming through the car once it was fed up with simply trying to punch into it. It chose to be solid when it ripped through the house. It could choose to walk through that door as beat its way into it. For now, it chose the jarring slam and slam again method. The beast tried everything to stop them all. Pure physically-induced terror was the quickest route to that.

Kaly's hands were madly searching the floorboard, her head pressed sideways against the steering wheel. She whispered in an embarrassed groan, "I dropped the keys."

The dog rocked hard into the side of the car, pushing his shoulder into the already flattened door, denting it far inward. This time the impact cracked the back driver's side window, where Janae sat, and Tryal knew it would be the last time before the dog ignored the physical barrier of the door and would pounce into the interior of the car.

"There, by your right foot. Quick! Go, go, go!" Tryal screamed. If he had been outside of the car, he would've just run. Left everyone behind and just run.

"Shut up! I've got them!" Roland said.

"Faster! You have to go faster," Tryal said. The dog pulled back for its final jump. The beast's dark hide faded. Its bark echoed in the small enclosure and Tryal clamped his hands to his ears.

Roland held the little girl close to his body.

Kaly slammed the key and turned the ignition, the car started with ease.

Tryal ignored Kaly and pulled at the gearshift, jerking it into reverse. The dog's teeth were in the car now, its eyes and body still partially intersecting the door and the cold air outside.

Janae wailed like a harsh siren in the dark as the teeth bit down hard on her arm. She had experienced the cuts of razors before and this was nothing like that. The pain was excruciating as the teeth penetrated deep into her flesh. Every dark emotion she had boiled to the surface and she squealed, agonizing pain roaring through her body and her psyche.

The car jutted back as Kaly's foot hit the gas pedal and the dog's teeth slid through Janae's arm, the car and out before it had realized what happened.

Blood poured out of Janae's arm, her stitches torn open anew, and Cody grabbed the pink jacket lying across her lap and wrapped the arm.

The Jetta jumped onto the street, stuttered and turned sharply. The specter had deciphered the situation quickly and was now bounding after them, its large, gaping mouth open again for a fresh bite.

Cody shouted from the middle-hump of the small back seat, "Steam." As quickly as he spoke, the snow between the front of the car and the running dog heated and rose into an opaque wall. Fujo was slowed by this unexpected apparition, and gave Kaly the few seconds she needed to push the gear-shift into drive and race off down the street, her tires spinning and slipping on the icy road.

Tryal turned around to see the monstrous dog crush through the wall of steam and follow after them, his speed increasing with each bound. Dark tendrils of foam sprayed from his harsh snarling mouth. The still-fading sunlight was just strong enough to pierce his thick hide. As they sped away, the dog faded with each step in pursuit of them until he was simply not there.

Roland whispered down at the girl who had appeared in front of his fireplace, "I hope you're this important."

Chapter Nineteen

A KENNEL

MICHELLE WAS ENJOYING THE FIRST of three nice days away from the hospital. Four back-to-back 12-hour shifts had made these initial free hours sweet. With a growing sense of regret, she'd spent the morning sprawled across her tan couch watching anything the DVR had picked up in the last four days. She then spent an hour at the World Gym a few blocks away and had returned to relax alone.

The three large phantom dogs walked around the small apartment room, ignoring the barriers of couches, walls and chairs as they paced. The largest of the three rested curled, half of its shadow body intersecting the Ikea ottoman. The smaller two, each larger than a cougar, paced from the bedroom to the front door, back and forth.

"Are we nervous today boys?" Michelle called from the kitchen, where she cut vegetables. At 22, she was the newest E.R. nurse at Incamna United. She brushed her long, red hair out of her face.

"I hate it when you get like this. Caliban's not all worked up. Why do you have two have to be?" The other two paused simultaneously, stared back up to her and just as quickly started pacing again. "Don't get me wrong—I hate you all the time. It's just that I especially hate you when you get like this." Her leg jerked out to kick at one of them and passed through its torso completely.

"Nevermind, my always-silent pooches. I'll figure it out soon enough." On cue, her cell phone rang, vibrating across the kitchen counter. "And here's fate on line one. Blast."

She grabbed the phone, looked at the number and showed it to the phantom dog, "Is this for you, Puck? Cause I don't know 'em." She circled the phone around and held it to the other, "Caliban?" The two dogs glanced at the phone and then back at her, the flames in their eye-sockets glowing more brightly. "And there's my answer. You two have been waiting for this. You stupid mutts."

She flipped it open and answered, "This had better be important, 'cause my carrots are starting to miss me."

"Michelle?" The voice was male and unfamiliar, although not displeasing.

"Yes. And you are?" *Don't be a freak. Please!*

"This is Cody." *Who was Cody?*

"Cody?" As quickly as she asked, she knew, "Cody from the hospital? The one with the sister and—" The answer would be yes. Of course it was Cody. From the instant the call came in for the E.R., she knew something was up with those kids. Cody, the oldest one, and the best-looking, was also the most normal. But even he had started her weird-meter to buzzing. She knew weird when she saw it. She lived with it. However, these kids were beyond weird. That spontaneous flood was Twilight Zone material. For hours she had questioned her sanity. She took an early lunch, called in sick, went home, and shivered in her bed until she fell asleep. She hadn't felt strange like that since she had first seen the red eyes in the cornfield. The rules of reality had been wadded up and tossed in the garbage.

She rubbed the head of one of the Cinders at her side.

I can't really judge when it comes to strange.

Michelle hadn't felt normal since encountering the Cinders. It was one of the reasons she had gone into nursing. She had developed a strange intuition. She'd walk into her emergency room waiting area and point out those near death, despite what procedure told her to do. Doctors were always stunned to discover she'd pulled in someone just on the edge of having their appendix burst or suffering from some unknown internal bleeding.

Yep, I'm all about strange.

She had asked to check in on Cody's sister the moment she saw her. There was just something strange about her. About them. That had been an understatement.

Michelle replied, "Yeah, it's me. I know you didn't call for a date. What's up?"

He didn't respond for a few moments. "I need to come over. I mean, not just me. Me and my friends. We need you to look at," Cody paused, "To look at a girl that's been hurt. She's only ten."

"Take her to the hospital."

"Please, can you just look at her?"

"I can't do that. You need to take her to the hospital."

"We can't. Please, can you just take a quick look at her?"

"No. If you show up here, I'll call 911. I can lose my certification if they find out I told you to bring her to me."

"No one's going to find out. Please, we can't go to the hospital this time. We need you. I hate to drag you into this but you're the only one we can think of." He paused and she heard him mumble something. He spoke back into the phone, "Just give us one minute."

"No."

"Michelle, please. I'll walk in with her for one minute, just me and her. One minute of your time is all you need to give me. I don't even have to walk in. I'll stay outside."

She had started to form the word "no" again, but all three of the phantom dogs crowded against her, their bright eyes sparking against the coal-black of their skin. Holding the phone away, she asked the Cinders, "You want me to say yes, don't you? You know, if it wasn't for the fact that you don't shed or poop, I'd have sent you all to the pound a long time ago."

"Please, Michelle, please don't say . . ."

"Yes." *I'm so going to regret this.* "Yes, it's okay. Do you even know where I live?"

"Seriously? Yes?"

"Yes. Don't ask again."

"We're on our way. Thanks!"

"I'm assuming you need directions. I live in those apartments across from St. Fessey's Park. #140. The fence should be unlocked. And bring some dog food."

"We're not far away. And what type of dog food? Bag or can?"

This guy is desperate.

"I'm joking. No dog food. Just be quiet walking through my complex. Don't wake my neighbors. The Asian lady next door is a grump after . . . Na, she's a grump all the time."

A girl's voice spoke in the background, "Tell her to turn on all the lights and open up all the shades."

Okay, that was a weird suggestion.

Yet, it was familiar. "What's that about? Should I make sure all of the faucets are turned off?" Michelle asked.

"Nothing. Uh, no. Its—uh—" She could hear him move the phone away from him and snap "shaddup" to one of the passengers with him. He moved the phone back to say, "We'll be there in five minutes."

"Yeah. Just great."

She hung up the phone, her lips turning outward and down as she silently cursed all three of the shadows in front of her—Macbeth, Puck and Caliban.

"Time to hide, boys," and the shadows twisted and retreated to the corners, brightening the small apartment considerably.

"He takes the form of a huge black dog,

and prowls along dark lanes and lonesome field footpaths,

where, although his howling makes the hearer's blood run cold,

his footfalls make no sound . . .

to meet him is to be warned that your death

will occur before the end of the year."

—W. A. Dutt, 1901

Chapter Twenty

NURSE MODE ACTIVATE

THE DOOR SPRANG TO LIFE WITH A THUD. Michelle had put the phone down a few minutes ago, walked over to the windows and opened them wide, revealing the fading winter sun and the constant flurries against the orange sky. She flipped on the dining room light before going back into the kitchen, picked up her favorite chopping knife and continued on the carrots. She'd sliced up two before the knocking started.

Her hand resting on the door handle, she scanned the apartment behind her. The living room was clear. The kitchen was clear. The bedroom door was shut. No shadowed snouts sticking out of walls.

Good.

She started turning the handle and looked back once more over her shoulder. The three dark dogs had been so anxious for her to accept this stupid request. They wouldn't stay hidden.

Michelle reluctantly opened the door while her other hand unhooked the chain-lock. "Come in. Try not to flood my apartment this time."

All five kids rushed inside. Wait, there were six of them now. It wasn't fair to call Cody a kid, but at the same time, he hung out with these little weird brats. The rest of the names escaped her. The next oldest boy, the big mouth of the group, held a pale little girl in his arms. Michelle had remembered he couldn't stop talking nor had been able to keep his eyes off her chest. Cody's sister was walking on her own, but gripping her left arm tightly and leaning against Cody's arms with most of her weight. She was hurt too. Again.

One girl? Just one minute? Just look at one sick girl?

There was blood on most of their jeans and shirts, and the smallest girl's jacket was soaked to the point of dripping.

Nurse mode to full. Two girls. Two injuries.

"Here, get on the couch," Michelle pulled at the loudmouth's arm and pointed him in the direction of her sofa. Crap, does microfiber even work against blood stains? It was the miracle material after all.

Michelle put a soft arm against Cody and said, "You need to sit over there." Her intuition sparked. His sister was going fast. Even so, the little girl on the couch pulled at her—some strange tug that seemed to say, *That one first.*

Michelle turned to the blonde freak, who sent her weird-o-meter into the red zone, and the girl, probably a cheerleader, who was obviously in love with him. The boy was still in the cast that he had received in the hospital. Michelle glanced at the cheerleader. It was odd that this girl hadn't managed a single scrape in their accident.

Okay, there's another thing for the weird total. Don't worry about that now. Focus.

Michelle continued with the quick orders as years of schooling and nursing took charge, "You get a basin of water out of the bottom cabinet and fill it with warm water. And you," her arm on blonde-freakie's shoulder, "Get in here, shut the door, and get me this girl's parents on the phone."

The loudmouth had been moving the little girl's weight off of him to the couch with precision when he heard these words and glanced up. He stumbled over his words, "I wouldn't know how to do that."

"You dial the number—" Michelle shook her head. He didn't know her parents. Likely none of them knew this girl's parents. That made this dangerous for Michelle. Legally, she was crossing some thick lines at this point. She had crossed some of those lines by opening her door to them in the first place.

Blondie stuttered out his words, "I—I don't know her parents. It's just that—we found her like this. An hour ago."

Michelle kneeled over the girl, grabbed her arm and handed it to the loudmouth, "Here, check her pulse." Surprisingly, he held her and pressed his two fingers against her radial artery and looked at his watch to count the seconds.

At least he's not stupid.

She turned the girl's head over and waved to Blondie. "Grab that towel and hold it here. Put some pressure on it. She's nicked her supraorbital artery."

The lovesick girl walked over carrying some clothes, a young girl's by the cut and the thread of the jeans, "Here, we grabbed these for her."

Michelle continued to inspect the little girl, "Put them down and grab the blankets out of the closet by the front door. We need to get her out this bloody mess and make sure she's not bleeding anywhere else. Then we need to get her warmed up."

The lovesick cheerleader turned to glance at Mr. Blonde and Weird, begging his approval for her next step. Crap. This one was a puppy-dog if she'd ever seen one.

Michelle said, "Don't look at him. Just do it. You're wasting my time." She ripped the seams of the girl's bloody dress by hand. The seams were worn and cracked open easily. She pulled the dress back, turned her over and examined her.

Moving her hand across the girl's back, Michelle said, "There's some nasty scrapes on her back, but nothing too terrible. She doesn't look like she's eaten recently, either. So where did you find her? And how did she split her head open?"

The blonde boy was obviously hiding something. He glanced around to the others before facing Michelle. He replied but didn't make eye contact, "She was lying on our porch. She was bleeding when we found her."

"And you can't go to the hospital because?"

Cody kneeled next to his sister, "I'm sorry we're bringing you into this. We didn't know where else to turn. A hospital just isn't safe for us right now. We need you to believe us about that and help us without asking any more questions. Please." Cody's eyes had never left Michelle's and she could feel him melting away her determination. A nurse in the E.R. plays detective as often as she plays healer and it was difficult to switch that off. Tonight, instead of struggling to ask the right questions, she struggled between which questions to ask. There were so many things wrong with all this.

But Cody had asked her to take the detective hat off and simply do her job. She wasn't being barked at or demanded of. He simply asked.

So she relented, "Okay."

Michelle nodded towards the puppy-dog cheerleader, "You grab that water and a towel and come here. I won't ask any more questions but you need to move when I ask you."

"My name's Kaly," the puppy said, rubbing the side of her temple and squinting. She picked up the bowl of warm water with both hands.

"Okay, Kaly. Please come over and start cleaning her up. We'll change her clothes later. Right now, just make sure she's not bleeding anywhere else on her head. And you," Michelle turned back to the loudmouth, "What's your name?"

"Whatever you want it to be," the boy said. Cody grunted from across the room. The loudmouth grinned, "It's Roland. Roland of 919 Wonder Avenue, Incamna, Nebraska."

"Roland, I need you to keep doing what you're doing. Don't let up the pressure on that wound. You have the most important assignment right now."

"And do I get a prize if I do good?" He smiled at her.

Michelle was beginning to hate that smile. "Shut up, hold that cloth, and don't move." She turned now to focus on Cody and his sister, the girl from the hospital, her former patient. She pulled one of the yellow plastic dining room chairs around and gave it to Cody, then grabbed another one and swung it around so that she could sit in front of the girl.

Michelle forced a smile. This one was awake, and good bedside manner was demanded if not valued right now, "I'm sorry. I've forgotten your name."

"Janae."

"And what's happened to your arm?" Michelle put her left hand under Janae's arm and started to pull back the girl's right hand with her other. Janae winced and pulled back as the wound was opened up to the still air.

"Bit by a dog." That answer came easily, not at all like the blonde freak's dodgy responses. Cody nodded in agreement. He didn't say much, but what he said without speaking was enough.

"What type of dog? Yours or a neighbor's?" As she examined the wound, she was surprised how well the girl was responding. She had been collected the entire time. She was exhausted, but that was to be expected. She hadn't cried and judging on the depth of the teeth marks, she would've had every right to do so. This girl had an incredible pain threshold.

Janae thought and then replied, "Don't know. Large. Dark. Not mine."

"Okay, I need you stand up and follow me over to the sink. We need to rinse this out and I'm going to have to use a little soap." Janae caught the unspoken warning of, "This is going to hurt," hesitated for a moment and then stood up, still allowing Cody to support her. The three walked over to the sink and Michelle turned the water on, testing it twice with her two fingers to make sure it wasn't too hot.

She pulled Janae's arm under the water and realized why the girl had developed a high tolerance to pain. Her arm was covered in scars from what Michelle instantly recognized as a razor blade.

This girl was a cutter.

Buried between the fresh cuts and this new wound were several cuts which were almost healed.

The water continued to wash through the wound, revealing a deep tear in Janae's arm. The water should be stinging her something awful but she barely noticed.

As the water continued to rinse the deep bite marks and the torn flesh of the girl's arm, Michelle noticed several thin dark lines branching from the wound and marching up her arm. One single line was thicker than the others and had already reached her inner elbow.

"This bite is infected," Michelle said. Her arm shouldn't be showing signs of infection this soon after being bitten. What infection was this dark? It appeared infected. Her blood had been tainted, that was a fact. But Michelle wasn't sure what foreign little thing raced through Janae's blood stream on a march to her heart. Add one more point to the weird column, which was quickly running out of space.

"I think I have some Amoxicillin in my medicine cabinet." Michelle knew that simply offering anyone, let alone a minor, prescription meds could get her RN status revoked faster than the infection on the girl's arm had spread. The girl needed to get some pills in her and she needed them about an hour ago. She couldn't say for sure, but Michelle was sure the mark had moved further up the arm in just the brief time they'd been standing and washing it off.

She turned to Cody. "Okay, grab a towel and dry it off then grab another one and apply some pressure just like loudmouth is doing for the little girl. Keep it up until the bleeding stops."

From behind her, the blonde freak shouted, "Help! Roland! It's back!"

CHAPTER TWENTY-ONE

THE LIGHT BRIGADE

THE SCREAM CAME FROM THE BLONDE BOY. As Michelle turned to the living room, she saw Tryal leap over the couch and stand guarding the little girl. His face was blanched. Roland left one hand on the girl's forehead and twisted around to cover her up. Kaly had moved behind the two boys.

Across the room, six feet away and moving closer, was the ghost dog Macbeth. The Cinder. The beast was simply walking. Michelle had seen him angry. She'd seen him in protection-mode. Now, he was simply interested, his flaming eyes dim and focused on the girl bleeding on the couch.

"It's back!" Tryal had said.

Back? Michelle heard the word in mid-stride and her mind raced in a mad game of connection. They've run into him before? Maybe it was another dog. How would they mistake Macbeth and his two buddies for just a normal dog? That's mistaking Big Ben for a stopwatch.

"Cody, get to the door. We've got to get out of here," Roland shouted out the orders.

Michelle replied, "STOP!" The two boys and the dark dog looked up to her, all three in confusion. She continued, "He isn't going to do anything!"

Attempting to bring her up to speed, Roland said, "This isn't a neighborhood German shepherd."

Michelle lowered her voice, "I know. Just stop. Nothing is going to happen if you just calm down." With each word, her voice dropped in volume, hoping to calm the room with her tone.

Roland said, "Listen! Just get to the door. This is the thing that bit Janae."

Was that true? Had her three done this?

She couldn't trust them, wouldn't trust them—although she had grown to know them each well. This wasn't normal behavior for them; first, to bite an innocent and, second, to appear to this large an audience. Then again, she had only opened the door to this group because the three dogs had in their own quiet and demanding way urged her to.

"He won't touch you," Michelle rounded the kitchen counter and grabbed Tryal's shoulder, then looking at the dog, "Macbeth, back off."

"Macbeth?" Roland eased enough to look her in the eye, "It's got a name?"

Tryal still stood between all of them and Macbeth. Despite the incredible revelation Michelle had delivered, he hadn't relaxed at all.

"Cody. Get to the door. Roland. Get the girl," Tryal pounded out each word with a strange boldness, a role he had never filled before.

Michelle reached forward and slapped Tryal across the head, "Don't you listen?" The odd move paused the tension. "I said he isn't going to hurt anyone."

"This isn't your dog!" Tryal's eyes were fixed on her, completely ignoring the slap.

She stepped between Tryal and Macbeth, "Pay attention. I don't know what you thought you saw tonight, but Macbeth wasn't it. Macbeth has been with me the entire day."

As if on some cruel cue system, Puck and Caliban, the two other phantom dogs, walked through the wall and appeared next to Macbeth. All three of them stood along the far edge of the room.

Tryal stumbled backwards, pressing against the couch just as a thump came from behind them. They turned in time to see Kaly slam to the ground unconscious. The thump had been her forehead smacking the wall as she fainted. Cody dropped to hold her.

"What next?" Roland asked. Three of the very beasts they had been running from were standing in the room, but this crazy nurse could throw them each a doggy biscuit and scratch behind their ears. Roland's mind raced. What was going on? The dogs are just standing there. Not tense, not enraged like Fujo. But they look the same. Heck, they looked identical. Sleek and shadowy. Dark, leathery specters sending tendrils of black smoke in the air. These three were different from old Fujo. There was a difference. He just couldn't grasp it. Not yet.

Their eyes. Their eyes were flames, as were Fujo's, but these were merely red dots against the black phantom fabric of their skull.

"They're not going to kill us, Tryal," Roland let go of the cloth on the girl's head and grasped Tryal's shoulder, "She's right."

Michelle couldn't contain her surprise. This was the one she thought the biggest idiot and here he was being the voice of reason.

"No!" Tryal's eyes were locked on the dogs in front of him.

"Tryal calm down. I don't think these are the same ones," Roland argued.

"They're not," Michelle couldn't contain her comments.

Lowering his voice to a little more than a whisper, Roland said, "Could you be quiet?" He glanced at Tryal and then back to Michelle, "Please?"

"No," Tryal said.

"Now you become courageous? Can you please listen?"

Tryal's mind had gone unusually cool. He had made a promise. The girl would be kept safe. So, he simply stood his ground, "If they're safe, then make them back up. I don't want them anywhere near her."

Roland turned to Michelle, his eyebrows raised, passing the request to her.

"Macbeth, Caliban, Puck, can you back up? Please?" She moved between Tryal and the dogs. Maybe if she was willing to get close to them, he'd get the hint.

The hellhounds simply stood there, the television and the wall behind them still visible through their oily skin. Smoke rose from their backs. Their eyes still a dim flicker compared to Fujo's.

Macbeth took two steps back, his body intersecting the television and its cart behind him. Caliban and Puck mimicked the action in an odd choreography.

Tryal's body relaxed, falling out of his defensive stance.

Michelle moved closer to the dogs and bent down. She whispered low but still clearly enough that Tryal could hear, "What's going on with you three?"

Macbeth took one step forward and nudged the side of Michelle's leg, looking up at her.

Michelle said, "Are you asking for permission?" Knowing what Tryal's answer would be, she shook her head. "No. They don't want you near her. Not yet."

"Not ever!" Tryal said.

Macbeth's hind leg muscles rippled. They each coiled back as puffs of smoke poured from their bodies. Their skin grew opaque and they stepped forward, out of the wall and the TV.

Tryal, a few feet away now, asked, "What are they doing?"

The eyes of Michelle's shadow dogs had gone a shocking blue. A bright, icy blue.

A moan roared from Janae. She clutched her arm and rolled onto the ground, shuffling her feet and pushing herself into the corner next to the set of nesting tables. Her face was tormented and her eyelids wrenched back against the sockets, causing her eyes to look engorged. The widening pupils grew fast past their edges.

Her moan still resonating in the room, Tryal heard a distinct voice in his head.

keep her safe

Door had spoken. Brief but clear. Not a memory. Not his imagination. Her voice was back for one small second. Wherever she was, she could still reach him if she wanted to.

The little girl on the couch opened her eyes. At the same moment, her mouth parted to a narrow sliver and a scream tore through each of them, a wave of sadness riding behind it. All of them dropped. Michelle felt as if all the reason for living had been pulled out of her. Tryal didn't hear her scream, at least not with his ears, but knew she had screamed in his mind and in his heart, as every bit of his emotions were electrified and then drained away.

Janae shook in the far corner. She slammed against the tables, collapsing picture frame after picture frame onto the carpet. She still clutched her arm as Cody pulled himself to her. He gripped her shoulders and she bucked his hands loose. From her left arm, black steam rose from the bite. The infected lines had marched up her arm and had disappeared under her shirt sleeve only to reappear above the collar and across her neck. The lines hadn't just moved up, they had widened. The one closest to her elbow was nearly an inch thick.

From across the room, the three hellhounds growled in unison and pounced. Caliban or Puck, one of them, Tryal couldn't tell, had in a single bound leapt onto the edge of the couch. The other small one had darted through him, sending an icy chill through his body and raising gooseflesh across his arms. The large one had also leapt to the far end of the sofa. It crouched positioning itself between the now-screaming girl and the door.

The fourth dog had moved next to the door across from Macbeth.

"No!" Roland screamed and instinctively turned and pulled Michelle backwards on the television-side of the couch.

A fourth. Four dogs where there had been just three.

The fourth was Fujo. His eyes were alive, flames leaping into the room, showering the carpet with cinders. His dark teeth were bared. His skin was a shadowy tempest of smoke. The muscles moved underneath like writhing snakes below his skin.

Then he barked. It was a hands-to-your-ears deafening bark that vibrated the room. It found an odd harmony with the little girl's spiritual scream. Ear, head, and heart all ached from the noise.

Kaly winced. Pinpricks of pain shot through her head. The voice in her head whispered.

Run!

The bark's echo receded. Just as it did, the little girl's eyes shut tight and her mouth clenched, muffling the scream into silence.

The haunting pain still stayed with them. For each of them, it took its own form. For Tryal, his mind still clouded with memories of childhood loneliness and late nights on the streets searching for food before he met Roland. Roland pushed back the deep memories of cigarette and stove-top burns. Michelle's mind flooded with pictures of cornfields and Patrick. The memories faded to phantoms as the scream stopped, but the pain was still fresh and faded much slower.

"Who is that?" Michelle shouted as she pushed Roland's arms off.

Fujo's back haunches were inches from the unconscious Kaly's head. His long neck had stretched as far as it could, putting its snout two feet from Macbeth's.

"That's freakin' Old Cujo. Fujo for short."

"He's a Cinder?" Michelle asked.

"What the heck is a Cinder?" Tryal's stupor had worn off.

"Those things. We named them Cinders," Michelle said.

"He's after her," Tryal said.

Roland asked, "Who's 'we?'"

Michelle took a confident step forward. She opened her mouth to speak but stopped as Janae moaned across the room and in a clean motion jerked her head back into the wall, leaving a distinct impression in the textured sheet-rock. Cody tried to hold her still and to hold back his own tears, failing at both miserably. Kaly kneeled to her side, muttering, "Janae?"

"What is your name?" Michelle pointed at Fujo and commanded. She spoke clear and loud and hoped that she appeared far more confident than she felt.

Without opening its mouth, the Cinder's eyes flickered and it spoke a single word that Tryal would later wish he had never heard, had never ever known about.

"*Shestlene.*"

It was a simple word, but the images of misery and pain that whipped out with its sounding slapped them each sharply. The beast's name was a word and a package of compressed terror. Tryal saw the moment of death of countless individuals in that one utterance. A woman's soul leaving her crackling, bound body. A child's tormented and tongue-less tears as spirit was yanked terrified from flesh. A man's head rolling across the ground, its mind shuttering in and out of the last moments of consciousness.

They would never say his name to each other again. He had been nick-named Fujo and that was enough. Tryal was sure he would hold a deep bit-terness towards Michelle for conjuring up such evil.

Michelle took one step closer and spoke, her voice noticeably shaken, "Leave this place, now."

Her three Cinders growled in agreement.

Fujo stared at her, the brightness of his eyes stabbing against her own, but he did not move.

"Leave this place! Now!"

Fujo cocked his head and considered her. Roland couldn't say for sure, but there was a bit of confusion on the dog's face, as if Michelle was some-thing he hadn't accounted for.

Once more Michelle spoke, her voice loud again, any hint of timidity gone, "I know you obey me. Leave this place. Now."

Macbeth lunged forward and snapped at Fujo. It was a warning shot, but near enough to reinforce her command.

"NOW!"

Fujo growled at Janae, who writhed to the dog's right. He barked his deafening bark at her and she lunged forward to meet him, pushing Cody away and slamming him against the kitchen cabinets, tearing one of the door's off of its hinges. Her eyes pulled open wide. Her whites had been masked within an ink-black smear. At the pupil, a sliver of a spark gleamed.

She moaned. Fujo barked in return, louder than ever, forcing Tryal, Roland and Michelle to clutch their ears. Cody reached back to her, placing both hands around her, his arms trying to lock into place against her writhing, rippling body.

She spasmed and evaporated into dark smoke just as Fujo faded from the room, his eyes once more gazing at Michelle.

Cody's hands slapped together, stirring the last dark and disappearing vapors. Kaly fell back to the carpet, stunned and grasping her head.

Fujo was gone and Janae with him.

Cody crumpled to the floor and sobbed.

"Shuck the Dog-fiend:

This phantom I have heard many persons in East Norfolk,

and even Cambridgeshire, describe as having seen a black shaggy dog,

with fiery eyes, and of immense size,

and who visits churchyards at midnight."

—REVEREND TAYLOR OF MARTHAM, 1805

Chapter Twenty-two

INTO SHADOW

TRYAL STRUGGLED WITH A CHOICE. Run or freeze. There were only two options. Tryal could see other options when in danger, but he knew that he would always choose one of those two. He dreamt of being strong and racing in to face the challenge, but he rarely did.

Right now, he'd chosen freeze. The strange moment of courage that had possessed him a few minutes ago was gone. He could hear the din of their voices. Kaly pinched the bridge of her nose. Another headache. Stress?

In the far corner, Cody was rolled in a ball wailing so loudly Tryal was certain Michelle's neighbors had already called the cops. Two houses in two hours and both times the police would arrive in their wake.

Around him, the smoke rose from the backs of demon dogs as they moved closer to Michelle. Roland stared at the front door, appearing frozen too. Tryal knew this wasn't true. Roland never froze. Roland acted. Roland chose. Often the wrong choice and the wrong action, but he rarely hesitated when actions were required. The two stood at the polar ends of that spectrum.

Michelle said, "He'll be back." She had stood staring where the growling beast had just disappeared, taking their Janae with him. Michelle turned around and walked into the kitchen. She finished her thought, "He'll bring others."

This comment snapped Tryal out of his fog. Janae's sudden disappearance had been the freezing event. So sudden. So unexpected. So. . . normal. Once again, something terrible had happened and he was at the center of it.

"Others?" Tryal's lips froze as the words escaped him.

Michelle pulled knives out of the knife block sitting on top of the apartment-standard white refrigerator. She piled them all on the kitchen counter, carefully but quickly.

"He wants the little girl and he'll need to bring back reinforcements."

"What reinforcements?" Roland had joined the discussion. His voice was loud over Cody's sobs. Kaly, dazed but awake, had moved to Cody and had been holding onto the rocking boy, adding her own tears to his. Tryal could make out only a few of the words Kaly threw out to console Cody. The only sentence he heard, repeated over and over, was "We'll find her."

Michelle already understood, "More Cinders."

"There's more than just Fujo and the three Shakespeareans here?" Roland asked.

"Yeah, plenty more. I've seen them. He'll need more to match my three."

"Your three? You said 'yours'? These things belong to you?" Roland pointed his finger at the three Cinders still in the room.

Tryal finished Roland's thought, "Your pets?"

"Yeah, they're mine. Definitely not pets." She chortled and coughed at this, "They're mine—on loan."

"On loan! For what?" Roland had moved to stand in the kitchen entrance.

"We need to leave now. He's coming back," Michelle nudged Roland aside, and opened the front closet, pulling out a dark-blue hiker's pack, "Soon." She picked up her phone from the kitchen ledge.

Tryal felt a small hand grab his. He twitched in surprise and looked down. The little girl was awake and standing next to him, her hand in his, her torn rags hanging from only one shoulder. Her face was empty except for her large dark eyes. He looked at them for the first time since they had pulled her free into this world. They were huge, with dark pupils, black as ink against the small whites of her eyes and her smooth, pale face.

Michelle paused to stare at the little girl. "Wow, she healed fast," then went back to racing around, grabbing things out of drawers, disappearing into her bedroom and returning just as quickly, and stuffing everything into her backpack.

Roland stared at Michelle, unsure that she was real. She fit into their weirdness so easily. And she had brought a heaping helping of the strange herself. Now, she was putting in with them for the next step, without argument. In fact, she was leading the charge.

Roland said to her, "We can just leave. You don't have to go. We don't need to get you more wrapped up into this."

"No. If you're here or not, they're coming back here first. If I'm still here, they'll rip me and my boys apart. They'll have enough of a force to guarantee we won't put up much of a fight. I don't like it, but I'm with you for right now. Besides, you have no idea what you're up against."

That was true. They didn't know anything. They had a mute little girl with a big bad wolf chasing her. Oh, and the wolf could walk through walls and take any one of them with him when he wanted to. What little knowledge they had scared Roland.

Cody's large frame shuddered in the corner. "She's gone. She's gone. She's gone."

Cody was right. Janae was gone. And Tryal had no idea to where. Cody was acting like a child who had lost his mother, crying in the middle of the grocery store. No matter how messed up Janae was, she had always been there. The backhand of their father could be endured for each other's sake. Misery loves company and the two had shared each other's. And now Janae was gone.

"Princess, we're going," Michelle said.

In the distance, pushing through the roaring winds, more sirens wailed.

"Cody, we have to go." Roland said.

"Shesgoneshesgoneshesgone," the words bled into each other as Cody rocked on his calves against the wall, his hands fumbling in the pockets of his pull-over.

"Yes. She is," the consoling words came from Roland, now leaning over Kaly and Cody, "But the hot nurse is right, we have to go now."

"She's gone. She's gone," Cody's mantra slowed.

Roland raised his eyebrows. "What the heck do I do now?"

Michelle came behind Tryal and the girl, her three demon dogs following. "If he's not moving, leave him."

"No!" Roland answered.

"No," Kaly was on her feet and her sudden rise pushed Roland back, "We can't!"

Michelle pushed past Tryal and stood in front of the door, "Pick him up and carry him. Once more, we have to go."

"Give us a minute," Roland said and bent back down, putting his hand on Cody's shoulder.

"No," Michelle said, "They will wait to see what we do. But not for long. They're coming back. If he can't stand and you can't carry him, leave him. In the morning they will be limited. Weak. But not now. It's night and they are going to be stronger than ever. It isn't safe here." Tryal found himself nodding once as the logic of her argument caught up to him. He was glad Roland and Kaly were looking at Cody.

"That's why we can't go without him," Kaly said.

Roland whispered in Cody's ear, "Come on, man. We've got to go. Stand up. I'm not going to leave you."

Cody's mantra picked up speed and volume in response, "Shesgoneshesgoneshesgoneshesgone."

"Michelle, they listened to you," Kaly said.

"Just the once. They won't again. It's not obedience," Michelle put her hand on the door and opened it before adding, "It's just a little respect. Very little." She walked out and her Cinders faded away as they followed her.

Tryal stood staring at the open door, the girl's hand still firmly placed in his own. There was no fear on her face. There was no emotion at all. This little girl, who was so important to Death, waited for Tryal to choose.

Roland spoke once more in Cody's ear, "Let's go, Cody." He pulled on Cody's arm as he stood. Cody jerked his arm back, rocking with a solid thud against the wall.

"Ahh, screw it!"

"Roland," Kaly stared at him as he stepped back, still staring at Cody, "We can't leave him. Tryal?"

Roland turned around, facing the door and added, "The bossy chick is right. Leave him. We might actually draw those things away from here. We have to go." As if to emphasize his conclusion, the sirens whoo-whoo'd louder, a block or two away at the most. "I'm going to stab whichever busybody neighbor called 911."

"Cody, please!" Kaly cried as she pulled on his large arm. She yanked, but couldn't move it now that Cody had determined to stay immobile. He rocked, chanted, cried, and his hand still fumbled inside of his pocket. He jerked back, bringing her almost down upon him. "Cody, please get up!"

Cody just repeated his mantra and closed his eyes.

Kaly felt Tryal's hand rest on her shoulder. "We're leaving, Kaly."

Kaly wrapped her arms around Cody's big chest and sobbed into his neck. "I'm sorry." Tryal's hand was there once more pulling her back up. With one hand he held the hand of the young girl and with the other he pulled Kaly tightly to himself and led her through the open door.

Chapter Twenty-Three

IT'S A TRAP

H E HAD TAKEN HER. The demon dog had pulled Janae away from him. She had been stolen by him.

To where? Where had he taken her? Cody's head smacked against the wall. The thing had left when Michelle had ordered it, and took Janae as payment.

Just give him the girl. Janae was gone and all we have is some little girl. The girl for Janae. Why hadn't they just given her up?

"Shesgone." To somewhere dark.

"I'm here. I'm waiting."

Janae's soft voice spoke in his mind. She had said that before, but when? Was he imagining her speaking? Where was she?

"I'm here. Come with me."

That was her voice. Those were her words. She had spoken it through the water. The water and the locket. He had heard her voice as his head fought against the rising water in the hospital room. He had looked at her then but she wasn't speaking although he could hear her voice.

"*Come find me.*"

He hadn't imagined them. She was somewhere dark, somewhere far from home. A somewhere that the locket opened up to.

His right hand fumbled in his pocket and felt the silver chain, cold and damp in his fingers. He had picked it up at the hospital and found himself looking into it whenever the others were gone. He would sneak off to hide in the bathroom and just stare at it, careful not to get it near any mirror. He kept it in his hand whenever he could, running his fingers along the raised carvings on its face, tracing the unknown letters and strange marks that lined its casing.

Now he knew why he had palmed it. Now he knew why he couldn't keep his hands off of it. Now he knew why he stared at it for hours.

"*Come find me.*"

She was on the other side of the locket and it was going to take him to her. She had called to him when the locket was open and now he was going to find her.

But the others wouldn't let him. They'd stop him as they'd stopped it once before. But they couldn't have stopped the water without him. His Voice spoke to the water. His Voice had saved them. Not Tryal's. Not Roland's. And not Kaly's.

This time, it would be his Voice that would drive the waters.

"*Come find me.*"

But not just yet. Soon, but not just yet. The others were leaving, so let them leave. Stay and wait.

She was gone and the dog was coming.

He'd kill the stupid thing and find his way to her at the same time, her own Voice pulling him through the water. When he found her, they would both be home. They would no longer be lost.

Cody could feel Roland pulling on his arm, but he just closed his eyes, pulled back and let Janae's voice wash over him.

"*Come find me.*"

But now I know a secret you don't. I know where she is. I'm going to find her and you can't stop me. I'm going through the dark. I have the locket and I'm going to use it and I'm going to find her and I'm going to drown that blasted beast as I do so.

"She's gone."

But I can still hear her calling to me.

He wouldn't move. They had to leave. They had to go, and go now. She was gone and that monster was coming back and Cody would be waiting for him.

The door to the apartment shut and he stopped mouthing the words, although his lips kept moving. He was alone. He opened his eyes and pulled the locket out.

It was beautiful. The light in the room rolled across its edges and reflected in bright wash on his face and the wall. He coursed its outline with his finger and rested it against his lips.

"I'm coming to find you." The locket vibrated in his hand as he spoke. He tightened his fingers around it. It was as if it tried to flee from him. Do this fast before it's gone.

He searched for the other ingredient in the magic-making. There were framed photos of the Santa Cruz boardwalk and various West Coast sights hanging around the room. They were all reflective and might do the trick, but they weren't right. Above the television hung a small mirror. It was framed in a dark-stained wood and had a small faux keyhole at its bottom. That would work fine. As he walked over to it, he glanced at the sliding glass doors that opened onto the small cement porch. It was now dark enough that he could use the doors as a mirror. He shuddered. If he started with the mirror above the television, soon after the doors would turn to inlets themselves and they were large enough to slam him against the far wall when they opened up fully. Those rushing waves would take out anything in their way.

He'd have to raise *his* Voice and the water would respond. *He'd* simply ask it to move faster. *He'd* say "please" and water, willing to be used, would obey. Cody smiled at the ease of it.

He heard a knock from the front door, followed by a slurred and pained voice, a voice he imagined belonging to a man who had smoked one too many cigars, "Anyone there? It's Detective Manning with the Incamna Police. We have a report of a disturbance."

Cody stood with his back against the television and the mirror that would serve as the real keyhole in a just a minute and the large, dark glass doors to his right.

Another knock and the request grew more urgent, "Please open up. This is the police." Was he reading that off of a cue-card he stole from cop show? Cody grinned and flipped the locket over and over in his hand.

The Officer knocked again and coughed, irritated by having to use his voice again, "Open the door. I've got two other officers here and we need to speak to you."

Cody stood and smiled, his finger running over the locket.

"*Come find me,*" echoed Janae's voice at the back of his mind.

———

Outside, Detective Manning stood there listening and waiting.

From the small apartment, he heard barking. It sounded far louder than one dog. It sounded as loud as a pound full of dogs, their barks bouncing off of the concrete of their cages while they stepped in their own crap.

There then came one loud, authoritative bark, silencing the others, followed by a quick and screaming "I HATE YOU! YOU TOOK HER!"

The voice was hoarse and bubbled on the syllables. Instead of more barking to answer the cursing, there was the deafening roar of water rushing like a waterfall. The lights in the hallway flickered and then went out, plunging the hall into darkness before the amber emergency lights high up on the wall clicked on.

The edges of the door sprayed water across the hallway, drenching Manning's thick glasses. He stepped back, pulled them off and slapped the junior officer next to him, shouting over the sound of the water, "Simon, get in there! Kick it open if you have to."

The young officer gave the edge of the handle a solid kick and was slammed back across the hallway as the door burst open. The wave of water knocked Simon unconscious as his head slammed against the wall.

The two remaining officers were swept down the hall, scrambling to keep their footing and falling under the river pouring out of the apartment door. Manning's arms lashed out, tearing at the plaster wall and ripping the skin off of his fingers in his desperate attempt to latch onto anything. His legs were pushed behind him and he went face-first into the rushing water. His head bobbed up, down, and he gasped for breath between each. Plunging below the surface the second time, he opened his eyes and saw not the darkened hallway, but fields and clouds and stars and in the final second before he came to a sudden stop, an overwhelming sensation of flying washed over him.

Manning, propping himself on one knee first and wheezing to plant his foot underneath him, pulled himself up and stared at the standing water, now only a few inches high. What the heck just happened?

He sloshed back across the hall to the shattered door and the unconscious Simon and fumbled under his wet jacket at the latch unholstering his gun. Still dazed, he kept the weapon at his side, hoping to see his other officer stumbling up the stairs. No such luck. He was going to have to do this by himself.

As if taking a cue again from a television police drama, Manning flattened himself back against the wall and raised his weapon, coiling his strength and courage together. Manning turned into the apartment, splashing with each step. The gun pointed ahead, he fanned from one side to the other of the small apartment. No one. Except for the water and the ruined furniture, the apartment was empty. He stood alone in draining water that was only a quarter of an inch high.

Well, not alone. Behind him and just at the edge of Manning's vision stood Mr. Mu and Mr. Hu and the limp, unconscious body of the mother, slung over Mr. Hu's shoulder.

"Late."

"*Yes we are.*"

"Again."

"*Yes.*"

"This whole job might be the undoing of our reputation, friend. I'm not convinced this was a good choice. So far, we've been to half a dozen places and all we have for it is this old woman who just wouldn't scream. A little screaming would've been so nice. Very poor etiquette on her part."

"*The boy. That's all we need.*"

"He was here. There were others."

Mr. Hu sniffed the air. "*Yes.*" The words coming from the thin man's mouth were slow and tired. They emptied the air of all life.

Mr. Mu sniffed, "Do you smell that also?"

Mr. Hu stood there, his lungs filling softly, "*Yes. This place, this girl. Not right.*"

"Add up the pieces and something doesn't fit. A boy. His companions. A witch? Their locket. A locket that's been used. Three times.

Mr. Hu asked, "*The question to be asked is why?*"

Walking past his companion, Mr. Mu said, "He might have some bit of knowledge. Perhaps he knows who lives here." Mr. Mu pointed his fat, stained fingers in the direction of Officer Manning, who looked at the calendar next to the refrigerator.

Mr. Hu reached far into Officer Manning's skull and grabbed tight, pulling a large chunk of the officer's brain out as he jerked his hand back. The officer fell to the floor with a thud and a splash. His ears, nose and eyes filled with and then drained of blood that leaked into the standing water, coloring it crimson.

"*Let's see.*"

"And her eyes have all the seeming of a demon that is dreaming."

—FROM THE RAVEN BY EDGAR ALLAN POE

CHAPTER TWENTY-FOUR

INCAMNA AT NIGHT

A GREEN TOYOTA FORERUNNER, which was now just passing the bar known as Winner's Circle, held in silence Kaly, Roland, Tryal, Michelle, and a little girl whom Roland had named "Hood". They'd been quiet for the five minutes since they drove away from the back entrance of Michelle's apartment complex. Michelle drove. Roland tapped his fingers against the frosted glass, Kaly sniffed and dropped the occasional tear, and Tryal stared out at the growing snowstorm while holding the little girl's hand tightly. The little girl leaned against Tryal and started to doze, her face empty of expression. Tryal had put Stacie's red jacket on her, a fleece Old Navy special with large pockets.

The streaming snowfall, now moving parallel to the car, mesmerized Tryal. In the short time since getting in the car, and owing no small part to the adrenaline rush of the last few hours, Tryal had twice nodded off. His eyelids shut and his body jerked an instant later, waking him up sharply. Crap! He shouldn't be sleeping now. There was at least one, and probably a host of those Cinders chasing them. He'd promised to keep the little, quiet girl safe and protected against those beasts.

Just for once, Tryal. Do what you say you'll do. Be who you want to be. Please.

Tryal's thoughts continued to race.

Cody.

His mind called out the question he had avoided, calling to Death as if it was right next to him.

Is he dead?

Nothing.

Is he dead? Please, tell me. Is he dead?

Underneath the beating of his heart, he heard.

no not yet

"He's not dead," Tryal said, standing.

Kaly turned to him, "Are you sure?"

Tryal said, "Yes. I asked."

"Can you find out where he is?" asked Roland.

At the same time, Michelle said, "Who did you ask?"

Where is he? Tryal asked again.

beyond my reach and beyond yours

What do you mean? Tryal thought.

Silence. No response came.

Answer me. Nothing again.

"Answer me!" shouted Tryal into the black air.

Michelle jumped in her seat, "What was that about?"

"Ignore him," Roland said, "Your creepy little friend is not talking again?"

Kaly put her hand on Michelle's shoulder, "I think we should go back for Cody."

Tryal spoke, "Don't. You won't be able to reach him. She's said that he's beyond our reach."

Michelle asked, "Who is 'she'?"

Kaly's face sobered, "What does that mean?"

Tryal said, "That's what I've been trying to find out. I was told that Cody's beyond our reach. That's all I know."

Roland grinned, "You can shut up now."

Michelle said, "What friends do you keep talking to?"

"Just tell her," said Kaly.

Tryal shook his head.

Roland chuckled, "She lives with demon dogs. I think she can handle your own brand of strange."

Tryal said, "Ours."

Roland said, "What?"

"Ours. You said it was my brand of strange. It's all of ours." Tryal stared out at the window.

"Why does that matter?" Roland asked.

"It just does," said Tryal.

"Whatever," Roland tapped on the dashboard, "Hey, you named them Macbeth, Caliban, and Puck. Shakespeare fan?"

Michelle smiled. "Just a bit."

"Okay, beautiful, here's the whole thing. Make sure you have your seat belt on. This will get weird."

Roland explained each of their friends—insects, the future, the weather, and water. He explained how they took Janae, bleeding, and their trip to the hospital. He explained almost everything but he did not tell her about Door. About Death.

Roland continued, "Then Mr. Tryal received a message from a friend, started a fire and . . ."

Tryal interrupted, "The girl appeared." He skipped over Door's demand to protect the girl. He explained how the dog appeared and chased them to her house.

Michelle had listened intently through the entire explanation. "I have to be dreaming. This isn't real."

Roland waved his hand, "Okay, question for you. Why'd you come with us? You could've kicked us out. Told us to grab Cody and get the holy heck outta there." At the mention of Cody, Kaly started to sob again.

Michelle shot a glance back at Kaly. A strange mixture of sympathy and irritation framed her eyes.

Kaly sobbed in a gulp and bleated, "We left him!" Tryal wrapped his free arm around Kaly and pulled her close.

Roland answered Kaly, "Yes, we did."

Again, Kaly said through tears, "It's just . . . we left him! I can't believe we left him."

"Kaly," Roland said soothingly, "He wasn't going to move and those things were coming after us. Besides, he's, well—he's the most powerful of us all."

Tryal agreed. Roland had said what they all had assumed but never spoken. They all suspected that Tryal could get his friend to do some pretty wild stuff, but they'd never seen it. Heck, they never wanted to see anything that Tryal could do. He was frightening to them. However, in terms of raw power, Cody was nearly Aquaman.

Roland continued, "We just couldn't stay. It's not like we're all *Super Nurse* who commands the animals of the wild, real or imaginary." He grinned at this attempt at a jab.

"SuperNurse? You don't have a clue about the Cinders," Michelle retorted.

Roland said, "You're right. We don't know crap about the Cinders. But you do. In fact, you're the only one in this entire world besides us who has a clue what those things are. You seem to be a freaking PhD on those blasted things, and we're still struggling with Play-Doh in kindergarten. What the heck is going on with you? Just by chance, we need a nurse and the one we find is the one nurse in this world who happens to raise those pooches. In fact, she's running her own kennel."

Those were Michelle's thoughts exactly.

Creepy.

"And more than that," Roland continued, "She's got some strange magic over them. '*Stop. You must leave. You must obey.*' What was that? What stupid voodoo do you have going on right now?"

"I don't know as much as you think."

"Huh?"

"I don't know as much as you think I know. I don't. I'll tell you. But first, we have to figure out where we're going. I'm not sure if you can tell, but I'm just driving without a purpose right now."

That wasn't exactly true and she knew it. She had been moving them closer and closer to a safe place. She had instinctively known where to drive tonight. She did know where they would spend the night, in quiet and safety. "I don't want to be traveling at night, but we just can't stay anywhere. Those other ones thrive at night. There aren't too many places they can't go."

"But there are places they can't go, aren't there?" Tryal asked.

"Yes," Michelle allowing herself a small smile. *He catches on quick.*

"And is there one close by?" Tryal said.

Michelle turned the corner at this and in front of him, silhouetted against the hazed light of the city and muted by the falling snow was the steeple of St. Thomas Aquinas Cathedral. Roland had been here twice before, Tryal once. Each was part of one of the Hartsell Home's service projects and the boys assisted in cleaning the Cathedral in appreciation for what the Home had done for them. They were told on the initial tour of the Cathedral that the Brothers of St. Tom's (the city's nickname for the place) had donated a lot of support to the Home.

Kaly sniffed. In the silence of the car, it was louder than she intended.

Roland turned to her, "We had to leave him."

Kaly cheeks were wet, "No. We didn—" She stopped short of finishing the admonition. "We should go back."

Tryal spoke, "No, we shouldn't."

"It's Cody," Roland continued, "At the worst, the cops showed up and he's in jail."

Kaly said, "No. That's not the worst that could happen. Those Cinders could've shown up."

Tryal said, "Yes, but after we left, I don't think so. They're after Hood. And, I guess us. But I don't think Cody."

"They're definitely after us," added Roland.

"And Janae? What happened to Janae?" Kaly asked.

The silence grew thick and no one spoke.

Tryal muttered, "I don't know." He felt the loss. Cody and Janae in one night. In one hour. In one moment.

"So these Cinders are like vampires?" The question had come from Kaly who had managed to stifle her crying to ask it. Her head throbbed as she spoke. Why had she asked that? Was it the other voice?

Michelle gave a small hoot, intended to be a chuckle and came out shorter and sharper. "Sorry 'bout that. I laughed 'cause that was what I thought when I figured out this little trick. I'm still not sure how wrong I am on that. There's a few things that are way different."

"For one, they don't need an invitation to come into your house," Tryal actually smiled, small and hidden in the dark of the car, as he said this.

"Second, they don't suck blood. They don't have a human form. What you see is what you get. They don't talk," Michelle paused, "Most of them don't, that is." Roland noted this, but didn't feel this was the best time to press on that piece of information.

Instead, he added, "And they can't go onto holy ground? Is that it?" The other eerie similarity, and the one Roland refused to say, was their bite. You might not turn into a blood-craving master of the night, but you definitely didn't stay yourself. Janae was gone, but he didn't think she was dead. She wasn't dead. He knew this, but wasn't sure how.

"As far as I've been able to tell, yes. With all of the crap of the last few years, St. Tom's become a bit of a sanctuary. Every time I've gone, my three have never gone in with me. They'll walk with me all the way up to the front doors but no further. They'll sit and wait on the steps until I'm done. So my guess is that this place is safe from them."

"So we just going to run from church to church?" Roland asked.

Michelle shook her head. "Maybe."

"Maybe I can find some shoes there," Tryal said, his voice calm again. "I mean shoe. Just need one."

Roland leaned back to look in the back seat at Tryal's feet. In all of the madness of the last few hours, he'd totally forgotten Tryal was barefoot except for the cast. All of that insane racing through the snow from burning house to house to Cinder house to this car without any shoes.

"Church, brother. We're going to a church. Not a Nike store," Roland said as he settled back into the front seat.

No shoes. All that running and no shoes. He laughed aloud at the craziness of it.

"They'll have a drop-box. We used to steal out of the Parish's drop-box all the time. That old khaki jacket I wore."

"St. Tommy's gonna be open this late?" Roland asked.

"This place never locks up. A holy 7-Eleven if there ever was one," Michelle said.

They pulled into the alley behind the Cathedral. Without wanting to, Tryal quietly asked Michelle, "Sure we should've taken this turn?" The alley was nearly void of light. The street light was soaked up by the darkness a few feet in. A haze reflected by the individual snowflakes filled the remaining space.

"Have to. The only other place to park is in the lot or on the street," Roland said. The sirens that were growing louder as they left her apartment weren't coming just because of the noise they had raised—Roland and his friends had been in trouble before they arrived at her place. Hopefully, the police wouldn't see the car in the dark alley.

Chapter Twenty-Five

SANCTUARY

T HE DASH FROM THE CAR to the front steps of St. Thomas's Cathedral was uneventful, except for Roland sliding around the corner on the snow and ice, and landing solidly on his butt. Tryal walked slowly, never leaving Hood's side. She moved at a steady pace even while the others ran. Roland's fall did not elicit a laugh or a smile from her. Tryal pulled a thin black windbreaker from his bag and pulled it over his head. He stood with the others before the large oak doors.

"Holy hades!" Roland jumped back several feet.

"Quiet," Michelle answered. Three Cinders had appeared on her left side, amassed closely together. Tryal flinched, but stopped, and guessed, from Michelle's reaction, that they were Macbeth, Caliban and Puck, her Cinders. They stood there, the sharp edging of the Cathedral's pillars and stonework visible through their flowing hides, puffs of ash joining the falling snow and dirtying the white layer at their feet. Tendrils of smoke wisped off of their backs and blew away against the wind.

"How can you tell these are yours?" Kaly drew close to Tryal, her left hand closing around his forearm.

"They didn't show up with their teeth around my neck," Michelle moved towards the large doors, "They'll stay out. It's not smart for us to be wasting time in the dark." If Michelle realized she'd been cold and sharp with Kaly, she didn't show it. Kaly herself ignored the thin reaction.

Michelle pulled open the large soundless doors. They opened to an amber-lit foyer sparkling with reflected light from a wall of stain-glassed windows. The rainbow of light danced across the fallen flakes.

"I am welcome here."

The words came as a shock. Hood had spoken. Tryal looked down at her. They all looked down at her. Michelle let the large door fall shut again. The little girl said nothing more. Her expression was empty.

"Did she just—" Roland leaked out the words.

"I think so," said Tryal. She had spoken, right? The voice was small, almost still, but it had been quite clear and he was sure it came from her. The quiet little mystery had uttered four brief words that would bang around Tryal's head for a long time to come.

"What did she say?" asked Michelle, although she had heard Hood clearly, as they all had. Tryal, however, would argue within himself for most of the evening whether the last word had come out "here" with a period or "here?" with a question mark. Statement or question?

"She said, 'I am welcome here,'" Kaly answered.

Until this point, Michelle had been iron in the whole drama, unbending, cold, and sometimes sharp. Michelle did something unexpected, even to herself. She bent down, her knee against the cold stonework of the steps, and said to Hood, "You are. You're right." She grabbed Hood's hand and pulled on the door again, leading the little girl inside the Cathedral first and the rest of them following.

You're wasting time! shouted the voice in Kaly's head. She paused and felt a stab of pain in her temples.

"Shut up," Kaly whispered.

Tryal paused, "What?"

Kaly shook her head, "Nothing." In her mind, the voice continued.

Get him to leave with you. Lose the girl. Lose the nurse.

The voice became louder and more demanding. Kaly ran ahead and grabbed Tryal's hand to reassure him and herself.

She thought to herself, *I'm definitely losing my mind.*

In surprise, the voice replied. *No, you're not. Stay focused. Mess up and you'll ruin a life of work.*

Kaly shook her head again, "I need some aspirin. Or Vicodin. Something," and leaned into Tryal. She felt reassured against him as if just being next to him answered all of her doubts.

She whispered into his ear, "Why is she with us?"

Tryal said, "Who? Michelle?"

Kaly said, "Yes. I don't trust her."

Tryal said, "I don't know. She's helping us, I guess."

Kaly pulled back, "You guess? You're leading this expedition. If you don't want her, tell her to leave."

Tryal stopped walking, "Leading? What are you talking about?"

"If you're not, who is?"

"We need a leader? I'm just trying to not to die," he dropped her hand, "I don't get you. This isn't—I don't know. We don't need someone in charge and we don't need to be deciding who comes along. This isn't the aquarium. This isn't one of our weekend adventures."

Kaly's head pounded and she shouted back, "I know! You conjured up the little girl. You started this! If we're about to die, it's your fault!"

Tryal, stunned, just stared back at her.

Roland, around the corner and out of sight, said, "Hey, you two. Shut up! You can have your little lover's spat later. Then you can sneak off to some pew and make up. Or make out."

Tryal growled and kicked at the snow, "I know. I'm sorry." He turned to follow Roland.

In Kaly's mind the two voices, her own and the other one, spoke at the same time.

Stupid girl!

Through the doors and quickly through the foyer, the five entered the sanctuary sans Cinders. Large, sky-scraping pillars rose and arched above, creating the sense of a forest canopy.

Tryal stepped back and stood, his shoulder bag balancing his stance against the opposite weight of the bulky half-cast. Pausing, he examined the ornate and meaningful embellishments scattered around him—carved ivy along the base of the pillars, dark wooden pews lined up as marching soldiers before their commander, the basin of holy water to his left, the cascading shelves of candles with their bouncing flames on his right, and towering nearly above him, the cathedral's pride—the twenty-five or more foot-tall stained-glass display.

Backlit to ensure a brilliant spectacle even at night, the stained panes featured the crucifixion of Christ prominently. Two smaller but still impressive scenes showed the Garden of Eden on the left, its green tree tinting the marble risers in front of it, and a reddened depiction of the Great White Throne of Judgement, a different Christ than the one in the center pane seated on a massive throne, his eyes calm but penetrating as they looked out at the mass of human civilization before him. The crucified Christ in the center hung limply from his cross. The blood was a bright crayon red. The figure of Christ was thin, pallid, and sad. Somehow muted.

Tryal was fascinated by religion, although he would never have called himself religious. Yet, the concept of the crucifixion disturbed him. A father sending his son to be carved up and killed. The Bible seemed obsessed with children-killing dads. Abraham tying Isaac to the rocks. God sacrificing Jesus. Tryal wondered what it would be like to be the son of a father like that. At least, they met their dads.

"Stupe—wake up," the whisper came from Roland who looked back as the others approached the front of the pews.

"You don't have to whisper. The priests are all asleep. It's okay," Michelle said, "We can hang out here until morning."

"Are you sure those things can't come in here?" Tryal asked.

"Do you see mine?"

"No, but your three aren't like that other one at all," Kaly said.

"It'll be fine."

"Isn't tomorrow Sunday?" Roland asked.

"Yeah, sure. Why?" asked Michelle. Roland stared back and waited until her face changed to awareness. Roland nodded as her realization came full.

Tryal walked up the aisle. "What?"

Michelle said, "Mass."

"And?" Kaly asked.

"And the priests will be up early to prepare. We'll have to be out right at dawn," Michelle explained.

"We need to be waiting at the front door looking out for the dawn," Roland added.

"It won't be as early as you think if that storm is still going strong then," Kaly said.

"Okay, so we camp out and we get caught by some sad little priest stacking songbooks."

"Hymnals," Michelle corrected.

"Huh?" asked Roland.

"Hymnals. Not songbooks. Hymnals. And Catechisms." Michelle said.

He continued, "Whatever. So we get caught by some sexually-frustrated priest. It's a helluva lot better than that dog or dogs. I'll take my chances with the priest. I'm not sure I can outrun one of those beasts, but I know I can dodge flying communion wafers."

Kaly had sat down and leaned against the wooden altar, her shoulders tugging against the cloth draped over its top. Hood sat down beside her, dark eyes peeking beneath their heavy lids. Michelle smiled and gave Kaly a wink. Hood might be completely otherworldly, but she still grew sleepy-eyed like any other elementary-aged girl. Kaly smiled as she leaned against her arm.

"Looks like you're on babysitting duty tonight," Roland said.

"Not too tough of a job," Kaly gently pulled her arm from under Hood and let her head rest in Kaly's lap, "Think I'll manage just fine." Kaly smiled as she realized her headache had vanished. No pain. No strange yet familiar voices. It was the first moment of rest she had felt in days.

"And she's out," Michelle said, looking at Hood.

"All of this for a little girl—this so doesn't make sense," Roland said.

"No, but maybe after story-time we'll put some pieces together. Don't think you're getting out of telling me what makes this little girl so important," Michelle said.

Tryal thought to himself, *I'm not sure if we know that any more than you do.*

Roland responded, "You neither."

"Gotta pee. Bathroom?" Tryal asked.

"Around that column and down the hall. Be quiet. Be respectful," Michelle said as Tryal walked quickly.

"So remember to lift the lid," Roland called after him.

CHAPTER TWENTY-SIX

ON HOLY GROUND

*T*RYAL ANSWER ME PLEASE

Tryal scrambled to make sense of the quiet voice that only he heard. Door was talking to him. Death was, well . . . alive. Until now, Tryal had been scared that she would be gone forever, that some dark and terrible thing, that thing that had frightened her, had caught up to her.

tryal please listen i do not have long please

Tryal raced around the column and stood by himself in the dark hallway, the only light coming from behind him and underneath the bathroom door.

"Door, are you safe? Are you okay? Where did you go?"

i am still here, Door's silent voice paused and then continued, *did you find her is she safe*

Tryal allowed a brief smile. He had managed to find her. He had kept her safe. His smile left quickly; he had kept her safe at the loss of two friends very dear to him. Janae and Cody were gone; Cody may be still alive but definitely absent and out of the story as far as Tryal could see it and Janae was—he shut his eyes at the thought. Janae was dead.

No. That didn't feel right. Maybe not dead. Somewhere else. Somewhere far away.

Or was that hope talking? Hope that his promise wasn't killing his friends?

Where he had expected pride to show through, only sadness did when he answered, "Yes. She's safe." One unknown girl at the cost of Janae and Cody. He stopped walking and opened his eyes to see shelves full of books surrounding him. He had walked into a small library without realizing it.

tryal be careful the other one you are with is not safe

Michelle? The nurse that Cody had led them to? As far as Tryal could tell, they were alive because of her. So far, she'd been the only safe thing this whole evening. And if she knows this, how did she not know he had found the little girl? "We can't trust her?"

you can trust her but she still isn't safe

What the heck did that mean? "Door, that doesn't make sense."

she is not all she seems to be

"What is up with Michelle?" Tryal asked. What did Door mean? She hadn't said Michelle, though, had she? "Door, which 'she?' do you mean?" She couldn't be talking about Kaly, could she? He asked again, "Please. What do you mean?"

i love you

She did and he knew that. He wasn't going to get anything more from here so he said, "I love you, too." He did and he had just realized it. He had missed her voice. He had missed their conversations. Her nagging presence had filled those empty places in his mind. She was water that searched out the low and empty cracks of his life and brought them to brim. He missed her.

keep her safe

Once more she was gone, and he was alone. Instead of protesting against the empty air, Tryal simply sat down in the quiet library and leaned his head against the books as his cheeks grew wet with his tears.

"Sleeping?" Michelle's voice came from the door. Tryal didn't open his eyes to acknowledge her.

"No," was his only reply.

"Then what are you doing?"

"Sleeping."

"Okay."

Tryal's head rested against the books, pushing several of them back on their shelf against the wall, his casted foot straight out and his arms curled around his one knee. Michelle sat down across the room on single wooden bench and waited.

Tryal broke the silence, "My mom is going to think I've ran away again."

"Are you?"

Tryal opened his eyes, "No. I haven't done that in a long time."

Michelle asked, "You've done that before?"

Tryal shut his eyes.

Michelle said, "Sorry."

"It's okay," said Tryal.

Michelle responded, "It's not that big of a deal. We're in no hurry right now. The other two were just wondering what had taken you so long. They thought you might've gotten lost."

"No. Not that," Tryal allowed a quick glance up at her and returned his eyes to studying his feet, "I'm sorry for all of this."

Tryal shifted and closed his eyes again, "I'm sorry for dragging you into this. I'm sorry for dumping all of this in your lap," he pressed his hands against his forehead, his eyes firmly closed. "I just feel—I don't know, as if all of this is my fault. I was the one who brought the girl here. Those stupid dogs. I was the one who led us to your door—well, Cody suggested it, but if I hadn't started this crazy chase you'd still be at home knitting or something. I'm sorry."

Michelle stared at him but he didn't return her gaze, "Knitting? Seriously? How old do you think I am?"

"You know what I meant. Not knitting, just something. Just I'm sorry. I really, really am."

"I'm here. It was my choice. You didn't hold a gun to my head. Besides, you're the only other people I've met who know about those things. You'll understand when you hear my side of this mess. I've known about them for far longer than you've probably been alive. So no more sorry. You're wasting your time feeling sorry for yourself." She nudged his foot, "So, why are you doing this?"

"Because I made a promise."

"A promise? To whom?" Michelle asked.

Tryal said, "The point is I've never kept a promise in my life. Now, I *have* to keep this one."

Michelle stood, "Okay."

He opened his eyes and looked at her for a long time before cracking a small smile, "Before I was born? How old are you?"

"Maybe that was an exaggeration. Not that old," she put a hand on his shoulder, "I'm going back, don't take too long." At the door she turned to look back to him, "Maybe I'm the one who should be sorry."

"Why? We came knocking on your door."

"I know, but I can't help to think I've got something to do with this. You were being chased by a Cinder—I just, I dunno, maybe after we've talked it might make more sense." She walked into the darkened hallway.

Watching her leave, Tryal whispered to himself, "Why am I doing this?"

His head still echoed with Door's voice, with the voice of Death herself, and he savored every last sound. He leaned his head back and closed his eyes again. Death's voice went silent and tendrils of smoke rose in his mind. Sleep carried him away.

Images of teeth borne out of smoking skin filled the empty spots. An ocean full of the Cinders clouded his mind. It was all he could see—their dark smoking skin, puffs of flaking ash stirred with each step, their phantom fangs translucent against the red of their throats, and their eyes, those glowing, flaming eyes shooting Fourth of July sparklers.

He jumped and let loose a sharp "Uhh," as he smacked his head against the shelf. His eyes focused on the room filled with books, a single wooden bench, and a faded gray and red-speckled carpet. His head hurt, but he was safe. He rubbed the aching quarter of his skull and scanned the empty room.

"I'm okay. I'm safe. I'm alone. No one's here." He tried to soothe himself with lowered tones, just as if he was talking to a scared child. Why did he always have to get so scared?

He picked up his shoulder-bag, flung it across his chest, patted the side, and walked out.

"Somewhere in sands of the desert

A shape with lion body and the head of a man,

A gaze blank and pitiless as the sun,

Is moving its slow thighs, while all around it

Reel shadows of the indignant desert birds."

—From The Second Coming by William Butler Yeats

CHAPTER TWENTY-SEVEN

STORY TIME

TRYAL ENTERED THE MAIN HALL to see Roland sprawled across the front pew, his left leg dangling and scraping the hard floor. Kaly leaned against the center altar. Hood was asleep, her head resting on Kaly's lap. Michelle stood to the side, her red hair glowing in the light of the flickering candles she watched. She turned as Tryal's casted foot thudded against the hard ground.

Roland said, "Did you fall in?"

Tryal sat down.

Grinning, Michelle said, "Story time boys and girls. Let's figure out what the heck is going on here." She sat next to Hood's bare feet.

"Flip a coin?" Roland's voice was a hollow echo in the large room.

"Nope. You go first. Besides, I'd win anyway. Coins like me," Michelle said.

Roland nudged Tryal, who had just sat on the edge of the pew next to Roland's head, "You wanna get this started or should I?"

Tryal shrugged.

"Okay, that settles it. Kaly, you start," Roland said.

Kaly lifted her head up but didn't make eye contact, "I'm not sure where to start."

"At the birthday party or the school assembly. Either one will work," Roland said.

Tryal said, "No. Start at the Safeway. That's where this all started."

Kaly smiled at Tryal and he smiled back.

He's not angry with me?

The voice in her head answered. *Don't mess up again. The boy is all that matters.* She shook her head again.

Roland said, "Uh-uh. Not where you guys got started. Where we all got started. Tell it right or don't tell it all."

"But you . . ." Kaly argued.

"Just start, please," Michelle said.

"I had only just met Janae and Cody before the weirdness started." At the mention of their names, their stomachs tightened, even Michelle's. "Should I skip the parts about them? I mean, there's a lot of them in this story and I'm not sure we can handle it if we all get, I dunno, choked up every time."

"Tell it all. It's okay," said Roland.

"None of this works without them," said Tryal.

Kaly took in a deep breath and continued, "Their dad had moved onto the block months after they lost their mom. Janae and I hit it off pretty soon after. We were good friends for nearly half a year before I ran into Tryal at the Safeway."

"Stop! I said no Safeway," said Roland.

"It's important," Tryal said, pulling his legs underneath him as he settled in.

Tryal and Roland stared at each other for several seconds. Roland thrust his hands up in a mock-surrender, "Loud and clear. Gotcha doc. The Safeway scene stays in. But I'm telling it now. I can't deal with any of your stupid awkward 'I wish your tongue was in my throat right now' looks at each other."

Tryal smacked Roland on the head but Roland continued without a pause, "These two ran into each other in Safeway. Flirting started from the first moment. I think they may have even messed around behind the produce counter."

Tryal smacked him again, "Tell the story right! It had nothing to do with the two of us."

Roland waved his hands above his head, "It had everything to do with you two. You were the only ones there."

Kaly leaned forward, "Stop it! The story does start at Safeway. Tryal had been connecting with the . . . other side . . . you know, ghosts, voices, and things like that, for a long time before I ran into him."

Michelle shook her head, "Be a bit more specific, why don't you? In fact, assume I'm stupid. What are 'things like that?'"

Roland answered, "What the SyFy channel would describe as 'paranormal experience.' We'll get into the specifics. Tryal's a regular freak show in himself. He's some sort of homing beacon for anything out there." On "out there," Roland mimicked quotation marks with his fingers.

"Ghosts?"

"Yeah," answered Tryal.

"Vampires?"

"Vampire. Not plural. And maybe. I think," Tryal shivered at this and shut his eyes. He didn't see Kaly twitch and shake her head. She fidgeted with a loose bang, curling it around her finger.

Michelle ignored this and asked, "What was it like?"

Roland laughed, "I think it sparkled before it tried to kiss him."

Tryal said, "Shut up. It didn't sparkle."

Michelle wasn't going to get an answer on that question, "Uh, demons?"

"Big yep," said Tryal.

Michelle had expected some hesitance on that answer. She was surprised to see there was none. His encounters with demons, or his definition of demons, didn't seem to have imprinted him as much as the vampires, and those he was still scared of. Deeply.

Roland smirked, "You think they were demons. You don't know."

Tryal shrugged his shoulders.

Michelle continued her questions, "Werewolves?"

"I don't think those are real. Movies and cheap paperbacks only."

"Seriously? Vampires and ghosts are real but werewolves aren't? That's a bit tough to believe."

"All of this should be tough to believe. I might've seen a vampire. Ghosts I've seen. Werewolves I haven't. Maybe they exist, maybe they don't. I've never seen them and I've seen a lot, so my guess is that if they do exist, they sure hide well."

"Cinders?"

"Until five hours ago, a big fat no. I've never heard of those walking shadows! Thought I was in a Harry Potter movie there for a minute."

"So maybe werewolves are real? Just maybe. I mean the Cinders are definitely real," replied Michelle.

"Maybe, but I wouldn't hold my breath. Besides, have you seen werewolves?"

"No. My supernatural resume is limited to Cinders only. Well, Cinders and a strange wizard in a yellow jacket."

"A wizard? This just gets weirder by the moment. Anyone seen Bigfoot? Unicorns? Nessie? The Moth Man? A smiling clown hanging out in gutters offering balloons to little girls? Voldemort?" Roland asked, motioning to each of them for each myth he listed.

"I'm joking. He wasn't a wizard. I just don't know what he was. It's part of my story and I'll get to it, but for right now we're still on yours. So what about the rest of you, has it just been Tryal that's experienced all of this? Not the rest of you?"

"Until we had all met, nothing that strange. I'd experienced a few things, but always when he was around." Roland sideways glanced at Tryal and back to Michelle, "Never, ever, without him."

Kaly continued, "I, on the other hand, was living the perfect little middle-class life: original mom and dad, kid sister, Lexus in the garage. I was into normal. I couldn't even sit through all of 'Paranormal Activity'."

"An American princess. Crown and all," Roland smirked at this.

Kaly continued, "I had run down to Safeway that Saturday—"

"It was a Sunday," Tryal added.

"I had run down to Safeway that Sunday. It was just a few blocks away. Tryal had gone there too."

"Mom had actually dropped me off on the way back from one of her work appointments. I told her I'd walk the rest of the way back."

"I was in the cereal aisle—"

"And I was looking at magazines."

Kaly said, "And I heard my first voice. I thought at first it was the loudspeaker and then it said my name."

"Tell her what it was saying before it said your name."

"Yeah, that's right. It was hard to hear at first, but after a while I could make it out. It sounded like 'The boy is near' and 'Tryal is the boy.'" Kaly rubbed her forehead. She thought, *You have heard the voice before.*

In response, the voice in her head said, *Yes. I've been waiting.*

"I'm on the other side of the aisle, flipping through the magazines, when I thought mom had come back to the store and had started calling my name," said Tryal.

Michelle interrupted, "You were hearing the same voice telling you that you were near?"

Kaly and Tryal laughed. Kaly continued, "No! I was getting so irritated after ten minutes of this senseless '*Tryal is near. The boy is near. Tryal is near. The boy is near.*' Finally, I just shouted out, 'What boy? What Tryal?'"

"I heard that loud and clear. Kaly's voice. At first, I just looked around. I gotta imagine we looked pretty stupid to anyone watching on the security cameras. I kept spinning around looking for mom. One time I think I actually called for her."

"You did. I remember hearing you say, 'I'm here' after I shouted 'Try-al?' for a second time. Scared me crazy. Imagine it—some weird thing starts talking to you and it's saying some boy named Tryal is coming to visit you and just after you ask for more information, he answers you. I almost peed my pants."

"Clean up on aisle five," Roland said.

Hood stirred and shifted in her sleep, almost rolling off of Kaly's knee. "Shhh! A little quieter."

Tryal, lowering his voice, continued, "But instead of feeling scared, we both did a bit of an Abbott and Costello routine."

"He raced around one end of the aisle and I turned around the other."

Michelle smiled, "So now you're on the opposite sides of the aisle, where you both started?"

"Yep. And she's shouting 'Tryal' and I'm answering 'I'm here.' Big, big idiots."

"I'm sad to admit it, but we did that two more times. Switching aisles, I mean."

"Finally, I just decided to stay where I was and I heard her footsteps running behind me. I turned to see her and . . ." Tryal smiled at Kaly.

"See! Look! I told you they would end up like this!" exclaimed Roland, who sat up, hands flailing in Tryal's direction and then Kaly's.

"I think it's sweet," Michelle said.

"Sweet? We're talking about some spectral voice talking to a cheerleader while she decides between Captain Crunch and Fruity Pebbles. Not sweet. Just weird."

"It was weird but I don't think we realized it for what it was right away," said Tryal.

"I didn't. I know I didn't. For some reason I kinda forgot about the voice until the birthday party," said Kaly.

"But you had to be wondering how she knew your name?" Michelle asked.

"Yeah, you'd think so. But, honestly . . ." Tryal said.

"Yes?" Michelle replied.

"Spit it out, my stupid brother," said Roland.

"Well, I guess, I kinda ignored the weirdness of it all because . . . well, she looked nice that day. It didn't seem like I hadn't known her until then. I introduced myself."

"And I introduced myself."

"We just kept talking from there. She checked out, I checked out and we walked back to our homes. The fact that we lived on the same street was the weirdest part of it all. We couldn't get over the idea that we'd lived about four houses away from each other for a year or more and never seen each other."

"Yeah, how is that possible?" asked Michelle.

"I'd never seen her either. I'd seen her younger sister and her mom and dad before. Heck, I'd seen her older sister a few times before," said Roland.

"Roland, you stood out on the porch and watched her sister sunbathe," Tryal said.

"Tiny little red bikini with white polka-dots. The way she spilled over the edges. I remember her very well," Roland smiled.

"But Kaly seemed to be—I dunno—not a part of the picture until the cereal aisle."

Roland smiled, "Now we can't get rid of her. She's not just a part of the picture, she's filled it corner to corner with that big nose."

Kaly curled up, bringing the one knee Hood wasn't resting against closer to her chest, tipped her head, and hunched her shoulders—anything to appear less noticeable. Roland's jab had hit something dead-on. Kaly hadn't liked that line and couldn't hide the fact that she was embarrassed.

Roland sat up and spit through the words, "Kaly, I'm sorry. I didn't mean to—"

Kaly, still balled up, replied, "It's cool." They all knew it wasn't.

Tryal spoke up, "Michelle. Kaly. Do either of you have a phone?"

Roland smiled, "This isn't the time to play video games."

Kaly pulled hers out and handed it to him.

"I just think it would be good to call mom. Check in."

Roland said, "We can't go home. We do and those things go after mom."

Tryal dialed and held the phone to his ear. "She's not answering."

"Did you call home or her cell?" Roland asked.

"Uh, home."

"Try her cell."

Tryal dialed again. "Not answering there either."

"Could be asleep. Ringer off," said Roland, "She'll be fine. We've done dumber stuff before."

"Dumber? She probably showed up to a house full of firemen," Tryal handed the phone back to Kaly.

"Maybe she thought they were a birthday present from us," said Roland.

"Where is she?" Tryal said.

"Relax," said Roland, "She's probably staying at a friend's." Roland had his arms crossed and didn't seem reassured.

Tryal said, "We need to go find her."

"No. We need to stay here. This is the only place we've been those dogs haven't shown up. Mom's a big girl. She'll be fine," said Roland.

"What if one of those things got to her?" asked Tryal.

Roland said, "They're after us. Not her."

Michelle spoke, and quite quietly, "We're safe now."

Tryal started, "No one else around us—"

Michelle interrupted, "We're safe. Just—we're safe." She stood to her feet, "Let's curl up and get a few hours of sleep before dawn. We need to be out early before the altar boys arrive to prep."

Roland laid down in the pew. Tryal watched Kaly and Hood. After a moment of hesitation, he moved over to her and put his arm around her. She leaned her head against his shoulder, Hood still laid with her head on Kaly's lap. Michelle stretched out on the altar, closed her eyes, and went fast asleep.

Outside, the sound of sirens drifted past, muted by the stone walls. Roland stayed alert until it was obvious the sounds were receding away from them. Only then did he relax enough to fall asleep.

Somewhere outside along the quiet, cold lanes, a howl echoed. The sleepers in the Cathedral shivered. A shadow fell across the front door and continued to prowl the grounds.

Chapter twenty-Eight

THE BREAKFAST CLUB

Sunday, February 12, 2012

THE PRIEST NUDGED MICHELLE with his foot. "Wake up," he said softly.

She stirred with a twitch of her head.

A bit louder, the priest said, "It's time to wake up."

"You're being too nice about it," Roland said from behind him.

The priest turned to see Roland sitting behind him with a smile on his face. Roland stood, walked over to Tryal, and kicked him firmly in his shin, "Let's go. Wake up, crap-head."

Tryal stirred.

Michelle had awakened, rubbed her eyes, and seeing she recognized the priest, scurried to her feet, "I'm so sorry, Father. We didn't mean to . . . I'm so sorry. There weren't many other options." Michelle was noticeably awkward and embarrassed. This was a new reaction for her. Michelle was the take-charge action-now type of girl. This place kept bringing out new sides of her.

The priest raised his hand, "Stop. You're fine. This is what this place is after all. A sanctuary." He smiled at this, "Did you sleep well?"

Standing up now and gently nudging both Tryal and Kaly, avoiding Hood's resting body, Michelle replied, "Yes. We did. Thank you. We're so sorry again. Oh, my!" Michelle glanced around, "It's about time for Mass! Crap!" At this, she blushed and the apologies streamed, "I'm so sorry! I can't believe I . . . I'm stupid. Tryal! Kaly! Wake up! I'm sorry, Father. We're leaving. We won't keep you any longer. Roland, wake them and let's go."

Roland sat, arms crossed over the pew in front of him, smiling at Michelle's growing discomfort.

The Priest said, "You're fine. We have some time before Mass commences Don't worry. You're absolutely fine. Wake the two, gently, and anyone entering will believe you are early arrivals as well. No harm at all."

Michelle was still nervous and continued to nudge Tryal and Kaly, "Wake up."

As Tryal did, words slipped from his mouth and his memory at the same time, "Minatare . . ."

"Minatare? What's Minatare," Roland asked, "Hey, sleepy, are you okay?"

Michelle asked, "That stinky old town? What are you talking about?"

Roland said, "Tryal just said it."

"He did?" asked Michelle.

"Talking in his sleep. You didn't hear him?"

"No. You guys go to the lake often?" asked Michelle.

Roland said, "Never been there. Never heard of it."

"Never heard of it? It's just a few miles south."

Roland shook his head, "Nope. Ain't much for nature."

Michelle replied, "You talk to bugs!"

Roland spun, "Hey!" He glanced at the priest who nudged Tryal. If he had heard Michelle's gaffe, he didn't show it. Roland stepped closer to Michelle and whispered, "Spiders are city nature. Not nature nature. And, um," he nodded in the priest's direction, "Keep it down next time."

Tryal stirred. Kaly stirred in response and pushed her head, nuzzling it, into his chest. His mind attempted to focus.

Minatare? Why had the voice asked that? Had I said it first? He couldn't remember. His eyes opened onto the nest of Kaly's hair. The light entered and his vivid, nearly lucid dream blinked out of his conscious mind. He took a breath and smelled Kaly's hair—a hint of flowers and sweat. It was Kaly and she smelled wonderful.

Tryal looked in the direction of the voice and was not surprised at all to see a short man in a flowing black cloak, a priest. He had tanned skin far darker than Tryal's light complexion, a bristly stubble of a beard, a hint of a double chin, all wrapped in the classic black and white collar of the priesthood. It was the morning of Mass and they had awakened late.

Tryal sat up, almost dropping Kaly onto the hard floor, and glanced around, fearful that he would see a full congregation in place, a hundred eyes all staring at the sleeping intruders. He shut his eyes, trying to adjust to the light, let out a slight moan and opened his eyes again to the grinning face of Roland.

"Kaly. It's time to go. Wake up." Tryal jostled her shoulder, pushing her long hair off his neck. She woke and smiled at him briefly before realizing they weren't alone. There was a priest standing above them. The voice in her head screeched, Not safe! She rubbed her forehead.

"Kaly, you okay?" Tryal asked, helping her to her feet.

"Ya, head just hurt a bit." She lied. No headache. Only that horrible voice.

Roland stood, "Padré, you'se might want to douse that spot there with some holy water. Not sure those two didn't do somethin' a bit profane in the night."

"Shut up, a—!" said Tryal.

He didn't get the word out before Michelle shuddered and shouted, "Tryal! Watch your mouth!"

The priest smiled, "It's fine."

Michelle said, "I'm sorry. I am. We'll be leaving now." To Tryal and Kaly, she said, "Let's go! Now!"

"You seem familiar. Have we met? I'm Father Trajan."

Michelle said, "I work at the hospital. I've run into you on my shift a couple of times. And um, in confession, I think."

Father Trajan rubbed his chin. She was familiar, but he couldn't remember much more than her face. "Ah, that's it."

Tryal and Kaly gently woke up Hood. She opened her eyes and froze, every muscle tensing.

"And who's the little one?" Father Trajan asked.

"Her name is Hood," answered Roland.

Hood looked at the priest, her body tense as she stood with that smooth motion only children can pull off. Her face was calm, though.

Father Trajan said, "Has she been here before? Do I know you?"

Hood said nothing, only smiled before turning to Tryal and Kaly and muttering one of the few other words they'd heard her say, "Hungry." She reached up and grabbed Tryal's hand and fell into place next to him.

"Ahhh, daddy Tryal and his wittle girl. What's she getting you for Father's Day?" Roland said.

Hood had started tugging on Tryal's arm.

Tryal looked down, "You okay? You need something."

Kaly shook her head. "She has to use the bathroom."

Roland tilted his head. "How can you tell?"

Michelle sighed. "She's near dancing."

Father Trajan nodded to the right. "Just through the hallway. It's the room past where the brick corridor ends and the drywall begins." Kaly stood up and led Hood by her elbow down to the bathroom. As she walked away, she rubbed the back of her neck and winced.

Father Trajan said, "So, what are you hiding from?"

Michelle looked at Roland, who looked back at her and to Tryal. They all sat silent until Michelle answered, "It's hard to explain, Father."

"Real hard to explain," continued Roland. "In fact, I'm pretty sure we're all delusional. Mass-hallucination most likely. If I was you, I'd be palming my cell phone under the table and calling the men in white coats. They need to lock us up. We're loony, especially the girl who just went to the bathroom; she's the most nutso of the whole bunch."

Father Trajan said, "Are you in trouble?"

"I can't explain. Seriously, you wouldn't believe us. Father, we'll just get our two friends and leave," Michelle wiped her mouth and dropped the napkin.

Father Trajan grew restless. "Please answer my question."

"I'm sorry. I hope we haven't caused you problems," Michelle stood and wiped her hands, "Stand up, boys. Let's go."

Tryal and Roland stood.

A scream echoed through the room as Kaly and Hood rocketed down the hallway, slamming hard into Tryal and knocking the two over onto the brick. Behind them, the door to the girl's bathroom launched forward, tumbling to the floor. A mass of shadow and smoke, snarling and sinewy, seethed. Fujo and another Cinder erupted down the narrow hallway toward them.

"All down the church

in midst of fire, the

hellish monster flew,

And, passing onward

to the quire, he many

people slew."

—FROM AN OLD NORFOLK POEM

CHAPTER TWENTY-NINE

WELCOME

THE HOUNDS CAME RUSHING and leapt at the scrambling bodies, still twisted on the floor. As if a glass wall had appeared, Fujo hit something mid-leap and fell back onto the tile floor of the hallway, whimpering. His two companions bounded next to him and snarled at the entrance, their noses hovering above the dividing line between tile and brick, sniffing at the barrier.

"Michelle! You said this place was safe!" Tryal shouted, picking Hood up and backing towards the rest of the group.

Michelle stammered, "I don't know. I don't know."

"Are those what you're running from?" Trajan asked and then whispered, "Demons."

"Yes! Holy Yes! A thousand Yeses!" Roland shouted.

Trajan moved first towards the corridor behind him, putting distance between himself and the beast. Tryal leaned down to help Kaly back to her feet. Both of them were moving as if they were in water, each action slow and deliberate.

Tryal and Kaly were the last to make it to the lip of the corridor. The others stood just inside, a hundred feet or more between them and the snarling Cinders.

"Hood?" Kaly looked around her. Hood was not next to Tryal.

Tryal spun, "Where's Hood?"

Michelle pointed back to the Cinders. Hood stood where they had first fallen, staring at the beasts. She was framed by the Fujo's frame, even as it clawed and hunched against the ground. She was tiny Red Riding Hood dwarfed by the growling Big Bad Wolf.

Tryal froze. Kaly nudged him, "Tryal! Get her!" He struggled to move. Kaly pushed him, "Get her!"

He stumbled forward. "Hood," Tryal said, the words shaky, "Turn around. Come here."

As if to answer him, she stepped towards the beasts, opened her small mouth and spoke for the third time, "You are welcome here."

The Cinders raging vaults paused. With a careful step, Fujo tested her statement by slowly placing one paw across the border. Then another and another, until he was fully across and walking slowly towards the little girl, the two others walking in pace behind him.

Kaly screamed, "Tryal!"

Tryal grunted, a hacking gurgle rose in his throat as his panic rose in a fevered pitch. As his throat cleared, he lurched and sprinted, hoping to clear the distance before the beast did, and screamed as he did so, "HOOOOD!" The girl turned, her face blank.

Fujo stopped, moved his focus from Hood to Tryal and launched forward as it realized Tryal's focus was the little girl. The beast snarled and Tryal's stomach tightened. Tryal closed within a few feet of the girl, outstretched his arms and realized the smoky beast was a second faster. It was going to get to her first.

"In the name of Christ, stop!" the words echoed from behind. Tryal still raced to Hood knowing Fujo was closer. The dog radiated a growing heat.

Tryal reached out to Hood and scooped her up. He turned his body in the same motion, pulling his momentum into the turn. He had her. He had made it there first. How was that possible? As he ran backwards, his heart raced. He was soaked with his own sweat. He had never run towards danger before, at least not knowingly.

How had he made it? How had the beast not attacked him? The dog was engulfed in flames, the air rippling around it as it stood snarling at him. The walls near the beast had caught flame. The fire moved through the room.

Father Trajan walked slowly towards the beast, his arm outstretched, a crucifix gripped tightly. The dog's strange reaction began to make sense. One more trick had been discovered to stop the Cinders. How long would this one last?

As if he had heard Tryal's thoughts, Trajan, his focus still on Fujo, said back at them, "Start moving. This won't halt him long. Up towards the altar. There's a door there. Now!"

"Go!" Michelle shouted as she grabbed Kaly's arm and pulled her away. Roland, Tryal, and Hood followed.

Tryal avoided the looks of the others. He had saved Hood, but, Kaly had to push him first. His first reaction had been to freeze.

Behind them, they could hear the raised voice of Father Trajan growing louder, "Leave this place now! In the name of Christ, I command you!"

The hellhounds seemed to waver, flicker in the dusky light and then they disappeared.

"This way," Michelle led them around the railing and up the stairs.

Father Trajan ran towards them, "There, past the candelabra, there's a door. It heads out back. Hurry!"

"Father, where does this go?" Michelle asked.

"The maintenance building."

"Why?"

"It's not where the demons are."

"Why not leave through the front door?" Michelle asked.

"Why not?" Trajan repeated.

Michelle breathed deeply.

Roland spoke, rushing his words, "Because the law is gonna come that way and we'se runnin' from the law. Thank real big fer keepin' us out de slammer, Padré!"

Tryal said, "Where did the Cinders go?"

The Priest turned, eyes wide, "Those demons? They just . . . Poof . . . Like smoke."

Tryal groaned and stepped into the hall. "Eyes wide everyone. They could be anywhere."

They turned to the left and to the right.

In the short hallway, Kaly wrestled with the other voice. *Don't follow him! Get Tryal. Run!* She muttered back, "Shut up."

"Huh?" said one of the others, quiet and indistinct.

She whispered back, "Nothing."

CHAPTER THIRTY

DETECTIVE WORK

MR. MU AND MR. HU SAT ON A WOODEN PEW that was just starting to burn. The smell of the roasting varnish wafted over them. The old building burned quickly. The fire ran through the dry wood under the floor, in every wall, across the altar, into the rafters. The adornments, mostly paintings, crackled as kindling.

"*Dangle her.*"

"Maybe."

"*She is our lure. Dangle her before the boy.*" Vera hung limply to the ground next to them, her hair curled around his fingers, her eyes and ears caked with blood. In the passing, the tall one played with a few new words. Where his companion simply used gestures to draw magic into the world, he used words. It took a simple word to cause her eyes to bleed. Now, she lay next to them, unconscious.

"Yes. But something has changed. I am smelling something in this hunt. Look around," the fat one gestured at the crumbling building, "and think with me."

Around them, the local fire department raced. Men shouted at each other, dragging hoses through the center aisle, spraying the altar. Flames reached and tickled the walls. The room was collapsing. Soon, the entire building would be ash.

"Think. A place of worship," he made a mocking hands folded gesture of prayer and continued, "and it looks like the flames of Sheol itself. Fitting, eh?"

He stood and continued his thoughts, "Smell the flames. Take a deep breath."

His tall companion breathed deeply and coughed, albeit nearly imperceptibly, "*What is that?*"

"I believe it is the smell of the hunters," he breathed deeply again, his nostrils flaring, and chortled.

Mr. Hu said, "*A bargheist? A hound?*"

Mr. Mu dangled a finger in the air and moved it through the smoke in sweeping pattern, "Yes. And they do not know we are hunting them."

The pew collapsed when the fire weakened its center support, but it was empty. Its invisible occupants had disappeared once again.

CHAPTER THIRTY-ONE

THE PENCIL

THEY SAT INSIDE THE VAN IN SILENCE. The wheels click-clacked off-balance against the road as they traveled south to the highway. They were moving through the streets, taking turn after turn quickly in a late '70s Ford Econoline van with scratchy tan seats and a cloth roof drooping down to their heads. Father Trajan had handed Michelle the keys and said, "The police aren't looking for a van." He had turned around back to the Cathedral as the van pulled away.

Tryal was tired. His sleep during the night had been shallow and brief. The rhythm of the van lulled him to sleep. His eyes grew heavy.

"Where are we headed, now?" Roland asked.

Michelle, driving, answered, "Out of town. For now."

"And then?" Roland continued.

Tryal heard only that and drifted into sleep. Hours may have passed. Minutes may have. There were images of teeth and water. He stood in front of a lake, dark and swirling, with shadows of dark wings thrown upon the waves. He leaned forward and touched the inky foam of the lake.

And woke up.

"Minatare," the words were out of Tryal's mouth before his eyes had opened.

"Minn-a-what, sleepy?" Roland asked.

"Minatare. I don't know. Isn't it a lake?" said Tryal.

Michelle said, "Why do you keep bringing that up?"

The air hung still in the speeding van. Roland asked the question Kaly was thinking, "Is that our destination?"

Tryal closed his eyes, the guilt of dragging his friends through this haunted chase stirring against his voice, "Yeah." He pressed his palms hard against his eyes, pushing and not rubbing, "It is."

Kaly said, "Okay."

"Just like that?" Michelle said.

"Like what?" Kaly responded.

"He points and says 'that way,' and you wag your tails and run off into the bushes?"

"He's never wrong," said Kaly.

"She's right. He's a chicken. But he's a correct chicken," Roland laughed.

Michelle sighed, "Whatever."

Roland said, "Just trust him. He really is strangely right most of the time. Well, so far, all the time." Roland's defense sounded more chosen and calculated than the leave-my-boyfriend-alone tone that Kaly's had carried, but Roland allowed his mind to follow Michelle's concern.

We do follow him. Blindly at that. He's not been wrong, not once. Not yet. It just takes once. Racing headlong with five people slammed in a Ford Econoline on the way to a lake named Mina-something, with a literal legion of phantom puppies who shoot fire from their eyes (and maybe their butts, too) in pursuit.

"And this, all of this crap you've pulled me into, this is 'right' to you? This 'isn't wrong'? Holy heck," Michelle said.

Tryal had been right when he conjured the girl up in the fire, but considering all of the damage and death that had happened since, wouldn't it have been better if he had been wrong? This trip was going further than they had ever gone before. Their house had almost burnt to the ground. Their mother was missing. He had acted unmoved by that fact, but it was now beginning to concern him that she hadn't shown up and hadn't tried to find them. He had no sense of what the day would bring, let alone the next hour. Their lives had been miraculously saved, but only by the sheerest of chance. All of this because Tryal made a midnight half-mad promise.

"Drop us here if you don't want to come. We didn't drag you, did we?" said Kaly. Her eyes were closed. The other voice echoed in her head.

Get away from the nurse. Take Tryal and run. She rubbed the bridge of her nose and grunted.

"You brought what's-his-name . . . Fujo, to my front door! Not a whole lot of other options besides running, were there?"

"So sorry, we didn't realize your kennel was full," said Roland.

"Minatare. Can someone get directions?" Tryal ignored the fight and pressed forward.

"Ah, come on!" Michelle slapped the front steering wheel.

"What's a matter?" Roland asked.

"My phone and my bag! I must've left them on the table at St. Thomas's!"

"Kaly has hers," said Roland.

"Uh," said Kaly.

"What?" Tryal said.

"I think I left it back there too. In the restroom. I had put it on the ledge above the sink when I was washing my hands and I," Kaly shuddered, "saw those horrible red eyes in the mirror. I grabbed Hood and ran. It's probably still there."

"No, it's probably a piece of ash right now. Fujo was doing his best Human Torch impersonation back there," said Roland.

"Oh," Kaly muttered. She shivered as the voice in her head spoke to her.

It's a phone. It's unimportant.

"An atlas then?" Tryal said.

They scrambled around looking under their seats.

Kaly spoke from the back, "Yeah, there's one under my feet here."

Tryal flipped through the pages, "Okay, umm, well, we could take 93 south or go find Boxen South Road and . . ."

"It's fine," Michelle said, "I know where Minatare is. It's a little town twenty miles from where I grew up and about thirty miles south of here. It's a crap-hole. Literally. The county's settling ponds are to the east. The smell of poop rolls in every morning. I hate it there."

Tryal spoke, "I don't think it's a town. I'm pretty sure it's a lake."

"It's a lake, too. Lake Minatare. It's pretty nasty, just like the town. Small and dirty with these ugly beaches. It's got this stupid tiny little lighthouse that all the old people thought was a great tourist attraction. We'd all go there in high school to get drunk and lay out on the beach. Smells like dead fish, but there was nowhere else to go. Hated that place."

"Good job, Tryal. Your little freako compass could point us to city, a mall, a Pizza Hut, even a Hooters, but instead you're sending us to Lake Friday-the-13th. Free chainsaw-wielding Jason included with three proofs of purchase. Blast. This vacation is turning out miserably."

Kaly muttered, "So now where to? Directly there?" Her voice was weak. She put her head on the back of Tryal's seat, "Ugh."

Tryal put his hand on her shoulder, "You okay?"

"Headache's getting real bad."

Tryal said, "Michelle, you have aspirin?"

Michelle didn't hear him, "You're all convinced he's right. I'm not sure. I'd take other opinions."

Tryal whispered to Kaly, "It'll be fine." He fished around his bag and handed her a bottle of water, "Here. Drink this. It might help."

"Thanks," muttered Kaly.

Roland smiled, "So can we hear your side of the story now? Been pretty silent."

"What are you talking about, Roland?" Tryal asked.

"Huh?" Michelle grunted.

"We told you all about us. We've still yet to discover where you got the puppies from or about that yellow-jacket wizard." Roland slapped his hand on the back of Michelle's seat. "Maybe trying to hide something."

Kaly raised her head up, "Who's not being honest?" The voice in her head spoke.

The girl! Get away!

Unseen by the others, Kaly curled up in her seat, her face tortured. Beads of sweat formed on Kaly's forehead with the pain of the headache. The voice yelled at her.

The girl is false! A trick! Keep her from Tryal! Without knowing why, she unbuckled her seat belt.

"I'm joking," Roland smiled, "Just want to hear your mesmerizing tale of your demonic little pound puppies."

Kaly grunted from the back seat. The buzzing in her mind was deafening. Voices rolled over voices and she struggled to keep her mind from being engulfed.

Michelle said, "She okay?"

Tryal said, "Her headache's getting bad. I asked you for aspirin."

Michelle said, "Didn't hear you. Is she going to be okay?"

"I don't know," said Tryal

The buzzing in Kaly's mind grew to a roar. The other voice spoke louder and louder and louder. Kaly's mind churned and roiled in pushing waves that broke the surface of the ocean. Memory and story erupted and she remembered. The voice in her head spoke.

My turn.

Michelle said, "Okay, I'll tell the important parts. We don't have time for everything."

"Start by telling us about your connection with those dogs," Roland said.

"I was getting to tha—" Michelle said but was interrupted as Kaly leapt across the van, grabbed a pencil from the seat next to her and jammed it into

Michelle's arm, her hand slapping hard against the skin. Black smoke and blood filled the van, rushing out of the wound as Michelle screamed. Tryal reached for Kaly and tried to hold her down. Michelle slammed on the brakes and jerked the car to the side, slamming Kaly forward against the side door.

Roland pulled the pencil from Michelle's arm. "Get her!"

Tryal unbuckled and grabbed Kaly's waist and pulled her back across the seat. Her eyes were bright, the pupils narrowed, and sweat stood across the fine hairs lapping at the edges of her face.

Hood stared blankly at Kaly. Tryal's hands gripped and strained against the increasing strength of the mad girl. Kaly was still focused on Michelle, her muscles tense and pulling against Tryal, her eyes bulging from their sockets as her lids twitched back, reddened and pulsing.

"She's not calming down!" Tryal shouted.

Michelle held her arm trying to put pressure on the wound. Her fingers were lost in the waves of smoke falling out of her gashed arm.

Why was there smoke coming out of my wound?

She had cut herself hundreds of times but never seen this. Kaly growled and whipped her head, splashing spit across Roland's face and the back of Michelle's neck.

"Blast! The freak has completely gone psycho!" Roland said

As Kaly pulled harder, Hood stood up and leaned across. Tryal saw her hand reach out to Kaly's face, "Hood! Get back!" He loosened his hold on Kaly to push Hood back but he felt Kaly tug and use the error to gain a bit more distance. Tryal gripped harder and yelled, "Hood! Get back now!"

Hood ignored him and instead, touched Kaly's quivering cheek with her hand. Kaly turned to Hood and her eyes rolled back into her head, every muscle relaxed and she fainted, drooping against Tryal.

Hood crawled over the seat, moving past Kaly's exhausted body. Roland jerked back as she moved near. Disturbed and terrified—it was an emotion Tryal had never seen in Roland. Roland pressed himself hard against the door, frightened as Hood moved near.

Hood stepped next to Michelle and placed her hand against her wound. Her left hand waved the empty space between the seats and, into the emptiness, the form of one of Michelle's Cinders took shape. Hood placed her hand on the smoky dog, tilted her head towards it as if asking a question. She smiled at the Cinder and it lowered its head. The dog jerked.

"What are you doing?" Michelle asked, staring at the Cinder. "What are you doing to Caliban?"

Hood said nothing but turned her eyes back to Michelle. The dark dog shuddered once more and then disappeared completely and Michelle pitched back in her seat. Her features relaxed and she turned to look at Hood, who now smiled up at her.

Michelle turned to the spot where Caliban had been. She grabbed Hood and shouted, "What have you done? Where is Caliban?"

Kaly lay sprawled across the seat, face down, unconscious.

Michelle shook Hood and shouted, "What have you done?"

Tryal placed his hand on Michelle's and said, "Stop." She didn't. She continued to shake Hood until Tryal reached forward and slapped her. The slap came so quickly, so sharp in the middle of the madness, that Michelle froze.

"Where's my dog? Where did he go? Bring him back!" Michelle had released Hood but still yelled.

"No!" Tryal's arm was on Michelle, pushing her back into her seat. "Stop!"

"You don't get it! You don't understand." Michelle's voice had dropped.

"Then tell us. But not now. She just saved your life!"

He turned to Hood, "Are you alright?" Hood didn't answer. Tryal shook his head.

Michelle stepped out of the car, leaving her door open, and walked out in a trance.

"Hood, sit here. I need to get her." Tryal started to move out and put a hand on Kaly. She didn't react. He nodded and left. Roland opened his door and got out, shaken at his own lack of action.

Roland caught up to Michelle as she marched across the snow. "What's going on?"

Michelle came out of her trance. "I'm sorry I snapped but . . ." Her red bangs were matted to the edge of her nose, wet from tears and sweat. Tryal couldn't see the tears through the haze of the snow blowing between them, but her voice told him they were there. She was crying, slowly, but still crying. "You just don't understand. I have to have all three. He said it's not safe for me if I don't."

"I thought you hated those things," Roland said.

"I do," Michelle sniffed, "I did. I don't anymore. I just . . . They've kept me safe."

"Let's go back. You can tell us in the car," Tryal said.

Michelle sniffed a tear back in response and asked, "Roland? You okay?"

"I'm fine. Blast!" Roland gritted his teeth, "I'm embarrassed. I don't know what came over me." Tryal felt a mixture of joy and guilt wash through him at Roland's admission. Roland was never the weak one. Tryal had seen something that, unknown to himself, he had been waiting years to see.

Roland looked at Michelle. "Are you okay?"

Michelle nodded.

They walked back to the van. Michelle sniffed again. She could burst at any moment. She could but wouldn't. As a nurse, she had learned to stifle the personal for the immediate. Late bills, family problems and broken relationships all were forced into the shadows when a twenty-year-old motorcycle accident victim came screaming and bleeding into the E.R. She had ignored her life then. She'd ignore it now and get them all somewhere safe.

"I just, wow and blast, that was weird," Roland stared at the ground as he walked back.

"Ya. For us even. Real weird."

"The little girl. I can't explain it. For a second there, I didn't see her. It was something else, something colder and pulling me in. I felt like I was standing on the edge of a cliff and I was leaning over and I wanted to jump," Roland stopped, "I was scared. I've never been that scared ever."

"I'm always scared. Sucks, doesn't it?" Tryal said.

They exchanged a look and Roland grunted an affirming "Uh-huh."

Tryal said, "Can you explain Kaly? What happened?"

"Maybe she hates nurses. Or redheads,'" Roland smirked, "I know I don't."

Michelle said, "Or she's completely insane and she's going to kill all of us in our sleep."

Tryal stammered, "It's Kaly!"

"Tie her up," Michelle said as she crawled into the driver's side.

"Huh?" asked Roland.

"Tie her up. I mean Kaly. Not Hood. Although I have questions for that little —" Michelle said.

Roland finished for her, "Girl. The word you're looking for is 'girl'."

"She's not a girl. Whatever she is, she isn't a girl. She made you run away like a scared cat, knocked Kaly out with a touch, and healed me." Michelle looked at the other two Cinders, "and killed Caliban."

Roland had started back into the van and moved to Kaly, "Tryal, see if there's some jumper cables in the back."

Tryal froze, "Are you serious about tying up Kaly?"

Michelle nodded, "I'm not driving anywhere with her if she isn't."

Roland didn't look back but said, "Yes. Everyone is back to normal but she started this mess." The snow blew between them and bit at their cheeks. "Now just get the cables and get in the van."

Tryal's voice grew firm, anger welling up, "No. You did."

Roland, helping Michelle back in the van, replied, "Huh?"

"You started this crap. Not her."

Roland turned and twisted the corner of his mouth in a crooked smile, a trick that drove Tryal nuts, "Find yourself a little courage now?"

Tryal grabbed the cables and slammed the door, "You brought up the subject. Kept pressing Michelle."

Roland said, grabbing the jumper cables from Tryal, "Seriously? You want me to not dig into these things?"

Michelle buckled the dry nylon seat belt across herself. Her fingers scraped against the cracks in the vinyl armrest.

"Give me that end," Roland grabbed the cable from Tryal and pointed at Michelle, "So, skip the dog question. What are you?"

Michelle tried to start the engine and groaned as it struggled, "What?"

"Okay, what the heck are you? Because last I checked, normal people spurt blood when stabbed. Not smoke." Roland had finished tying the jumper cables around Kaly and crawled back into his seat.

"I was bleeding," Michelle said. Although, when she glanced around the van, there was no blood anywhere.

Kaly lay tied up across the far back seat. She was more calm and peaceful now than she had been in several weeks.

What's wrong with her? Tryal thought.

Michelle had started the van after a few tries and pulled away from the edge of the street. "We're going. We can talk later."

No one said a word. Roland clenched his hands. The world was now a far stranger place for him and there were things in it that he could not comprehend nor move by his will—and he was scared for that.

Tryal pulled off his black windbreaker and laid it across Kaly's unconscious body. Still peaceful. Still beautiful, he thought. He kissed her cheek and whispered, "What's happening with you?" He grabbed her loose hand. "What's been happening with you?" Of everything, this had scared him the most. He had never realized how much he cared for her.

Kaly, please, be okay.

He just wanted another late night talk. Another safe adventure of sneaking in somewhere, her holding his hand and pulling him along.

Just one more time. Please.

Hood sat there, smiling. Smiling? But there she was, sitting calmly, hands at her side, looking ahead, and smiling.

They drove in silence, the snow still falling outside. After several miles in the quiet van, Michelle spoke, "Okay, I'll talk. I need to talk." And she did. She told of the cornfield, of her first sighting of the Cinders, of the horrible night in the driveway when the Cinders burst through their invisible barrier, of Patrick's death. She paused in the sharing after that.

After a few minutes, she said, "And then I met their handler."

"And a dreadful thing from the cliff did spring,

and its wild bark thrill'd around,

His eyes had the glow of the fires below,

'twas the form of the spectre hound."

—From an old Welsh poem

Chapter Thirty-Two

FORTUNE COOKIES

CHINESE TAKEOUT WAS SUCH AN ODD MEAL to be bringing back to the house. General Tso's chicken, fried rice, potstickers, won-tons, and a big bowl of hot and sour soup. Marissa couldn't imagine the hosts of Heaven dining on this food, spreading out those cheap foil wrappers, squirting out soy sauce from the stingy plastic envelopes it was inconveniently served in, wiping the salt and grease onto their flowing, bleached garments, between sips on a plastic straw. No, there was nothing in her memories of Sunday school that even suggested this. Yet, the angel in the basement ate this exact order everyday. It was the only thing she could get him to eat. Oh, and don't forget the fortune cookies. He would never forget the fortune cookies.

Marissa waddled through the snow with the handles of the Chinese take-out bags hooked in her elbows. Her puffy pink snow coat was a bright marker against the white sheet of falling snow. The house was on the edge of the growing snowstorm and she hurried, knowing her mom would want her home soon.

She walked up the porch stairs of the old house. She hadn't been concerned about others seeing her enter the house until she caught those boys sneaking around. Now she glanced across the cornfield and around both sides of the porch. It was all clear and she nudged the front door open.

She shut her eyes against the darkness of the inside and blinked before crying out, "Oh, Mr. Angel Rasul!" She snickered. He hated being called an angel. He insisted he wasn't one, but Marissa was sure he was. He was large, glowing, and she felt happy around him. Oh, and she could see completely through him! And he had wings or something like wings. The wings didn't have feathers. They were like large plastic wing shapes that floated behind him. He insisted he was simply something he called a "Watcher." She just called him Mr. Angel. He finally confessed that his name was Rasul. "Mr. Angel Rasul, I have your food!"

Rasul awoke to the young girl's footsteps on the floor above him. He raised his head, which had been resting against an old Kenmore washing machine.

He twisted awkwardly in order to sit up. Legs crossed, his back and head were still hunched and turned down in order to fit in the basement.

"Rasul! Rasul, you down there?" the young girl shouted down the stairs as the door parted, spilling the warm evening light across the steps, the concrete and the stone wall.

"Yes. Just napping, friend. Did you bring dinner?" He asked, knowing she had the wok-tossed goods in the white takeout bag.

"Why are you down here?" She walked down the stairs, unknowingly shaking snow from her boots upon the boards with each step.

"Just making some preparations. Gathering a few things. Happened to fall asleep."

"Mrs. Raby says you have narcolepsy." Marissa was halfway down the stairs and leaning over the rail, able to look him directly in the eyes, her smile as warm as the light now splashing across his wings.

"Your teacher knows about me?"

"Don't you want to know what that is?"

"You didn't tell someone about me, did you?"

"No. I'm good at keeping secrets. You know that. It means you can't control when you fall asleep. You also need to sleep all the time. Even in the middle of the day. Even if you've slept all night. Mrs. Raby is right."

"Narcolepsy? Bring me something to read about it tomorrow. I might just agree with you. Now, back to your teacher—how did you get her to answer your question if you didn't tell her about me?" He began to pick at the chicken with his chopsticks, a delicate act with his large fingers. He shrank a few feet in size and the task became more manageable.

"I told her my uncle kept falling asleep whenever I talked to him. Told her that he'd start talking to himself and fall asleep. Told her he'd be working on something in the afternoon or the morning or at lunch and he'd fall over, completely out. She said it sounded like my uncle had narcolepsy." Her smile widened, pushing her cheeks into her eyes, "You have narcolepsy. She had to write it down before I could pronounce it. A really weird word."

"Well, thank you for your concern."

"I asked if there was medicine you could take and she said she didn't know. Jody, that boy that sits behind me, the boy with the girls' name, he said I should get you a Red Bull. He said it's supposed to give you energy. He drank one the other night and didn't fall asleep until two in the morning, so I picked one up for you." Her hand reached into the other bag, fished around, and pulled out a thin silver red and blue can and held it up.

He reached out, his long arm covering the distance, and picked the can out of her hand with care.

"Wait." She reached back for the can and popped the tab on it before handing it back, "You might have problems with that part."

"Thank you once more." He took the can and drank all of it quickly and in one drink. He sighed afterwards and smiled at her. "Tastes fruity but I still feel a bit tired. When you leave, I might turn in for the night."

"Maybe you're just bored, you know?"

"I have narcolepsy and I'm bored? Might I have the measles also? Or the AIDS?" He pulled out a potsticker and ate it.

She frowned. "Do you even know what that is?"

"The measles or the AIDS?"

"The . . . AIDS. You picked that up on TV, didn't you?"

"This TV doctor had a special on it on Monday. The doctor on TV seemed to care, but I wasn't convinced."

"But you don't know what it is, do you?"

"No, other than it kills people."

"You don't have AIDS. I'm pretty sure angels can't get that. Don't say that again."

"I'm sorry for offending you. Your pardon, lady?"

"It's not that bad. I'm just thinking you either have narcolepsy or you might be bored. Maybe it's that you just don't do anything. You sit in this house all the time. Maybe you're tired because you're bored." She sat down on the stairs and fished through her backpack, "Or maybe you have a little of both. Why don't we go do something fun right now?" She stood up and walked the remaining stairs to the cement floor of the cold basement. She approached him and tilted her head up to look him once more in the eyes.

"Not tonight, I'm . . ."

"You always say that! Stop it!" Her finger was in his face and she stood as tall as she could, still shorter than him by at least five feet. "I keep coming up with ideas and you always say 'Not yet.' Why not? Give me one good reason beyond the 'I'm an angel and I can't go outside' line. I know you can make it so people don't see you. I've seen angels on TV do that and I know you can do much more than they can. So why can't you go do something with me?"

He had finished his meal and cracked opened a fortune cookie, gingerly, his large transparent hands pulled the white strip out of the stale cookie. He held it up and read aloud, "'You will soon have very important guests!'" He frowned, "What does yours say?"

She narrowed her eyes, "Answer my question first! Stop ignoring me!"

He smiled, "I will. Just read the fortune to me first."

She pulled out the cookie and broke it open. She read it, "'Your great journey is soon to start.' What does that mean?"

The glow around him brightened, "It means the time has finally arrived."

Marissa tilted her head, "Time to go out of this house and actually do something fun?"

"Not today. Tomorrow. Today, I'm busy making preparations. But tomorrow I promise that we will begin a great journey."

Her head turned to the right, her finger dropped and her smile returned. In the two years she had known him, he'd never left this house. He lived in the cramped rooms, often ignoring the physical barriers of the walls and floors, descending into the basement and retreating entirely into the physical realm when he grew depressed by things she couldn't begin to understand. His only contact outside of the dilapidated house was his black and white television, a large free-standing unit with wooden sides and top.

"Wait. You just repeated my fortune to me. What's going on?"

He smiled, "The time that I have been waiting for is here. So many years of waiting and finally, our special guests will arrive tomorrow. They are on their way now."

Her questions came tumbling out, one on top of the other, "Tomorrow? Who are these guests? They're coming here? What do we need to do?"

"You yourself will need to go home this evening and make preparations for a journey that will start tomorrow night. Use your backpack so your parents will think you just have a lot of homework." His eyes were gleaming and they were far wider than she had ever seen them. His smile was not forced, which was unusual, and matched her own in size. "Oh, and make sure you bring a few of the potstickers with you."

"I'm going with you?" Her throat tightened.

"Please don't be late, and please be ready. The travelers will be here tomorrow night. When they get here, we will only have the briefest of minutes. Be here before twilight, please."

"The travelers? They're coming here?"

"Yes, they have made certain choices and those choices will now lead them here."

"I can't believe you're not more excited. You've been waiting for them forever."

"Not forever. For a long time. I am pleased. Maybe even excited."

"And I get to be here with you!" She leaned in and hugged his broad torso, a gesture he returned.

"Go make your preparations and come back tomorrow afternoon. Be ready."

Marissa let go of him, grabbed her backpack and raced back up the stairs.

Before closing the door to the basement, she leaned back in, smiled one more time and promised, "I'll make sure to bring extra Orange Chicken!" She closed the door and he heard her feet race across the ground floor and out the front door, back into the evening snow.

He smiled, finished the remaining rice and chicken, then laid back down and promptly fell to sleep.

PART 3

THE CARVINGS

CHAPTER THIRTY-THREE

THE NURSE'S TALE: FAIRY TALES

SUNDAY, OCTOBER 31, 2004

HARVEST CAME AND THE CORN STALKS lay flat, the field naked and empty. There was no place for the Cinders to hide. Michelle would stand and look out across the empty field and wonder where they had taken Patrick.

Then one day, she crossed the line and walked across the ditch in the early morning into the empty field, its stalks broken as old, dry bones beneath her. The old fright filled her and she hesitated before taking her next step. Were the Cinders watching, their limbs tight and their ghastly grins gaping, waiting to see what happened next?

She walked determinedly down the cornfield until she reached what was Lantern Waste.

"Good morning," a hoarse voice said behind her.

She fell forward in a clumsy attempt to leap and turn. Her mouth filled with snow and soil. She sputtered and looked up. It was a man in a yellow jacket. A man with incredibly long fingers, long ears and nose, and a billowing, old banana yellow duster. Its edge dragged across the empty mounds of the corn rows.

He held out his hand to help her up. She stood up on her own.

"Who are you? What are you doing here?" she asked.

"I see them, too," the old man said. He smiled with only one corner of his mouth.

"Who?" Michelle asked.

He snickered, "The beasts, the dark ones that stalked you and your brother."

"Those things killed Patrick," Michelle said.

He picked at the frozen kernels, pulling each one off one at a time, "There is something in this backwoods town—something new, wonderful, bright and full of Color. I can smell it. At first I thought, only a few thousand people—this shouldn't be that difficult. But it was. The individuals passed by and I struggled to see them clearly. They were all heaps of emotion and dread and despair." He tossed the ear of corner on the ground, "Then I saw you." He spun and pointed his finger at her, "You are different, Michelle. You are a beacon to things not of," he twirled his finger in the air, "not of this world. The beasts saw it. I saw it."

"'Not of this world?'" she sat back down on the ground, her jeans cold in the wet dirt.

He laughed, "You still don't know, do you?"

"Know what?" Michelle asked.

He spun around and his yellow jacket flowed out around him, "You have a spark in you."

"A spark?"

"Can you do anything but ask questions?" he paused and she continued to glare. He broke the silence, "Fine, fine. Let me tell you a story." He waved his hand, "Once upon a time . . ."

"Fairy tales?" she asked, "I don't want to hear a story."

"Oh, yes, you do. This one is about you."

"It's about me and it begins 'once upon a time?'"

"It's a good start. May I?" Yellow Jacket sat down next to her and picked up ears and stalks of corn. "There was a boy who wanted to sit on his father's throne. To reign. So he worked and worked but his father ignored him—the old man refused to die; he was convinced he was to rule forever. The boy, greedy for the throne, schemed and played with some very, very dark Colors and turned the clock ahead. To move time requires quite a lot of power—to turn the clock to the end of the world took all of the power in the world, everywhere. War came. Everyone the boy knew died. This didn't sadden him. He had what he wanted. Once a person goes to great means to achieve something, they will go to great means to keep it. Knowing the power that had helped him turn the clock ahead and bring the great war to his old man, he knew that same power could turn the clock back, so he drained the magic away. From everywhere. He killed everyone who had a spark of Color." Yellow Jacket picked each of the corn cobs that had made up the castle and began throwing them out into the empty field.

"Is that the end?" Michelle asked, "No, 'They lived happily ever after?'"

Yellow Jacket stood up. He leaned close to Michelle and she could feel his hot breath on her face. He spoke slowly, "He killed everyone who had a spark. Not a single ember was allowed."

Michelle took a step back, "Stop. What does this have to do with me and the Cinders?"

The old man whispered, "That boy is still on the throne and his, ahem, workers still hunt for all who have a hint of power. And you, little girl, you are the first bright spark I have seen in years. And if the dogs, my dogs, saw it, and spared you, soon that boy's workers will see it. They will come for you and kill you."

She turned around, "Magic isn't real. There is no such thing."

"Oh, it is real. But it has been a very long time since anyone actually had any magic to work with. Well, except for now. You are a light, and you might be able to create great magic. Something flipped that switch on when you attracted my hounds' attention—and soon, others will follow. We must find a way to keep you quiet and keep you dim."

"Are you saying the Cinders were my fault?" Her eyes filled with tears, "I brought them here? Are you serious, you freak?"

He put his hand on her shoulder and she jerked away. "No. Blood and death in an old place like this, stacked up through the centuries, that was enough to open the doors and let them walk through. No, it was your own Color that kept them from eating you up like a Happy Meal."

She sniffed and rubbed her eyes, "You keep saying 'Colors' and magic? Like Harry Potter?"

Yellow Jacket smiled and a small chuckle rolled out, "No, then not magic. You're right. Magic is a tired word with far too many odd, childish images carried with it. Color is a much better word. When I say 'Color,' I mean the currency of creation. Red, green, blue, black. White. Many more. Power, the spark, the force of life, the dunamis, magic, whatever you wish to call it—the fuel of the universe has long been vanquished. Don't you ever feel as if the world is simply moving but contains nothing of substance? Nothing of import? Do you never feel the weariness of this world as if in one small moment, all that is could simply stop running? That we teeter along as a car on the last fumes of gas before chugging to a stop? Then you have felt its absence—whatever it is, the 'it' that makes this reality run is gone. The tank is empty and has been empty for a long time. Oh, but here you are, a small drop of that fuel, a spark of Color, burning small but bright. Given time, the Colors would flow from you like a river. But before that, others will be racing to suck you dry."

"Did you practice that? How many times have you said that? Because that was Oscar-worthy," Michelle rolled her eyes.

He roared, "You stupid child. Your world has gone stale—a corpse drained of all its blood. You're too important, little red drop, for you to kill yourself by your own foolishness. Forget this masquerade. I cannot lose you. If you will not protect yourself, then I will. He snapped his fingers, and drew a circle in the air as if outlining her face. "Seton. Cor."

The dark beasts were there. In the field. She screamed and threw herself against Yellow Jacket. She wailed until she was hoarse. Three of them. Sitting. Wait—they were just sitting. They weren't trying to kill her. Their eyes were red but not glowing. They just sat there looking at her. No glinting teeth, no radiating hunger and dread. They just sat there, like dogs. They were less real than they had been at night. She could see the leftover corn through them, through the air of their body. They were outlines against the cold sky. Would they be invisible in the sun?

Yellow Jacket stepped away from her and said, "They are yours until I solve you. Moreover, you are theirs. Their lives hang in the balance if something should find you or harm you."

She stared at him, anger and panic welling, "I don't want them!" She teared up; her fists tightened together, knuckles white against the throbbing redness of her bleeding palm. Fear crept across her and she went limp and felt faint. She collapsed to the ground, her hands dug into the soil and stalks. And everything went black.

She woke with the smell of wet, cold dirt against her face. Minutes? Hours? How long had she been out? She sat up and saw the black molten faces of the Cinders. She was too drained to conjure fear and so she just looked at them. They stared at her with their humming red eyes. Those eyes— she felt herself being pulled into them. The pupils flickered into flame. There was something in them she hadn't seen before. Emotion. Beyond ferocity, there was a look of anger. She was reminded of the dogs she had had growing up. She discerned something in the Cinders that she had seen in her own dogs: loyalty. These were the demon dogs and she was applying memories of past pets, of her favorite dog Watson, onto these beasts.

Stupid! They are monsters!

"Monsters!" she shouted, "Get out of here!"

They obeyed. They were gone, or rather out of sight. She could still feel them near, walking around her. There were hints of the dark forms, like vapors, twisting the air.

The field was empty. Yellow Jacket was gone. She could see for miles and saw not a hint of his blazing yellow jacket. She left the field, her head down, feeling the beasts follow behind. Shadow and blood fell in her wake.

"The blood-dimmed tide is loosed, and everywhere

The ceremony of innocence is drowned."

—From *The Second Coming* by William Butler Yeats

CHAPTER THIRTY-FOUR

REGGIE'S JUNKYARD CAFE

HOOD ONLY SPOKE TWO WORDS since encountering the hellhounds at the Cathedral. "I'm hungry."

Her voice was faint but exact. It wasn't a question or a request, simply a fact.

Her words broke the silence that followed Michelle's story. Michelle had shared everything and felt drained when she finished. Roland had started to comment but only succeeded in producing a frail, "Holy…"

For miles, no one muttered. Tryal felt ashamed to even breathe loudly. Michelle's path had been as strange, and perhaps worse than his own. He tried to wrap his mind around it, looking for some part of it that would shed light on their current experience with the Cinders, when Hood spoke.

"I'm hungry," she had said again, and the tension broke. They argued about the need for food and decided to pull off at a roadside hamburger joint when Michelle had observed that Hood had not eaten all of her breakfast and they had never properly fed the young child they were so determined on protecting. They went southeast on Boxen South Road, a back road, towards

Bridgeport, Bayard and far out of the city, crossing over Highway 385. Reggie's Junkyard Cafe stood at the intersection between Boxen South Road and Hidatsa Road.

Roland's response had summed up all of their guilt, "Oh."

The tires crunched across the snow-packed gravel lot. "What about Kaly?" Tryal asked.

"Leave her. If she wakes up she can join us," said Roland.

Outside a hand-painted sign, in three different fonts, its letters fading in the many years since it was hung, declared "Reggie's Junkyard Cafe—Open when the Sun is Up." The Cafe was wide and flat and Tryal already knew he'd be able to smell the grease caked into the faded carpet and red plastic booths before walking in. It was a roadside restaurant; hitched to a gas station that tried to be a Walmart in an 80'x80' space—everything was for sale and none of it worth buying.

Tryal, shamed by what he was about to say, asked, "What if she's still switched to crazy?"

Michelle had come around to help Hood out, "Unbuckle her. If someone looks in, they'll think she's sleeping—we don't want them thinking she's been kidnapped." Michelle crossed to the restaurant holding Hood's hand.

Inside, they found a booth against the window and started scanning through the menu.

"You think they wash these glasses?" Roland's cynicism had returned, a positive sign for Tryal. Tryal had felt uncomfortable with Roland's silence. If Roland was truly deflated, if he lost his edge, Tryal was lost himself. Tryal disliked the image of the little brother trailing after the big brother, but it was an apt painting of their connection. Wherever Roland went, Tryal followed. He might whine and complain, but with Roland in the lead, at least they were going somewhere. It was always Roland leading, even with Tryal's "strange sense" giving them directions.

"No. Drink and die of Hep C. Please. For all of our sakes," Michelle spoke, and allowed a slight upturn of her mouth.

Roland stopped his inspection of the empty glass, "You and me all goody, now? Everything just water under the bridge of friendship?"

Michelle smiled, the first time in an hour.

They all ordered hamburgers, except for Hood. They ordered chicken fingers for her. The waitress circled around them, taking their order with one eyebrow raised in concern—a look that made Roland chuckle.

Michelle said, "It's bright in here. We shouldn't worry about the other Cinders." Tryal now realized why they had chosen to eat here. The windows were large and the restaurant was filled with the soft sunlight pushing through the snow clouds. He had hoped they could hide in some corner where they couldn't be seen. His fear of police, one which he had fostered with a series of bad decisions in the years past, had started to rear up. The dogs or the cops? He wasn't sure which he was more scared of.

Tryal turned to Michelle, "I just can't get through what the guy in your story said."

"Yellow Jacket?" Michelle said.

"Ya," Tryal said, "Just what did he mean by that 'once upon a time' story? Did he mean real magic? I've encountered some crazy things, but true, honest, wizard and witch and warlock and Merlin magic is new to me. And he called it Color?"

"Ya. He talked about it like it was some untapped water source." Michelle studied the table. "I've thought about it a lot myself and I haven't been able to come up with much more than . . ."

Tryal interrupted, giving words to the questions that had been stirring in him since she had told her story, "And are they really yours? And who is coming hunting for you? Do you think he meant other Cinders?"

"Woah, hold your horses, big boy!" Roland put his hand across Tryal's mouth, "Let the pretty lady answer one at a time. Gonna spook her if you keep up."

Michelle giggled, "Um, let's see. They're mine. Kinda. They do what I say most of the time. They definitely protect me. Territorial and loyal."

"You named them," Roland said.

"Took me a few years. At first, I ignored them. Then they became butthole #1, #2, and #3." She thought of the Cinder that Hood had touched in the van. "Caliban."

Michelle looked at Tryal, "And you? Can you fill in the gaps? I still feel like you're holding back."

Tryal sighed. "You sure? Cause this is the weird part?"

Michelle nodded.

Roland said, "Just tell her."

Tryal explained, with many starts and pauses, of his relationship with Death herself, how he had come to know her as Door, of their conversations and her visits.

Michelle sat still and listened. After some time had passed, she asked, "Are you sure this being you talk to is actually Death personified?"

Tryal replied, "I've never questioned it, I don't think."

"I honestly can't accept that the end of life is an actual thinking person. It just seems impossible."

"We had just gone with it. The insects were real. The water too," said Roland, "We had no reason to think otherwise."

"Did the voice you call Death tell you that the Cinders would be chasing the little girl?" Michelle asked.

"No," replied Tryal.

Roland added, "She just told us to watch her. To protect her."

"Keep her safe," finished Tryal, a string of Death's tone inserting itself into his recitation of her words.

Michelle continued, "Since I was given my Cinder, I've done some digging. Spent hours in libraries and floating through Wikipedia. These Cinders show up in many stories. The Welsh call them the *Gwyllgi*, the dogs of darkness. They're also called shucks and padfoots. Hellhounds. The earliest legend was spot on. Says they were enormous, halfway between a dog and a calf."

Roland swished his finger in the air, "Check."

Michelle took a drink, "This is what freaked me out—the stories said they would hunt silently in the night and would serve as the forerunner for death. They would bear the souls of people to the afterlife. It is said that they are hunters of lost spirits—ghosts who have avoided their destination—and that they hunt the living who have found a way to escape death."

Tryal set down his french fry, "What are you saying?"

"This little girl might be just that. A wayward spirit," Michelle said.

Hood continued to chew her french fries.

Michelle said, "She's detached."

"No," said Tryal.

The little girl smiled at Michelle and then continued to eat her french fries. Michelle said, "Look at her. She is, at best, imitating what a little girl should be—nothing seems natural when she does it."

Tryal said, "No. I mean . . . that doesn't seem right."

"That might be. Whatever she is, the Cinders are chasing her." Michelle waited for Tryal to return her gaze. "And they will find her. They don't stop."

Resting all of his weight onto the table, Tryal spoke, firmly and loud enough that several booths turned their direction to him, "No! They won't!" To add the exclamation point to his sentence, Tryal's weight tipped the loose table top and the plates slid. He let up and the resulting spring clanged the plates and Hood's glass of water tipped over, splashing water into Michelle's empty seat.

Roland spoke, "Crap! Good job, Dr. Banner."

"Sorry!" Tryal was red-faced and scrambling to fix the spill.

Roland gave directions, "Ya, ya. Get a napkin please. Or a mop." Tryal stood and walked to the counter.

Roland turned back to Michelle. "Tell me a bit more about the Cinders. I want to know everything."

"There's a hellhound on my trail,

hellhound on my trail, hellhound on my trail . . .

Every old place I go, every old place I go

I can tell, the wind is risin',

the leaves tremblin' on the tree . . ."

—From "Hellhound On My Trail" by Robert L. Johnson

CHAPTER THIRTY-FIVE

QUESTIONS

WITH A FIZZLE AND A PETITE POP, two figures appeared in front of the cafe, the snow sizzling around them. The pavement's oil-stained top was fully hidden under the fast-falling snow now piled high. The tires of a Ford Explorer and Dodge Ram crunched across the snowpack as they maneuvered slowly into the gas station adjacent to the hamburger joint.

Mr. Mu looked around. They were near their prey. He sniffed the air. Very near. Yes. He sniffed again. He sighed. There it was. The smell of Color. Pure. Unbridled and untapped.

"Blast! It's been a long time." It had been. They had been scraping together bits of Color, carvings that contained small amounts of barely usable magic. But here they were, outside a simple hamburger joint, with no defenses, no armies standing in their way between them and their prey, a soul brimming over—a natural, untapped flow of Color.

Mr. Mu spoke again, "Let's go. I'm tired of this hunt and I am very hungry." He trounced in a dark rage, the snow melting in his wake.

"*No,*" spoke Mr. Hu.

Mr. Mu stopped and slowly turned. "What do you mean?"

"*Very unwise to apprehend a potential ember with a direct attack,*" said Mr. Hu, looking through the glass of the cafe.

Mr. Mu looked up into the sky and replied, "I'm going to regret this, but what do you mean?"

Mr. Hu said nothing in reply.

Throwing his arms above him, Mr. Mu shouted, "How could that possibly be? The boy has no knowledge. Otherwise he would've used his reserves by now. We are discovering him in the raw. No one else has noticed the runt. He is unused and inexperienced. Let's be done with this blasted business once and for all."

"*He has yet to be acquired.*"

Mr. Mu stared at Mr. Hu's emotionless face and then said, "And you think there's a reason for that?" Mr. Hu said nothing so Mr. Mu continued, "Of course there is. You're right. Very clever way for him to hide."

Mr. Mu stared at the cafe, "So then, what now? Do you have a plan?"

Mr. Hu spoke, "*No. Another concern—you smelled hunters before.*"

Mr. Mu smiled, "Oh, you are good. I had forgotten!" He waggled his cigar at his companion, and then turned back to the cafe and breathed deeply, sniffing sharply at the end of the breath. Then he spoke, "There is something here but it isn't as strong as earlier. Maybe they haven't caught up yet. That's curious."

His sentence was punctuated with a gust of snow that blew fast through the street and into the parking lot. The temperature dropped sharply. Mr. Mu sniffed the air. He waved a finger in front of him. Three slanted lines glowed before him and faded away.

Mr. Mu cursed, "Oh, bloody no!" Before he could finish the statement, he was on the ground, scribbling in the snow, pushing into the dirt.

Mr. Hu spoke, "*It won't hold him long. Not again.*"

"Anything is better than nothing. That stupid beast we released is on our heels! I won't let him divert us when we are this close. Not now. We will have the boy!" He scribbled like mad, dragging his foot one moment and then etching against the snow with his cigar the next. Mr. Mu cursed again, "Blast! This one is going to drain me. We'll need to depend on all you can muster to get the boy."

To their side, the limp body of Tryal and Roland's mother, Vera, stirred. She uttered a pale moan.

Mr. Hu breathed at her, "*Hush.*"

Mr. Mu nudged him, "Quieter! You'll put everyone to sleep. We need bodies to throw at him if this doesn't hold."

Mr. Hu scanned the bluffs and hills northeast of them. The wind built up force and beginning to squeal in pitch. The sky darkened and the clouds twirled.

Mr. Mu spoke, "He's getting closer!"

Mr. Hu replied, "*You are overlooking something.*"

Mr. Mu coughed, "Speak, blast you! I don't have time for riddles!"

"*Why is he here?*"

"For the boy of course!"

"*No. He has no need for Color. He's beyond it.*"

Mr. Mu stopped drawing on the ground and stood up. He examined the designs in the ground and motioned at his friend to back up, "Move away!" Then he clapped his hands twice, twirling them in circles after each clap. The shapes drawn in the ground shimmered for the briefest moment. He grinned and spoke again, "It works. Now what were you saying?"

Mr. Hu's mouth pulled into a tight grin, "*He's not here for the boy.*"

"One of the boy's companions?"

"*Likely.*"

Mr. Mu turned his attention away from the blowing wind and back to the cafe, "What could more valuable than the boy?"

"*That is the right question.*"

CHAPTER THIRTY-SIX

ABDUCTION

THE BLOWING SNOW OUTSIDE THE CAFE mesmerized Tryal. It spun in whirls and danced by the windows. He could hear the muffled noise of people at the gas pumps and the trucks driving in and out, but he couldn't see them. The snow was a veil to the action outside. From beyond the window, he heard a frightening voice, thin and sharp, "*Sleep*."

Michelle had started to speak but was interrupted by a large thud as Tryal's forehead impacted the yellowed linoleum of the floor.

Roland rushed out of the booth and pulled up Tryal's head. "What's wrong with him?"

Michelle turned Tryal over. "He's completely out." She put her hand on his forehead and then against his neck, "He seems fine."

"What just happened?" Roland asked.

In answer, a growl rolled out from the booth behind them. Hood turned around and gave a muffled, "Shh." She gazed into the empty space between them and the booth and held a finger to her lips to silence the growl. She turned back to her plate, oblivious to the commotion in the restaurant, and splashed her remaining french fries into the pile of ketchup.

Michelle shook her head and said, "Roland, grab him. Something is very wrong here."

"No crap, Sherlock," muttered Roland, slipping his arm under Tryal, "Small little guy can cause some big problems."

Michelle said, "We need to get out of here."

They had made their way to the restaurant door when a large man, a corn kernel clinging to the bib flapping on his overalls, said, "That boy sick?"

Michelle, smiled, "No, just tired. All okay."

Mr. Mu looked and Mr. Hu, "Can you ragdoll this woman?"

"*Is she still alive?*"

"She has a pulse."

"*She sleeps?*"

Mr. Mu picked up her head and let it drop with a thud under its own weight, "You could call it sleeping."

"*Then yes. She will work well.*"

"Tryal."

The word was a whisper, a creaking word tortured from the throat of something barely alive. Tryal lifted his head. The effort to do so was enormous, as if bricks were stacked on his head. He looked around until he saw her. His mother. Standing in the restroom doorway. He blinked. What was mom doing here? The door to the restroom shut.

"Mom." he whispered, shook free of Roland and raced to her, his cast foot thudding against the hard floor.

Roland called after him, "Hey, not the time for a pee break!"

Tryal burst into the bathroom. It was empty. He saw only himself and his reflection in the cloudy, cleaner-streaked mirror above the yellow sink.

And then they were there. The two men were standing behind him, blocking the only door out of the restroom. There had been no Roddenberry-inspired glow. No sound or light at all. No nothing. They were just there. And between them, held by the tall man, was his mother. Her short, ash gray hair was caked with blood and her dress was torn at the bottom. Her feet were bare and bloody as well.

He squeaked, "Mom."

"We'll be taking you now," the shorter of the two garbled. He stepped into the broken fluorescent light, "Come here."

Tryal froze. He could imagine several things to say or do, but he just could not rally the courage to do them. There was his mother. She was hurt.

Do something! But he couldn't move.

A small mouse crept from under the cabinet filled with detergent. In a few quick steps it had moved near the two men.

Say something! Refuse him! Don't be such a coward!

Tryal railed inwardly at himself. Roland's words echoed in his mind, *You're the biggest coward I know.* It was right. He was. He scanned around the room—a small window, the toilet? These routes were absurd, he just couldn't imagine himself to be lucky enough to get out of this restroom breathing.

Mr. Mu sniffed.

"I'm peeved now, boy." Mr. Mu thumped his cigar against the stall door.

"Mr. Hu, give me your sword." Mr. Mu held out his left hand to his tall companion. Mr. Hu's limbs looked like pulled taffy wrapped under a wet sheet. Each arm was lithe and appeared frail. His face was still covered in shadows and his head almost touched the panels of the dropped ceiling. His long, slender fingers pulled his sword from his scabbard and handed it to Mr. Mu. The sword was short and marked with curves and strange symbols that reminded Tryal of the locket.

Tryal blinked, The locket? Where was the locket? How had he forgotten about the locket? Had their world been so crazy that he had completely overlooked the one true otherworldly item they possessed? Stupid!

Mr. Mu stepped forward. His foot shattered the small mouse in his way. Tryal stared at the blood leaking underneath Mr. Mu's boot. A pink bubble formed against the heel and Tryal was sure it was the mouse's stomach.

Tryal shivered and retched at once. The sword pointed near him but not at him. That fact didn't ease Tryal's fears any. He was sure the man holding it could place the blade wherever he needed it to be when the moment was right.

"*Tired, aren't you?*" The words hadn't been spoken by the tall man so much as they had leaked out from him. They filled the room like smoke and Tryal felt his stomach unclench. His muscles relaxed, if just slightly. Mucus inched out of his left nostril and his nasal passages cleared.

"*Walk here.*" The air grew thick.

As Tryal obeyed, his legs gave way and he stumbled, slamming his head into the concrete floor. He was far too relaxed to feel much more than a jolt. His vision quivered, the room went out of focus and darkened.

"*Get u—*"

Mr. Mu pushed the sword sideways against Mr. Hu's chest. "No more. You'll kill him." He reached over and pulled at Tryal's blonde hair. Tryal's eyes wavered as he tried to look at Mr. Mu but found he stared at the ground. Blood pooled from underneath his head and met the mouse's.

"Come along peacefully, now," Mr. Mu let out a grin as he spoke. Tryal's head thudded as it was dropped again.

I feel so happy, he thought and then blacked out.

Mr. Mu gently wiped his hands clean against a white handkerchief. He raised his left index finger and began to move it through the air, slashing in odd motions. He stopped and stared around him. He sniffed the air. Nothing happened. Something should've happened, he thought. They should be on the other side. They weren't. Mr. Mu and Mr. Hu stood in the bathroom with Tryal at their feet, anger washing over Mr. Mu's face.

"This is the wrong time! And the boy's too real. The walls are too thick. My craft is a bit weak now. It is all too much," Mr. Mu said. He glanced around the room, sniffed the air, and continued, "We need to find a thin place."

"*And a thin time.*"

"Yes," he pulled out a pocket watch, "We have three hours until twilight. We need to find a beach—a place between places at a time between times."

"*I can piss in the dirt for you.*" There was almost a smile on Mr. Hu's face as he said this.

Mr. Mu stopped, his brows dropped, and he glared at Mr. Hu, "You think this is funny? That stupid beast is nearly here and we're stuck! Fine, you carry the boy and his mother."

Mr. Hu hoisted both of the bodies over his shoulder in a placid motion. He tore Tryal's bag off of him, tossed it aside, and glanced at the sleeping boy. "*Familiar.*"

A rumbling sound came from outside.

Mr. Hu said, "*He's here.*"

Mr. Mu raised his left index finger and motioned a few symbols in the air. "Let's go. I might not be able to move us across worlds, but I should be able to move us at least out of this place and a nice distance away." He spat, "This is getting blasted expensive!"

There was no sparkle. No hum. No pop. No nothing at all. The restroom was empty except for Tryal's Doctor Strange bag and the large red puddle underneath the flattened mouse, slowly mixing with the water pouring down the drain.

"Of the thing that is neither god nor beast . . ."

—FROM THE GODS OF PEGANA BY LORD DUNSANY

Chapter Thirty-Seven

THE MIDNIGHT MAN

H E WALKED IN LIKE A BOLT OF THUNDER, a twisted deity. The people sitting in the small vinyl-seated cafe jerked their heads up. Across his dark form, carved images of crawling cities and worms squirmed and wrestled against each other in filth. All eyes fastened on him. He was the Midnight Man.

Roland could not stifle the creeping fear. They had faced demon dogs but nothing like the dark hulking beast that had just walked into the Reggie's Junkyard Cafe. Roland blinked and tried to reconcile the images—the shape of a man, his skin enflamed under a roiling surface, and then, the shadow of a dark wolf, hungry and raging behind gritted teeth. No matter how many times he slammed his eyes shut, Roland could not lock down the monster's shape.

"Behind me!" shouted Roland.

The Midnight Man chortled, a gravelly snarl followed, "So, the little moon has guardians?"

Hood latched herself onto Michelle's leg and buried her face against Michelle's side. Hood appeared at her door a day ago. Now, hours later, Michelle would do anything to protect Hood. She did not know why.

"What is that?" Michelle stammered.

"I don't kno—" Roland tried to say.

"A hunter who has found its prey," the churning darkness growled through a frightening grin filled with hundreds of razor teeth, bright and sharp against the dark lips around them. The number of teeth was staggering. Each one was a needle, white, glowing and embedded into a blood-red gum line. Before Michelle could unlock her gaze from his teeth, he moved towards them with haunting speed from the other end of the cafe. He moved inside the doorframe and in less than a blink he had covered half the distance, forty feet or more, to them. He was upon them and she did not know what to do.

The Midnight Man flew sideways. Michelle did not see what hit him. The coals under his skin glowed and churned like a rolling sea—she glimpsed dark shapes swimming under the glowing surface of those coals. There were dark things moving, beasts in the murky substance. His fall crushed a booth, the table flattened against the floor and the glass window above spider-webbed.

The Midnight Man fell again. Above him, Michelle's two Cinders took form. Their jaws clamped to his glowing arms, sparks sprayed from their eyes, and smoke rolled off of their fur. The two tore at the Midnight Man. The monster, more than twice their size, dwarfed them.

The image shifted. No longer two beasts attacking a man, it became three wolves locked together. The dark creature stood on his haunches and snapped his wolf jaw, with teeth like countless needles. He lurched at the shadow dogs and struck at Puck, the smaller of the two. Puck leaped back but the Midnight Man snagged him and tossed him into the bar stools. The counter erupted in flame. Every place the Cinders touched burned. There were pad-footed scorch marks across the linoleum.

The Midnight Man snapped at Macbeth. The two creatures locked onto each other's neck, tearing at each other. The boundary line between them swirled. Michelle felt a sharp pain in her side. Something was happening to Macbeth. Something was happening to her Cinder! Her guardian!

She hunched over and grunted, "Macbeth!" She was not just chained to them. She cared for them. She was connected to them deeper than she had ever grasped. They were not just her haunting spirits, they had become her. She understood her rage in the van after Caliban's death. Now this demon was destroying another of them. She howled, "Stop it!"

Roland pulled at her arms. She had been trying to run towards Macbeth, to help her Cinder! Macbeth was losing himself at the edge of the monster. Where there had been Macbeth's side, pressed against the Midnight Man, there was a swirling ink-splot against reality. He slowed his frantic attack and faded as he was pulled into the raging horror. The two still fought. Macbeth tore at the monster. If Macbeth continued much longer, he would be gone, forever stolen into the the Midnight Man. Michelle wondered, for the smallest of moments, if the dark hulking shapes that swam under the glowing surface of the Midnight Man might be former enemies it had consumed. Were they locked in there? Souls stolen and imprisoned in the thing that ended their life?

Michelle knew what she had to do. She could not allow Macbeth to be destroyed. She breathed deeply and shouted. A word rose from somewhere beyond her own mind—she had never heard it before but knew it was right.

She shrieked, "Creltes!" and a ripple of space, their reality, crested into a wave that slammed against the dark forms grappling with each other. Macbeth rolled off of the Midnight Man and the monster loosened his grip and collapsed, struggling to regain his footing. He pushed with his hind legs back into the the shadows of a table.

What is he doing? Healing himself maybe? Maybe there is something found in the shadows.

The Midnight Man spasmed. He wrenched himself up and stood motionless. His eyes rolled up to Michelle. He shifted and was no longer a beast but a man, a man filled with a demonic and murderous rage. Five words, like snakes, slipped from his mouth, slid past the thousand needles, "How did you do that?"

She did not know. She glanced at Roland. He was shocked, staring at her. She had done something but she did not know what it was or where it came from. Hood still pressed against her side. Hood seemed fascinated with Michelle, perhaps even awed.

The Midnight Man made a step with a short and arduous stride. He was hurt. She scanned behind them, hoping for room to retreat. They were pushed back against the far wall of the cafe. There was nowhere else to go. Roland had pulled them back and had moved in front of her. When did he do that? Michelle also noticed—time felt so slow—that she had stopped viewing Roland as a boy. His shoulders had drawn tall and she followed the tension in his arms, his legs. He meant to protect them, her, with his life.

Michelle reached down and picked up Hood and a shock of fear rolled through her. Hood had begun to sob again. Earlier that day, Hood had stood before the Cinders and invited them into the Cathedral but she was terrified of the creature in front of them. What was this thing? What was Hood?

From behind the Midnight Man, a shape moved—one of the truck drivers that had been sipping coffee at the bar, a large man with stained overalls. He swung at the Midnight Man. Drained and hurt, the monster swiped at the man's neck without a glance and sprayed blood across the huddled cafe patrons behind him. His lifeless body slumped into a large glurp as he struck the ground.

The Midnight Man took another step, and then another, and the distance between them and him was down to a few feet. Michelle's mind raced.

If he plunges at us, we won't survive. Roland will die. I will die. Hood will—

She was not sure what would happen with Hood and that disturbed her.

Hood is a little girl. Hood is frightened. Hood could die.

But she knew that that would not happen. Hood would not die. At least not simply die. She would do something far different than Michelle could fathom. Something beyond death. How do things that seem beyond death die? Michelle did not know.

The Midnight Man snarled, his eyes narrowing in rage. He stepped to within striking distance of Roland and went rigid. His face contorted in a flash—from barbaric, vicious rage to genuine surprise. Surprise? What could surprise this walking nightmare?

The giant Midnight Man struck the ground with a stick lodged in his back. His head smashed into the linoleum at Roland's feet.

Michelle's Cinders descended upon him, ripping into his limbs. In seconds, they had shredded him and the few scraps faded into the air.

Roland and Michelle gazed up. Where the Midnight Man had been stood Kaly, her face fierce and her eyes dark, wearing Tryal's black windbreaker.

Roland whimpered, "What the—"

Kaly interrupted, "Let's go. Grab Tryal and get to the van."

They stood frozen against the back of the cafe, their eyes wide and their mouths drooped open.

She barked, "Now!" and they followed, still disturbed.

Roland looked back at the scratches on the tiles where the body of the Midnight Man had collapsed. A stick, burnt and blackened at one end, lay on the ground.

Roland said, "Did you stab him with a squeegee handle?" Strange carvings reflected from the handle's surface—letters and twirling shapes, and they glowed first blue and orange and then faded as it rested on the tiled floor.

Kaly reached down and picked up the handle with its strange markings, gripping it as a spear. Roland gaped. The girl who stood in front of him was dressed the same as Kaly, had Kaly's face, hair, and shape, but she was no longer Kaly. She appeared to stand inches taller than he had ever seen her before. She was not taller but every muscle was taut, every sense on full alert. Frightening. Something new in Kaly's body.

He couldn't stop himself, "Who are you?"

Kaly glanced back over her shoulder. Was she holding back a smile? She said, "I'm Kaly, Roland."

Before he could catch it, he replied, "No, you're not."

She spoke paced and deliberate, "I'm Kaly. Still Kaly. I just remember everything now."

Michelle peered into the kitchen, "Where is Tryal?"

Kaly's eyes narrowed. Tryal couldn't be found. She grabbed Roland's shirt, "When did you last see him?"

Roland struggled to remember. It caught up to him, "The restroom. He passed out just before that thing came and everything went straight to hades. He woke up and raced off to the bathroom, maybe to pee, maybe to, um, get a drink and wipe the blood from his face." He was rambling, but he couldn't control it. "And that is when everything went totally insane."

CHAPTER THIRTY-EIGHT

SLEEP

MR. MU SCREECHED, "WHAT IN HADES!"

Sploosh. The snow splurted away as Mr. Hu and Mr. Mu appeared in the field outside the cafe. Behind them, they heard the sounds of the cafe's front glass doors erupting inwards. There were screams. Two people scurried from the back door and raced across the asphalt parking lot.

Mr. Mu twirled his large body around and screamed, "What the holy Hades?" Mr. Hu stood there, Tryal limply draped across his shoulder. The boy's mother laid on the ground, Mr. Hu's hands wrapped tightly around her hair.

Mr. Mu turned once more, taking in their spot. They had barely moved more than a hundred yards from the cafe. This was nowhere near where he wanted.

"A lake. A river. That's all I'm asking for! Why the heck are we here?"

"*Technically, this is between.*"

Mr. Mu glared at the gaunt and emotionless Mr. Hu. Here in the field, the white snow around him, he resembled a piece of chalk. Mr. Mu retorted, "There's not much of a flow to tap into here! Color comes in motion. From violence and contrast and change! Time and change! This is snow and dead ground. It is still and lifeless. This is not what I was aiming for! This was not part of the plan! What the blast went wrong?"

From behind them, inside the shattered door of the cafe, a large crash echoed.

"*He's arrived.*"

"And we're out just in time. At least one thing has gone right." Mr. Mu looked down at the boy's mother, her bloody body sharply outlined by the white snow.

"It's a matter of weight, you fool. Drop her. We have the boy—we don't need her now."

"*Yes we do. If he awakens, she might be our only shield.*"

"If we stay stuck too long in this hellhole of a world, then we'll be dead anyway. What good is a shield when you're locked up? Worse yet, what if that monster catches us? You barely escaped with fragments of your soul last time. That thing is unlike anything we've ever encountered. You still wear the scar." Mr. Mu nodded at the scar along Mr. Hu's hand—a small, nearly impercep-tible scar had formed.

Mr. Mu continued, "Drop her. We need to move now!" He sniffed the air, "There's a lake nearby." Mr. Mu pointed with his smoldering cigar towards the eastern horizon. "There. Just a few more miles."

Mr. Hu loosened his fist and allowed the strands of her hair to unwind from his fingers. With a thud, her head dropped heavily into the snow. Her breathing was slow and imperceptible, but she still lived.

Mr. Mu spoke, "There let's try this again. And hopefully, we'll get a bit further."

He waved his hand in the air, turning and spinning the wild characters that instructed reality to bend its rules for them.

On the last move of his hand, a shout resonated from the cafe, "Creltes."

It was followed by rush of air that smacked the two to the ground and sent them rolling through the snow. Tryal landed hard, a sharp breath escaping his unconscious body.

Mr. Hu looked back at the cafe, "*That was odd.*"

Mr. Mu rolled into a kneeling position, his breathing hard and fast, "Odd? That was right scary! What did we leave behind in there? That was a very old word."

Mr. Hu picked up Tryal again, hefting him over his shoulder, "*And not from this world.*"

Mr. Mu commented, "That was a waste! This had better work. Let me try this again." He swiped through the air but stopped sharply after the first half-circle. With a slow precision, he reached his hand into his pocket and brought out the small glass vial, its side etched with carvings to channel the flow of Colors. He stared at it and brought it close to his eyes, turning it slowly over and over. He waved it in front of Mr. Hu. It was empty. He balled his fist and threw the glass container far into the field, "Bloody no! It's empty! We're out. None." He waved his arms and stomped on the ground. In the middle of the wet field, the killing machine known as Mr. Mu threw a tantrum. "We are dead! Dead! Dead! What are we going to do now?"

"*Walk.*"

Mr. Mu turned to the chalk-white face of his friend and spat onto the ground. "Walk? You have no clue do you? We have to traverse three miles by twilight! We can't miss this." He pointed across the field. "There, past the nest of trees, the lake is there."

"*Then walk now!*" Mr. Hu took a step in the direction Mr. Mu had pointed, leaving the enraged Mr. Mu and the slowly freezing body of the boy's mother.

———

"The bathroom's empty," said Roland, "But here's his bag." He held up Tryal's

Doctor Strange bag.

Kaly cursed, "This has all gone wrong! I found him. I found others. Tryal, Cody, Janae, and Roland. Find him, keep them safe, and the others will follow. I was doing that fine. And then this little girl appeared." Kaly looked at Hood.

Roland shook his head, "What are you talking about?"

She turned to Michelle, pointed her finger and yelled, "And I have no idea how you've gotten involved or how we missed you in the first place."

Roland grabbed her arm, "Hold it! What are you talking about?"

Kaly tore away from him, gripped the handle tighter, her knuckles white, and glared at Roland, "We have to find Tryal! Now!" She marched through the front doors, uprooted from their hinges, the glass shattered across the tile flooring.

"There!" Kaly pointed and ran across the snow-packed parking lot, her attention stuck on the horizon. Roland strained to see what she saw. There, in the field, three shapes—no, four—moving across the hard-packed snow. They were visible in contrast.

Kaly's pace quickened and she sprinted across the snow, her feet deft and precise. Each foot barely touched the ground and then she would vault. Roland struggled to keep up, the snow dragged against his stride. The gravity that impeded Roland ignored Kaly. His feet dragged and sloshed through the snow. He pulled himself over a wood barrier, decorated with signs shouting "FARLEY'S MUSHY-SLUSHIES! THE SLUSHIEST," that separated the pavement from the field. The snow had drifted and Roland sank down much farther than he had anticipated when he landed on the other side. He kept pulling his legs out of the snow and barely making any distance. Kaly anticipated the drift and leapt far past it, landing in a thinner patch of snow, and continuing her race towards to the two men carrying Tryal. Roland was stunned at her fluidity. She raced ahead like a warrior into battle, confident and determined, towards her target with nothing impeding her.

Kaly bellowed, "Tryal!" and the heads of the two standing in the field snapped in her direction.

———

Mr. Mu grimaced, "Unneeded!" He waved a fat hand in their direction, flicking them off like a fly, and turned away from the running people and continued to walk.

Mr. Hu's long white form stood taller. He moved like a shadow amongst the snow drifts and the corn, like the shadow of a bird flowing across the peaks and valleys of the snow. He took a step in the direction of the girl running towards him. His eyes locked on her and he opened his mouth.

———

Kaly was closing the ground between her and the two figures. She saw Tryal clearly, his blue hooded sweatshirt and his white casted leg thrown over the tall one's shoulder. The two in front of her were oddly dressed. Both looked as if they had stepped from a ballroom dance that had been invaded by gypsies. Full suits covered in odd knick-knacks and emblems. The taller one's skin was as white as the snow in front of him. His face was blank and smooth, like porcelain, and he was walking in her direction. The fatter and shorter of the two made a slow but steady pace towards the trees.

The tall one opened his mouth. Not now! She knew that something was going to happen—she was so close! She had to get to Tryal. He was what mattered. All of these years would've been a waste if she lost him now!

Mr. Hu spoke.

And then she heard it.

"*SLEEP.*"

Mr. Hu had breathed only one simple word, but it moved as a ridge in front of him, slamming first into Kaly, Roland, and then into Michelle, and Hood.

Kaly's body went limp and she saw the blurring of the sky before all went dark. Her head and body smashed into the snow with a loud *smoosh* sound as the wet snow splattered away. Behind her, Roland and Michelle lost their hold on consciousness and fell forward into the snow, like bowling balls dropping into the hard soil. They were raw weight with no reason to stay up. All fell to the ground.

All except for Hood. She stood there alone looking at the bodies face down in the snow.

Mr. Hu studied the little girl in the field. Except for her, all of the ones who had raced after him and Mr. Mu lay unconscious. Except her.

What had the monster been pursuing? A greater prize than the boy?

"Stop staring! Pick up the boy and let's get moving." Mr. Mu's fat body trudged through the snow. "Oh. And thank you." He continued muttering, "Blast. Keep forgetting to say that."

Mr. Hu couldn't stop staring. This little girl had resisted his words. In thousands of years, no one had done that. It was an impossibility. Forget the brat of a boy. This girl was the prize! This girl was of something far greater than this battery of a boy they had been toiling over.

"*We should get her. She's—*" He stumbled for the word. "*New.*"

She was new. In all of these years, in the endless repetitive cycle of history and nature that had become their lives, here was something new.

Mr. Mu turned his obese self and sputtered, "Of course she is! And that hound of hell we released is on her trail. That's a beast we can't wrestle with. So, no. We won't invite danger of his type anymore. Let's go." He turned back around and trudged through the snow, "Leave her! Twilight is coming and we must be at the water's edge if we're going to escape this blasted waste of a world!"

Mr. Hu looked at the little girl once more. Wait—did he recognize her? Yes, he did, but he could not decide from where. She was familiar. Very familiar. A scent rose from his memory. The smell of iris flowers.

"And leave the woman. We have the boy. She'll slow us down," Mr. Mu shouted, refusing to look behind at Mr. Hu.

Mr. Hu picked up the boy, hoisted him over his shoulder. The woman on the ground was almost dead, and in this snow, she'd be gone before they had walked out of the field. To make sure, he moved his fingers across her throat. Nails like blades, like talons, tore her neck open. He dropped her and she stained the snow red as she bled out.

Chapter Thirty-Nine

TIME BETWEEN TIMES

NOW THAT THEY WERE MOVING through the trees, Mr. Mu and Mr. Hu's pace had slowed noticably.

"Move faster! I must have time to carve him. Every second is worth our lives," huffed Mr. Mu.

Mr. Mu's large frame constantly encountered difficulty, stumbling across the bare branches, moving sideways between tight trees, and crawling over fallen ones. Mr. Hu had no such difficulty. His tall frame and long legs stepped over every obstacle with grace. And even though he was adorned with far more trinkets, totems, and talismans than Mr. Mu, he made barely a sound.

Mr. Mu continued to huff, "Almost there. Almost there. A few more steps. Blast it!" He had tripped and fallen hard against a tree, putting a huge rip in his suit jacket. "Blast this entire world! I hate all of it. Curse this world." He stood and slammed his fist against the tree, causing it to splinter. "Fa! This waste of a forest is impossible to see through. Impossible to navigate. And it's impossible to gauge the time. Move! We might have already lost our chance."

Mr. Mu had picked himself up and trudged through the forest again, moving towards the shattered and fading light breaking through the tree line ahead of them, the promise of the edge of water, the promise of their destination.

"*Then we wait until morn*," said Mr. Hu, who walked alongside the struggling Mr. Mu.

"Bloody! No! We have barely acquired this boy. We are almost drained of magic. Smell the air! This is an old place and there are beasts that will soon prowl this night. Neither of us is up for another fight."

"*A very old place*," said Mr. Hu. And to himself, he thought, *And a very well-traveled place—there are traces of great ones in this forest. Of the Princes themselves. We will be lucky to survive the next hour.*

They stepped through the tree line and came out on to the edge of a nearly frozen lake. Its waters were calm; the cold had stilled all of its rocking motion. The water sat, rolling glass, moved only by the breathing of the earth itself.

It was not night. It was not twilight, but it soon would be. The cold sun had given up a bit of resistance and splashed the sky with amber tones. This was a tired and ignored beach, roots and limbs and debris of forest and plain life had piled upon its shores. Each step towards the water made a crunching sound under the snow. On the far side there were a few houses, ranch-style, with twisting and fleeing smoke trails coming from warm chimneys.

And there, on their side of the lake, half-crumbling into the shore and the now still waters, was an old house, wooden edges, paint all but torn away. Mr. Mu saw it, and, despite feeling little of the cold, shivered. The house was wrong. The house shouldn't be here. This was just a lake in the middle of a god-forsaken parcel of land on this ugly rock of a world.

He stared at the house and sniffed. The air made him shudder. The smell of ebony, holiness, and blood struck his nose and he gasped. He glanced at the house and then, with great will, forced himself to truly look at it, past the veil, past the illusion—this was a truly old magic, crafted with delicate care like a seamstress lacing a wedding dress. He saw past the magic and he saw the house for what it was—a great cave in time and space, a cavern leading to a tunnel of reality.

"A Gate," Mr. Mu muttered, his senses still clearing themselves. This was a Prince Gate, to be used only by the Lords beyond the Blend and their ambassadors. To bend time to move over into the Blend just once took great magic, and certain talismans (he remembered the cursed lockets that had been dispersed as bait) were able to do it with severe violence and great cost; but the magic to permanently inscribe and, also, veil a Gate—that was a wealth of magic he had dreamed of but would never possess.

The Princes were the gods' gods. There were distant, rarely seen, and even more rarely interacted with. Mr. Mu was quite happy with that arrangement. In the world of the Blend, the Princes were occasionally glimpsed. A Gate in the Blend was avoided as it was sure to be a point of high traffic of the Princes and their consorts. The Princes disdained daily use of magic—they much preferred a permanent installation where they didn't have to deal with any magic whatsoever. Thus, the origin of the Gates. They made traffic to this world from the Blend and the worlds beyond much easier.

Mr. Mu was jostled by Mr. Hu, "*Focus.*"

Mr. Mu realized he had been entranced. It was noticeably darker and the flames of sunlight were dwindling. *Almost time. Almost twilight.*

"Bloody, stupid Gate! Stupid, blasted Princes!" He sputtered. He pointed to a spot on the edge of the water, "Lay the boy there, feet in the water, head on the sand."

Mr. Hu dropped Tryal onto the beach and dragged his feet around until they were in the cold lake water.

"Not like that," Mr. Mu said. He walked over and flopped Tryal around so his back was up. "I need a canvas to do this. He'd bleed too fast and die before I could finish this. Aim his head due west!" Mr. Hu grunted and, with a nudge, aligned Tryal's body, aiming him towards the west. Mr. Mu had already leaned down and cut open Tryal's shirt, revealing his bare back to freezing air. The snowflakes melted as they landed on his skin.

"Must write this precisely. On paper is one thing. On flesh is another." He picked up a stick and drew figures in the snow and muttered, "Galto, Om and then…No, Om, then Galto, Stoval, Aie, and finally Cor." He leaned in close and sniffed Tryal's limp body. He shook his head and sniffed again. He turned towards Mr. Hu, "If he is a source, what type of Color is it?"

Mr. Hu replied, "*Your domain usually.*"

Mr. Mu glared, "Take a guess! I'm not getting anything. The smell is all wrong. This boy is a puzzle." With that, he kicked Tryal hard in the stomach.

Mr. Hu walked over to the water's edge and scooped up water in his white hand. He moved back to Tryal and squatted down, slowly pouring the water across the boy's head. He studied the water for quite some time, "*I do not know.*"

Mr. Mu had lit his cigar and drew deeply on it. He waved it over the boy, "Doubtfully not Black. So Blue? Red? Green? The White? Some other? I have to know or we could be two dead crows after this!"

"*Surely not Black. Play safe. Draw for Blue, ward for Red.*"

"Hmmph," Mr. Mu pulled deeply on the cigar again and exhaled in a long stream of smoke, "Wise beast you are. Wise. Dig for the deep and hidden and protect against the worst. Oh, this is going to be a long cord. Ha! And this boy is going to be sore when this is over!" He laughed again and pulled out a thin black and crooked knife.

Mr. Hu interjected, "*He could be of the White.*"

Mr. Mu hacked and shuddered. The White. The source of the Princes' power, although they would never dare to call it part of the Colors. The White was not normal.

There was something wild at its core. Mr. Mu whispered, "Yes. Yes. He could be. But let's hope he isn't. I don't have the time to craft a cord of that strength." Mr. Mu pulled his cigar from his mouth and huffed the words, billowing with smoke, "And I will not draw as deep as to pull White." This was hopeful at best. The White didn't limit itself to the rules of the other Colors. He could scratch the boy, magically speaking, and release a fountain from the White. He hoped this didn't happen. This close to a Gate house, the unfocused release of White would draw the attention of whatever haunted there. And they'd be dead before that happened. Either way, this boy was dangerous. But what choice did they have? They were broke—not an ounce of Color between them. They had released a First One, a Foundation Beast, one of the beasts that had been formed before this world took its first breath, and he had their scent.

Move fast. Move now. Forget the risks!

He pulled the knife across Tryal's back and winced as the blood flowed. It wasn't the blood though—he was scared this boy might just explode. It was like carving into dynamite. Nothing but blood though. He continued to cut Tryal, arcing the blade, pulling it and carving into the boy's skin.

"There, one down." In Tryal's back, laid across his upper spine, Mr. Mu had drawn the aleph of *Om*.

"A twelfth one I see,

up in a tree,

a dangling corpse in a noose,

I can carve and color the runes,

so that a man walks

and talks with me."

—Hávamál

CHAPTER FORTY

THE BIRDS ON THE SHORE

TRYAL'S MIND WAS FILLED WITH KALY. Kaly was his closest friend. She was also a psycho. But Kaly was still Kaly despite her freak-out in the van. Why had she done that? She had never acted that way before. What she did was so not the Kaly he knew. And loved? Yes. She was Kaly. He loved her.

But now he was alone. All around him, shadowed by the starless and moonless night, he saw nothing but corn.

He was dreaming. Again.

A shadow moved ahead of him.

Tryal croaked, "Hello?"

There was no answer. The shadow moved between the stalks. It was pulling corn from the stalks. He knew it was female, but not from any physical features. The shadow was draped.

Tryal staggered closer. He still had the cast on, even in the dream. With each step, she appeared to get further away but she did not move. He could not bridge the gap. He moved at different angles but still could not glimpse her face, hidden in shadow.

The shadow turned and opened her mouth. He heard Door's voice.

i am that star of babylon

Tryal's face sagged. He had a thousand questions, but this was a dream and only the one he had wondered a thousand times before escaped his lips, "Why me?"

Her voice was calm and quick.

because you listened

"Tell me that I'm special." Tryal spoke the words before he understood them. He reddened.

no you are mine but i can not assure you anymore than that

"There's nothing else?"

He words came without pause, a cadence devoid of inflection.

i spoke you heard i spoke again you listened you spoke back you were the only one that has ever listened

"The only one?" Maybe he was special, he thought.

many hear i keep speaking and many hear but no one ever listened

"But why did you want them to listen?"

i wanted a friend

"Oh."

i am scared

"Of what?"

i am scared of something i do not understand do not know what i am scared of

"Not at all?"

i am scared you will not listen i need you to listen and to be my friend

"I am listening. Will you tell me everything?"

no i do not know anymore than i have told you i do not know anything else and i am always honest

"So what do I do now?"

wake up shut your ears and run

"Nnn," murmured Tryal.

Mr. Mu paused his cutting, "Did he just say something?"

"Nnnghh," gurgled Tryal again.

Mr. Mu growled at Mr. Hu, "I thought you said the boy would be out. Completely out. He's moving."

"*Cut faster, then.*"

"'Cut faster', he says. Why that's novel! Blast! I still have three alephs left. *Pilo. Guars. Taleps.* This is taking forever! Stop wriggling you beast and let me slice you open!"

"*Slow down. He's bleeding too much.*"

"Now you say to go slow! This is not easy. I don't know what I'm working with. I don't know what this boy is. Too many pieces," said Mr. Mu. He continued to draw the knife across Tryal's back, cutting the symbols one after another in a widening spiral from the center, "And it's long. Tough to be precise when I'm having to carve so small! If this works, it'll be a miracle!"

"*All for a gate?*" Mr. Hu asked.

Continuing to cut, Mr. Mu said, "No! Not all for a gate! Do you think I'm stupid? If this boy is the one to return the Colors to the Blend, he's a treasure worth more than anything. If we carved him for a gate only, all we would have is a fancy door opener. No. I'm tapping him to draw out everything for whatever I want. I'll finish the cord for the gate in the sand—not on him."

tryal wake up close your ears and run

The voice of Door echoed in Tryal's head. He thought to himself: *I need to wake up. Wait—I'm asleep. Where am I? The bathroom. Mom. The two freaks. My feet are wet. Where am I?*

"*Should you enslave him?*" Mr. Hu asked Mr. Mu.

Tryal's thoughts stirred, *Wake up. Get up. Something about not listening. What am I not to listen to?*

Mr. Mu stood up from his stoop, dangling the knife in Mr. Hu's direction, its end dripping Tryal's blood, "Oh, you're right! You are a smart one! There you go, proving yourself useful! All this power and I was about to turn it over to him. Nope. Nope. Can't allow that to happen. Quick, turn him over—that one should be carved over his heart."

Mr. Hu flipped Tryal over with a single hand. The grains of sand cut into Tryal's open wounds as he bled. He grunted.

His thoughts focused on the world outside of the dream. *It's bright! What am I seeing? Ow! My back is in pain.*

Door's voice echoed.

wake up run

Mr. Mu spoke, "What is the aleph for servant and slave?"

Mr. Hu replied, "*Kryeth.*"

Mr. Mu said, "Kryeth! Yes, you're right. So, now, let's carve Kryeth over his heart and then—"

Mr. Hu interrupted, "*Do not leave my mark off.*"

wake up

And Tryal did. It was just before twilight, his head on the sand and his feet in ice cold water, his blood pouring into both. Finally awake, his eyes flew open.

CHAPTER FORTY-ONE

CINDERS IN THE FIELD

THE TIN SMELL OF COLD AIR STUNG ROLAND as he awoke. It was a painful emptiness. No moisture. No hints of other scents. Just the cold nothingness of frozen air. He opened his eyes and saw a corncob, bruised, speckled, snow-covered, laying across from him, a mottled yellow texture framed by the whiteness of snow.

His next thought was "I'm in snow." That was followed by a sharp shiver and sudden conscious grasp that he was bitterly cold. He came to his knees fast, looking across the snow-covered field. It was near twilight but the sun still peeked over the horizon. In the darkness of the shadows along the tree line ahead of him, the first fireflies, orange and sparking, were turning on, just above the ground, and moving out of the trees.

There were dark mounds in the snow next to him. They were clothes. No, they were people. He shook his head—why did everything seem so out of focus? So difficult to comprehend? Those people were his friends. Kaly. Michelle. There was someone missing. Where was Tryal?

He remembered Tryal being carried across the field by two men. He was running, behind Kaly, to catch them. He had lost consciousness. He had let Tryal down. Stupid Tryal always getting himself into problems and stupid Roland couldn't rescue him this time.

Kaly lay closest to him and he stumbled towards her. He jostled her and she turned over, her eyes flashing open, sharp and full of violence. He jumped back, surprised at her reaction. Far quicker than he had done, she was on her feet looking around. On the ground was the squeegee handle she had impaled the Midnight Man with. She picked it back up and and asked with a weak voice, "Where's Tryal?"

"I don't know." Roland picked up Tryal's messenger bag from the snow. Roland had dropped it when he had collapsed.

Kaly ignored him and was already walking across the field to where Tryal had been. Roland finished his thought, "We need to get the others up and go look for him."

Michelle lay in the snow behind him. She stirred, lifting herself out of the snow with one arm.

Roland helped her up, "Are you okay?"

Michelle shivered, "Ya, I'm fine. I just . . . Everything seems so fuzzy. What happened?"

Roland said, "Same for me. That bleached beanpole did something and we all went out. I don't think it's completely worn off."

Michelle hunched over and heaved, throwing up her entire lunch in several retching juts, marking a yellow splash on the white snow. Roland held her steadily as she puked, one arm around her back. He said, "It's fine. Don't rush."

In answer, behind them, a police siren sounded.

Roland said, "Blast!" The cafe, several hundred yards back, sat still. He stared and saw an SUV with a few people outside it. Some family must've come along hoping for food and found the scene. The Cathedral's van they had borrowed was still outside. It wouldn't take a smart officer long to put the pieces together. There would be no going home tonight.

They were all awake now. Michelle had finished heaving and wiped her mouth on her sleeve.

Michelle said, "Where's Kaly going?"

Roland, "She's got Tryal on her mind. Who knows?"

Michelle turned. "Where's Hood?"

Hood wasn't next to them. She wasn't anywhere to be seen. Ahead of them, Kaly had stopped and leaned over something on the ground.

Michelle shouted, "Kaly, is that Hood?"

Kaly turned her head and slowly shook it. Roland was puzzled. It wasn't Hood. It was someone else. Michelle ran towards Kaly and the mound. Roland followed.

Kaly stood up and stepped aside as she heard them approach. In front of her, laid flat, her eyes to the sky, barely breathing, was Vera, Tryal and Roland's mother. Roland collapsed, scooping her up in his arms.

Michelle leaned down and put a finger against Vera's neck, "She's not dead, but she's cold and—"

Roland pulled her tight against him and shut his eyes, her blood staining his shirt, his hot breath warming her cheeks, his tears dripping into the caked blood of her face. The others stood silent as he wept. Roland spoke, his words were a whimper, "Blast you Tryal."

Kaly retorted quickly against Roland's accusation, "This was not Tryal's fault."

Roland looked up at her, his arms holding the cold body of his mother, "Yes, it is! It's always Tryal's fault." Roland had been protecting Tryal since they first met in the large bunk room. The kids had cornered Tryal and Roland had stood up to defend the runt. He later discovered Tryal had stolen one of the boys' iPods. Roland punched him for that, made him give it back, but they were friends from then on. Roland's tears became a sob as he hugged his mother.

Michelle knelt and put her arm on Roland, but Roland gave no sign that he noticed. He continued to weep.

A quick wind picked up the snow and blew it across their faces like a whip. It grew darker and colder.

Michelle stood back up and asked, a quiet voice against the quiet field, "Where is Hood?"

Kaly scanned the field. Kaly pointed towards the tree line. There, amongst the fireflies was the silhouette of a little girl. Hood just stood there, arms outstretched, palms up towards the glowing pinpoints of light.

Michelle yelled, "Hood!"

The girl turned around and walked towards them. Michelle trembled. The mass of fireflies followed her, leaving the safety of the trees. The image shifted and solidified. Those weren't fireflies. They were eyes. Eyes of fire. Hood walked towards them and following her was a mass of Cinders.

The beasts were a cloud of darkness beside and behind her. A steady flowing form of shadow.

Next to Michelle, Puck and Macbeth formed, their hair bristled and their fangs bared against the army marching towards them. They all moved in closer to the kneeling Roland. Roland was gripped by fear as he choked back tears.

Twenty feet in front of them, the little girl walked with the line of hellhounds. Roland could hear their feet pad against the ground and the clicking snap of sparks flickering from their eyes. The Cinders were all he could see. He looked past the ones closest and back towards the tree—the beasts poured from the forest, eager to walk as night fell. The day had become twilight and the beasts continued to come. They were an ocean spread before Roland, Michelle, and Kaly.

Directly behind Hood, one Cinder seemed larger than the others, its eyes bright against the mass of shadow. Roland knew it in his heart that it was Fujo. Next to Fujo walked a shadow dog much smaller than Fujo, smaller than the others around it. Its frame was thin and its snout was gaunt. Roland hurt to look at it—it radiated sadness.

Kaly hunched into a fighting stance, holding the squeegee handle like a sword, and prepared to fight. Michelle blinked. Were the strange marks on the handle glowing?

Hood was only a few feet away from them and the dogs were just behind her. Puck and Macbeth growled but they were not answered from others. Were there just too many of them? Did just two Cinders not even seem a threat to be bothered with?

Michelle spoke, a request, "Hood come here. Please." Michelle shivered as she, with great effort, reached her hand out to the little girl. "What's happening, Hood? What are you doing?"

Hood turned towards the beasts following her.

Kaly shouted an empty threat, "Not one step more!"

Hood smiled a thin smile at Kaly and turned back to the Cinders and raised her hand.

"Stop," Michelle whispered to Kaly, "Look."

The line of Cinders was backing slowly up. The entire army moved away from this small girl.

All except one. The small Cinder that had stood next to Fujo took deliberate but slow steps in her direction. The young girl held out her hand as the creature sniffed it and then put its head on the ground. Fujo repeated the gesture, lowering his head and front haunches but not closing his eyes. In echo, the others behind did the same. Hundreds of the dark shadows bowed, lowering themselves in obeisance to Hood.

Roland stared at the smaller Cinder next to Fujo. It was familiar. He had no idea how but he felt a strange sense of connection to the small shadow dog.

Puck and Macbeth stepped forward, passing by Roland and Kaly before standing next to Fujo and the smaller Cinder. They lowered their heads as well in Hood's direction.

"They're bowing," said Michelle.

"Why?" asked Kaly.

Hood turned her small body and walked towards Roland. Roland held his mother's unconscious body closer. Hood approached and looked him in the eyes. As she had done to Caliban in the van, Hood placed her hand on Vera's forehead. The woman's eyes sprang open and locked on Hood's face.

Hood spoke, a quiet word, "Welcome."

Vera smiled. She closed her eyes. She breathed a soft breath, one small raspy breath. Her body grew limp in Roland's arms and he knew she was dead.

Hood still had her hand on Vera's forehead. In one horrible choir, the Cinders howled, a cry that shook them all. It was a cry that they heard not with their ears but with their souls.

Roland's mind spun. Inside, he ached. He saw glimpses of his mother's life. As a young girl. As a teenager. Adopting Tryal and Roland. Working late at night. Happy moments—birthdays, first dates.

Sad moments—Vera being beat by her father. Images of fists and screaming mouths. These rolled through him as the howl grew louder. He saw her life, her joys, her hurts, her hopes. He knew she loved them. Deep inside, as the howl roared and he crumpled back into the snow, he knew she loved him. He had been without a mother and was without one again, but he knew she had loved him.

The howl grew. It found a rhythm and a melody. There was harmony in the strange tones. It had become a song, Vera's death song. The Cinders were singing her life—in honor, in sadness. In front of him, Hood kneeled and placed her arms around both Roland and the lifeless body of Vera and she cried.

They stayed like that for what seemed like days in Roland's mind. The howling choir stopped, Hood slowly released him and Roland opened his eyes. Michelle and Kaly kneeling around him, their cheeks wet from tears. The hellhounds stood at attention, behind Hood, the rolling smoke from their bodies and the sparks of their eyes were their only movement.

Michelle spoke first, "I'm sorry."

"I can't leave her like this," Roland said.

Kaly said, "Tryal is still out there."

"I can't leave her like this," replied Roland through streaming tears.

"Fine, mourn your dead. I'm going after the living." Kaly stood and took two steps, stopping at the wall of hellhounds in front of her. She tensed but they stood motionless.

The wall turned around. Not out of response to Kaly but to Hood. Hood walked towards the trees. The dogs parted in front of her and allowed her to pass. Fujo and the small Cinder followed close behind and then flanked her.

Michelle spoke, "The Cinders weren't chasing her. They were trying to protect her. This whole time." She looked at Kaly. "They weren't chasing her. Even my Cinders bowed to her." Her faced reddened. Was she jealous? She pushed the thought away and said, "All of them bowed to her. And now they follow her."

Kaly spoke, "Yes."

Michelle nodded at Hood, "Who is she?"

Kaly said, "Better yet, where is she going?"

Roland had lowered his mother to the ground. "She's going to Tryal."

Kaly jerked, "She is? How do you know that?"

Roland said, "She came to him in the first place. He's the magnet for weird. You want to find Tryal? Follow her."

Michelle turned to Roland. "If they're here now, what are they protecting her from? Not us. They don't seem to be at all concerned with us now."

Kaly asked, "That thing back there?" She pointed at the cafe which now filled up with police cars, ambulances, and fire trucks.

Michelle said, "Maybe. What was that thing?"

Kaly had taken a few steps in Hood's direction. "I don't know. There's a myth I heard when I was a child. That thing, if it's what I think it was, is on the level of a god."

Michelle said, "But you just killed it."

Kaly's face grew somber, "No, I don't think you can kill it. I slowed it down. That's all."

Michelle shook her head, "I'm not sure how you know these things, but—" She hesitated to call it a man despite what it looked like. "That thing is still after Hood?"

Kaly walked after Hood. "Yes."

Michelle looked back at Roland and asked, "Roland?"

Roland's eyes were red and his voice weak, "What do I do with her?"

Michelle put her hand on Roland's shoulder, "You can stay but Kaly is right. Your brother is still with those two and we do not know what they have planned. You should come with us. If you come with us, you'll have to leave her."

Roland's bravado was completely gone and he said, "We'll come back." Roland stared at the blank expression of his mother's dead face. After several minutes, he stood up but stumbled on his rise and Michelle had to steady him.

Roland murmured, "Walk with me?"

She said, "Yes."

CHAPTER FORTY-TWO

RUN!

MR. MU WAGGED HIS KNIFE, "What, you question my loyalty? We don't have time for both marks." He did not see Tryal's eyes open, blinking against the dimming light of day. "*Both or none,*" Mr. Hu said firmly.

Tryal peered in the direction of the voices and saw the two men from the bathroom. The tall one had said something and he blacked out.

That's it! The tall one can do things with his voice.

But it was the short one that was truly frightening to him. The eyes of a butcher deep in that fat skull. Tryal clamped his hands to his ears and rolled over, stumbling to his feet.

Mr. Mu spoke, "Alright, have it your—" He spun around as he caught Tryal's movement out of the corner of his eye. "What the Hades! Stop you stupid child!" He took an off-balance swing at Tryal with the knife but stumbled in the wet sand, landing on his knees.

Tryal looked at the tall one who had started to open his mouth. Tryal held his hands to ears and screamed.

Mr. Hu spoke, "*Sleep*," but the words were lost among Tryal's screams. He then reached out with a long thin arm to grab him, stepping over Mr. Mu in the sand.

Tryal remembered that he was supposed to run, but where to? Tryal, still screaming, saw an old house a few hundred yards up the beach, surrounded by trees and a dilapidated white picket fence. Hands still to his ears, his back blazing in pain, Tryal ran as fast as he could towards the house.

Mr. Mu scrambled to his feet just as Mr. Hu stepped over him. He tripped up Mr. Hu and the collision sent both of them to the ground Mr. Mu looked up to see the boy running away, running to the Gate House.

Mr. Mu shouted, "No! Blast you! He's going to the house!"

Mr. Hu had regained his balance, "*Worse, you finished the carving.*"

Mr. Mu spun to face Mr. Hu, his eyes widening with understanding, "You . . . You're right! Curses on you! The carving is done without the lock! He's awake and it's probably starting right now—the cord will be active and we don't control him! No!" He turned back to pursue Tryal, running as fast as his short legs could move.

"Get him, you tall bird! Get him! Fly!" he shouted at Mr. Hu.

Mr. Hu, in only five steps, moved past Mr. Mu and was closing in on Tryal, who was just over halfway to the house.

Running!

That's all he has been doing the past couple of days and this run was the toughest yet. His soles were bare, numbed from the icy water. The fact that his feet were numb might be the very thing keeping him moving. His feet were sure to be bruised and when he rested, he knew they would start bleeding, but for now, he could run and not feel the pain. His leg was still in a cast and this run was going to destroy those few weeks of healing. He used that hard leg as a vault and bounded across the snow in an arching odd rhythm. He couldn't run a cross-country distance but he might make a few more yards. Just a few more. Ignore the pain in your feet. Just keep moving. Don't stop! But his back—he couldn't shut that pain off. They had done something to his back.

He was bleeding. They had shredded him. He started to reach around to feel his back and remembered—don't take your hands off your ears! Remembering that, he screamed louder again! That freak with his voice was behind him.

Mr. Hu hoped that the boy would let his hands down and stop screaming, "*Sleep. Stop,*" he intoned repeatedly.

The green farm house was suffering from neglect. Paint was peeling off the sides in small and large curls, the wooden shingles were water-cracked and scattered, the windows broken, and the loose rails of the porch were splintered. It even came with a standard picket fence, several slats broken and leaning. The front yard had decayed into weeds and those weeds had decayed into dirt, now covered with a grimy snow, still growing from the persistent snowfall.

It was old, ignored and, from Tryal's glance, uninhabited for decades. He bounded up the stairs, his cast leg thudded against the planks.

He looked at the front door and feared he'd have to take his hands off of his ears. The door was cracked open. Just a slight crack, and the darkness of the house lay beyond. He pushed the door with his shoulder and in a blur, swept his eyes around the interior of the house.

The walls were yellowed, the furniture was shockingly ugly, a white floral pattern on a vomit-green design. With his other shoulder he slammed the door shut. Could he take his hands off of his ears? Should he? There was a lock. What was a lock to those two things? They could cause him to sleep with a word. A lock is a lock, he reasoned.

He risked a quick movement, shoving his ear against his arm and, imitating an elephant, he reached over and locked the deadbolt. It was stiff and initially resisted his use. The entire time, he continued screaming.

Hands back on his ears, he tried to orient himself in the house. He was in a large sitting room with a wood-floored room on one side, and the kitchen on the other. There had to be stairs to the second story. Yes, there they were. He searched around for aid. A weapon. A hiding place. A teleporter. *Crap!* He needed something. His heart slammed itself against the inside of his chest and his ears throbbed. He coughed—no more screaming. No more. He was done.

Once more he felt something strange in his observations. He couldn't see anyone there, but he felt something. This house was different. The floor was clean. In the old carpet, a small path had been worn from the front door to the right, left around a corner to another open door.

Through the door he could see a single stair-step, leading down into darkness. There was a basement and if something had visited this house it had made a direct path from the front door down those stairs. He glanced down again. The carpet was damp in a few places from melted snow. He wasn't alone. But it didn't matter. Whatever was in this house could not be worse than what was outside.

He searched for weapons, tools, anything that he could swing. Nothing but thin slips of paper taped to the yellow walls, taped to every wall.

That's strange.

He needed to find something to hit those things with. He glanced down the hall to an empty room and saw a floor to ceiling crimson curtain with an odd purple light reflected around it. His memory jogged.

There was something about a red curtain. He couldn't focus, his head pounded and every part of him struggled to not collapse against the pain.

Keep looking!

There was a fireplace but only a small hand broom lay near. He had hoped for a poker. Something to stab the stupid bastards!

He paused as he felt something in his pocket. Without needing to see it, he knew what it was. He reached in and pulled it out. As he did so, he glimpsed above the fireplace a large oak-framed mirror. Without thinking, he walked up to it and began to pull the thing from his pocket.

Wait!

He glanced to the basement as he remembered the Aquarium.

Better.

Could he risk the time to get it down? Could he get it and get to the basement? Would they follow him? Of course they'd follow him. He might just be able to pull it off. But first, he needed something around his ears. A sheet laid across the white-flowered pea-green couch would do it. He picked it up. It was fresh and clean. He ripped a long strip from it and tied it around his ears.

Will all of this even work?

"Face to face

Show me to my brother.

Between two worlds,

I'll open another."

—Tryal's Locket

CHAPTER FORTY-THREE

GATE HOUSE

MR. HU STOOD AT THE EDGE of the porch staring at the front door when Mr. Mu waddled up, panting. He put his thick, fat hands on his knees, as his breathing descended into a fit of wheezing and coughing. After a spasmodic minute, he regained enough control to mutter, "What are you standing around for? Get the blasted boy before it gets dark. We can still pull this off!"

Mr. Hu said nothing. Mr. Mu grunted, wrinkled his nose, and pushed his way up the stairs with a rumbling wheeze.

"*Stop! This is a Gate House.*"

Mr. Mu turned his head, his lips pressed tight together and he pushed out the words, "I know."

"*A Gate Holder may be in there.*"

His hand on the door knob, Mr. Mu spat, "We've killed Princes before."

"*Through subterfuge.*"

"Nothing matters without the boy. We'll deal with the blasted guard if we have to."

"With what, exactly?"

"The boy! Just get the dumb boy. To hades with everything else!" Mr. Mu pushed against the door to no use. He was drained. He looked up at Mr. Hu in expectantly.

Mr. Hu sighed, cutting through the air like two pieces of sandpaper rubbing together, and moved past him. With a small push, the front door cracked at the locks and opened, swinging limply. Mr. Hu stood unwilling to cross the threshold. The wood frame above the door entry was etched with strange markings rolling out in a spiral. He read aloud, *"Stemz hacte stra'lee—"*

"Shut up you fool," Mr. Mu said fiercely. "I know what it says. 'Bring only what is necessary. Leave all else before.' Princes and their awful cryptic mutterings."

Mr. Mu entered the house, wheezed, then sniffed the air deeply, and followed that with a coughing fit. He glanced at the floor and saw footprints. He sniffed again and confirmed that the boy had gone in and the footsteps were his, along with several noticeable drops of blood. That was a good thing—the boy was still bleeding. Fresh wounds. Fresh Color. At the least, they could draw on the Red if the boy wasn't a storehouse for much else.

"Do they know we are here?"

Mr. Mu roared, "It is I, Mujon of the Woden Throne, the Great Roving Eye, Hunger Unbound, and the Swooping Darkness." He looked back at Mr. Hu, "They know now. Get in here, coward." Mr. Mu walked toward the darkness in front of him, "This way, into the basement."

Mr. Hu reluctantly followed as Mr. Mu walked towards the stairs leading into the basement. Mr. Mu shouted, "Come on, boy! We don't want to kill you! Not at all. In fact, we'll let you stay awake. We just want to go home."

When Mr. Mu arrived at the top of the stairs, Mr. Hu reached around him and flicked on the switch inside the stairwell. A single bulb dangling at the base of the stairs shot harsh light through the extraordinarily long staircase. Mr. Hu estimated nearly thirty wood steps from the top to the bottom. At the bottom, they could see nothing but a few boxes and a white sheet laid out upon the concrete floor.

Mr. Hu reached down and picked up a small crumb from the floor and ate it. "*Odd. Fortune cookie.*"

Mr. Mu spoke, "You're hungry? I want to leave this wretched place. Focus." Ambling down the stairs, Mr. Mu announced again, "Come on boy. We've been through this before. If I was going to kill you, I would've done it by now. We saved you back there. That monster would've devoured you."

From his hiding place in the dark basement, Tryal had seen the single light come on. He hurt all over. His back was in piercing hot pain and he couldn't stop the blood. Between his feet, a splinter of light from the single bulb illuminated a small pool of blood that was forming there.

Could he do this? He would have to be fast. Crazy fast, but he could do it. He had to do it.

The two had reached the bottom steps and were looking around the large basement. This was a room built for a giant.

Mr. Hu shivered at the thought. This was a house built for a Prince. One of the guardians of the worlds.

So where was the monstrous thing?

Was this the type of Prince to defend and kill without talk or was this a pitiful reservist—forbidden by oath to engage in petty issues? Mr. Hu hoped it was the last. They had killed Princes before but it was always so messy. So difficult. One of the two of them usually died and the other would have to work twice as hard until the other one could pull himself back together.

In habit, Mr. Mu sniffed the air, and instead of coughing, he gagged. "Holy ground! Hades! This is holy ground. Ugh, that smell will be with me for days."

"*There*," said Mr. Hu, pointing ahead of them into another room with the door cracked open.

"Found you, you little brat!" Mr. Mu shouted. They had the brat cornered. Now, just to grab him and get back to the beach. They could still make it. A few more minutes and this nightmare of a job would be over. And he'd be bloody rich to boot.

Mr. Mu opened the door and strode into the room. It was up to Mr. Hu again to flip the light switch, turning on another single bulb, casting light into a room filled with nothing but a few old toys—a rocking horse, few dolls—all shoved against the wall. The smell of abandonment filled their nostrils. There was nothing in here and there was nowhere the boy could be hiding.

The door slammed behind them and they heard it lock from the other side.

"Blasted stupid boy! You're just ticking me off more!" Mr. Mu yelled.

Tryal limped as fast as he could from the door to the base of the stairs. He pulled the sheet off the ground, revealing the large mirror that had been hanging above the fireplace. In his right hand, he held the locket. He wasn't sure how it had come back to him. Cody had it before. But it had returned. It always returned. He opened it and slammed it face down against the other mirror. The mirror's surface bubbled and water crawled over the sides.

The door of the room burst at its hinges, smacking the ground and bouncing just as Tryal scrambled up the stairs. The cloud of splinters and dust settled and Mr. Hu stood in the doorway. "*STOP!*" He shouted the word and the house rattled.

Tryal stumbled. *What was that?*

The room went out of focus and his stomach lurched. He hadn't heard what the tall man had said but even the garbled sounds had slammed against him and were now scrambling his brain.

Tryal saw the open door at the top of the stairs. A young girl in a puffy pink coat stood there. Was he dreaming? He took another few steps.

Mr. Mu's horrible teeth flashed—a mouth of daggers, all fangs, sharp and blood-stained.

Mr. Hu stopped at the base of the stairs and looked down at the mirror and the locket laying on top of it. Between his feet, in the mirror, instead of his reflection, he saw the azure depths of a great ocean. Large dark hulks swam in the darkness below his feet. "*Oh!*"

Mr. Mu grunted, "Blast!"

The ocean water pushed against the mirror's surface broke and a geyser slammed against the two, throwing them across the room. The basement filled with water quickly.

Tryal was down on his hands and knees, his cast anchoring him. Just a few stairs more. His vision had gone dark but he could still see the outline of the girl at the top of the stairs. He heard the tall man mutter something again and everything went black just as reached for the little girl. He felt her hand on his.

Behind him, the two struggled in the swirling water. Mr. Hu heard the deep voice from the Blend echo through the waters, "*Come over*," and he succumbed. It was a terrible and frighteningly uncertain way to cross over but it would work. He stopped swimming and allowed himself to go completely under the surface, hoping that when he broke through again, he'd be somewhere else, somewhere far away.

As he was pulled under the water, a large, black wing broke the surface, struggling, before it was pulled back down, leaving black feathers floating across the surface.

Stupid, stupid boy! was Mr. Mu's last thought in this world.

Mr. Hu's had been, *Well done you little beast.*

CHAPTER FORTY-FOUR

A WALK THROUGH THE TREES

THE WALK THROUGH THE TREES WAS SLOW. Hood moved like a ballet dancer weaving between each tree, avoiding the fallen logs and limbs. The dark dogs walked around her, flowing in and out of the shadows, their bodies passing through the trunks, showing no concern for obstacles.

Kaly followed Hood and her army, but lagged behind, avoiding their attention, each step wary of drawing their ire. Roland still cried and Michelle had waited with him, an arm around his back to walk slowly beside. They trudged through the rising snow.

Michelle hurried to catch up to Hood. As Michelle ran, Puck and Macbeth formed beside her, in full run. She came to the back of the mass of Cinders and could see Hood ahead of her, moving delicately between the trees. Now was the time to be bold. She pushed ahead and the group of Cinders broke apart for her, allowing her and her two dogs a clear path to Hood ahead. So, they considered her safe? She heard Puck growl deeply inside and glanced down at him. He stared back up at her. She caught the flash of a personal argument between Puck and another Cinder.

Did these things have true personalities? Arguments? Opinions? Maybe a society? What were they?

And what did it mean for Hood? She was being protected by them. Again, so was Michelle. She felt an odd connection with Hood now. Michelle had lived with the oddity of Puck, Caliban and Macbeth for years as they watched her every step, guarding her like a porcelain doll. She had stumbled upon the only other person to be protected that same way. She was drawn to protect Hood before, but now it was matched with an insatiable curiosity.

Michelle brushed past Kaly, who was hesitantly staying behind the mass, and caught up to Hood. Fujo hugged Hood's left side closely, not letting anyone to come too close to the little girl.

They left the mass of trees and walked onto the beach. The fading sunlight, now completely behind the horizon, and the darkening sky blurred the details of the shore. Hood had stopped a few feet from the edge of the water. The Cinders parted and stepped back, as if responding to an unheard command, and allowed Kaly and Roland to join them.

Kaly kneeled and examined the upturned sand. She spoke, her voice low in fear of the hellhounds—no reason to startle them, "This is recent." She ran her finger through the depressions. She brought it up dark and wet and smelled it. She said in a quiet voice as well, "Blood." She ran her palm across the depressions and added, "And a lot of it."

"Tryal's?" asked Michelle, "Do those two guys that took him even bleed?"

Roland's voice was little more than a mutter, and he spoke directly towards the dirt, "What happened here?"

A water spider, its legs long and lithe, crawled through the sand and stood directly under Roland. No one interrupted.

Roland quoted, his voice betraying his grief at losing his mother, "Two birds spread out their prey, draining him, but the prey still lived, and escaped their trap, fleeing, towards there."

He stared across the snow-covered beach at the outline of the farmhouse, its color and details shrouded by the evening. All was dark except for a small flicker of light against the window and soft smoke rolling from the chimney. Roland felt a steady vibration in his mind as he gazed—as if a great drum pounded upon his soul. Fujo howled a mournful cry and the other Cinders, the throng of hundreds, joined in, sending a rush of pain through them all except Hood, who only stood there looking at the house.

Roland strained to speak, "Please stop."

Hood nodded and the Cinders quieted.

Regaining his composure and rubbing his head with his hand, Roland leaned slightly towards the sand. Struggling to not lose his balance under the extra weight he spoke quietly to the arachnid, "Honor to you, great walker." The spider wriggled, lowered its front legs and scurried away.

"Time is the hound of the gods; but it hath been said of old that he will one day

turn upon his masters and seek to slay the gods . . ."

—FROM *THE GODS OF PEGANA* BY LORD DUNSANY

Chapter Forty-Five

STALKING TOWARDS BETHLEHEM

AMANDA HOLLOWAY WAS CURLED UP in the front seat of the police car, an orange blanket wrapped around her shoulders. She was still shaking. She couldn't stop shaking. She felt like a soda can about to blow—scared of what might explode out of her.

Officer Jody Palinski crouched next to her, a pad of paper open in his hand. It was too cold to be doing this. Incamna was a sleepy town and since he'd been on the force little had ever happened here. A break-in here or there. A stolen wallet. A drunken driver. All spaced far apart.

Twenty-four hours ago, everything had changed. They quickly had two arsons and a murder on their hands. Now this. Yes, this was twenty-eight miles south of Incamna, but the local sheriff who first responded called for assistance—this was out of his league. Jody would've done the same thing. Reggie's Junkyard Cafe had been devastated. There were seven dead when they arrived. But that was the odd thing—only two of those showed signs of a physical struggle—heck, one of them had been ripped in two. The others all showed signs of cardiac arrest. Five heart attacks! Eight had survived, but several of them were catatonic—unable to speak, shaking the same way Mrs. Holloway did, their eyes dilated and their hearts racing. Reggie, the owner of the Junkyard, had survived but he wasn't any help. He kept muttering nonsensical sounds.

Jody spoke carefully, "Mrs. Holloway, could you try again to tell me what you saw?" He rested his hand on her shoulder. She twitched but her eyes stared across the empty field ahead of the car. The wind blew snow in waves across the harvested ground.

Her words came out soft, "Wolves."

Officer Jody hadn't expected that. *Wolves?*

"Did you say 'wolves'?"

A voice shouted at him from across the parking lot, "Jody!" It was Mitch, an officer who had been with them for about a year. He waved with his hand in the air, a motion stifled by his large winter jacket.

Jody shouted back, "What is it?"

Mitch pointed behind him and back out of the way, "Look at that!" Behind him was a white Ford Econoline Van. Jody did not catch the point. Then he read the cracked vinyl letters near the back of the van: "St. Thomas Aquinas Cathedral." He knew it—this much crazy didn't happen all at once without being connected. We have a maniac on the loose.

"Three wolves," said Mrs. Holloway, her permed gray hair flattening in the cold air.

Jody turned back to her, "What was that?"

"Three wolves," she said again, her voice soft and without life.

He had to move this along. He just wanted to go home and sleep. Just a few hours. He said, "No, Mrs. Holloway. A person or several people did th —"

Mrs. Holloway screamed, "What is that?"

He jumped and followed her gaze. She stared far across the field. His eyes adjusted to the darkness. What was she looking at? He squinted, blinked, and thought he saw it. A row of red lights, like Christmas tree lights, moving into the trees. They twinkled. Tiny candlelights in the field.

At once, the ground moved and he lost his footing, falling hard onto the icy concrete. Mrs. Holloway screamed again and curled up into a ball in the front seat of his cruiser. Everything shook again and he had a strange thought—it's an earthquake.

This is Nebraska! We don't get earthquakes here.

But it was happening. The ground shook. The entire building rattled. The few remaining windows blew out, spraying glass into the snow. Officer Jody blinked again. The shaking stopped but the shadows in the cafe moved. Officer Blake burst out the front door.

"What's happening?" shouted Jody.

Blake didn't respond. He just ran across the parking lot and onto the road.

Jody stood up, drew his gun and clicked the safety off. Ahead of him, the shadows around the building swayed.

The metal frame of the building screamed. From inside the cafe, a bone-breaking yowl rolled out. Jody's hand slipped on the trigger and he fired a shot. The report was loud and turned everyone's heads. He wasn't aiming at anything. His palms were sweaty. He fumbled to get a good grip on the gun.

The entire cafe grew dark on the inside. The few lights shut off. The shadows surrounding the building rushed into the interior. If it were possible, the darkness inside the cafe grew darker.

A hulking, monstrous, jet-black creature crashed through the broken door frame. It resembled a wolf but was something far different. It was not something—its form twisted and churned as it charged.

Unthing.

The word sprang to Jody's mind. The Unthing racing towards him, Jody emptied his entire clip in the few seconds it took the monster to reach him, one shot after another, and did not slow down the beast one bit. Its spinning eyes stared down at him just before it turned its jaws and bit clean through his neck.

Unthing.

It consumed Jody's body in two more bites.

Unthing.

He had tasted Jody's last thoughts as he consumed his body and soul. Unthing was a new name. It served as well as any other.

Unthing. Midnight Man. Monster. He was all of these and more.

And he hungered.

Food.

He struggled to gain balance and form. He stayed as a wolf for pure hunger's sake—easier to hunt.

Next to him, a woman screamed. The Midnight Man turned his large shaggy head to see an old woman scrambling to shut the door of a car. Her fingers tried for the handle but kept missing. In a step and a chomp, he ended her life and fed on her body.

He had to get back to the hunt. His prey was so close. He couldn't let himself fail. The Final One would be coming and he had to prepare the way. There would be a new world soon, a new world that required all of the foundations of the old to be removed, starting with Death. The Final One would be all the new world would need. Beginning and end in itself.

The Midnight Man snarled and shook his charred mane. Just a few more and he would have enough strength to continue the hunt. But he wouldn't go blindly this time. He had been caught off guard earlier. That would not happen again. There were wise people protecting his prey. She had guardians.

He saw a small pair of eyes beneath a car. His smoldering body cleared the distance, with far less speed than he should have been able to muster, pressed his snout under the car and flipped it. Revealed, Mitch shivered on the ice. The Midnight Man devoured him, staining the snow-packed parking lot with the officer's blood.

Soon.

Soon he'd have his strength. Soon the hunt would begin again.

CHAPTER FORTY-SIX

APPROACHING THE HOUSE

MICHELLE COULDN'T TAKE HER EYES off the house, far across the field, "I don't like that place."

Kaly replied, "It's night time and we're out in the woods surrounded by an army of doom hounds."

Michelle said, "Point taken. Still. There's something not right about that house. I can't focus on it. It's there and it isn't and I feel a pounding in my brain whenever I look at it too long."

Roland sniffed, "They've lit the fireplace. Someone's there." He tugged at Tryal's messenger bag slung across his shoulder.

What did he keep in this thing?

Kaly said, "If Tryal went there, we go there." She pointed at the house with the squeegee handle still gripped tightly in her hand.

Roland said, "If those two things followed him, we'll be just like before—asleep before we know it."

Michelle said, "I don't think they can affect Cinders. Puck and Macbeth didn't seem at all dazed when I woke. I don't think they were hit."

Kaly said, "We have an army of Cinders."

Michelle frowned. "We?"

Roland spoke, "What are you going to do now?"

Kaly replied, "Get Tryal back and then take him to…" Her voice trailed and she broke eye-contact with him, staring at the ground. "It's the only thing I know to do."

Michelle spoke, her voice perplexed, "Take Tryal to who?"

Kaly spoke, "The seidr, the witch, said to go and hunt Tryal. And I guess you two, maybe. I don't know. That's what I've done. If I go back, someone will know what's next."

Michelle said, "Go back? You are making no sense." She shook her head. "None. But I think Hood is with you if you're going after Tryal and I'm not leaving her alone."

Roland asked, "Why?"

Michelle replied, "Why what?"

Roland said, "This isn't safe. Tryal's my brother, Kaly's something, and Hood's whatever, but he's nothing to you. And you've only known Hood for a day. Why not pack up and leave?"

Michelle started to reply, "Seriously? After all that's happened, you're ques—"

Roland cut her off, "I'm not being a jerk. I'm serious. This is dangerous. I can't see why you should put yourself in any more danger."

Michelle glanced down at Hood and felt gooseflesh rise on her skin as she found Hood already staring at her. They looked at each other for a breath and Michelle continued, "Sorry. I'm coming. I've found more answers in the last day than I have in the last ten years. I think Hood…"

She struggled to explain this connection that had been brewing in her heart. Hood was a little girl. Was Michelle putting too much into the similarities? She said, "Hood needs someone. Macbeth and Puck watch out for me. Tryal's not here right now for Hood, so I will be."

Roland took a breath and muttered, "Okay."

Kaly stamped impatiently. "Can we go now?"

Michelle said, "Ya. I think we're all trying to avoid the house, but I don't think we can."

Kaly said, "Tryal's there and he's hurt. Figure out the whys later." She lowered her voice and dropped her gaze, "Please."

Roland put his hands on Kaly's shoulders. "You're not alone. We'll get Tryal."

Kaly felt awkward. Despite Roland's reassurance, she couldn't respond back in kind. If it came to it, she would still do what she had to do alone. She wanted to tell him that she'd be there for him, for each of the others, but she knew she couldn't. It wouldn't be the truth.

Roland leaned into Michelle as they walked and whispered, "Please be safe."

Michelle said nothing in return. She just nudged him away and smiled.

They came to the edge of the white fence outlining the house's property. Fujo walked to the front porch, turned and sat his back haunches down. The remaining hellhounds, as if conducted by an unseen director, flowed out, encircling the house and facing outwards. In the growing darkness, their eyes were frighteningly bright and hypnotic.

Roland gazed at Fujo and saw the flames in the dog's eyes, saw the flames past those, an ocean of fire falling out into an eternity behind the eyes. He wanted to fall into the never-ending spark, the purifying flame of those eyes. They were the last stop of this life—a final stop that removed everything wrong about him, sending him clean into the endless void of the next life.

He felt an elbow in his ribs. He shook his head to see Michelle nudging him again. She said, "Stop staring at their eyes. You'll go mad."

He squinted. "That was odd."

"And wonderful," she said.

"Yes," he put his hand on her shoulder "And frightening."

This time she didn't pull away. His hold was comforting, reassuring. He had been right earlier—this was dangerous, but she had lived for a long time assured that she was the only one to face the weirdness of this world. Now someone else normal who knew everything she had experienced was real. Just to know that there was someone else who saw the world the same way she did was a wonder. This was truly why she had stayed with them. She had been hungry for this connection for all her life and finally had it.

The curtains were drawn and the inside of the house was obscured, but there was light inside, small against the darkness of the night. A flicker of light, probably from the fireplace, shined against the curtain. Kaly walked up the steps and tried the door. It was locked. She examined the lock, pulled out a small sheet of paper and a pencil from her back pocket, and drew an awkward scribble, a large oval and an arrow, in one smooth motion. She muttered, close against the door. The door clicked and unlocked. Realizing that every one else was staring at her, she said, "My mother taught me that little trick."

Roland spoke, his words still a whisper, "You are strange."

Kaly glared at him. "So says *Speaks To Spiders*."

Had she grinned a bit there? Was the new Kaly softening?

If she had, her face had already snapped back to its original fierce mold. She turned to open the door and paused as she examined the molding above it.

Michelle said, "What is it?"

Kaly nodded. "There's something carved above the door." There were strange shapes written as words in the wood on the door frame. Kaly muttered, "I think I remember some of these. It says something about 'leave all' and the last thing says 'before.' That's all I can make out." Kaly put her hand back on doorknob and started to open the door.

Roland leaned into Kaly and whispered, "Stop. We don't know what's on the other side. Those two might be waiting. Open it, but stand back. Michelle, can your two Cinders be up here?"

Michelle looked down at Puck and Macbeth and spoke, still in hushed tones, "Can you?"

They responded by walking up, almost rising through the air, and standing on either side of Kaly, who shivered at their approach.

Roland spoke, "Now, open it and stand back."

With one hand, Kaly gripped the squeegee handle and, with the other, she turned the doorknob and threw it wide open, letting the light spill out onto the porch.

PART 4

THE HOUSE

CHAPTER FORTY-SEVEN

THE HUNTER'S TALE

THE AGE OF WIND: YEARS 1723–1735 OF THE TNOSCANN

THE STORY OF KALY'S BIRTH WAS TOLD OVER and over, a legend forming into myth. It began with a wailing, screaming, bloody, dripping baby pulled quickly from her mother's womb under the flickering candles that formed the birthing tent of her clan. The Meyjar were nomadic and now, despite their past glory, were forest scavengers.

In the corner of the birthing tent, its walls made of knit skins, leaves and stolen cloth, in the darkness of the motley construction, sat the Seidr, the witching woman. It was custom for the Seidr to be at the birth of every child. At each birth, she did nothing but sit and rock. Every tribe had one and every tribe was embarrassed of theirs. They had been useless for centuries, but it was customary for the Meyjar to travel with one, in hope that her blind eyes would see through the veil and predict a good future or warn of tragedy.

Kaly was born to a clan that still had their Seidr. And she shook at Kaly's first wail. Her eyes filled with a dark hollow and her head bobbed and strobed beneath the dynamic of the candles.

She shook, and whispered, her hot, foul breath rolling over the newborn's face, her lips close to the child's ear, "She'll hunt. She'll search. She'll find. She'll return."

The others in the room—Kaly's mother, her aunts, a few other women—grew silent to hear the Seidr's soft words, the first from her mouth in years.

The Seidr's voice was rough, and she gagged on her own dry throat, but forced the words between gasps of breath and heaving coughs, "Her hunted will be her other. He will undo the dark day. They will return the Colors to the Stratoich, to all the worlds. Send her out, into the pathways, and she'll find and return the Solas Emrys to us. Her spear will be sharp, her eye keen, her purpose set. In their wake, others will awake and follow. Name her Kalypso. Name her Oski, the wish-finder, wish-hunter. Clothe her in the skill of the Escielenn, so she may hunt in shadow. She is the hidden and subtle huntress." The Seidr, the first to speak a true word of prophesy in ages, choked on her final word and fell to the floor, dead.

It did not matter. Kaly's mother and all those present remembered every word. Some wrote them down immediately. Kaly's youngest aunt rubbed her own fingers in the birthing blood and wrote the words on the animal hide lining the tent. This canvas was displayed in the open wherever the clan traveled. And the legend of Kalypso-Oski spread.

Kaly was not old enough to remember this, but she had been told the story from the moment she could understand words. She had no reason to live other than to find the Solas Emrys, the last, hidden, source of true Color waiting to be fanned into flame again. She would find and return with him. And he would bring others with him. But, he would also be her other, her companion, her mate. It was to be. The Seidr had said it.

Kaly nursed, crawled, walked, and her training began. She learned her first words and her first Color carvings together. The carvings rarely worked at first, but by age five, she knew all the local Seidrs could teach.

When she awoke, when she went to sleep, she was reminded of Kalyspo-Oski's Great Hunt. The story was spoken as a ward against darkness wherever she went. Every day began with the words, "We do this for Kalyspo-Oski's Great Hunt. She will succeed because we do this today." She was the Kalypso-Oski and she was prized.

At age three, she was taken from her tent in the middle of the night, blindfolded. She was sat down and heard the words again, "We do this for Kalyspo-Oski's Great Hunt. She will succeed because we do this today." When the blindfold was removed, she found herself in the forest, alone. Kaly had cried for most of the morning. Out of tears, she stood and rubbed into the dirt a simple carving for direction. Above her head, the leaves shook and the branches bent, pointing behind her. She followed the tree's directions until she walked into the clearing of her village two hours later. Her mother stood on the edge, wrapped in hides and armor, her large eyes like beacons across the gap.

At age four, Kaly was handed a roughly carved and bent spear and was taken out again into the forest, this time at night. She cried for only a few minutes this time. She did the carving for direction, the grass at her feet bent in the direction of the Meyjar village. The air was cold and the night sky was dark, the light from the moons veiled by the treetops. She heard the snap of a branch behind her. The glowing eyes of a hunched animal floated between two trunks. It grunted. Fear washed over her. She scratched in the dirt. The beast leaped and slammed against an invisible wall. She scratched on the spear with a piece of chalk she kept in her pocket and the spear erupted into light. The creature in front of her was a shaggy brown mass of hair, teeth, and dumb scheming. It fled towards the safety of the dark underbrush and far from the strange girl. She returned to the village's crying, smiling faces, and her mother's hopeful stare.

At age five, she was removed again and sent to the Escielenn, the men of shadow. The next few years were grueling and wonderful. She learned tricks that all children crave to know. She learned tricks of deception, of imitation, of cunning. She learned to change the course of men's minds with a few words. She learned to hide behind people's own memories so they saw not her but a long-forgotten friend or enemy. She learned the shadow men's ways.

At age nine, she returned to the Meyjar. They had been busy in her absence planning for her Great Hunt. They had sent out trackers. They had gathered tools, weapons, and secrets. They had scrounged for every small piece of knowledge of the whereabouts of the Solas Emrys. Every dream, every stray vision, that spoke of his appearance was chased and jotted down. They had brought tales of every possible world where the Solas might be found. They had gathered maps of every secret, silent door between the possible worlds. Kaly was told all. She was taught secrets that had been pulled from other tribes, other peoples, from the Princes and the other great powers. They had even brought secrets held by the Court of Danor.

They had scraped pieces of raw, flowing Color, mostly red (to their shame) to fuel her carvings. She never told them that she rarely had need of fuel for her carvings. Her carvings worked. Every time.

The day arrived. She had trained for twelve years. She knew everything the Meyjar, the Seidrs, and the Escielenn could teach. She did not feel ready. She walked through her village and the rituals of the day, numb to her own emotion. There were prayers and blessings. She embraced each as she left. Their faces were filled with a desperate, fearful hope. Her success was all they had. They had all lived the last twelve years for Kalypso-Oski's Great Hunt. Today, there would be no more training, no more words of affirmation. She began her Great Hunt with a step out of the village and towards one of the silent doors into darkness. She turned back to look at the wall of people, her people, one last time. She twirled her finger around a lock of brown hair, bowed her head to whisper a prayer, then lifted her spear and shouted her own name "Kalypso-Oski." It was echoed by the throng and she walked into the deep forest with her name shouted by everyone she ever knew. She glanced back once more and saw only her mother at the front, her large eyes like a beacon. Those eyes burned. Those hopeful, demanding, desperate eyes.

"Who knows but the world may end tonight?"

—ROBERT BROWNING

Chapter Forty-Eight

THE SECRET

WHEN THE DOOR OPENED, light poured in the house. Tryal lay face-down on the ugliest couch Michelle had ever seen, a monstrosity of gaudy white flowers against a pea-green background. Tryal's back appeared to be sliced and gouged. The first image that sprung to her mind was that of shredded beef.

A little girl was next to him, a cup of water in her hand. She was maybe ten or eleven years old and wearing a massive, very pink winter jacket. They were lit by the warm light of a fireplace to her right. The heat reminded Michelle that she had been trouncing through the blowing snow and was freezing. The warmth overcame her apprehension and pulled her into the room.

There was something else in the room. Michelle could not grasp what she saw. The light shimmered in the room as if she stared through gasoline fumes.

"Hey guys," slurred Tryal, his eyes barely open and his arms dragging across the floor. He pulled himself up into a partial sitting position.

Roland pushed past Michelle and slammed his fist into Tryal's face, sending him flopping back to the couch with an "Ooomph!" Roland raised his fist again, "You stupid little— "

Kaly rushed through the door, dropped her squeegee handle on the ground, pushed Roland aside hard, and landed on her knees while wrapping her arms around Tryal. He screamed and retched in pain, sitting straight up and then falling face forward onto the couch cushion.

Roland fell against a wooden chair, tripped, and landed with a crash. As he picked himself up, Michelle went to him. "Roland! Stop!"

"No! It's his stupid fault!"

Tryal groaned, his eyes struggling to stay open, "My fault?"

Roland was on his feet and Michelle leaned against him, holding him back from Tryal. "She's dead! Do you get that? You killed her!"

Michelle grabbed his arms. "Roland!"

Tryal blinked. "Mom?" He pushed himself upright as Kaly helped steady him.

Roland screamed, "Mom! You. Killed. Her."

Michelle pleaded, "Roland, calm down."

"No!" He stabbed his finger at Tryal. "You. You're always thinking about you. Always trying to save yourself. You! It's always you! And you killed her. You little self-centered coward!" He seethed, spitting the last few words.

Kaly put her hand around Tryal to steady him further and felt something wet. She pulled her hand back. It was covered in Tryal's drying blood. Kaly blanched, unsure and confused, "What happened to you?"

Roland saw the blood on Kaly's hand. He stopped fighting Michelle. "Tryal?" he murmured.

A booming voice answered, "He's been injured, carved by those two monsters." The voice was melodic and deep, echoing through the house. "Come in. Calm down. Come and dry out by the fire."

Kaly scanned for the source of the voice but before her eyes could focus, Michelle whispered behind her, "What is that?"

Kaly saw what had spoken. In the center of the room, there was a large man, only his translucent torso and upper body were visible. His waist started at the floor and his head scraped against the ceiling.

She knew what it was. Her true memories bubbled up. This was a Prince. Here, in this world. And it was speaking to her! She had heard of them as a child, maybe even glimpsed one far on the horizon, but she had never hoped to be so close to one herself, ever. They did not involve themselves in the lives of the common, mundane things. They used her world as a way station and, according to the stories, as neutral ground in their wars.

The little girl in the pink jacket dropped the glass of water she had been holding. It shattered on the ground, spraying water and glass across the carpet, the couch and Tryal. She glanced at the Prince and asked, her voice wrinkled with fright, "What are those?" She pointed past Michelle where the Cinders had moved into the doorway, advancing before Hood, who still stood outside.

Michelle moved back to the front door. "It's okay. They're with me!" Michelle nudged Hood directly behind her, hiding her from the view of the two new people.

Kaly inspected the carnage that was Tryal's back.

What did they do to him?

His back was cut as if by a razor blade, blood still caked to the butterflied sides of flesh. He had been cleaned up, and she noticed the bloody towels in the corner of the room—these two had been helping Tryal. She stared at the cuts.

Were these letters? Can I read these? Were these alephs? What were they trying to do with him? Why did they do this?

She could feel an answer far in her true memory but it remained indistinct. She began wiping the glass from his back, picking a few shards up.

The little girl in the pink jacket started picking up the pieces of glass on the floor, her voice apologetic, "I'm sorry. I didn't mean to do that. I was just startled."

The voice of the Prince rumbled again, "Let us all stay calm." As he spoke, Kaly could feel herself, her very being, grow warm with each word.

Roland said, "No!"

The voice spoke, "Please, now, all of you, come in, shut the door. Warm up."

Tryal mumbled, "Mom?"

The voice sounded, "Tryal, you of all people should know she is on a new journey now. She has left this world, escorted to her Path. Let me allow you a minute to gather your thoughts, to face your grief." The man shimmered and faded away.

Tryal began to cry.

Janae. Cody. And now Mom. Roland was right.

Tryal turned his head to Roland, and choked out the words, "I'm sorry."

Roland stood fixed. "No."

Michelle started to interject but caught the look of rage in Roland's eyes. He sat down in the wood chair he had tripped upon earlier and hung his head, wrapping his arms around himself.

Was he crying?

Michelle went to the door and pulled Hood in, shutting and locking it behind them. Out of habit, she stomped the snow from her feet. Kaly glanced at her. Michelle pushed Hood behind her, keeping her as much out of sight as possible.

The room stood silent for several minutes except for Tryal's soft sobbing and whispered, "I'm sorry." After a few minutes, Tryal stopped and lay back down, prone against the couch and Kaly's lap, exhausted from their ordeal, pain, and the shock of his mother's death.

The fire flickered, dancing shadows across the inside. Michelle examined the room. It was filled with mismatched furniture. To her left, past the table Roland sat on was a hallway that led to an open room. A crimson curtain hung across the wall, a purple light sparkled from its edges.

On every wall, small pieces of paper hung. She leaned in and read from one, "'You will be happily surprised by a long-time friend.'" Michelle read another, "'You will obtain your goal if you maintain your course.'" She pointed at the walls. "They're fortune cookies."

Kaly scanned the room, "What the?" Almost every inch of the walls were covered with the scraps of paper.

The young girl in the pink coat said, "He likes Asian food. He keeps the fortunes. Says they're always true, always right."

Michelle read one more, "'The time is right make new friends.'" She shot a look at the girl, who sat down in the chair opposite the fireplace.

She read another, "'You will find your solution where you least expect it.'"

The girl's soft voice spoke, "He says they're always right."

The deep voice of the translucent Prince spoke, and Michelle jerked in surprise. "The two *skrikers* should wait outside with the rest of their kind."

Michelle made sure Hood was behind her. "The *what* should wait outside?"

The voice spoke again, seeming to come from all corners of the room, "The two doom wolves."

"You mean Macbeth and Puck?" Her Cinders' ghostly bodies intersected the wall beside her. She was sure Fujo and his cohorts stood only a few feet away outside. "How many names do these things have?"

The voice spoke again, and Roland stirred in his seat. Like Kaly, he felt warmed by it, calmed by it. "They are known by thousands of names. They are in every world, in every culture, in every age. They are the constant hunters. They are not tame. They answer to only one Master and even I couldn't hope to summon Her. Please, I ask again, have them wait outside."

Michelle spoke, pushing Hood, further behind her, "No."

The voice replied, "No? So be it. I shall not be tame myself if they make any move towards violence. Until then, let us continue. First, I am Rasul, a servant of the White and the Gatekeeper of this Hold. And this little one is Marissa. We've been waiting for you."

Tryal stirred and moaned. His casted foot slid from the couch and landed with a thump on the floor.

Rasul spoke again, "Your friend entered our house in an attempt to escape the two ravens. Through his own cunning, he eluded and vanquished them. Mind you, through wit alone! However, they had been attempting to use him to return to the Blend and in doing so, had hurt him greatly. We had just finished cleaning him and moving him to this couch when you arrived. I was hoping to work on healing him a little. There's little I can do here, but I believe I can work at a bit of repair. I'd like to have him at rest before we discuss our plans for this evening with you. Tryal is a very important part." He nodded at Roland. "As are each of you, I'm beginning to see."

Michelle muttered, "What?"

Rasul closed his eyes and laid one of his large, translucent hands on Tryal's back. It moved like a cloud through the air—drained of color but full and expanding. Tryal moaned and moved his leg up, just a small amount. Tryal's back no longer looked bloodied and bruised. It quickly turned white and glowed. Soon, the room filled with a sharp white light. Not blinding but overwhelming the small candles placed throughout the room and the flicker of the fireplace. The light faded, and Tryal still laid on the couch. But he was different. His wounds, still red, weren't flayed open. His color had returned and he was no longer wincing in pain. His voice growled in his throat, as if struggling to discover words again.

Rasul turned to face Roland. Roland stood up and stepped back, his eyes wide in fear.

Rasul nodded at him and lifted his large, clear hand. "Please."

Roland dropped his head and plopped down in the seat.

Rasul moved his hand across and through Roland. Purple shimmered across Roland's body and he sighed, looking into Rasul's huge eyes.

Rasul said, "I can only quiet your pain. Not remove it."

Tryal started to stand but fell back into the couch. As he sat down, he fell against Kaly once more, resting his weight against her.

Roland asked, his voice slow and in awe, "How did you do that?"

Rasul replied, "I am a Prince. It is our nature to heal and restore. It is the nature of the White."

Kaly spoke, "He's an angel."

Roland's mouth gaped, "What?"

Marissa piped up, her voice was bright and fast, "He really is an angel. He hates being called that. He can do much more! Well, except for staying awake for more than an hour. He has narcolepsy."

Roland said, "Wait, are you referring to the type with fluffy wings and halos? And he struggles staying awake? See, told you church was boring." It was the first joke he had told in hours. Michelle smiled a bit.

Kaly coughed nervously and spoke, "Roland! Shut up! This is a Prince."

He glared at her. His anger was still alive. "A what?"

Rasul smiled, "He's fine. I quite enjoy the banter."

Tryal tried to speak up, his voice still raspy and dry, "Rasul has been helping me. They saved me."

Tryal was still sitting on the couch with his head in his hands. Kaly sat next him, her arm on his shoulder, avoiding the still raw scars on his back. She kept glancing at his back, trying to read the scars.

Roland studied his brother—he did not seem cautious around Kaly. In fact, he was taking comfort in her presence. Tryal had not seen the warrior Kaly in the cafe and she was not eager to comment on it. Tryal knew only of the freakout in the van.

Roland turned back to Rasul and said, "Nice. But enough about you. Back to Rasul. Are you an angel?"

Rasul smiled. "No."

Marissa nudged him. "Rasul . . ."

"We have responded to that name before. We are of the White. We serve the First."

Michelle said, "You've said that."

Rasul said, "Angel. Maybe. Probably. There is some truth in that word. Not much, but there is some. I am of the White and I serve the First of Caelum."

Michelle spoke up, "Do you mean God?"

Rasul said, "That name is not correct. At least, no longer."

Michelle said, "He isn't God anymore?"

Rasul replied, "No, that question isn't right either. Your world has forgotten the meaning of that title. You have removed it from meaning."

In this exchange, no one had noticed that Hood had moved around Michelle. She stood directly in front of Rasul, her eyes looking up at him and her mute lips pressed tightly together.

Marissa was the first to notice her and said, "Oh, and who are you?"

Tryal exclaimed, "Hood! Wow! Have you grown?" Tryal was right. She had grown. She was taller. How had Michelle overlooked that?

Tryal started towards her but was taken back by Rasul's reaction. A look of dread flashed on his features and then faded.

Rasul spoke, "Now, you are truly a surprise." He laughed deeply, "My apologies, mistress, but your presence was completely unexpected." He lowered his voice, "Dangerous, too. We must move more urgently now."

Looking towards Tryal, he said, "I didn't realize she was with you. I couldn't anticipate that she would walk with you. You had her mark on you, that was clear, but I wouldn't have imagined this."

To Hood, he said, "You have hid well, little queen."

Rasul leaned in close to her and then there were two of him, one a smaller, normal-sized version within the larger one, like a nesting doll. The smaller mimicked the larger one in perfect synchronicity. The smaller brought his hand to grasp hers, and bowed, his head coming to her level, and spoke, "Ahh, little queen. You now complete the puzzle but open up a far larger one. May I ask, why are you here?"

"You know her?" Tryal asked what all of them were thinking.

"You don't?" Rasul's eyes washed over Tryal, "Her chosen companion and still you don't know?"

Tryal's face was blank.

Know her? How could he know her?

He had been asking that question himself since he made the promise.

Who was this little girl? Why was she worth risking his life over? Why was she so important?

"No," Tryal admitted.

Rasul was now just the smaller version, closer in size to a normal man, although still large and transparent. Fire light twisted through him. He smiled broadly, "Well then, this is a treat. Tryal, she is your mistress. She is the Great Mistress."

Tryal stared, his brow furrowed.

"Tryal, she is the Gatekeeper. She is Death."

Death.

Tryal's mind whirled with the news. He kneeled to look her in her eyes, both knees digging into the grain of the wood floor.

Door.

Hood. Door. Death. His friend.

Tears formed in his eyes. She had been gone. Missing. Death had been his friend and he thought her far away.

She had put herself in his hands from the beginning.

Hood stepped towards Tryal. He wrapped his arms tightly around her. In her ear, Tryal whispered, "Door, is this really you? Why didn't you tell me?"

Hood remained quiet, but Death's voice spoke in Tryal's head.

i am sorry

He pulled back and said, "Just sorry?"

yes you could not know, Hood closed her eyes, *i had always protected you i needed you to protect me i still do*

"Okay," Tryal replied. He then hugged Hood tightly and said, "I'll try."

Chapter Forty-Nine

FEEDING TIME

THE MIDNIGHT MAN, THE UNTHING, lapped his sharp tongue through the pool of blood at his feet. His lunatic mind was filled with dark hopes.

I'm coming for you. And when I find you, I will pull your limbs, bone from bone and splinter your bones in my teeth, sucking your marrow.

But he was still weak. And angry. What had that girl done? It was as if he had come unplugged, forcibly and unwillingly removed from this world, and left searching through the dark edges of existence, scraping for an opening back in. Yes, that was it—he had been ejected from this world, pushed, just a few feet into the nether curtain that surrounds this reality.

There, he had felt fear for the first time. In the darkness, he had begun to lose himself. Perhaps he had. Perhaps he had left part of his rolling spirit back in the great hugging ocean of black that feeds the shadows and nightmares of this world.

Yes! He hated them for introducing him to fear. He was the beast that prepared the way for the Final Destroyer. He was beyond fear. He had been beyond terror. Those stupid morsels had done the unthinkable!

His lips pulled tight from his snout and he yelled into the darkness, forcing all of his liquid rage into that howl.

Feel me coming! I want you to know I'm coming!

He needed more. He was hungry and he could feel the hunger pushing him. He had to eat. The hunger would drive him and direct him when he found his prey. He had let his hunger reign last time and that was his mistake. These were smart little creatures he was chasing, cunning and wise enough to push him out of this world. Must not let hunger be the conductor. Must be satiated and think clearly.

Scraps of people lay around him. Mrs. Holloway. Jody. Mitch. Reggie. He did not know their names, only their taste between his teeth. There was not enough to fill him. He would have to hunt before pursuing his ultimate prey. He scanned around. Hunt with its mind and not with its hunger.

He listened.

There. Behind the propane tank.

He splayed his claws and leaped over the large gray tank, surprising a small, screaming boy. His monstrous maw chewed through the child, blood splattering across the drifted snow.

More. One more.

He had not searched everywhere in the café. His paws crunched across the shards of glass. A fluorescent light flickered above and the light from inside the pie display still shone, reflected in the small shards. A thousand tiny stars across the dark floor.

He sniffed. So many dead. Decay already starting in. He would not scrounge from carcasses. It must be fresh. He slid his massive body behind the counter and brushed against the body of a waitress. She was bent across the cash register at a horrific angle, her spine snapped in two, blood draining from her back. Her eyes and face were blank—a body far into death. The Midnight Man paid the corpse no further heed.

A gurgling sound came from the waitress's mouth, blood bubbled across her lips. "Who are you? Why do you chase?"

The Midnight Man bent his head and snarled. "Is that you? Speaking through your collected souls?"

The woman's eyes did not move but she spoke again, "Why are you chasing me?"

The beast stepped back and said, "You only need to know that I am coming for you."

He bit the head of the waitress off and spat it across the rest room. The voice from the head spoke once more, muffled as it rolled across the floor, "Who?"

She's scared. Good.

Fully restored, the Midnight Man retraced the path of his prey through the field, slowing to smell the ground where Mr. Mu and Mr. Hu had dropped Vera. There was a pool of blood at the spot, cold and lifeless. He ran a shadowed finger across the frozen surface, causing it to boil with his touch. He resisted the urge to lap up the liquid.

"I am not a scavenger. Live prey only. Hunt with your mind."

His muscles crawled under ebony skin until he was back in the form of a man. He stood and followed the path of his quarry into the trees.

Chapter Fifty

STORIES BY THE FIREPLACE

TRYAL SAT ON THE GROUND HUGGING HOOD.
He spoke again, "Thank you. I understand."

Roland interrupted, "Am I the only one hearing Tryal talk to himself?"

Tryal replied, "It's okay. I understand why she didn't tell me."

Roland threw his arms in the air! "This is your ol' buddy, Death? Death. Where's the hood? The bone fingers? The big old knifey stick thing?" The old Roland was returning.

Michelle smiled and answered, "A scythe?"

Roland glanced at Michelle and said, "Ya, that thing. Seriously, the Grim Reaper is a little girl? Even with all the other weirdness, I can't be the only one who finds that tough to believe."

Michelle said, "I'm a bit taken back by it myself." As she said it, though, she knew it was a lie. She wasn't shocked. If she was truly honest, somewhere inside, she had known it. She was not sure how but she had.

Tryal answered Roland, "It's true."

Roland stood up, "Little brother, I don't get you. This innocent little girl we've all been risking our lives for is actually the great Grim Reaper. How are you okay with all this weirdness? This might be just a bit too much for me."

He turned, yelled and slammed his fist against the wall, "We lost mom for this!"

Tryal leaned back against the couch, releasing Hood. She took a step back to stand next to Michelle.

Michelle put her hand on Hood's shoulder. "For Hood. Yes."

"For the great bogeyman? We lost mom to protect some all-powerful creature hiding out in a little girl's body?"

Tryal said, "I don't think she's all-powerful right now. I think she's scared and vulnerable."

Rasul spoke, "I concur. When dawn comes, we will need to hurry. With her along, we must go even quicker."

Roland said, "What does Death have to be scared of?"

Hood's voice was soft in their minds.

there is much beyond me worlds beyond and after me

Roland shivered and then winced. "Don't do that."

They heard her voice again.

your mother is on the path she is far happier now

The anger that had been raging in Roland burst apart and he collapsed sobbing. Tryal crawled from the couch and wrapped his arms around his brother. The two cried and everyone stayed still, watching.

Tryal helped him back to the couch where Kaly sat. Roland pulled Tryal's messenger bag from his own shoulder and handed it to his brother. "Here. Found this."

Tryal flipped up the front flap. "Thanks." He placed it at his feet.

Michelle said, "You said 'go even quicker.' What did you mean?"

Rasul said, "Speed is a bit elusive. We must wait a bit more. But we can not miss our opportunity. The timing must be perfect. It must be the clock perfect tick of dawn before we can play doors."

"If you know of a place to keep Hood safe, I'll go," said Tryal.

"It is safe," said Rasul, "For her too, I believe."

Tryal said, "You're not sure? We only came here because everything pointed us to this lake to keep her safe."

Rasul rubbed his chin and moved back towards the fireplace. "Michelle, Roland—our friend Tryal knows little of your part since he was abducted. Can you fill him in?"

Michelle sat on the arm of the chair Marissa occupied. Marissa scooted over, patted the seat for Hood to join her. Hood plopped down and looked up at Michelle.

Michelle began, "You had blacked out and then everything went insane." They told the entire story: the Midnight Man, the Cinders help, Michelle's strange outburst that had staggered the creature, Kaly's appearance, the two men in the field, waking to discover their mother's body, the mass of Cinders surrounding Hood and their trek here.

Tryal looked at the window. "That thing was hunting Hood? It was hunting Door?"

Rasul nodded his head.

Tryal turned on the couch. "Kaly?"

Kaly hung her head and tugged at a loose bang.

Rasul continued, "You made a promise, correct?"

Tryal's mind raced back to the night in the hospital bed.

keep her safe

"Yes."

"Now is when you keep it," said Rasul.

Michelle pointed to the door, "Tryal, look outside. You're not the only one."

Tryal went to the window, his cast clopping along the ground. He pulled back the curtain to see the sea of red, fiery eyes. He jumped back.

"Lot of them, huh?" Michelle said.

He pulled back the curtain again and stared at the throng of shadow dogs, all looking towards the house. "There's so many." Tryal's face fogged the pane of glass. Over the last day, this scene had been his worst nightmare. He feared they'd get stuck somewhere and be surrounded by hundreds of the hellhounds.

And now it's a good thing?

Rasul said, "The skrikers are difficult to explain. They are said to be the guardians and huntsmen of Death herself."

Sudden realization slammed against Tryal. The hellhounds and he shared the same purpose. They had been there to keep Hood safe. They had each thought the other was the enemy.

But there was something more frightening coming for Hood. She wasn't safe now. They had reached Minatare, they had made peace with the Cinders, and she still wasn't safe. In fact, until now, she had not been in danger.

"Where are we going? What place is safe from things like that?" Tryal asked but didn't wait for an answer. "Kaly killed it."

Rasul waved his hand at Kaly, "Did you?"

Kaly did not answer. Instead, Michelle said, "I don't want to go anywhere else. This is so much more than what I had thought I was getting into."

Rasul turned his gaze to her, "Do not think that because you are not part of the original circle of friendship, you were not destined to be here. It is no accident. The only surprise in this fellowship is the young girl, and even that is beginning to make a certain sense to me now."

"No. Destiny can go get lost. I'm done." The wind at her back roared in response. It grew so loud that they each turned to look into the gray depths of the evening, expecting to see something there. The storm behind them raged.

"I would think that you would be most eager to go over."

"Keep talking," Michelle's confidence in the matters of the strange surprised Roland again. She was still holding back. Here they were, standing before a towering angel, a living, breathing, gleaming white, huge-darn-monster wings floating behind him. Only trumpets and a halo were missing. She spoke to him as if they were equals.

"Michelle. Where do you think the man who gave you the doom wolves is from? If you wish to hold him to his promise, you will need to find him."

Michelle's clenched hands dropped open, her posture caved and her lips folded back as her jaw opened wide and then closed slowly.

Rasul said, "Not in this world, that's assured."

Tears formed along the edges of her eyes. "How did you know about him?"

Rasul nodded at the fortune cookies on the walls, "I've received updates."

Kaly traced the figures carved in Tryal's back. "Where to?"

Rasul smiled at Kaly, "You know where."

"Home? The Blend?" Kaly said, sitting up.

"You are going to the Blend."

Roland spoke, "The Blend? That sounds like an ice cream store."

"Ha!" Rasul's laughter rumbled from him. They all felt a wash of warmth and sudden joy roll over them. "That's funny! You are going to the Blend. To the mix of all worlds," Rasul bent over to Tryal and poked a finger into his temple, "You've been there before, haven't you? You have the look." Rasul glanced around and met Roland's eyes and then Michelle's. He grimaced and spoke, "You've all stood at the threshold. Your eyes tell that story. But you didn't go in? Why not?"

The locket. He was referencing the locket. Tryal fished in his pocket and hauled it out, dangling it in front of him so they all could see. The light from the flames danced across its curves and it glowed like molten gold.

Rasul smiled and held out his hand for the locket. "So, they're still fishing with these?" He held it up and let it swing lazily on its edge, "To answer your question, I think this one is bound to you—it was made to find you and having done so, it will be able to always find you whenever it's removed from you. So, how did this one come to you?"

Tryal began, "We were leaving the aquarium ..."

Roland laughed, "You were running from the aquarium, like a little girl." He glanced at Marissa. "Um, no offense."

Tryal said, "I was running from the aquarium. I ran into Kaly and there was this old guy there."

He told of the two times they had accidentally used it. He left out its loss and reappearance, two things Tryal still was not sure about. Tryal finished, "It said 'between two worlds, I'll open another.' Is that the Blend? Is that where it was pulling us?"

Rasul nodded.

Roland waved his arms, "So the place we've tried to avoid is the place we have to go?" He glanced outside at the Cinders. "And the things we thought were chasing us were actually trying to protect us? Were we doing anything right?"

Tryal asked, "You said something about the doors swinging open slowly. That thing seems to work quickly. Can we use it to get wherever we're going?"

Rasul replied, "No. I cannot trust where it will open up. You see, this locket and many others before it were meant to find you. Specifically, you. But I don't know who sent it and their aim. This is an unknown, and probably quite deadly. Besides, they do not work by themselves."

Kaly interjected, "They require contact with a source of power."

Rasul turned the locket over and held it up, pointing to its back, "Do you see this symbol here?"

Tryal had stared at the symbol for hours. It was a claw that had a finger shaped like a demonic key. He had memorized it.

Rasul continued explaining, "That is *Galto*. It draws power from somewhere else—the user of the locket."

He pointed it at Tryal. "This mark is the same that the two carrion-crows carved on you. You are a source."

Roland interjected, "A source?"

Kaly spoke up, "The power is the flow. It's what fuels life."

Roland grinned. "Oh, like the Force, Obi-wan. Or do you mean magic? Are we magic, Mr. Jedi Master Rasul?"

"Maybe. But not all of you. Not her." He pointed his finger at Hood.

"Actually, she's more like a shield. It's likely her connection to Tryal is what has kept you hidden all these years." Rasul handed the locket back to Tryal, and he slipped the chain around his neck.

Kaly glared at the little girl. She had done a terrible job of protecting Tryal and this little girl, whom she had wanted out of the way, was actually the one who had been keeping him safe.

"And maybe not Kaly," Rasul continued. "I'm not sure. She's a daughter of the daughter of the great powers. A Meyjar. But, from what you've told me, she might once have been the source the locket fed from. Hmmm."

The angel continued to study Kaly, "There is no reason she couldn't be one. We've not been told that it had to be from this world. I think we just assumed."

Roland had had enough. Too many mysteries. Too many veiled references. "What are you talking about? One of what? What is going on? We just wanted to keep this little girl safe. And even that seems to be a complete weird mess in itself. Now we discover that the great Grim Reaper is wrapped in a tiny little girl body, complete with curls, cute button nose, and a flowered shirt. What is going on here? Kaly is the daughter of something called a May-jah?"

Rasul looked at Kaly, "You know much of this, but you haven't explained to them?"

Kaly gritted her teeth, "Since I have remembered, there's been no time! And it wasn't important. I'm supposed to keep Tryal safe. If possible, the others, although I didn't know that at first. I've failed on two of them." She stood up and stamped her foot. "Come on! We're wasting time now! If you have a way over, open it and let us go through!"

Rasul released a small growl in his throat, but the effect, slight as it was, was enough to cause Kaly to sit back down. She twirled her hair with her right hand. He spoke, "We can do nothing until dawn. The door is locked until then."

Rasul gazed hard at Kaly, "I'd like you to begin, young lady. Tell your part and tell what you know. I have been here many a year waiting. You might have fresher knowledge than me."

Kaly, barely audible, said, "No."

"And what rough beast, its hour come round at last,

Slouches towards Bethlehem to be born?"

—From *The Second Coming* by William Butler Yeats

CHAPTER FIFTY-ONE

THE PLAN

T RYAL STARED, BAFFLED. "Kaly, what is wrong with you?"

"She's not Kaly, stupid," said Roland.

"What do you mean?" Tryal asked. But he had already seen the change. It was more than her being more defiant. Something inside of her, deep inside of her, was different. It was as if a missing part of her had been switched on. Yet, she still did Kaly-like things. She played with her hair, twirling it when she was confused or unsure.

Kaly spoke, looking only at Tryal, "I'm still Kaly." He could hear the pleading in her voice. She desperately wanted him to believe that. "I'm just not who I told you I was."

Tryal started to speak and Rasul interrupted, "Perhaps that's the story you should tell."

"No," said Kaly. "Tryal, I need you to come with me when we go over to the Blend. Rasul's destination is right. But, I've been lying to you for years. I've been lying to everyone, including myself. I just don't think you'll follow me if you know everything."

"Why is it so important that I come with you?" asked Tryal.

Kaly pulled Tryal's jacket tight around her. She was still wearing it from the van.

Tryal was her purpose. The seidr witch of her clan said that he was to be her hunted. When she caught him, they would return the Colors to the worlds. Tryal would not understand that.

She said, "You're important Tryal. You're the one who can change everything. I don't know how." She lied.

"And I don't know why it's you." She lied again.

"But I know it's you. I can't return without you." That was, finally, a true statement. The Meyjar did not allow failure to return to the clan. Her mother's eyes burned at her in her memories. Those hopeful eyes.

Tryal shook his head, "You're a girl who lives across the street and shops at the mall. You like striped socks and those stupid fuzzy boots girls wear. I even know you only buy panties with pink little bows in front. You listen only to hip-hop music and you can't sing at all. You hate your mom's Monday night meatloaf but you love her Thursday night lasagna. You have A's in every class but history. Stop talking crazy! You're Kaly!"

Kaly kept her voice low and her eyes towards the carpet. "I like those things. I really do. But that's not my mom. That wasn't my dad. They were a family that moved in next to you. I carved a memory onto them. They thought I was theirs."

"What?" Tryal asked.

"And I thought I was theirs. I carved a memory cord into me. It worked. Sort of. I had moments where the real me kept peeking out."

Roland, "A cord?"

Kaly replied, "A sentence of power. Similar to what you would call a spell."

All eyes were on Tryal now, except Kaly's. Her hand went to her hair and she started twirling it.

"Stop that," shouted Tryal, "Are you faking that?"

Roland blinked.

Had the lamp in the house grown brighter? Were Tryal's eyes glowing?

Tryal said, "Kaly, can you please help me understand? Who are you?"

Rasul placed his large hand resting across Kaly's back. "I don't think you have any choice but to explain it all."

Kaly never moved her eyes from the ground as she told her story, "I was born in Trevenske Forest, 930 years after the Draining."

"Stop!" said Roland, "Dictionary, please. What is the Draining?"

Michelle raised her hand. "I know this one."

Rasul said, "Allow her to tell the story completely. However, let me fill in a few facts first. The Draining is important. In fact, it is why you are here. Roughly 70 years ago, most of the Colors, the flows of power, were drained from reality."

Kaly spoke, "It's been more than 70 years! It's been nearly a thousand since that day!"

Rasul continued, "Yes, quite correct. Nearly a thousand years have passed in Kaly's world, the Blend. However, time is different here. It's been slightly over seventy years here. But they've been devastating. This world doesn't run on the Colors the way the Blend does, but the loss has been noticed. This world is dying because of the dying of the Blend."

Roland said, "What is the Blend? Seriously, is there a Wikipedia article on this?"

Rasul said, "A what?"

Marissa's mousy voice squeaked, "Just keep talking. I like this. You haven't told me any of this before."

Rasul continued, "The next world over is properly named Treday e' Stratroich. It is also known as the Par'Daes. Or the Zwischen. It is commonly referred to as the Blend."

"The Blend, roughly speaking, is an in-between of worlds. It exists as the transition point between the many worlds of existence, between the world of the Princes and the Daevs. Between your world, between many other worlds.

There must be neutral ground and the Blend is it.

"The forgotten of your world, lost children, often fall through the cracks into the Blend. Many of the myths that persist in your world find their origin here. It is a pulsing, ebbing reality. The doors to there are growing fewer every day, and they are brief. True entry, like this house, requires enormous power. After the Draining, travel between the worlds slowed. Only the Princes could do so at will and without hindrance. Their power came from the White and was unaffected by the Draining. This house is of the White."

Michelle spoke, "So how did he do it?"

"Do what? Who is he?" Roland asked.

"The Draining. I don't know who. Whoever it was, how did he do it?" Michelle said.

Rasul said, "That has remained a secret. No one knows. There have been rumors but no answers."

Michelle spoke, "Why are we going there?"

"It is the safest place I know," said Rasul.

Roland said, "You said there's a war. How is that place safer?"

Rasul sighed, "Because there are many there who will fight for Kaly and Tryal," he nodded toward Hood, "And for her. The Blend is—"

Roland laughed, "Wait, maybe I'm slow here, but is the place we're going to the universe's butt-crack?"

Kaly jerked her head at him, "You are an idiot! The Blend is the home of gods. Your ancestors have worshipped its citizens," she stood and faced Roland. "The Blend is dying and it's my task to save it! Say another wrong thing and I will gut you, dear Roland!"

Roland froze unable to reply. Rasul spoke, "Young lady, calm yourself. If he is one of the embers, then you will do no such thing."

Kaly lowered herself back down and Rasul continued, "She is right, however. Your world used magic for games and grew bored with it. The Blend was a world that ran on the Colors. Everything was fueled by it. Magic was its currency, its industry, everything! And in one day, it all disappeared. The

Blend fell into chaos and has been unable to find its way out."

Michelle spoke, "Can I ask a question, and I mean no offense Kaly, but, why does this matter to us? Everyone in this world lives without magic or Color or whatever and they live fine."

Rasul continued, "I'm not too sure that they do. All worlds are linked to the Blend. Nonetheless, your world and the Blend are linked. In the chaos, tyrants seized power and domains. The High Throne was seized by a tyrant, and he used the chaos to cement his power. In the years since, the Blend had dried up as if it were a discarded snake skin."

Rasul nodded at Michelle, "You ask why it matters? Simply, as goes the Blend so goes your world. If it dies, your world dies with it."

Roland couldn't contain himself, "Oh, come on! Seriously, the end of the world as we know it?"

Rasul looked at Hood, "The presence of Death herself in flight is proof alone. Your gods are leaving you. If Death doesn't survive, there will be nothing between your world and the chaos beyond the worlds. Imagine—if Death dies, what would that mean?"

Roland said, "No more Death. Wouldn't that be a good thing?"

Rasul said, "Everything would unravel. Death is necessary."

Despite the chill that ran through her, Michelle wrapped both of her arms around Hood. She leaned forward and whispered in Hood's ear, "I won't leave you."

Hood reached her hand up and gripped Michelle's wrist and spoke in a hushed voice, "I know."

Rasul held his hand out to Kaly. "I've stolen the stage from you too long. Please, continue with your tale, young warrior."

Kaly continued, sitting back down, "My people . . ."

Roland interrupted, "Your people? Like a tribe? The Village People?" Kaly glared in his direction. She gripped her makeshift spear squeegee handle.

Tryal sighed. "Let her finish, Roland."

Kaly took a breath and continued, "We have sought to return the flow of Color to our world."

Kaly told her story. She told of the night she was born. She told the prophecy that was spoken by the seidr. She left out that Tryal was to be her companion. She told of her training and her life growing up. She told of leaving on the great hunt. She told of the great hunt.

After she had shared it all, she turned to Tryal, her eyes wide and pleading for understanding. He just stared back dumbfounded.

She whispered, "Tryal?"

Tryal spoke, "I just . . . That is just so bizarre." He shook his head frantically. "Ugh. I just can't comprehend it."

Roland spoke up, "Was this whole 'hunter' thing why you attacked our poor, defenseless nurse in the van?"

Kaly hated the question but welcomed the break from Tryal's awkward response. "I don't know. I guess. Ya. Actually, I don't remember. I heard you talking. I heard myself say 'Tryal's in danger' and then everything went black. I woke up with the seat belt around me. I think I was just frantic to protect Tryal. Maybe there was something more, but I don't remember it."

Rasul spoke, "If it means anything, you did well. You managed to bring four of the embers together. I was only able to find and protect one." He nodded in Marissa's direction. "No one else has done any better. With yourself and Michelle, you had six together at once. Remarkable, young lady!"

Marissa chirped up, "What?"

Kaly ignored her and said, "But I didn't do any of that. When I started living with the Zicks, Roland and Tryal were already living across the street. Together! A month later, Janae and Cody moved in a few blocks away. I didn't do a thing. They were all drawn to each other."

Rasul explained, "Yes, deep calls to deep."

In a squeaky voice, Roland said, "You're a wizard, Harry!"

Tryal ignored him. "Those two things that took me. What were they?"

Kaly glanced at his scarred back. The cuts were now pure white and stood up from his skin. They were definitely letters. Alephs. They had been cut to slave Tryal to those two monsters. But it wasn't finished. She could read them well enough to know that.

Rasul grew serious, "I'm not sure. They were knowledgeable and had the smell of the Red over them. Very cruel and powerful. You only survived by tricks and luck, Tryal. Don't hope to do that again. They should be avoided at all costs."

Michelle said, "I still don't understand why we all have to go anywhere."

"You are special. I cannot protect you on this side any longer. The two who took Tryal, that thing you faced back at the cafe—these are proof that whatever hid you before is no longer working. There are darker forces than those that will be pursuing you. There are those in the Blend that have been waiting for you Tryal, and for the rest of you. It'll be easier to hide you."

Michelle said, "But if it's bad as you say..."

"It is. Over here, you are a bright spot in a dark ocean," he turned to Hood, "Which is likely why she, in her constant search over this world, focused on you, Tryal. You were a light house and she couldn't avoid you. Which, in the end, was a good thing. We've all been searching for you. Well, not you specifically, but any of the embers. My apologies—I have forgotten much. Your friend hid you well, even though I'm not sure she meant to."

Roland motioned around, "Hide us? The Cinders are on our side now. Tryal got rid of those two buffoons. Kaly killed that thing once back at the cafe. Who is left to hide us from?"

Rasul replied, "Everyone. Many will seek you. Many are seeking you now, to kill you, to use you, to abuse you."

"Stop rhyming." said Roland.

Michelle smacked him, "Stop interrupting."

Rasul continued, "Thank you. Things have accelerated far faster than I anticipated. The hellhounds are still here because she is still here." He motioned at Hood. "If they are still protecting her, then something is likely on its way right now. She is still in danger. The thing Kaly killed at the cafe is beyond death. And I suspect a spear through its heart only slowed it down. Before it returns, you all should have left this world."

Michelle turned to Kaly. "You stopped that thing. You must know what it was."

Kaly said, "I have an idea."

Roland twirled his fingers, "And?"

"A Foundation Beast."

Roland said, "More, please."

Kaly sighed. "From what I was told, a Foundation Beast is one of the original creations that haunt the flow of time, guarding the order of the worlds. They are like the Cinders there, however, on the scale of the gods. But they were corrupted."

Marissa tapped Rasul's arm. "Wait. You didn't say 'we.'"

Rasul nodded, grasping the point of her statement, "I didn't. I am not going."

"I'm not going with them if you're not! I don't know them!" Marissa demanded.

"My girl, on this side, I have been honored to guard you. However, I can not travel there. To go there would be to leave here and to leave my post. I am appointed to this Gate and I must stay here."

Marissa buried her head his side again, sobbing, and said, "I'm not going!"

Rasul held her, "It is your choice, although I would encourage you to go with them now. Your destiny will take you to the Blend one day. If not now, later. At least you will have them as guides. Together, you'll do much better."

They held each other for awhile until Marissa's crying stopped. She stepped back from him. He smiled at her and placed his hand on her head, "You are a good friend, little Marissa."

Kaly stood. "Where is this Gate?"

Rasul waved his arm in the direction of the hallway beyond the dining room table. "There, in that room, behind the red curtain."

Tryal sat up, "Red curtain?" He remembered something about a red curtain. "Wait, something, um, 'behind the red cloth, is one more door back. Go there. She can only be safe there.' Ya, that's it."

Roland smacked Tryal. "What was that?"

"I was told to find the house with the red curtain."

"Who told you that?"

Tryal stammered, "Um, a dead lady. In the hospital."

Roland smacked him again. "Nothing can be normal with you, can it? And could you put on a shirt?"

Tryal reddened. His naked chest and torso became the focus of attention. Michelle giggled. Tryal fished in the bag at his feet and pulled out a red shirt. It fit snugly as he brought it over his head. The room erupted in laughter.

Tryal raised his hands, palms up. "What?"

Roland, laughing, pointed at Tryal's chest. Tryal glanced down to see Justin Bieber's face adorning the front of his shirt. "Ah, come on! Kaly, this is your sister's shirt."

Kaly reddened. "Uh, it's my shirt."

Roland roared. "How did he—" He couldn't finish.

Kaly leaned across Tryal to slap Roland.

Tryal explained, "I must've grabbed it when we went in her house to find clothes for Hood."

Kaly continued. "It must've been mixed up in her clothes."

Michelle waved her hands. "Wait, wait. Kaly, you have a Beiber shirt?"

"No. No. No." Kaly saw her shirt on Tryal. "Yes." She fell back against the couch, covered her eyes with her arm, and laughed.

Roland nudged Tryal. "You skinny little wierdo, you can fit in your girl-friend's shirt!"

Tryal glanced at Kaly. Was this Kaly still his girlfriend? He didn't know.

They all continued to laugh. Tryal put his arms in the air. "It's way better than being naked."

Roland said, "Ask Kaly that!"

More laughter erupted. All except Hood who stayed sitting next to Marissa, her face serene but still.

The laughter died. Roland wiggled his foot at Marissa. "Wait. Isn't it past her bedtime?"

Marissa smiled and kicked her feet. "I'm up past midnight every night. I've got insomnia." She pointed at Rasul. "He's the one you should be worried about. He has, um, narcolepsy."

Michelle said, "She has insomnia and you have narcolepsy. That's a bit odd, isn't it?"

Rasul gave a mock stretch, said, "Speaking of, I feel I'm growing tired and need to sleep before we attempt to open the Gate. We must wait until dawn before it will fully open."

"It's a door. Just open the door," said Roland

Rasul held his hands up. "It only opens when the worlds are thin. Time between times. It can only open when someone from the other side responds to my opening of it on this side. It's a delicate procedure."

Roland asked, "How often does that happen?"

"In three hundred years, it has only happened twice. Only very important matters would bring a Prince to this world through the Blend. Again, I grow tired. But before I do, you might be wondering why I have been waiting for you?"

Roland said, "You'd think on the weirdness scale that would definitely be up there, but right now, I hadn't even thought about it. You know what I would like to know? Why aren't there any bugs in this house?" Roland had sensed it since they walked in. The house was devoid of any insects. In a large house this old, far into the country, there should be thousands of spiders, worms, and other creepy-crawlies. It was empty. Not a single spider anywhere in the entire structure.

Rasul continued, "Fair enough. I think I can answer that but first you must know why this house exists. I have waited and I have slept in this house for several hundred years."

Tryal spoke, "I'm fifteen."

Rasul replied, "Truth be told, I was not waiting for you exactly. We knew that the embers would be kindled. But we weren't sure exactly when. We weren't sure where, either. We had a few clues. I believe that guessing within a few hundred years and a few miles isn't too bad considering we had the entire world and all of eternity to choose from. Nonetheless, you should know that some of us, despite our pledge for non-interference, have, um, developed opportunities to return the flow of Colors. While we cannot war for anyone outside of the prime realm, we have still felt that the current situation was not an accident, and thus we aim to—"

He was caught by a sound outside, and a chilling roar echoed through the hellhounds. A single harrowing howl reverberated in reply.

CHAPTER FIFTY-TWO

FANGS AND FEAR

WITH THE MOTION OF A HAWK, the Midnight Man dove at the nearest Cinders. He snatched a dark dog, bit at its neck, and pulled at the ethereal membranes in its skull, lifting it up, away and back into the trees.

The dog writhed within his clutching jaws. Teeth straining to clamp together, the Midnight Man, in the deep shadow of the trees, hidden from the revealing reflection of the moon, drank the beast's core—its life ebbed away from it and into the emptiness that was the Midnight Man. He shook the dying creature's shadow body and dropped it. It dissipated into the night.

Then one after another, the next Cinder in line struggled but lost its life as well as the Midnight Man descended upon them and pulled them into the trees. The green needles scattered patches of moonlight on the snow. The struggle between the ancient beast and the Cinders moved between the shadows. The sparse moonlight briefly revealed the smoking borders of the dogs as their souls were drained by the Midnight Man.

On the front porch of the house, Fujo went rigid, scanning his army. Six had been taken.

Inside the house, the curtains were pulled back. The army of Cinders amassed in the empty field. Tryal and Kaly stayed seated, and Hood stood alone in the room. Tryal kept his head down, his hands at his temples.

Through the hazy window, at first, Roland saw nothing. He focused in the direction of the dogs gaze. At the edge of the tree line, the Cinders were frantically attacking the nothingness of the night air. The moon waxed crescent, a pale porcelain blue cast across the snow field.

Roland turned to Tryal, "Hey, cheer up! Last time we didn't have an angel fighting on our side."

Marissa kicked Roland's foot. "He hates that word."

Michelle turned from the window, "You weren't listening."

Rasul added, "Roland, I'm sworn to not raise arms in your battle."

Roland's arms dropped, his mouth agape, "What good are you then?"

Rasul said, "I can open the Gate at dawn. That is all."

Roland's face grew red and he demanded, "When's that? Six in the morning?" He mocked a glance at his watch. "We're about to die and you're telling me the best you can do is open a door?"

"This was unexpected. I'm not sure I can do even that. The skrikers must delay him long enough for me to find a way to open that door or you will all die."

Ignoring Roland, Rasul floated through the floor in the direction of the hallway. He pulled back the red curtain. The room was bathed in a purple swirl of light. Behind the curtain was a mirror that reflected in a violet hue a great starry expanse.

A Gate to the Blend. He spoke again, "This might be quite difficult."

Roland yelled, "Open sesame."

Rasul, unperturbed, replied, "This is an old Gate to an old world and it opens quite slowly, if it opens at all."

Roland walked to the window. "Useless!"

Rasul continued, "Tryal, I could use your assistance."

Tryal sat up. "Yes?"

Rasul said, "Quiet your brother for me. He's become a distraction."

Tryal stood and glared at Roland and said, "Ya, that tends to happen. Roland, let the man work."

Roland sighed and pulled back the curtain again. He blinked and then pressed his face to the glass. He thought he saw, for just a moment, in a patch of moonlight, a man in bright yellow jacket standing far across the field, leaning against a tree. He blinked again. There was nothing but trees. He rubbed his eyes. "Gah! Need sleep! Six hours in two days. Not enough."

Marissa had moved up next to the Prince. "Rasul, I'm scared."

Rasul put his phantom arm around her. "I know."

"Like a roaring lion your adversary the devil prowls around,

looking for someone to devour."

—1 Peter 5:8 (ΠRSV)

CHAPTER FIFTY-THREE

FUJO'S ARMY

OUTSIDE, FUJO ROARED IN ANGER, flashing from one shadow patch to another, his body flowing into smoke and scarring the ground where he went. He was in front of the house and out near the trees and back within seconds. The dark dog bristled with anger. The Midnight Man wasn't seen and yet, one after another, the other Cinders were being snatched and destroyed. He could feel their souls leaving this world. His army was growing smaller.

Fujo disappeared and reappeared in the center of the other Cinders. With a bone-boiling sound, he roared across all of them. Each of the other Cinders backed away from the tree line, pushing into each other and closing in on the house.

Draw the circle smaller. Make the targets harder to find and hit. Make the Midnight Man come to them. He'd be seen, and when he was, he'd die.

Fujo had served his great mistress for eons. In the secret language of the shadow beasts, he was known as Iotnar, the Hastener, and, most recently, as Shestlene, the Fleet Hunter of Gods. And he protected her. Death.

To the Nords, she was called Hel, a name of which she was fond. Others called her Shiner and Counter of Years. The gods called her Fiery One and Gleamer. She was the mystery that was at the core of all existence. The great and eternal unanswerable question. The door past which no one can see.

Now, she was truly in danger, hunted by something far more dangerous than both of them. So Iotnar, the great beast Fujo, would fight.

He roared into the gray sky, the clouds shimmered and rolled back in the wake of his roar. He roared again. Children for miles around woke crying. He roared once more and across the world, children who normally slept soundlessly had nightmares. His huge claws scrabbled at the hard earth and he snorted through snuffling breath. His lean, dark form stretched. He stood fully on his haunches, and shook free the patterns this world had placed on him.

Each world had burdened him with their own metaphors of the supernatural. In some worlds, he and his kin were seen as great serpents. In others, they came as stalking spiders. In this world, they were known and feared as the hounds of death. Hellhounds. He shook free and became a raging mass of rolling shadow and flaming eyes, roaring as he charged.

Inside the house, they all heard Fujo's howling and all felt the pain of the beast's anger. Marissa sobbed. Hood stood alone in the room, frozen. Her pale features went white.

Michelle gazed at her.

She's scared. Death is actually scared.

Michelle glanced around at the others in the room. "She has arranged us. Her army, her hounds, her friends, even me. All of us to fight this thing." She pulled back the curtain, and felt a pang of guilt and desire as she stared at the mass of Cinders. She saw them prowling around the house, randomly baying at the sky. "I want to help them."

She felt a small hand grab hers and squeeze. Hood mouthed the words "So do I" and turned back to the window.

On the far edge of the Cinders, the snow spun, flowing up and around in a cyclone motion. In the center of that, the Midnight Man walked toward the house. He grew with each step. A Cinder launched at him and the Midnight Man turned at it, his jaw forming into that of the wolf, snatching the Cinder in mid-air. Instead of flinging its dry husk to the ground, the Midnight Man shimmered and yanked the body of the Cinder into his own, each smoky tendril dragged through the air into his own form.

One by one, each Cinder threw themselves at him and he snagged them, caught them, ripped them in their attack and pulled them into himself.

Fujo roared in anger, his bark commanding the Cinders to stop their attack and move beside him. The dogs trampled the ground in response.

There was now a mere hundred feet between him and the Midnight Man. The Midnight Man smiled and lowered his arms, their form shifting between the hands of a man and the sharp claws of a feral wolf.

The Midnight Man spoke, "Little cousin."

Fujo growled in response and took a step.

The Midnight Man spoke again, "You are to chase wayward raeth, not to fight an elder god for what is justly his. Stand aside."

Fujo growled again and stepped closer. He crouched against the ground, coiled to strike. His shoulders rose above his snarling head. His body had lost its definition as a wolf and stood like something that might have provided God himself inspiration for both wolf and lion: teeth-filled mouth, flowing dark mane, taut muscles under a thick, dark hide, all in a cloud of rolling shadow.

The Midnight Man ran at Fujo, his arms swept out wide to strike.

The two smashed against each other. Fujo swiped a large claw at the outstretched arm, ripping into what would've been skin and tendon in a mortal. Instead, a flume of smoke erupted, filling the already dark sky. Fujo turned and chomped hard on the Midnight Man's side, dragging him onto the snow with a thud. The Midnight Man's hissing snarl divulged injury. The two rolled and their bodies strobed as they fell into shadow—echoes of their form shadow-jumped into different dark patches between the forest and the house. The

Midnight Man raked a gnarled hand across Fujo's back. Fujo pulled off in agony.

The Midnight Man rolled away and stood up quickly. His skin cracked as fissures of flames etched out in splintered lines.

Again, the two lunged at each other, grappling in the snow. Fujo bit again and again, hurting the Midnight Man. Between bites, he barked. Several other Cinders came chasing after, all aiming to latch on to the Midnight Man and end his attack.

Fujo released his grip and drew back on his haunches. The Midnight Man stumbled. Fujo launched himself slamming his full weight into the beast again. He bit into his throat. Fujo constricted his bite as they thrashed through the trees, shattering them in their path. The Midnight Man dug both hands deep into Fujo's side and lengthened his claws once inside. The beast wasn't choking him as he had no need for air, but the beast's grip on his throat still hurt and it took all of his focus to stay locked on this reality and in this shape. Fujo was a powerful foe and the Midnight Man drew on Fujo's essence as he had done with the Cinders before him. He drank on Fujo. Fujo released his grip on the Midnight Man and pried himself away.

Fujo growled in anger and lunged anew. This time the Midnight Man was prepared and dropped his weight against the Cinder's thrust. Fujo bit hard on the Midnight Man's leg and yanked him along in his tumble. In seconds, the speed of their roll had landed them in the lake, splashing water in a torrent around them.

Fujo let go and relaunched at the Midnight Man.

And missed.

He crouched and growled. He had to win. This enemy has to die. This has to end. He could feel his strength ebbing away. That last trick had hurt him—the Midnight Man had done something to him. Yet again he lunged at his enemy.

Fujo had started to become one with the beast. He could hear the thing's dark, vicious thoughts, and its murderous dreams. In the darkest reaches of the Midnight Man's fears, Fujo had seen an even darker face, a face more fearful than anything he had ever encountered in his hunts. The Midnight Man was vicious but he was also enslaved to someone else.

They twisted. One snapped. The other dodged. Distinction between the two was lost in the shadows and the waves of night.

Inside, as the entire house rattled and creaked, it was filled with the sound of the two titans grappling outside.

CHAPTER FIFTY-FOUR

PAINTING
WITH KETCHUP

ROLAND MOVED TO THE WINDOW OPPOSITE of the fireplace. "I think they're down here."

Tryal peered out the window by the dining room table. "The Cinders are moving your way. I think they're trying to push him from the house."

Michelle shouted, "Rasul! What's the safest place in this house?"

Rasul continued to stand motionless in front of the large violet-mirrored door in the other room. He said, "The entire house is as safe as any other. If that monster gets past your Cinders, nothing here will stop him. We must hope they are enough."

Michelle cursed, "They are only delaying him. What do we do?"

"Wait for the door to open or for me to open the door," Rasul said.

Roland shouted form the other room, "Get the Gate open now!"

Rasul's voice stayed level. "This door swings open slowly . . ."

Roland said, "We've heard this. I want to live! Think! What can we do?"

Kaly stood up, "I need a pen or pencil."

Roland asked, "Writing a letter? The post office might be a bit slow for this one."

Kaly's voice grew stern and urgent, "Get me something to write with!"

Marissa spoke, her voice weak against the thundering of the fight outside, "Here's a pencil." She pulled a perfect number two yellow pencil from her backpack and handed it to Kaly.

Kaly started sketching on the ground but struggled to leave a mark. Her voice was full of frustration. "This isn't working. I need something darker. A marker. Paint? A crayon?"

Marissa replied, "I don't have anything. I have a paintbrush but no paints. I can't think of anything else."

Kaly said, "Anyone?"

No one replied.

Kaly turned to Marissa, "Uh, anything in the bathroom? Soap?"

"No."

"In the basement?"

"No, just old toys," replied Marissa.

"Upstairs?" Roland asked.

Rasul barked, "Don't go upstairs."

Everyone stopped what they were doing.

Roland said, "What's upstairs?"

Rasul said, "Don't go upstairs."

"Why?"

"Roland!" shouted Michelle, "Leave it alone."

Kaly returned to her focus, "Anything in the kitchen?"

"No, just all the leftover ketchup packets."

Kaly said, "How many ketchup packets?"

From the other room, Rasul actually laughed, "Many, many ketchup packets."

Kaly raced into the kitchen with Marissa and Roland following.

Michelle said, "Where?"

Marissa opened a cupboard and out poured ketchup packets, hot sauce packets, oriental mustard packets, and more restaurant sauce packets in every size and shape. She opened the next one and more came tumbling out.

Roland's mouth hung upon. "What the heck?"

Rasul answered, still in the next room, "I like fast food."

Marissa smiled, "And he hates throwing anything away. Says you never know when you'll need something."

Kaly smiled back, "He's brilliant. Quick, get these open!" She grabbed the packets and threw them on the front table. Packets slid across and rained onto the carpet.

The house shook again as a large boom rattled from outside. Michelle shouted out the play-by-play, "Fujo just tossed that thing back into the trees. They've moved away from the house."

Kaly said, "Good. Let's move. Is there a bowl?"

Marissa reached underneath the sink and pulled out a lime green Tupperware bowl and held it up for inspection.

Kaly said, "Perfect." She started ripping the ends off of the ketchup packets and squeezed the contents into the bowl. Roland and Marissa helped.

Kaly looked at Marissa, "We can do this! Where's that paintbrush?"

Marissa ran out and back in holding up a large paintbrush.

Kaly took it and the bowl of mixed sauces and went back into the living room. She said, "Get back from the windows. Go to Rasul. I need space." She bent over and started painting large symbols in bright ketchup red across the floor. They were tight and resembled some of the ones on Tryal's back.

Roland watched her for a minute and asked, "Are those spells?"

"Kinda. I'm hoping to slow him down. I don't think they'll stop him permanently—just give us some more time."

"Do you think that'll actually work?"

Kaly said, "It did at the truck stop."

Roland said, "You got him by surprise. And you stabbed him. In the heart. From behind."

Still wildly painting the symbols along the edge of the wall and floor,

Kaly said, "The stabbing had nothing to do with it. I don't think any of the carvings I know could actually stop something like him but he is still vulnerable to a focused flow of Color."

She started on the east wall of the house, doubling around.

She spoke loudly, "Oh, and these will also keep us from leaving. So, umm, we're stuck here until Prince Rasul gets us out. Once I've done the outer wall, I'm going to double up and carve the border of the room."

Marissa's eyes grew wide and fearful as she asked, "We're going to be stuck in that room? But what if we have to pee?"

They all stopped. There was honest concern in her face.

Michelle spoke, "It'll be okay. Go now. Quickly."

Marissa raced away shouting, "Okay!"

Kaly held out her paintbrush to Roland, "I need more ketchup. I still have to do the inside of this room."

Michelle looked down at the symbols as Kaly continued to paint. She spoke, "It's odd, but I feel like I can almost read them. What do they say?"

Kaly continued writing and said, "It's a repeating cord in some places. I'm actually carving a few different cords. They should reinforce each other. If not, I'm hoping that if some don't work against that thing, the others will."

Michelle bent down and placed her hand on Kaly's shoulder, "How much do you know about all this? What you told us in the church about meeting Tryal wasn't true. Why is that thing chasing Hood?"

Kaly replied, "Why are you involved? Why did we show up on your doorstop and pull you into this?"

Michelle could not think of a response.

Kaly said, "I don't know either. That wasn't part of the plan. You weren't part of the plan."

Michelle replied, her voice sarcastic, "There's a plan?"

They met each other's gaze. Kaly said, "No. Not really."

Michelle smiled, "Do you think this will work?" She motioned to the symbols.

Kaly said, "I think so."

The house rocked again as the fight once again drew closer. They all stumbled and struggled to gain their footing except for Rasul and Hood. Roland's foot slipped underneath him and he landed on his butt.

Roland interrupted, "Ugh! It's starting to smell like a collision between McDonald's and Khan's Chinese Buffet in here."

Tryal, ignoring Roland's joke, asked, "Don't finish the edge."

Kaly stopped and asked, her voice indignant, "What? You mean don't finish the warding? Why?"

Tryal replied, "Because Marissa is still in the bathroom."

Kaly replied, "Oh. Ya. Okay." She stood back up and went to the kitchen, "I need to get a bit more ketchup anyway. Almost out."

A large vibration slammed the house. The glass in the front window facing the porch shattered in. The boards creaked and the snarl of the beasts outside echoed through the room.

Hood wrapped herself around Michelle's side and began to shake.

"What the . . ." said Roland.

"Marissa!" said Rasul, turning from the door and looking for her.

"She's in the bathroom."

"Marissa," shouted Michelle.

Between snarls outside, a faint voice squeaked, "I'm hurrying."

"Marissa! Get in here now!"

Marissa shouted back, "I'm not done yet!"

"She's not done yet," said Roland, waving his hands in the air.

Michelle said, "Kaly, are you ready to finish those symbols? We need to be fast."

Kaly replied, "Get her in here and I'll seal up the full carving."

Several of them shouted at Marissa again but without response. The house shook and one of the Cinders smashed through the front door, its body flattening as if hitting an invisible wall and it turned to smoke and dissipated into the night air.

Tryal shouted, "What just happened?"

Kaly replied, "The carvings work. At least on the Cinders. Hopefully, on that monster out there too."

Michelle was shocked. "Macbeth and Puck are outside. They can't get back in."

Roland said, "Ah, crap! Seriously, Kaly? You couldn't have warned her?"

Kaly held her hands out to Michelle, "I'm sorry! I didn't remember. They'll be fine. They're Cinders. Not German shepherds."

Michelle walked to the window. "They're my Cinders."

As if called, three dark dogs appeared next to her. Puck, Macbeth and the smaller one that had accompanied Fujo pushed close to Hood and Michelle. Michelle wrapped her arms around the creatures.

Kaly coughed behind her.

Michelle glanced back, "Sorry. Overreacted."

Kaly grinned, "It's cool."

Chapter Fifty-Five

SPLIT PERSONALITY

THE MIDNIGHT MAN STRUGGLED TO FOCUS and grew tired. The hellhounds, at least in a pack, were far more cunning and determined than anything he had ever fought. They continued to leap at him from all sides, ripping into his sides. He healed fast but even that drained him. He had to break this pack up. All he could see was the dogs. He was no longer in control.

Fujo rocketed at him again and clamped down hard on the Midnight Man's neck. The two slammed against the ground. Fujo tightened his bite and dug into the beast's flesh. He continued to bite until he felt that vampiric pull from the Midnight Man. He released. Hurt the monster but don't feed him. It was a difficult strategy.

Contact must be sharp. Painful but brief.

The Midnight Man siphoned off of them every time they made contact. Fujo saw several of his companions were limping—the pull had been too much and they were at the end. Their numbers were dwindling. This was now a battle of time. Can they hurt him and outlast him? Or would he ultimately drain them all?

The battle was in and out of the icy water and moving closer to the house. Cinders had been thrown against it, smashing through its walls. Fujo pulled back and stared at the house. The last Cinder had completely evanesced as he struck the house. That was disturbing.

Fujo observed closer, past the crumbling porch and he saw the flowing Color along the inner wall. His Mistress's companions had carved wards into the house. That was good and it was bad. It would protect them but it meant that he and his dogs had another threat in this battle.

He pulled back and roared his anger into the night—this battle didn't need anything else. It was brimmed. Now they had to move the battle away from the house completely. He launched again at the Midnight Man but didn't fasten onto the creature. He dropped back and launched again. Over and over, driving the Midnight Man away from the house. His companion dogs had seen what he was doing and they were following suit. One after another, they heaved themselves against the Midnight Man, pushing him away from the house and in the direction of the forest edge.

Once they reached the edge, Fujo stopped his volley, growling commands to his army. They stopped and reinitiated their attack from all angles. They needed to keep him here. Back in the forest, the Midnight Man was far too able to pick them off one-by-one and hide from their attacks. Keep him here, in the open, far from the house and away from the trees. He would have to be finished here.

Fujo launched again but the Midnight Man met his attack, more coincidence than strategy. Fujo fell back and the Midnight Man gripped tight onto his neck, drinking on the Cinder's soul, slight at first, but slowly ebbing the dog into himself. Fujo flailed, his skin erupted in flames, spouting huge arcs of fire against the snow-filled night sky. The Midnight Man fed, his hands locked on Fujo, draining Fujo's twisting shadow form, extracting every bit of his soul, wrenching his memories free and slurping on each one.

He contorted his head, turning to the side and transforming into the wolf form, biting hard into Fujo's neck. As he sunk his teeth in, tendrils of fire leapt from the openings and stained the ground—blood of fire sprayed against the snow like a torrent of sparks, a child's firework sparkler in the dark sky, each drip melting the white earth.

Fujo was dying. The wounds had plunged deep. The other Cinders stepped back, confused. Fujo was caught in the grip of the Midnight Man, his soul draining and his body spraying across the ground.

The Midnight Man shook the body in his mouth. Fujo lashed out and drew his claws across the Midnight Man's face, ripping into his hide. The Midnight Man flung Fujo's body to the ground. His limbs flayed out and he sprawled into a snow bank. His eyes strained to stay open.

He had failed.

The great Shestlene had fallen in battle. The other hellhounds bayed into the snow-crested night sky, singing to their leader. His eyes shut and he drifted from this world with a single thought on his mind.

Mistress.

The Midnight Man scanned the remaining army. The other dogs were distracted.

Plunge now to the house. Crash through it and secure your prize.

He streaked over and around the dazed Cinders towards the house. The beasts chased him across the ground scarred from their battle. The Midnight Man was a flurry of ice and shadow spinning in a widening gyre. The dogs behind him flung fiery sparks in their wake.

The Midnight Man vaulted against the side wall. The inside wall erupted in a cloud of plaster. He pulled back, fuming and flailing—the house had burned him. How had that happened? He charged again. Inside, the far north side exploded into a blossom of wooden shards and splinters.

The impact with the house had felt like a rushing burn, a pain the Midnight Man had never experienced. His left flank blistered and bubbled. Before he could puzzle through what was happening, the Cinders were on him, biting and snapping. The mass rolled into the porch's supports, shattering them. The structure crashed down upon them. A canopy of wood erupted into flame as the sparks from the Cinder's eyes caught hold of the dry wood.

Two Cinders rolled into Kaly's barrier. They howled as their forms sizzled into nothingness. The weight kept pushing and the closest one scrambled to get away. With a hiss, he dissipated into the air. The other limped away, his right side completely gone. He writhed in the snow, baying a vicious howl, and, as the thin moon fell behind a cloud, melted into shadow and out of this world.

───────

"Marissa!" shouted Kaly, pounding on the bathroom door.

"I'm almost done! I'm sorry! I'm sorry!" she said.

Roland said, "Just say it. She's taking a dump."

Michelle held Hood close, kneeling. "Roland!"

Roland said, "Little girls do that too."

Kaly replied, "Roland, stop it."

Roland responded, "You're missing the point. She's a kid taking a crap. You're not going to hurry that by yelling at her and pounding on the door. Shut up, let her squeeze it out, and she'll be out here faster for it."

Neither Kaly nor Michelle replied. Roland was right. Rushing Marissa wasn't going to help. Roland grinned.

"Rasul, how's it going?" asked Roland.

Rasul took a few seconds to reply, "I am not sure." In front of him, the large mirrored doors reflected the images of those in the room overlaid on a sea of stars spinning in the dark expanse. Their own reflections were sobering—dirty clothes and dirty faces, tired and pale.

Roland squinted. "You're not sure?"

Rasul said, "The opening of the Gate requires a response from the other side. If we open this Gate and it does not open on the other side, then we will find ourselves floating in the gulf between worlds. It is an old world. Time moves different there. The doors open very slowly."

Roland said, "As long as it's not here, I'm happy. We'll figure out the rest when we get there."

Rasul responded, "No! You don't understand what the gulf is. It is the darkness that spawns the worst horrors of your world. I will not venture there. It is the abode of everything cast out from the White. Abhorrent souls, caco-daemons, creatures that make that thing out there look like a poodle." Rasul turned back to the mirror, waving his hand along its edges, tracing his finger through various circles and forms. "No. We will not go through unless we have a response from the other side. Wait. It will come."

Roland said, "Fine! If you've sent the message, why don't you go out there and kill that thing while you're waiting?"

Tryal spoke, "Roland! He's explained he can't. He's made an oath."

Roland said, "Seriously?" He turned to Rasul, "You're . . . You're supposed to be an angel! That thing is going to kill us! It's just a promise."

Rasul stared into the rolling reflection of the mirror. "No."

Roland slammed his hand against the wall, "Blast!"

The other Cinders held the Midnight Man to the ground, biting and clawing at him, in short bursts, avoiding his vampiric pull. Underneath their mass, the Midnight Man struggled to gain coherence. Torn open, his soul leaked into the air. He had come this far, escaped from his pit, pursued Death across the world to here, defeated their Cinders captain, and now he was dying mere feet from his prey.

Shrieking, his claws shot out and snapped two of the beasts' necks. He could no longer fight this fight alone. If he was to bleed out his soul, he'd bleed *into* them. They writhed as his dark, twisted dreams flooded into their minds, snapping at their own identities, smothering them in a miserable, hated darkness. He poured himself into the beasts.

One Cinder bit at the Midnight Man's arm, trying to release his companion. The two beasts held in his hands stopped struggling. All held still.

The one in his left hand snarled, followed by the other. He dropped them into the snowpack, baring their teeth and growling. Their flesh flowed shadow but the shards of fire that flowed underneath each Cinder's skin, seeping through in cracks, was gone. The fire was replaced with a cold, frozen darkness.

The Midnight Man chortled a tired laugh. He clawed against the snow and brought himself up on his feet.

He was now three. And he could do it again. Oh, he was not full anymore. He was spread across three bodies. His strength was split by three. But his turned dogs could distract their former companions and now he would destroy his prey. Death's end had come. He screeched and his two turned-dogs surged at their former brothers. The others joined the fight, and soon, the tangle of Cinders moved away from the Midnight Man and the house.

Through the collapsed wall, the Midnight Man peered at the people inside. He couldn't see his prey, but he knew she was there. As he moved up to the hole in the house, he carefully held up his hand and pushed closer. A sharp bolt raced through his him and he jerked back. There was Color here, a barrier, but it was less painful than before. Was it weakening?

"The monster was in that darkness . . .

Its eyes glowed amber, alive with stupid cunning."

—From *Cujo* by Stephen King

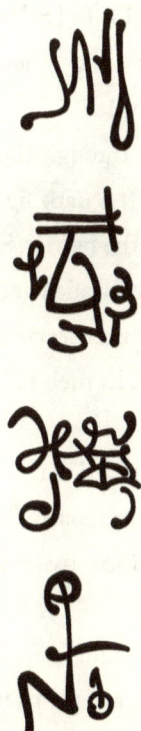

CHAPTER FIFTY-SIX

DEATH OF ANGELS

ROLAND SLAPPED THE WALL BEHIND HIM. "We've got a problem! That thing is here and none of those Cinders are doing anything about it."

"What?" Michelle glanced through the space and peered at the empty hole in the side of the house. The dark figure of the Midnight Man stood there, his hand pressed against the barrier. She screamed.

"Come on! Shake it off!" She wailed at the Cinders on the snowy ground outside. Three of them perked their ears in her direction. They tilted their heads and came up to their feet. In their failing strength, they snapped at the Midnight Man's heels.

Roland stammered, "They heard you."

Michelle's hand was over her mouth. "Uh."

The Midnight Man's livid form twisted into the beast and struck out at the two on his right flank.

Michelle shouted, "No! Hit him from the other side."

The third obeyed, although her words were a din against the roar of the battle outside. It thrashed in a ruthless attempt to hurt the monster towering above.

The Midnight Man was surprised. Its jaws missed the two it aimed at and the blow from the third sent it staggering.

"Now. Hit it now!"

All three responded to the directions and in a synchronized leap, piled against it. The grappling mass of beasts rolled out of her view.

"No!" She raced to a window. "I can't see them!"

Roland's eyes were wide. "Those things were obeying you."

"I know. I know."

The Midnight Man was dragged by the inertia across the ground, his hind claws failing to catch hold. The snow fell sideways. The world beyond the house was momentarily obscured by the white of the tumbling snow.

The Midnight Man twisted his body and let the momentum of the roll pull two of the Cinders underneath him. He clamped his thousand teeth across the head of one and stabbed his fore claw into the body of the other. They went limp in the Midnight Man's grasp.

The third had caught itself on a small stone. It drew back as the monster descended on it in a hellish fury. The gleeless jaws ripped through it and it fell into shadow bits across the snow.

The Midnight Man bounded around the house and lurched to the entrance, landing with a dull thump that shook the house again.

The Midnight Man pressed his hand against the barrier, felt the terrible stab of pain, but did not pull back this time. Instead, he pressed into it. It did not move but the pain was bearable—it was horrendous, but he could endure. He placed his other hand up, both burning against the current of Color. He felt the so slight, nearly imperceptible move of the wall. Not much but it had moved as he strained against the torture.

"Rasul! That thing's trying to get in!" screamed Michelle.

"Everyone, close to me. Put the skrikers between us and him. Quickly now," Rasul said.

Michelle commanded the three Cinders still in the house to move to the front room.

Kaly said, "Wait. Isn't Marissa still in the bathroom?"

The barrier budged.

It had moved. No, it had shrunk. Considerably.

This hurt him but he was close. His prey was near. It would all be over soon. The Midnight Man steeled himself against the burning force and shoved harder, his legs formed into claws and dug deep into the wood planks and the dirt along the collapsed porch.

The house hummed. The sound was small and rippled across every wall and floor. As the hum grew, the invisible barrier glowed red. The Midnight Man snarled.

The hum ceased. Pop! And boom! The house rattled. Plaster and paper burst as a cloud into the house. Like the snow outside, white specks of paper, the fortune cookie sheets, fell in lazy paths through the air, oblivious to the torrent outside.

Kaly, kneeling against the the doorframe of the Gate room, a paintbrush in one hand and her squeegee in the other, read one of the fortunes as it fluttered to the ground. "'A good time to finish up old tasks.'" She spoke the words out loud. Another gently descended next to it. "'Change is happening in your life. Go with the flow.'"

The Cinders in the field felt the boom echo across the plain. They had made a mistake. They had ignored the Midnight Man. Leaving his two turned-dogs behind, several of Fujo's Cinders raced back to the house.

The Midnight Man was carried by the rushing implosion and fell against the couch, smashing down the wall along the staircases. The barrier was down. He shifted fully into his wolf form and scrambled up, wobbling in his speed to reach Death. He fell against the wall of the hallway leading to the back room. His hulking frame rammed through the wall, broke through and tumbled into the bathroom. He crouched, all snarls and smoke. His hunger clawed back into his mind.

Mine. Now.

Marissa screamed as the wall above the bathtub fell down and the largest, darkest creature she had ever seen fell in with it. She looked into its eyes and it glared back with a startling sternness.

She screamed again and clambered for the door handle. It wouldn't open. Her hands were still wet from rinsing—she hadn't had time to dry them. She couldn't get a grip. Her panicked yelps shot through the house.

Rasul turned from the mirror doors at her scream. "Marissa!" In an instant, he covered the gap between himself and the raging Midnight Man, passing unhindered through the wall that separated the bathroom and the Gate room. His hands tightened into fists and as they formed, he gripped a suddenly appearing and massive scimitar, its edge caked with dried blood and scorch marks. He held it firmly in front of the Midnight Man.

Rasul's voice was as thunder. "Stay. Do not touch the girl."

The Midnight Man growled a hoarse sound. His eyes locked on Hood and a dark string of drool fell from his lips.

Michelle shouted, "Marissa!"

The Midnight Man moved his foot forward and was greeted by Rasul's deeply curved blade as the he swung it hard into the monster's chest. The room filled with inky smoke erupting from the Midnight Man's wound. The beast crouched back and roared. It struck out at the sink, shattering it with his touch. Rasul moved Marissa to what had been the bathroom door frame, struggling to get her out of the confined space.

Rasul spoke again, "I will not attack. I will defend. Leave the girl alone."

The Midnight Man howled, beckoning his turned-dogs to find him.

"Rasul, kill him!" shouted Roland.

"No," responded Rasul.

The Midnight Man tilted his head and questioned, "No?"

"Leave." said Rasul.

"You're one of *them*," hissed the Midnight Man. He took a deliberate step towards Rasul. His toe tapped before settling solidly onto the floor. "You might beat on me but you won't remove me, will you?" He raised a foot and took another hesitant step and spoke words in a strange language. "*Kaerth ski trupe, lea toore.*"

Rasul didn't answer. The Midnight Man grinned mirthlessly and took another step, moving close, his chilled breath blowing across Rasul's face. He spoke, "Strike again. Your child is within a bite's distance. Strike and break your oath."

Rasul held his sword firm but stepped towards the beast, moving Marissa behind him and into the Gate room. She fell into Michelle's arms, shaking in terror.

The beast lunged after her, shouldering Rasul into the corner, missing her ankle as she fell into the room. Kaly drew a single swipe with her ketchup-dipped brush. The beast grunted and pushed its snout at the prey a foot away. It smacked into another barrier. A gravelly sound pushed from its throat. Marissa screamed again and pushed Michelle on the ground in a frantic attempt to escape the monster.

Rasul was a blur of light, bringing the broad blade across the Midnight Man's side. With another hand, he picked up the monster and flung it back, through the dangling shower curtain and wall, into the kitchen. The cabinets split and the shattering of plates and cups filled the room.

Rasul charged the beast. Roland's heart raced and he jumped to the doorframe. "Woah." The strange overlay image of the nesting doll angel appeared. Rasul was the large, gigantic translucent man they first saw; his torso intersecting the floor and his head touching the ceiling. In that image, in simultaneous motion, was the man-sized Rasul they had seen in the Gate room moments before. Beyond those two images was a third. It intersected wall and ceiling. Roland saw huge, rolling limbs. Harsh wings against the dullness of reality spread out above him, moving into view and out as they flapped. A large, tree-trunk tail swiped the room they were in, passing through each of them. It reminded him of some story-book dragon he had scene as a kid. "Wow."

The two turned-dogs crossed the threshold of the house and were met by Macbeth and Puck. Just a few feet away, Rasul fell upon the scrambling hulking body of the Midnight Man. The cascading forms of Rasul moved in a disturbing synchronicity. He struck the beast and three fists impacted the creature's body.

The Midnight Man contorted his form and twisted into the man, sliding out from Rasul's giant grasp. Rasul swung his blade and the edge flew above the beast's head. Rasul swung again and the scimitar struck its hide again. Sticky oil-like smoke poured from the wound and the Midnight Man went livid as the pain shot through his side.

He quivered and stomped forward, his back legs were the powerful haunches of the beast. Rasul misjudged and went to grapple what he anticipated to be the creature's large frame. The Midnight Man moved between the grip and into Rasul's unguarded torso. His fingers dug into Rasul's side, pushing under his rib line. He flashed a cruel smile and furrowed his brow. The Midnight Man's fingers thrust out as spear-long blades, shooting through Rasul's abdomen, all of his abdomens, and piercing out his back. Rasul went rigid, dropping his blade to the ground where it rattled in a momentary stillness.

Marissa, still held by Michelle, had watched this from the doorway. Tryal and Roland stood next to her. She howled, "Rasul!"

Hood stood watching. Rasul was dying against the beast's blades.

He is frightened. He was right to be. He will not survive. She saw his death.

The moment would come when she would open the Door for him.

That was always the greatest confusion about her—she was simply the Door Holder. She could not always prevent a person's passing from this world. Death arrived when the time was right. And after she held the Door open for him, he would have to pass through, and he would be different. She could occasionally find them past the Door but it was rare. She had caught glimpses as to where each person's Path would take them, but she never knew for certain. It was as much a mystery to her as it was to them.

She could delay his death, though. She had to give them time. Her options were limited. The hallway was blocked. The room was square and the walls still secure. Kaly's barrier in the room still stood strong. Behind her, the Gate to the Blend was opening slowly. But there was the window, open to the snowy field outside.

Michelle felt a tug on her arm. Hood leaned up to whisper and Michelle bent her head. Instead of words, Hood breathed deeply in Michelle's face, a cold stream of air that caused her to shiver. Michelle started to ask but turned as she hear Marissa scream again, "Rasul!"

Light poured from the long gouges in Rasul's back. He spasmed and went limp, falling into the Midnight Man's arms. Sharp tendrils of light twisted from Rasul's wounds. The Midnight Man staggered against the weight of the body and fell back to the far wall. He coughed and hacked, spraying Rasul's lifeless face with black, sizzling droplets. He flung the bright body to the ground. It ignored the ground and the entire form, all three nesting doll forms fell through the floor and out of sight, taking their bright light with them.

The Midnight Man teetered forward, over the heap of the bathroom, and swiped at the wall, tearing a long stripe open. He peered through, his dark coal eyes leering at the room's occupants. He coughed again. Rasul had hurt him. He gargled out the words, "Has my prey fled?"

Tryal spun around, "Where's Hood?" Michelle glimpsed behind her. Hood wasn't there.

The Midnight Man scanned through the room and there, through a small angle of the window, he saw a flash of red. The girl ran across the field into the corn. The Midnight Man spun, dark tendrils warped and it was down on its haunches, baring its thousand needles of teeth. It trailed drool as it charged back through the hole in the front wall, tearing across the rubble and snow chasing after Hood.

"Hood!" Tryal struggled to crawl through the window.

"Stop!" Kaly pulled on his shirt. "Stay here!"

"No! She won't make it!"

"She's Death!"

"She's a little girl, too." Tryal kicked at her. "Let go!"

"The thing chasing her is a monster. She should've stayed here." Kaly grabbed his leg and yanked.

"What are you saying? Let her face it alone? What's happened to you?" His legs flailed in the air. He kicked at her again and fell through the window.

Roland snapped, "That thing just killed an angel!"

Kaly watched Tryal roll through the snow, come to his feet and hobble after. "No! No. No. No."

Roland leaned out the window. "Tryal!"

Kaly scrubbed her ketchup markings from the door, picking up her squeegee spear, and bolted out through the hallway.

CHAPTER FIFTY-SEVEN

PROPHECY UNWOUND

HOOD FELT THE CORN STALKS CLOSE TIGHTLY around her. The leaves slapped across her face as she ran, reddening her skin. It had gone unharvested years past and had grown wild in the remaining years. The stalks were dead and empty in the snow. She could see only a dim, carved path between the stalks from the light of the moon. Behind her, the roar of the wind carried the stampeding footsteps of the Midnight Man. She ran faster.

This will all be over soon.

The Midnight Man huffed, white clouds of steam billowing from his nostrils, in his race after Hood. *Hela. Her name is Hela. The children had called her Hood.* Her red cloak had disappeared into the corn across the field. He fell into full wolf form and plunged into the cornstalks, smashing them down in his wake. The wheezing monster flattened the corn with each step. He was a monster without control—frantic in his search for his prey. His limbs hurt, he bled his dark essence from cuts across his hide. The battle with the Prince had almost destroyed him. He staggered as he ran with imprecise balance.

End this.

Hood darted between the rows, racing away from the pounding noises of the beast.

The Midnight Man jumped across rows hoping to surprise her. There! He caught a glimpse of red and leaped, only to slide through wet cornstalks and the turned dirt. Wet soil flew up in his wake.

Maybe he was being too loud. She could run from the noise. She couldn't see him but she could hear him. He crept low, turned back into the form of a man. He glanced back at the house. Across the snow and under the moonlight, he could see two figures running this way. They would be a few minutes, sloshing through the snow—long enough for him to catch and eliminate her. No matter that there was no difference between his forms, he always felt he acted more unbridled when he was as a beast on its four limbs, his haunches perched above his sinewy back. Less precise. More determined. Now was the time for cunning and precision.

Hood sprinted. She could not hear the monster behind her. She turned towards of the house. A few shingles of its roof peeked above the top of the corn. The stalks filled all angles of the view. She was deep in the cornfield and he was in here with her, with nothing between her and him but the dried frozen stalks. No Tryal. No Rasul. No Michelle. Just her, a little girl, and the big bad monster.

She took careful steps, alert for his black form. She would not be able to see him. He was not reflective—he was simply the darkness of nothingness. Looking around did her no good. He could be anywhere. This thing was her end. Her millenia of walking the worlds was ending.

no

i don't want to

get out of the corn

go somewhere else anywhere he isn't

But that would do no good. you can't escape your end when it has come for you. Maybe it was time. All the pieces were ready. She shut her eyes and saw a room of books, Tryal in the center, but not alone.

they are ready they are here

Maybe confrontation was upon her. Maybe her end was here.

She stopped. Her tiny voice alone in the emptiness of the rows, "I'm here!"

The Midnight Man's head jerked. There! His charred, fuming form slid across the corn rows and peered down each one after another. His tongue lapped out and rubbed across his thousand sharp teeth. Her red jacket was a beacon. Smoky drool slipped across his lips.

Finally.

She was here and there was nothing in the way. He took a slow step forward.

She straightened her body up. "Stop."

He did not.

Hood spoke again, "You are one of the first. Formed at the time of the Foundation. I'm a daughter of the White. Before you move further, you are obligated to announce yourself and your purpose."

His front claw wriggled into the cold soil. She was right. There is a protocol to these things. Not that he had to obey it, but it was proper. He had always shared before devouring gods in the past.

Fine. Let's do this properly. "You stand in my way."

Hood narrowed her eyes attempting to discern him from the darkness. "You could move me aside with no effort."

The Midnight Man said, "No. I am to remove you."

"Today is not that destined day."

"This world and all its inhabitants were promised me."

"But not today. You are empty."

"What do you mean?"

"Devour all of us, devour this world, and you will still be empty. The grave has not surrendered its dead. I have not surrendered mine. Body and soul are forbidden you. You are empty, desolate, hollow. The Pit of Hell is empty today and will be until I choose to give up all in my care. That is not today. You should not be here. You can not cross over. Go back, you dumb beast."

He coughed and hacked into the soil, flinging dark spittle. He laughed, howled, "Dumb beast? Dragging Princes and Daevs back to the Pit?" Coughing and hacking, he took another step. "No. Not some beast from the shadows that hunts for sport."

Hood stepped back and covered her mouth with her hand.

The Midnight Man chuckled, "Speak of me if you know me. Tell them who it is they face, dear Hela."

They? Does he mean Tryal? "You are greedy." She shut her eyes and searched. "Unthing. Midnight Man. A new beast—a prowling maw."

"Listening to rumors on the wind?" He shuddered and slackened, his front quarters dropping into the ground. Hurt! End this soon!

The world was silent as the girl that was Death searched. Her body grew, a slight stretching but she was now two inches taller than she had been. She opened her eyes. "You are known by many names but today and yesterday you have lived under an old banner. You are Häti. You are Crom Dubh, the dark and crooked man. The bent man. Cruach. But you are early. You come as a man but you should not walk this world as a man yet."

"All true. If you know me, why do you stand against me?"

"I am Death."

He snorted. "Hela! Stop using cheap titles!"

"Death is my station! Do you know yours?"

His lips pulled back in a gruesome grin. "Station? I prepare the way for the one to come. The Final One to come."

Hood took a step, slipped, staggered and caught herself before falling. "No."

The beast moved forward, deliberate in its pace, no longer pausing between steps. "He is coming. On my heels is the Final One, the Great One on the Final Day, the Mouth that will close on all Creation." It shook its flowing mane. "And you stand in his way. You stand in my father's way, dear aunt!"

Hood inched backwards. "You aim to bring my brother to this world?" She grew taller again, an inch. She screamed, "Are you a fool? Do you not know who he is? What his coming means?" She stared and lowered her voice as she recited, "He is the final destruction, the abyss, the devourer, the maw and center and end of time." She balled her fists and wailed, tears flowing down her reddened cheeks, the snow twisting around her. "You plot to bring Hell itself to earth? His arrival starts the clock! You are a fool!"

"This world is dried up. It is kindling for the fire. Hell grows bright and all that keeps him locked away is you. Remove you and he is free . . . free to remake this world in his image."

She stood, sweating and shaking, but silent. The winds howled and the snow churned in sharp rivulets above them.

Her silence gave him the approval he needed. He charged, splashing dirt and snow under his claws, and was upon her in seconds, leaping, mouth open wide to devour her.

She whimpered as he neared, but, like a gust of air, she moved away and he tumbled forward under the force of his own momentum. His snout plowed into the soil.

He bent and twisted. There! He lurched again. Once more, she slid past him. She danced between his charges. How can she dodge me? He aimed and moved faster on his next lunge. In the instance before they would impact, she slipped to the side. He roared in his rage.

Tryal drug his cast through the snow. He could see the arching back of the beast, a shaggy creature above the corn stalks. Had it cornered Hood? Tryal's heart pounded in his chest. He had to get to Hood! Why had she run out? What was she trying to do?

Tryal heard their voices. Were they talking? What were they saying? He had heard him call her Hela. Was she lying?

The beast lunged at Hood again but she moved out of his way like water breaking across rocks. Where he grazed her, her touch on his hide was acid, a coursing iciness chased by nothing. He felt something missing from himself, as if a part of him had been erased. He might destroy her but he would be consumed in the process.

The Midnight Man lunged at Hood. Tryal shouted, "Hood!"

She turned in his direction, her eyes off of her attacker. The beast twisted, lurched, and snagged her between his jaws. His teeth sunk into her small flesh.

He had her! She squawked as the monster wrenched into her. She was being torn apart. He convulsed as stabbing pain pierced him. He shuddered but held tighter. She was nearly impossible to hold onto. His mind was in agony as he tried to draw her in. She screamed and writhed in his grasp, like a floundering fish in the mouth of a grizzly.

Tryal saw Hood's glance and then saw the beast bite her. Everything stopped. The world shuddered. A ripple of darkness moved past him as if the universe had blinked.

His eyes stung and he howled. The cut marks across Tryal's skin glimmered. A wave of warmth rolled over him, through him. What was torn flesh became crisp outlines as the carved shapes in his flesh moved. The glow reflected against the falling snow painting an aura in the air swirling around him. His path lit before his feet. But he took no notice of the light. He only saw Hood writhing between the monster's jaws. The Midnight Man was hurting the one he had promised to help. It was his fault.

His feet struck the ground. He raced forward and his image blurred. Like an arrow, he struck the beast, grabbing its hulking body with both arms. His life vacuumed out of him. The markings in his skin flashed, strobed and a white glow engulfed everything around him until the pulling sensation stopped. He screamed. He heard his friend's names pour out. "Janae! Cody! Rasul! Mom!"

Tryal howled at the beast, and with both arms gripping the monster's side, he pushed. The entire field was like the surface of a star bathed in white boiling light. The Midnight Man seethed as a surge of lightning stabbed through his side. Layers of flesh and shadow and soul peeled open under the pain—unimaginable, scarring pain ripping through him. The beast's jaw slacked and Hood tumbled to the ground with a soft thud.

Tryal beat against him again. Harsh light exploded like a bomb and lit everything in the field like the noonday sun. The explosion hit the Midnight Man and sent him rocketing down the corn row. He tumbled out of the field and rolled end over end uncontrollably down into the water.

Tryal slumped to his knees. No, Hood is still not safe. He turned towards her. Her body lay limp on the broken stalks of corn. He slid over to her. He was already crying and his breath came in huge, gasping pulls. "Sorry. I'm sorry," he whispered as he bent down to pick her up. He cradled her in his arms and pulled tight.

Her eyes were closed and, at his touch, she shook. At first small spasms, and then she seized sharply. Another wrenching jerk followed this and she rested limply against him. He felt her shallow breath against his skin and stood to carry her out of the field, his feet sloshing in the melted snow.

"*There are things known and there are things unknown
and in between are the doors.*"

—Jim Morrison

CHAPTER FIFTY-EIGHT

A CANDLE IN THE DARKNESS

TRYAL, WALKED OUT OF THE CORNFIELD, a nimbus of light around him like a candle in the darkness. Snow spun in the air above him but it melted beneath his steps. Kaly and Roland stood at the edge of the field, their mouths open, rubbing their eyes. Tryal walked between them, carrying the limp body of Hood.

Roland struggled with his words, "What the heck just happened? I'm almost blind here."

Tryal glanced back to the lake. A mound crested out of the water. It was the Midnight Man, its flesh smoldering on the bank. Tryal said, "I don't know. I was running and then there was Light. I don't know where it came from."

Kaly stepped close. Her hand hovered over his back. She traced a cut with her finger. The marks still glowed. "You did that."

Tryal stopped. She gingerly pulled her hand back.

Kaly muttered, "A supernova in skin."

Roland interjected, "What happened to your clothes?"

Tryal looked down. He had no shirt and no pants. Something else was missing. His cast. Everything on him was gone, burned off from the light, except for the locket hanging across his neck. He glanced at Kaly and at Michelle and felt his cheeks burn with embarrassment.

Roland took off his own jacket. "Aren't you freezing?"

As odd as it was, he wasn't the least bit cold. He was surprised by that fact and muttered an unbelieving, "No." Roland laid the jacket on Tryal's shoulders.

He glanced back once more at the heap that had been his enemy. Wait. Had he seen it move?

No. That was wrong.

The body just lay there. Tryal turned back to the remains of the house. "Quick, Hood's hurt."

Kaly glanced down as she heard a small splash when she stepped forward. The snow underneath Tryal's feet still turning to water. She asked, "You sure you're okay, Tryal? You're melting the snow. And you're glowing." His nakedness had caused them all to avoid looking at him. Now that they were walking, it was difficult to ignore that he was the source of the light. The lines that had been the cuts across his back and chest still shone a faint white and lit the ground. Along the cut's edges, the lines were settling into a light blue, reminiscent of tattoo ink.

He glanced at Kaly and she shuddered. His green eyes flashed with a brilliance she'd never seen, sharp and radiating. She shut her eyes and turned away, falling in step behind him.

Tryal's thoughts drifted to the little girl cradled in his arms.

Death itself was about to die and it was his fault. His friend was about to die. Was she Death? What had that thing meant?

Roland understood Tryal's silence. "Let's get Hood to the house, get Tryal some clothes, and we can get this figured out in there." They walked up the snow-covered hill, three figures sharp against a white lamp in the black night, leaving a path of melted snow behind them.

CHAPTER FIFTY-NINE

OPENING THE GATE

SINKING INTO THE BROWN WATER of Lake Minatare, the Midnight Man struggled to draw his thoughts into order. Pain ripped through his skull. The tingling unreality that had started eating him from the inside when he bit the girl was still ravaging him, shredding every sinew and synapse. Then there was what the boy had done.

What had the boy done? He had never been hit that hard. His right haunch, where the boy touched him, was numb. The girl was still alive. She still existed.

Hela.

He hadn't done his part. He was designed for this one moment and he had failed. Of all things, that thought hurt the most. He had failed his lord.

So, he moved. He must stand. He pushed against the ground with his one strong leg and collapsed again. He was still in the shape of the beast. To flow into a man would exhaust what little strength he had remaining. This form was larger and failing him. Instead of standing, he pushed with his back left leg and rolled forward to face the house. All was dark except for a single white light moving atop the snow.

The boy! Kill him. Rend him. Snap into his bones, slurp his blood. The boy!

Tryal reached the edge of the house, still carrying Hood, and flanked by Kaly and Roland. He stopped abruptly when he heard Door's internal whisper in his mind.

he is coming

Tryal scanned across the hill and through the cornfield. The body of the beast was gone from the bank of the lake. Where was he? On its far edge, between the lifeless rows of corn, the mass that was the Midnight Man shambled towards them. The thing was barely on one foot at a time but it was moving.

"Why'd you stop?" asked Kaly.

Tryal whispered to himself, "He's coming."

They followed Tryal's eyes to see the massive Unthing slide-stagger across the ground. It would gain its footing, collapse with a thud, and stood back up to repeat the process.

Roland touched Tryal's back, his hand warmed by the glowing cuts. "Tryal, just do what you did to before."

Tryal closed his eyes. "I don't know what I did."

Roland pointed back at the destruction that had been the cornfield. "You hit it with some of that white flashy crap. Look, you're still melting the snow and glowing. Just focus and punch that guy all Dragon Ball-Z style."

Tryal said, "I don't know how to do what I did. I was angry. He was hurting Hood. All I could think about was getting to her. It just happened."

"Then get in the house!" Roland slapped Tryal's back.

They shuffled up the edge of the stairs that weren't shattered and stepped carefully through the smashed entrance. Inside, near the splintered table, sat Michelle on the ground leaning against a wall with her eyes closed. Marissa lay curled in a ball at Michelle's feet, sobbing. Near them were two of the dark dogs, the small Cinder and Macbeth. Puck was nowhere to be soon.

Michelle muttered, her eyes still shut, "What happened?"

Kaly said, "That beast had Hood, but Tryal hit it and there was a flash of light and when we could all see, Tryal was like this, carrying Hood." The field in front of the house was empty. "Where are the rest of the Cinders?"

Michelle looked up. "When that flash of light went off, we couldn't see anything. When we opened our eyes, all of the ones outside the house were gone. Macbeth and that small Cinder were all that was left. Marissa was looking out the window watching you."

Roland interrupted, "Fine, cool. That thing is still alive and Wonderman here doesn't think he can do his 'skin supernova' thing again." He looked out the window and could see the body of the Midnight Man at the edge of the cornfield, starting to move up the snow. He had hoped it was over.

The Midnight Man wrestled against his fear. The terror that he had infected others with for so long was now devouring him. He would not survive another attack if the boy chose to hit him again. But he could not let his lord down. Máni must be ended tonight. Destiny promised that he would kill her, his lord and the end for this world would come, only to birth a new world in their own dark image. His hour had come round at least. His slow thighs moved and slouched up the hill.

Michelle took Hood's body from Tryal, "Let me. You get dressed."

Roland shouted, "That thing is moving faster. It's halfway across the field!" He slammed his fist against the wall, "Blast! Did Rasul get the door open?"

Kaly walked to the mirror and held her hand against it, "No. I don't think there was a response from the other side."

Michelle replied, "Maybe we can stop him in his state."

Tryal stood there, eyes locked on the barely breathing Hood cradled in Michelle's arms. "I'm sorry." He lifted his head. "Hood won't make another fight."

Kaly inspected the markings she had painted on the ground, "Most of the Cinders have left and my carvings seem to be done. There's nothing between him and us now."

From outside, growing rough grunts of the beast rumbled as it rounded the house. His glowing eyes were visible from where they stood. His flesh was like boiling tar—as tortured faces clawed their attempted escape from him only to fall back into the abyss, stretching along his skin. The beast was here.

Hood's shy face was obscured by the locket dangling from Tryal's neck, the only thing to survive the flash. The Midnight Man was dragging himself up the shattered stairs. Tryal snatched up his Doctor Strange bag, still resting against the couch, and yelled in the direction of the beast. "No!"

The Midnight Man gargled and spat. "Mine."

Tryal yanked the locket from his neck, snapping the chain, sending small links clinking off the wall. He grabbed Roland's forearm. Roland was already shaking his head in anticipating. Tryal nodded. "Do you trust me?"

Roland replied, "Barely."

Tryal shouted, "Grab them and follow me." He started to walk across the room and down the hall, into the Gate room, stepping over the planks and rubble of collapsed walls. "Everyone in here now."

Marissa sniffed. "What's he doing?"

The beast coughed and hacked as he shuffled across the shattered porch and across the threshold into the house. His distorted breathing was loud and harsh.

Tryal focused on the beast and commanded them, "Get in here, now! All of you. Marisssa."

Marissa didn't move.

Tryal spoke and the lines across his back flared brightly again, "Please."

The beast snorted in the front room, coughing a poor growl, dragging itself across the splinters that had been the table. "Boy!" it coughed.

Kaly looked between the beast and Tryal and said nothing. Tryal shouted, his lines glowing, "Now! Kaly, grab her."

Kaly grabbed Marissa while keeping an eye on the beast. Marissa kicked. She slapped Kaly and cried, "Rasul."

Kaly handed her to Roland, "Here. Carry this."

Roland wrapped his arms around Marissa's shaking, fuming body and her pounding fists smacked against his chest. "It's okay. You'll be safe." He braced himself for what he knew was coming.

The Midnight Man saw Hood in Michelle's arms and growled, "No more! Give me my prey!" The smallest Cinder, the one that had shadowed Fujo, and the only one of Fujo's army to stay, turned around and stood in the crumbled doorway facing across from the fierce Midnight Man. It barked once and followed it with a howl. The snow falling around twirled around the beast, forming an icy shield which moved across the front edge of the house. The small Cinder yelped again. The wind roared outside, moving fast across the lake, slamming against the house. The wind broke through the open gaps in the ruined house and slammed against the Midnight Man, stopping him in his approach. The wind buffeted the beast.

Kaly pointed at the small Cinder, "Is that—?"

The Midnight Man bellowed. He pushed forward with all of his might and took a step into the wind. Each step was a colossal effort but he gained against the wind conjured by the Cinder. The winds circling around him churned with the intensity of a tornado.

Tryal answered by pulling the locket over his head, flipping it open, and slamming it against the mirrored surface of the Gate. A twisting spray of water poured out of the door, faster than ever before.

Roland shouted, "What the heck is happening?"

Kaly replied, "This is a Gate. You just used a gate on the Gate." The wind cycloned through the house, deafening the rest of her sentence. The sound was greeted by a second rush of water pouring from the Gate, submerging the entire room.

As a wave slammed against them, the voice from the deep called again, "Come over."

Before Tryal ducked his head into the water, he yelled, "Grab hold!" He gasped as the surge washed over him and a burst of yellow flew past. The others followed him through.

The water coursed down the hall, dragging the Midnight Man out of the hallway. It carried him far out of the house, into the rubble that had been the porch. Claws feebly struggled under the torrent and then were seen no more.

The house windows broke as water coursed out of every opening, through the holes in the walls, the broken doors. The house supports, already stressed from the earlier battle, collapsed under the weight of the water. The house snapped and slid into the lake. An ancient creation, clothed in hewn timber, sunk under the sad waves of Lake Minatare.

"Come away, O human child!

To the waters and the wild . . ."

—From *The Stolen Child* by William Butler Yeats

CHAPTER Sixty

THE OTHER SIDE

THE AGE OF WIND: THE 19TH OF RAL, YEAR 1880 OF THE TNOSCANN

WITH ONE HAND TRYAL GRASPED MICHELLE, still cradling Hood, with the other he held tightly to Roland. The iciness of the water had reached to his bones and shred through the fabric of his muscle on its way back out. He somersaulted within his skull as his inner balance cavorted. The yank of the moving bodies next to him supplied only a momentary absolute. The chain of the six of them rushed upwards to the surface—he hoped.

Above him, now just a few feet away, Tryal saw light. It speckled as bugs floating through a cracked door and beaded out of view as he moved near. He felt locked in a refrigerator, its light shut off as the door has closed. He scrambled through the cave-like darkness with an unnerving panic. They were going to die. He was going to die. He was dying. His lungs pounded and his legs had already begun to cramp.

The voice had said "Come over."

He wondered, *Come over and die?*

He was inches from the light and rushing upwards, when his face smacked against something hard. In desperation, he let loose of Roland and pushed against the surface. It was cold, colder than the water, and smooth. He could see the moon, blurred and refracted, above him. What was this? Why couldn't he push through?

He kicked the surface with both of his legs. His lungs rippled with sharp pains. This was it. His eyes bulged and ached.

Inches away? Tryal could see the outlines of shapes above the water and knew that he was at the surface. He pushed, then realized he had let go of Roland. Through the dark waters, his hands thrashed, searching for his brother.

No. You moron. You had to do one simple thing right and you failed at that. You let go. YOU LET GO.

He railed at himself. *YOU ARE DYING.*

If he could just go a few more inches. Just a few more inches.

Ice.

They were under the ice. They were trapped in a lake, in the ocean, under an icy surface. Surely, he had fallen into a dream and would awake to find that they had simply upped the dosage of painkillers in his I.V. and everything since the hospital had been a dream. The sun would set and then rise. He'd be in school next Monday, being ignored by the other kids in class. There would be no ice, because there was no ice. This was a dream.

Kaly floated near him, her body limp in the water. He pulled Kaly closer with his free hand. Was she alive? Her face moved close to his and her eyes were blank. She was unconscious and swallowing water. She could already be dead.

Why? How could this have happened? Nothing made sense and he fell into pure terror.

His body jerked. He was being pulled. Michelle still cradled Hood in her arms—she was in danger and now he had plunged her into icy water.

Instead of moving back to the surface, he was being pulled under, down into the darkness. He pushed away. His legs ignored him. They were numb from the cold. Unresponsive. With his one free hand, Tryal pulled to the surface, but it was useless. Whatever had him was strong and not about to let go. He consented and found himself fading as he did so.

Michelle's grip on Hood went lax and the girl's body floated away. With his last waking thought, Tryal reached out and pulled Hood close, wrapping his arm around her and put an arm tight to Kaly's wrist. If he was going to die, it was with her, his closest friend next to his side.

Something felt weird about that. A hushed thought rose in his mind, Was this the real Kaly? Why had he thought that? Of course it was Kaly. Kaly was Kaly.

The creeping, numbing darkness washed over him and he drifted into unconsciousness.

"Wake up!"

He heard someone screaming. Pain rushed through his chest. Again.

He gasped and sucked in a rush of air. He could breathe. He gagged. Water sputtered out of his throat and he rolled over, coughing furiously. His eyes were filled with red pinpricks and he couldn't focus.

"Are you alright?" It was Michelle's voice.

"Say something stupid." The next voice was Roland's.

"I'm," cough, cough "Oo," more coughing followed, "Kay." The words pained him to say. He was going to live. Tryal shivered.

Something was wrong. He shouldn't just be sitting here. He should be panicking, trying to fix something. What was it? He quivered. The cold rushed through him and he felt as if he would never be warm again. Shivers flowed like waves from his feet to his head and back down.

"Blankets. We need something warm. Quickly."

"How's Hood?" he heard Roland say. Hood? What was wrong with Hood? Wait—that's it—Hood! He struggled to stand up but the dizziness pushed him back down.

Michelle responded, "She's still out. She's cold. Her lips are blue and she's barely breathing. She's shaking and something is happening."

"What?" asked Roland.

Michelle's voice continued, "I don't know. But unless my eyes are playing tricks on me, she's flickering."

Tryal's words were garbled, "What?"

Michelle said, "It's like she's there for a second or two then starts to disappear." Michelle's voice firmed, "Roland, get them out of their clothes, now!"

Tryal rolled over again and dropped his head. It slammed against the rocky surface below him. He puked. Cold sea water belched out of him. His stomach knotted. He heaved again.

"What'd you do?" shouted Roland, oddly panicked. Sobbing. Roland was crying—what was happening? Everything was upside down.

"I'm okay. I hit my head." Tryal realized he was calmer than he expected. At least he was alive. Everything was minor at this point.

He forced his eyes open again. The taste of salt was still on his lips and it burned his eyes. Wherever they were, it was dark. There was a faded light several feet away and he could make out stark figures against it. There was Roland, standing over a body on the ground.

Tryal shivered again. His body shook. He was still naked and the scars across his skin glowed a faint light. Tryal saw the edge of the water splashing against the rocks they were on.

Marissa's voice sounded small in the large room, "I want Rasul."

No one answered her for several minutes. Marissa whimpered, a sound that built into a full sob. Michelle spoke, "I'm sure he's alright. He's an angel."

Marissa sobbed. "He hates being called that!"

Michelle held her close, "It'll be okay. Come on, we need to help the others. Here, you can help me. We have to get her warm. She's younger than you."

Marissa tried to hold the tears back and replied with a timid "Okay."

Who was younger than Marissa? Tryal thought. Then the daze left him. He jumped to his feet, slipping on the wet stones, caught his balance and sprinted to them.

"I can't touch her." Marissa tried to grab hold of Hood only to have her hands pass right through her. Just like before the fireplace. She was leaving them the same way she had appeared.

She was leaving.

She was dying.

Tears ran down Tryal's cheeks. He had failed.

She spasmed and her image strobed—there one moment, and, in flashes, disappearing the next.

Michelle asked, "What's going on with her?"

Tryal's knees rubbed against the stone floor. He didn't reply. He had no answer to her.

To Hood, he spoke in a small voice, "Hood? Door? What do we do?" Even now, when she was the one he tried to help, he turned to her for answers. He glanced at her bite and cringed at the tears in her flesh. Staring at her torn side, it seemed as there were bodies superimposed on each other. There was her body, now older than the little girl he first met, bleeding and ripped open by the monster, by the big bad wolf. There was a second body, a body made of her shadow, full and real but also shredded and bleeding its own darkness into the world. It was the same darkness he saw bleed from Michelle when Kaly attacked her.

He now sobbed and paralyzed at his inability to help her.

Hood opened her eyes and spoke. The words were indistinct, small sounds, and Tryal leaned in to hear her better. She did not repeat what she had said. Tryal filled the silence with his small muttering of "I'm sorry. I'm sorry."

my tryal

Hood spoke again, a bit louder, but not vocally. He heard her in his mind, they all heard her in their minds.

i love you tryal

He sobbed harder at this and spoke loudly, "I love you. I'm sorry. I didn't keep my promise."

yes you did

Hood's eyes slowly moved to Michelle.

you are me and it is now yours

Hood closed her eyes. Door's eyes.

Michelle replied, "What is mine? What do you mean?"

Hood opened her eyes partly, looking at Tryal.

stay with her

Tryal pressed his face against Hood. She was there and then she wasn't. He felt the interminable bursts of warmth against his skin when she was fully there and the sharp chill of the air when she wasn't. He wept, frustrated at his inability to cradle her, to hold her. She was truly leaving him.

you awoke between death

Then she was gone. And she didn't appear again.

Tryal collapsed on the floor. Michelle crumpled against him, one hand across his shaking back. No one mentioned that the marks across his body were glowing a dull red.

As they sat there, Michelle's mind filled with images and memories that were not her own.

From person to person, she saw each of their moments of death. She glanced back to Tryal and saw nothing. He was the only one who brought no images to her mind. She could not see his death. She closed her eyes and saw the distinct glow of each of them as they surrounded her. Roland shimmered a deep violet. But Tryal did not glow.

In her mind's eye, it was as if he was not there—an emptiness where he should have been. Is this why Hood chased after him? Is this why Death became his friend? Was he the only one that was truly a mystery to Death?

Chapter Sixty-One

DARK SHAPES

A SCREAM WOKE TRYAL.

Kaly. Kaly had screamed. Kaly was awake.

He sat up and saw her racing out of the room, her pounding feet fading in the distance. Tryal wasn't sure how long they had been asleep but there was sunlight reaching into the stone room.

"What the heck was that?" asked Roland.

Tryal was up and through the door. "No idea."

Behind them, Marissa squeaked, "Wait. Don't leave me." Michelle turned around and grabbed her hand.

Tryal was running as hard as he could and still struggled to catch up to her. The corridor was circular and nothing but granite stones and walls, dank and dreary. The walls were hung with the same tapestries and torches as the room they had stayed in. Each tapestry was filled with the strange images. There were fantastic creatures riding on clouds, battling against each other. Some showed strange cosmic images of a solar system gone mad. One after another the images grew wilder. All around the edges, there were symbols much like the ones carved on his chest.

Kaly stood looking up at a wooden, twisting staircase.

Out of breath, Roland asked, "What is broken in your head?"

Behind them, Michelle slowed her pace. An image flashed across her sight. She saw the others standing on a wooden deck, all in chains, locked at the wrists. She stared down at her own hands. She held a set of large keys. The vision faded. Her five companions stood there, in their makeshift toga gowns, arguing with Kaly.

Kaly took a step up. "Stay close."

"What's up there? What are you freaked out about?" Tryal grabbed her arm. "We thought we had lost you."

Kaly said, "I don't know." She shook loose his grasp and took a few mores steps. "We're in the Blend. Everywhere is dangerous."

She ascended the steps, each stair cautiously reached.

Roland spoke up, "Again, warrior princess, what do you think is up there?"

Kaly whirled around, her face taut with rage. She whispered through gritted teeth, "I have no idea. Anything could be here. Anything! That's why I'm trying not to draw attention to us."

Roland pushed past her, and through cupped hands, shouted up the stairs, "Hey, it's us. We're . . . Um . . ."

He looked back at Kaly and asked, "What was that name you made up for us?"

Tryal answered, "The young gods."

"Ya. That was it." He turned around and shouted again up the staircase, "We're the young gods. And we're coming up." Roland started to to turn and ask for everyone's approval but he remembered and shouted, "And don't kill us!" He turned, a smile stretched across his face.

Kaly cursed, spit on the ground, and marched past him. "Loser," she breathed in his face as she walked past.

Roland looked at Tryal, shrugged his shoulders, and said, "Classy."

Tryal glared, stifling a smile. "Better hope you're right and not her. Otherwise, you just killed us all."

Roland slapped Tryal's back, "Hey, watch it. Getting us killed is your job."

Kaly spun around again, fire in her eyes, "Shut up now."

She moved up the stairs carefully and they followed. Tryal spoke, "Kaly?"

Kaly turned but did not answer. Her face was irritated that anyone else had spoken.

Tryal ignored her obvious anger and asked, "Why go up? Shouldn't we be trying to find our way out? Maybe search in the other direction of the hall?"

She turned around marching back up the stairs. "I need to find out where we are."

The passage brightened considerably until ahead of them they could see the sharp white light of the sun shining through a door. The stones glimmered like molten gold.

"Go slowly, please." Kaly whispered.

She inched out of the door, covering her eyes against the glare. They all followed her out onto a small stone ledge.

Roland spoke, "Holy … Okay, freaks, where are we? Did any of your little friends tell you about this? Kaly?"

Kaly didn't reply. No one replied.

Tryal asked, "Kaly, where are we?"

Kaly turned around and around, looking out past the edge. They were at the precipice of a stone tower. Stretching beyond the tower, the blue of crashing waves shimmered. An endless ocean. No islands, no ships, and no land.

They were in a solitary tower standing in the ocean. The clouds rolled far across the horizon and flashes of lightning danced between the billows. In the blue-green of the sky, the faint edges of three moons carved their bright arcs—two quite large, and the third one half their size.

"Are those moons?"

Kaly muttered, "Yes, three of them." A cold breeze blew across them, filling their lungs with the sharp smell of sea water.

Marissa looked up. "Wow."

"There's more?" asked Tryal.

Kaly spoke, "Nineteen." The word "nineteen" ended in a mutter.

Roland spoke, "You okay?"

Kaly replied, "We're in the Blend but I don't where we are. This is wrong." She stared down the side of the tower. "All wrong."

Tryal spoke, "Well, how many oceans or large lakes are there? We're in the middle of one of those."

Roland smiled, "At least nothing with fangs is chasing us."

Michelle shivered.

Kaly turned slowly and replied, "That's just it. The oceans are of the Black! That thing was of the Black. 'Never go to the oceans. Stay far from the oceans, far from the Black, and keep your soul.'"

Michelle stayed silent. She saw something else. She saw death on the waves—corpses floating over every crest. The surface was covered with the bodies of a mass extinction. Death had claimed these waters and only Michelle could see it.

Roland smacked the ledge. "Time to hunt down a spider and have a conversation."

The ocean's glass surface was a mirror reflecting the sky above. Tryal stared at the mirror, and under the reflections, dark shapes moved.

"Then from the throng did three come forward,

Two without fate on the land they found,

The fetters will burst, and the great wolf run free;

Much do I know, and more can see

Of the fate of the gods, the mighty in fight.

Brothers shall fight and fell each other,

And sisters' sons shall kinship stain;

An axe-age, a sword-age, (and the sun rises)

shields are sundered,

A Wind-age, a wolf-age, ere the world falls;

Nor ever shall men each other spare

Now do I see the earth anew

Rise all green from the waves again

There comes on high, all power to hold,

A mighty lord, all lands he rules."

—The Poetic Edda: The Wise Woman's Prophecy

(The Völuspá)

To be continued in

BOOK II: THE CHILDREN
UNDER THE SHADOWS

ACKNOWLEDGMENTS

"Write with the door closed,

edit with the door open."

—Stephen King, On Writing

When the door was open, there were several people whose advice, watchful eyes, and ideas were very, very welcome.

Karen, my first reader, was always there with the scalpel to slice away the junk. The entire novel was shaken firmly by the capable hands of J. Scott Wilson—he woke the entire thing up and made it walk straight!

Several people gave spot advice which helped move key passages along. Chapter 20 would've been a shadow of the thing it is now without Cana's medical advice. Christina's keen eye made several of the initial chapters cleaner than I could've hoped. For Don's great catch of all the bugs that made it through—this edition benefited from his effort.

For those that gave me a kick in the butt—Rick, William—thank you! All of my writing, far beyond this work, would have lapsed had it not been for the constant encouragement of Jody.

To so many that have enjoyed the first read of this book and sent messages begging for the next adventure . . . thank you.

FOLLOW US TODAY

twitter.com/JDanielBatt

facebook.com/YoungGodsSeries

www.JDanielBatt.com

www.StoryJitsu.com

STORY
JITSU

www.ingramcontent.com/pod-product-compliance
Lightning Source LLC
Chambersburg PA
CBHW051314250626
47155CB00007B/2312